"YOU HAVE A LOVELY SMILE . . .

. . . although," he mused, fingering the plain gray fabric of her gown, then lightly touching the hair she'd scraped into a tight bun, "I did prefer your appearance as a young lady of the ton."

Elizabeth did not have time to be offended at the implied insult, for he continued in that thoughtful tone. "Odd, isn't it, how in Society women strive to appear soft and inviting, when underneath they are hard and brittle? Yet you, as a warm-hearted governess, are expected to appear utterly proper, even drab."

"I'm sure that is appropriate for a governess," she replied primly, though his lingering touch on her hair sent little flutters throughout her body.

This was wrong. But she was powerless to stop him.

"Perhaps." His hand covered hers again. "But it makes me wonder . . . what would happen if I pulled those pins from your hair? Would I have a woman before me who was soft and warm both inside and out?"

BOOK YOUR PLACE ON OUR WEBSITE AND MAKE THE READING CONNECTION!

We've created a customized website just for our very special readers, where you can get the inside scoop on everything that's going on with Zebra, Pinnacle and Kensington books.

When you come online, you'll have the exciting opportunity to:

- View covers of upcoming books
- Read sample chapters
- Learn about our future publishing schedule (listed by publication month *and author*)
- Find out when your favorite authors will be visiting a city near you
- Search for and order backlist books from our online catalog
- Check out author bios and background information
- Send e-mail to your favorite authors
- Meet the Kensington staff online
- Join us in weekly chats with authors, readers and other guests
- Get writing guidelines
- AND MUCH MORE!

**Visit our website at
http://www.kensingtonbooks.com**

Nothing But Scandal

ALLEGRA GRAY

ZEBRA BOOKS
Kensington Publishing Corp.
http://www.kensingtonbooks.com

ZEBRA BOOKS are published by

Kensington Publishing Corp.
119 West 40th Street
New York, NY 10018

All Kensington titles, imprints, and distributed lines are
available at special quantity discounts for bulk purchases
for sales promotion, premiums, fund-raising, educational,
or institutional use.

Special book excerpts or customized printings can also be
created to fit specific needs. For details, write or phone the
office of the Kensington Special Sales Manager: Attn. Special
Sales Department. Kensington Publishing Corp., 119 West
40th Street, New York, NY 10018. Phone: 1-800-221-2647.

Zebra and the Z logo Reg. U.S. Pat. & TM Off.

ISBN-13: 978-1-4201-0825-5
ISBN-10: 1-4201-0825-5

First Printing: July 2009
10 9 8 7 6 5 4 3 2 1

Printed in the United States of America

To Miles and Alexis,
who still believe in fairy tales
(and hopefully always will)

Acknowledgments

Thank you to Megan Records, my editor at Kensington, for your enthusiasm and flexibility. Also thank you to my agent, Kevan Lyon, for valuable input on this book and for finding it a home.

A special thank you to Donnell Bell, Robin Searle, and Tracy Seybold, my fellow writers and critique partners. Without your insight, brainstorming, and encouragement, this book would not have been possible.

Chapter One

Family expectations—and the guilt that came with not living up to them—were going to be the death of Elizabeth Medford.

Given that her father, Baron James Medford, had hardly been a bastion of familial responsibility himself, having amassed a mountain of gaming debts prior to his untimely death, it seemed unfair that the remaining members of the family should expect that she, Elizabeth, would salvage them by marrying Harold Wetherby. Her third cousin might have a respectable income, but the memory of Harold's sweaty hands pawing her at a picnic when she'd been a mere fourteen years old was enough to convince her she simply could not, could *not* marry him.

And since she'd otherwise been a resounding failure in the marriage mart, Elizabeth had devised a new plan—one to be implemented that very morning.

The moment breakfast was over, she'd hastily ushered her younger sister, Charity, and their maid, Emma, out the door of the Medford town house and into Hyde Park for a stroll, ignoring her sister's nonstop stream of questions as they readied themselves.

They'd been in the park no more than a minute before Charity faced Elizabeth and thrust out her chin. "*Now* will you tell me what's going on? If you continue to tease me this way, I shall simply perish." She placed a melodramatic hand to her heart.

Elizabeth glanced behind them. Emma, acting as chaperone, trailed discreetly, close enough to keep up appearances but not to overhear conversation.

"All right. For the past weeks we've thought of only one thing: getting a man, any man but Harold, to propose marriage to me. Now that we're out of full mourning for father, Uncle and Mother are anxious to accept his suit. I am running out of excuses to delay. But perhaps there is another way out of this after all."

"I don't understand."

"Think. What does Harold stand to gain from marrying me?"

"Your connections. He wants respect, social advancement, obviously." Charity raised an eyebrow, making it clear she thought Elizabeth was cracking under the strain if she believed this was new food for thought.

"Exactly," Elizabeth confirmed with glee.

"I don't see where this is going."

"I don't want to marry Harold, right? Well, we *were* thinking I'd need a better offer in order to get out of it. But I don't. I simply need him to withdraw his offer."

"But what would make him do that? He already knows about father's financial situation, and even that miserable fiasco didn't make him cry off," Charity pointed out.

"No, it didn't, because, poor or not, I am still a *respectable* member of the ton."

Charity's eyes widened. "Ooohh. Elizabeth, I'm not sure I like what I think you're thinking."

Elizabeth ignored her. "If I were no longer respectable, if I were, say, ruined, Harold would withdraw!" She nearly tripped over a root on the path in her excitement over the idea.

"It's wonderfully daring," Charity conceded, not looking quite so pleased. "But how would you do it? And, oh, think what Mother and Uncle would do! They'd toss you out for certain. You'd be disowned, dishonored. Where would you go?" She tugged at her hair, an old habit and a sure sign of her concern.

"I could work for a living, I suppose." Elizabeth bit her lip, aware her plan had more bravado than substance. "I'd have to. I'm good with a needle, so I could work for a dressmaker. Or be a governess. Anything would be better than being married to Harold. I'd be forced to endure his touches and . . ."

She shuddered, then fought to regain control of her emotions. Her little sister didn't need to know how badly their distant cousin frightened her. He'd tried to force his attentions on her years before, and now that she was actually within his reach, he would stop at nothing until she married him. Unless, of course, marrying *her* would thwart his grasping ambition and hurt *his* precious reputation.

There was, however, one problem. "It's you I'm worried about. My marriage was supposed to support you, too."

Charity patted her sister's arm, her eyes softening with understanding. "Do what you must, E., and don't worry overmuch about me. For heaven's sake, don't marry the beast just because he's offered to keep *me* fed and clothed.

"But in order for your plan to work, your reputation would have to be utterly destroyed, and soon. You seem to forget that in spite of Father's penchant for scandal and debt, you, Sister dear, have no such objectionable deeds to your name."

"So far," Elizabeth said.

Charity's eyes narrowed. "You've already thought this through. You're plotting something."

"Of course."

"Well, for heaven's sake, tell me! You know I can't stand it when you don't include me in your adventures." Charity nearly bounced in anticipation.

Elizabeth smiled serenely, though inside, her heart raced. "You didn't think we came to Hyde Park merely to stroll, did you? No, Charity, I've decided the best way to destroy my reputation—and in a way that will ensure Harold never again approaches me—is to be caught in a compromising situation. With a man."

Charity stopped in her tracks. "Elizabeth, you couldn't."

"I could."

"But . . . but," Charity spluttered, "you'd need a man willing to take part. No gentleman would ever do such a thing."

Indeed. No gentleman would.

Right on cue, Elizabeth spotted him. Alex Bainbridge, Duke of Beaufort, striding along an adjacent path. He was no gentleman. Even at this early hour, he had the sleek appearance of a night predator, a beautiful but deadly jungle cat. Since she'd held a tendre for him since childhood, following his every move with fascination, Elizabeth knew he had a reputation to match that of his predatory look-alike. It was also how she knew he had a habit of walking through the park at nearly the same time each morning.

"I'm going to do it."

"Now?" Charity squealed. "Wait. Are you sure there isn't some other way?"

"Now. Can you make yourself scarce?"

Charity glanced around. "Mary Sutherby and her sister are just over there. I'll join them. E., do be careful."

"Careful, Charity, is exactly what I am *not* going to be."

Her sister's eyes grew wide with apprehension and admiration. "In that case, good luck." She hurried away.

Elizabeth turned. One pointed look at Emma was enough to make the poor maid shrink even farther behind.

Elizabeth hurried just enough to intercept the duke as he passed her way. She tugged her walking costume a bit lower on her bosom, remembering her prey was accustomed to bold women. Tracking him down and initiating a conversation—let alone the one she planned—were bold moves she would have never considered even a week ago, but Elizabeth was desperate.

"Your Grace?"

"Miss Medford?" He slowed his pace as she fell into step with him.

"Might I delay you a moment?" Her heart quickened at his proximity. She had to tilt her head up to meet his keen glance, and his thick dark hair fell forward to brush knife-sharp cheekbones as he bent his head in return. She swallowed weakly. Did he remember they'd waltzed at the Peasleys' ball? It had only been the highlight of her life.

"Of course. Do you need some sort of assistance?"

"Of a sort."

The duke looked around, as though there might be some emergency.

Elizabeth took a deep breath. How best to approach this? The etiquette books did not cover how to properly destroy one's reputation, only how to preserve it.

His dark brows drew together in question. Elizabeth swallowed hard. Best just to get it over with.

"Right. Well, thank you, Your Grace, for allowing me a moment of your time."

"A very brief moment." His features took on an expression of bored tolerance now that it was apparent no one was in dire distress.

"I'm not here to join the ranks of simpering females who usually surround you, hoping desperately for your hand," she announced bluntly, surprising even herself.

"No?" He gave her a lazy grin. "My skill at the waltz must be slipping. Usually it takes no more than that."

Absurdly pleased he remembered her, Elizabeth squelched the desire to respond in exactly the way she'd just promised not to.

"If it is not another dance you're after, and you've met no misfortune in the park, then how can I be of assistance?"

"Actually, I have a proposition for you."

"Really? A proposition from a lady? That hardly sounds proper." His voice was teasing, but his features were alert.

"Just wait until you hear it," she muttered.

The duke laughed, spearing her with a roguish

glance. She felt a wicked thrill at what she was about to do.

"You see, my mother is forcing me to marry and . . . never mind." She needn't bore him with details. "I would like you to ruin me."

"What!" The word was an explosion.

Elizabeth thrust out her chin.

"Let me get this straight. You *want* to be ruined?"

"Yes."

"By me." His face took on a masklike expression. Cynical appraisal replaced the open laughter of a moment before.

"Well, yes. I haven't much experience in such matters, but I thought you would know how to go about such a thing."

"I see. What's in it for me?" he asked bluntly.

Elizabeth fought down panic. She hadn't considered that. But now that she'd gone this far, the only thing to do was see it through. "Er, I imagine the benefit to you would be whatever it is gentlemen are usually after when ruining a woman."

The duke gaped at her.

"Of course," she challenged, determined to brazen it out, "if you're uncertain as to how to go about it . . ." She knew he wasn't. There'd been rumors enough.

"It's not my knowledge in that area that gives me pause," he snapped. "It is the foolishness of your proposition. Do you even know what you are asking?"

She arched a brow. "I have a fairly good idea."

"Then you know what will happen to you."

"Absolutely." She smiled. He might not understand, but those consequences were *exactly* what she was hoping for.

"Sorry, I'm not interested." He turned to go.

Elizabeth's mouth fell open. She'd been so sure this would work.

"Why not?" She couldn't help but ask.

He turned in the path, faced her squarely. "It may come as a surprise to you, but I'm not in the habit of seducing innocents, then failing to claim responsibility when I do so."

"I see." But she didn't. Hadn't he a reputation for just that sort of thing?

Heat flooded her cheeks. "I don't appeal to you in that way. Well, you wouldn't have to seduce me, then. We could simply have it whispered about—"

"I told you, I'm not interested." He glanced over his shoulder as though he had somewhere to be.

Crushing embarrassment swept through her, and her throat grew thick with the threat of tears. It was time to accept defeat.

"In that case, I thank you for your time, Your Grace. And I would appreciate it if you did not mention this, er, conversation, to anyone," Elizabeth said with the last scraps of dignity she could muster.

He gave her a stiff nod. She turned and fled as fast as her skirts would allow.

Alex stared at the quickly retreating redhead. The whole Medford family must be mad. It was the only way to explain it. Yes, he'd danced with her at the Peasleys' ball last week. She'd looked quite fetching, and a bit lonely. And, of course, he hadn't known who she was until too late.

He knew about loneliness, having grown up with it. But he'd never imagined the seemingly innocent girl he'd held in his arms had been planning to ask him to engage in an illicit liaison. Where on God's green earth had she gotten such an idea?

Mad, entirely.

Alex knew he had a reputation, but all his affairs had been with widowed or otherwise independent women. Well, there had been that one unfortunate incident in his youth, but in that case, the young lady in question had actually been teaching *him* a thing or two, so he could hardly be blamed for her ruin. He knew how the ton gossiped, though.

To tell the truth, it bothered him. He'd have preferred Elizabeth held him in higher regard, if she was going to think of him at all. In spite of her family, he'd been attracted to her refreshing wit. But once again, his judgment failed him whenever the Medfords were involved.

Some men would consider ruining Medford's daughter the perfect revenge, or, as the feckless baron himself had suggested, an appropriate repayment of debt, but Alex was not one of them. There was no satisfaction to be had in getting revenge on a dead man.

If anything, he pitied Elizabeth. Because of her father's reckless management, she now suffered. He'd not failed to notice her brief mention of an unwanted engagement.

His pity, however, did not extend to the point that he was willing to become personally involved. In fact, he'd promised not to.

Alex blew out a breath. Fortunes were made and lost all the time, and Elizabeth's was certainly not the first noble family to find themselves on the outs.

What would the chit have done if he'd said *yes?* He grinned at the idea. He'd been tempted enough. Her wildly colored hair, her slim curves, and her defiant bravery held definite appeal.

No doubt she'd have tried to back out at the last minute.

Unless, he speculated, she was using him.

Perhaps she was foolish enough to believe that if he "ruined" her, as she'd so boldly offered, he'd be forced to offer for her in return. Perhaps her father had even planted the scheme in her head before his demise. It was a far more daring approach than the coquettish looks he endured from dozens of other hopeful misses, but he was not so easily fooled. And there was nothing Alex hated more than being used.

He ground a heel into the dirt, then strode down the path that would take him out of the park.

She had his reluctant admiration for her daring, but Elizabeth Medford's problems were her own.

"Elizabeth, a word with you," Lady Medford said, accosting her daughter the moment she stepped through the door to their town house. Charity, whom Elizabeth had rejoined at the park before seeking the sanctuary of home, heard their mother's tone and disappeared like mist in the wind, leaving Elizabeth to fend for herself.

All Elizabeth really wanted to do was run to her room and hide her mortification under her bedcovers, but instead she schooled her features into a polite expression. "Mother."

Lady Medford started down the hall, and Elizabeth resignedly followed, dragging her feet over the polished wood floors. They entered the salon, a room decorated in delicate shades of rose—a room Elizabeth had always found completely uncharacteristic of her mother.

Lady Medford turned and faced her daughter like a general dressing down a private. "It has come to my attention that you were seen dancing with the Duke of Beaufort."

Elizabeth stifled a groan. The duke was the *last* person she wanted to talk about right now.

"Yes, at the Peasleys' ball," she answered cautiously. Her mother had chosen not to attend, pleading a headache. Elizabeth had been chaperoned instead by Lady Tanner—an older lady of venerable reputation, who would surely exact a favor in return for having performed the duty of chaperone, in spite of having performed said duty in a rather lax fashion. Just one more thing Elizabeth had to look forward to.

"Is he pursuing you?"

Elizabeth's attention snapped back to her mother. "I don't believe so." She nearly choked on the understatement. Beaufort had made it abundantly clear how little intention he had of "pursuing" her.

"Good. I think it would be best if you did not get involved with him."

Now Elizabeth was truly confused, for Lady Medford's statement surely qualified her as the only mama in the entire ton who didn't want her daughter pursued by the extremely wealthy, handsome, and eligible Duke of Beaufort.

Reminding herself her mother had no idea of what had actually just transpired, she replied, "Mother, I assure you there was nothing untoward; it was merely a dance."

"Nonetheless, the man has a reputation. Why, he's practically predatory. Any involvement with him is likely to end in disappointment on your part."

Well, that much was true. But since when did Lady

Medford care about her daughter's hopes getting crushed? That would be a new development in their relationship—if it was true.

"Also, I don't believe your father would have approved."

Elizabeth looked up sharply. Her mother had meticulously avoided unnecessary mention of her father since his death, so why would she bring him up now? None of this made any sense.

It really didn't matter whether her father would have approved, given that she would not be seen consorting with the duke again any time soon. He'd made that abundantly clear.

"It's all right, Mother. I've no hopes of snaring the duke's hand," she said in a tightly controlled voice.

"Right." Her mother sniffed. "Very well, then." She sniffed again. "I believe this room needs airing. The servants are becoming intolerably slack in their duties."

Elizabeth kept her mouth shut. The servants weren't becoming slack. They were *leaving*. They knew as well as anyone that her father had died with no heir and considerable debt. Slowly but surely they were finding employ in other, more stable, noble homes. If her mother chose not to recognize that, Elizabeth wasn't going to be the one to point it out. She turned to go, assuming her mother's change of topic meant she'd been dismissed.

"No, don't leave. You have a caller."

Elizabeth closed her eyes briefly. Could her day get any worse? First that humiliating and unsuccessful scene at the park. And now, when she wanted nothing more than a moment's peace, she had to entertain. And to what purpose? Her mother would announce her engagement in mere hours, and Elizabeth had run out of ideas for avoiding it.

"Wetherby is waiting in the drawing room. I wanted to be certain you had no foolish yearnings for Beaufort before I sent you in to see him. But I see that, in this matter at least, you are a sensible girl."

Elizabeth cringed. She'd been wrong. Talking *about* the Duke of Beaufort was infinitely preferable to talking *to* Harold Wetherby. At least her mother hadn't seen her "sensible" daughter's behavior thirty minutes ago.

"We can afford to wait no longer, Elizabeth," her mother told her. "Wetherby's lack of title may be lamentable, but his income is not. I've given him every reason to expect his suit will be accepted, though of course he'll want to hear it from you as well."

Elizabeth nodded woodenly. Yes, her day could definitely get worse. Her plan may have failed, but she was not yet ready to face her volatile cousin.

"Yes, Mother. I'll be in to see him as soon as I've had a moment to tidy my appearance." Her mother was a stickler for propriety, so Elizabeth knew she would approve of the short delay. One did not meet one's future husband looking mussed from the outdoors.

The baroness nodded. "I'll have the butler give him your message. Don't dawdle."

Fifteen minutes later, Elizabeth entered the drawing room, having dawdled only a little. The panicked whispers she'd shared with Charity had given her no new inspiration.

Her unwanted soon-to-be fiancé stood by the window, tapping his expensively shod foot. He did not look especially pleased to see her.

"Harold." She said it with as much politeness as she could muster, forcing her lips into a semblance of a smile.

"Elizabeth."

She stiffened her shoulders as he strode toward her.

"You're looking well," he told her, stopping only when they were separated by a scant few inches. "Better than I expected for someone distraught with grief."

"Right. Well. One must go on," she lamely replied. What was he after?

"One must. Though to hear it, you've been doing a bit more 'going on' than I would like."

Elizabeth held her chin up but said nothing. If he was going to accuse her of something, she wanted to know exactly what.

"Nothing to say for yourself, my sweet?"

"Your meaning is unclear." She managed to keep her tone modulated and polite, though she clenched her fingers in the folds of her gown.

"No? Then let me explain." His voice was silk but his quivering jowls gave away his simmering rage. "Why do you think I offered for you?"

Elizabeth had several theories on that, but as Harold wouldn't appreciate any of them, she kept silent.

"Respectability, Elizabeth!" He was openly angry now. "Your lack of dowry I can tolerate—I've sufficient funds of my own. But I plan to go places in Society, and I damn well want the respect that comes with marrying a nobleman's daughter!"

"I see." She was a means to an end for him. Well, she'd known that. "But that doesn't explain why you chose me."

"You know bloody well why. Your father, gambling fool that he was, left you within my reach."

"I see," she repeated. She refrained from mentioning that for someone who claimed to want respectability, he didn't seem to have any qualms about using vicious language in front of a gently bred woman.

"Obviously you *don't* see, or you would have more care for your reputation."

"My reputation is my own to worry about."

"Now see here, Elizabeth! I won't have a wife who speaks back. Or one who has sullied herself." The acrid scent of sweat assaulted Elizabeth's nostrils as he railed at her.

Insulted though she was, a ray of hope filtered through her anger. She hadn't done anything inappropriate—a fact she was all too aware of—but if Harold believed otherwise, perhaps she could convince him she was not worth marrying. She'd have to play it right.

"I am not your wife yet, and you overstep your bounds if you dare accuse me of impropriety."

"Oh? Then what is *this* all about?" His fleshy finger viciously prodded the bustline of her gown.

"How dare you! You should leave. Now." She stepped away, furious, her glance flicking down as she thought about the alterations she'd made to the gown earlier that spring, when she'd still hoped to attract a more desirable suitor. The ploy hadn't worked.

"Why shouldn't I dare?" He advanced again, giving her a nasty leer. "You've gone to great lengths to put yourself on display. Why else if not for a man to touch? A respectable woman would take more care to cover herself. You will do so, at least in public, as my fiancée and my wife."

"I will most certainly not—"

"And furthermore," he cut her off, "you should take more care in the company you keep."

"What is that supposed to mean?" Now he really went too far. She stepped beyond his reach.

"The Duke of Beaufort!" he exploded, face red and eyes bulging.

She folded her arms. "If you're so concerned with advancing in Society, you should be pleased to be marrying someone sought after by more prominent personages than yourself." Elizabeth couldn't help firing back at him, though it filled her with disgust to refer to their impending marriage.

Harold blew past her retort. "For all the duke's prominence, he's a known libertine and rake! Everyone knows it, yet you cavort with him as though you were a common serving wench!"

Perhaps her plan was working. She tossed him a deliberately provocative look. "His Grace appreciates me."

"Bah. He appreciates how gullible you are, perhaps. But from now on, you'll keep your flirtations, and that delectable little body of yours, for me alone." Spittle flecked his lips as he raged at her.

"I hadn't realized you were so, er, old-fashioned. Hardly anyone in the ton expects a faithful marriage." That wasn't *entirely* true, but it was accurate enough and suited her current purpose. "Perhaps we aren't so well suited after all."

"We're well suited enough." He stepped forward, closing a meaty fist around her arm. "I won't have you sullied by another man. The right to your body is mine alone. I'm marrying a baron's daughter, not a tavern slut."

Bile rose in her throat at the idea of enduring

intimacy with such a beast. Without thinking, she reached up and slapped him with all the force she could muster.

Her hand connected with his beakish nose—the only part of him where bones were more prominent than flesh—with a satisfying *crack*. He released her so swiftly she staggered.

"You vicious little bitch!" he bellowed, holding his nose.

"Get out. Just get out." She pointed an imperious finger toward the door.

He stalked over to the door, then turned. "Don't think this is over, Elizabeth. You may get away with this now, but as my wife you'll learn to bend to my will. Bend, or break." He shut the door behind him with enough force to leave it reverberating in its frame.

Elizabeth sat, limbs quaking, on the nearest available piece of furniture—an uncomfortable beige settee she usually avoided. She pressed a hand to her heart, then hugged herself tight. Her flesh still burned where he'd prodded her. There would be bruises tomorrow.

She'd thought for certain that Harold's railing at her meant he was about to cry off. He couldn't possibly treat her that way and still expect to marry her!

But, apparently, given his exiting remark, he did.

Rage and humiliation coursed through her. How could her mother care so little for her eldest daughter that she would see her married to such a pig?

Well, she wouldn't have it. Elizabeth stood with renewed purpose. She'd told Charity she could work for a living, and so she would. Her mother might announce her engagement to Harold in every one of London's papers, but Elizabeth wouldn't be there to fulfill it.

* * *

Alex stared at his brandy. Darkness closed in on the windows of his study, his business for the day long since concluded. He'd thought to spend the evening at home, but the morning's incident in the park kept replaying itself in his mind. Weakness. Why couldn't he simply block it—her—out? The red-tressed chit was as mad as her father, for certain, but the hint of desperation he'd seen in Elizabeth's misty green eyes ate at his soul.

She'd never have come to him if she'd known what he'd done. Or maybe, he reflected after a long swallow of the brandy, she would have. After all, he'd had a hand in the family's destruction, however unintentional. Why shouldn't he be the one to finish the job?

No. Irredeemable though he was, he'd not stoop that low. It went against his code.

The Code, as he liked to think of it, was a sort of modified creed of honor. It wasn't going to get him nominated for sainthood, but there were lines even a dissolute rake such as he shouldn't cross. Don't hurt anyone, and don't get involved with anyone who doesn't know how the game is played. It had worked for drinking, gaming, and women. Except that once, last fall. And there was no atoning for it now.

Elizabeth's hurt green eyes flickered into his mind. If only she knew.

It would have been no hardship, her suggestion. He could easily envision himself kissing the fullness of her lower lip, or the corner of her wayward smile. He'd explore the slim column of her body, the ripe curve of her breast, that impossibly smooth skin . . .

Alex tossed back the rest of his brandy and stood. Even thinking of her aroused him. Damn Medfords.

"Hanson!" he bellowed for his valet. He needed diversion. A night of cards and drinking. Since he'd pensioned off his last mistress, and had no liking for the bawdy houses, he'd restrict himself to the gentlemen's clubs. Besides, another woman would only remind him of the one he was trying to forget.

Chapter Two

Alex arrived at White's later that night, only a little drunk, and went immediately to his regular table. Lords Stockton, Wilbourne, and Garrett, veteran gamblers all, were already seated, engaged in the pleasurable pastime of betting obscene amounts on the trivial fall of the cards.

As Alex sat, a waiter appeared with a glass of his usual brandy. He quaffed it eagerly, as the three he'd drunk before leaving home had not sufficiently dulled his memory of the tempting minx who today had rashly offered up her own ruination. Nor had they dulled the memories of that same minx's father.

The other men dealt him into a game of five-card loo. They played several hands, but Alex's mind wasn't on the cards.

"Do you ever wonder," Lord Wilbourne joked as he raked in the cards after winning a hand, "how wealthy Beaufort would be if he didn't insist on losing such large sums to me?"

Alex grinned, the additional brandy having softened his mood. "I won twice that sum from you last week, Wilbourne."

Wilbourne's bushy brows lifted. "Quite right. I'd forgotten. I suppose I'll have to hope my luck holds a while longer tonight."

Alex knew Wilbourne didn't care one way or the other. The man was wealthy in the extreme, as were the others at the table. Playing with such companions made the game far more civilized.

They played some more, and Alex's mind drifted back to a pair of beautiful but desperate green eyes. A waiter appeared to replace his brandy, and he mindlessly took a swallow of the new one.

Lords Stockton and Garrett began discussing some of the more outrageous bets in the book at the front of White's.

Stockton, the eldest at the table, had a stodgy sense of propriety. Cards were well and good, but he couldn't understand what possessed people to bet on such foolish things as the type of jewels a certain courtesan would wear to the theater, or whether Lady X's garden party would be rained out—the latter of which Lord Garrett had bet in favor of and was devoutly hoping would come true, as he'd promised a friend to attend that unbearably dull annual affair.

"I just don't see how you can engage in such trivia," Stockton averred.

Garrett grinned. "I can afford it, and it keeps me entertained. What else is a man to do during the Season? Attend Almack's?"

"God forbid." Wilbourne shuddered at the mention of the marriage mart. "Even betting on the weather is better than that." He dealt the cards again.

Alex picked his up and tried to concentrate, both on the game and the conversation. His friends could afford to bet on whatever ridiculous whims they chose, but their conversation reminded him too much of those who couldn't but did anyway. He took another swallow of brandy and leaned back in his chair, allowing himself to float peaceably in an alcohol-induced haze.

"All right then, what's the strangest thing you've ever won at cards?" Wilbourne asked.

"A small estate in Scotland," Lord Stockton offered. "Way up in the highlands. Wild place. No Englishman in their right mind would live there."

Lord Garrett, the youngest at the table, shrugged. "Still, land is land, and is gambled upon often. That's not so strange. I, on the other hand, recently laid claim to a prize-winning sow."

Wilbourne laughed. "You, owner of a pig?"

"For as long as it takes my man to sell it, at any rate."

Stockton shook his head. "A man who resorts to betting his livestock ought not be betting at all." A longtime gambler, he dealt only in cash and land.

"Whyever did you allow the man to bet on it?" Wilbourne asked curiously.

Garrett shrugged. "I was enjoying the game. Didn't want it to end."

"A pig." Wilbourne shook his head. "Beaufort? Anything you've won that can top that?"

"A woman," Alex said, and almost immediately regretted it. He should have stopped drinking about three brandies ago, if he'd reached the point where his mouth functioned faster than his brain.

The other three men looked interested. Wilbourne set down his cards. "Do tell."

"A servant?" Stockton asked.

"Someone's mistress?" Garrett guessed.

Alex shook his head, wishing he didn't have to explain. "Someone's daughter."

To their credit, the three men looked horrified.

Alex raked a hand through his hair. "I was gambling with a man who got in over his head. I didn't know it, or I'd never have played with him. Anyway, suffice it to say, when he realized he couldn't pay off his many losses, he offered up his daughter to work them off."

"Who would do such a thing?" Wilbourne breathed.

"The man's deceased. I'd rather not name him and tread further on his memory."

"Barbaric," Stockton grunted.

"Positively medieval," Wilbourne confirmed.

"Did you accept?" Garrett asked.

"Of course he didn't," Wilbourne answered for him.

A man at the table closest to theirs—a man that Alex, in his brandy-induced haze, couldn't place— stood and brushed past, headed for the entrance. The stranger glanced at Alex a little longer than polite behavior dictated. Clearly, he'd overheard their conversation.

Garrett looked at Alex for confirmation.

"No. I didn't," Alex said shortly. Was his reputation truly so bad even some of his friends thought he'd stoop so low? He'd had any number of mistresses and lovers, but he'd never taken a woman who hadn't come to him willingly. Although, if this morning's encounter had been any indication of Elizabeth's willingness . . .

He stood. "I'm sorry to dash your hopes, Wilbourne, but you'll have to content yourself with winning these other gentlemen's money for the rest of the night."

"Leaving so soon?"

Alex shrugged. His fogged mind tried to come up with a decent excuse, since he usually played cards well into the wee hours of the morning, but the only thing that came to him was a vision of a red-haired temptress with hurt green eyes.

"Sorry," he said to the men remaining at his table, and left.

Elizabeth reached the temporary sanctuary of her room, paced for a few moments, then threw open her wardrobe and trunks. She contemplated which things were most essential to bring with her. The wild anger and fear she'd felt toward Harold had receded, leaving behind a steady resolve.

"He's a horrible man. An animal."

Elizabeth started. "You do have a way of sneaking up on people, Sister dear."

Charity managed to look mildly abashed, then gave herself away by grinning. "How else is a body supposed to hear anything worth listening to?" She sobered. "Did he hurt you?"

"No, not really. You heard what happened in the study?"

"Most of it." She tugged at her blond hair, distressed.

For a moment Elizabeth felt a pang of jealousy. Charity had golden hair and wide blue eyes, and she was irrepressible and fun. She'd have been an instant success in Society—if their mother hadn't held her back this year, embarrassed by their circumstances. If Charity had been the older sister, she'd likely have found a bevy of pleasant suitors, and their whole family would be out of this mess. Or perhaps not. As the eldest, Elizabeth had sheltered her sister for most of their lives. She'd always been the responsible one, the one to deflect their parents' displeasure over childhood foibles, and the one to try desperately to atone for not having been born a boy. Was it any wonder they'd turned out so differently?

Yet Elizabeth loved her sister far too much to remain jealous. Gently she pried her sister's hand from her hair. "You'll ruin your lovely curls."

Charity shrugged. "I don't know why I let Emma bother with them today anyway. E., how can you stand it? He's just too awful. Income or no, I can't fathom why Mother and Uncle wish you to marry him. I, for one, am glad you slapped him."

Elizabeth cringed, embarrassed when she recalled all Charity must have overheard. "It wasn't my finest moment."

"You're wrong. He deserved that and more. You just *can't* marry him."

"I know."

Charity glanced around, seeming to notice for the first time that Elizabeth was packing. "I take it you're leaving."

Elizabeth nodded.

"As well you should. But where will you go?"

For that, at least, she had an answer. "I'll visit Beatrice. She'll take me in until I can figure something out."

Lady Beatrice Pullington had made her bow to Society the same year as Elizabeth, and they'd been fast friends ever since. Bea had married almost immediately, for her family had made prior arrangements with Lord Pullington, an older member of the peerage. That gentleman had survived only six months of his marriage before his failing heart gave up entirely, leaving Bea a wealthy young widow.

For the past two years, Bea had kept her own house in town—a privilege afforded her by her widowed status. She was certainly pretty, and wealthy, enough to attract another husband, but she had no desire to relinquish the independence she felt she'd earned during her brief but stifling marriage.

Elizabeth knew she could find a temporary haven there. She had too much pride to prevail upon Bea's generosity forever, but she could at least hide there while she formulated a new plan. Bea knew how to be discreet.

Charity nodded, her eyes wide. "Shall I compose a message to her while you pack?"

"No. It would have to be delivered, and it's better if fewer people know my whereabouts. I can trust Bea not to leave me standing on her doorstep, unexpected though I may be. And I know I can trust you not to speak of it to anyone."

"Of course. See, you can do this on your own. You didn't need Beaufort to ruin you at all."

"Ugh. Don't remind me. Whatever was I thinking?" Elizabeth pressed her hand to her forehead. The fight with Harold had one benefit: it had made her temporarily forget her humiliating and short-lived foray into wickedness.

"Oh, don't be so hard on yourself. Perhaps you just wanted a bit of fun before consigning yourself to a life of drudgery. The duke is rather, um, red-blooded, isn't he?"

"Charity!" Elizabeth giggled in spite of herself.

Her sister grinned back. "When will you leave?"

"This evening, after Mother has gone out or retired for the night."

"Perfect. I'll simply say you sneaked out while I was sleeping. And I shall act hurt, as though I'm disappointed you didn't confide in me." Mischief lit Charity's eyes as she warmed to the falsehood.

"Thank you." Her sister's love for drama had gotten them into more than one awkward scrape, but Elizabeth was grateful for it now. She gave Charity a quick hug, then snapped her valise shut. There was no point in packing more, since she had no idea what her next step in life would be. If she needed additional items later, she could always have Charity sneak them to her.

The two sisters moved aimlessly about the house for the next several hours, pretending all was normal whenever the servants were near, and making plans in whispered exchanges when they weren't.

The darkness of night now lurked at the windows, but neither girl showed any inclination toward sleep. Charity was staring out Elizabeth's window, unconsciously gripping the curtains until her knuckles turned white. Elizabeth, oddly calm, sat near her dressing table.

"I heard Mother say she was attending a gathering at the Jameson residence this evening," Charity said. "As soon as she goes, you can be on your way. There. That new man is preparing the coach."

Elizabeth nodded. Their old driver, Fuston, had disappeared shortly after her father's death. He'd been driving the night of the accident. Presumably he'd been too guilt-stricken to remain in the Medfords' employ, though from what Elizabeth understood, there was little he could have done.

"There. Mother's climbing in. He just closed the door."

Elizabeth stood.

"They're gone. The coach just turned the corner. You can leave now and not be seen. I'll find a hired hack and tell them to pull around back, if you want. That way no one else will see you leave either."

Elizabeth looked at the golden-haired little

sister she loved with all her heart. "Charity, are you absolutely sure you'll be all right after I go?"

Her sister grinned. "Of course. Oh, I know they won't be happy with me, but I can stand it, E. You don't have to protect me anymore."

Elizabeth gave her a quick hug, then quickly composed herself. "I'll miss you more than anything. Go ahead and hire a carriage. I'll finish here and be ready by the time it arrives."

She gathered a few last things as Charity left the room. She debated leaving a note, then decided against it. Better to simply let them wonder.

Her mother would be furious, especially when Harold cried off, but Elizabeth was long past the point of caring. She was strong enough to make it on her own, and Charity was wily enough to withstand their mother's interrogations. That was all that mattered.

Elizabeth took one last glance at the lovely green-and-gold bedroom she'd known for years, then shut the door on that former life.

The Derringworth stables, located just outside London, catered only to discerning customers—mostly the nobility. The firm raised everything from racehorses to ladies' mounts, with only one stipulation: any horse the Derringworths signed off on was of highest quality. The operation represented the epitome of what Harold Wetherby aspired to be. Which was exactly why he was on his way there to purchase a new mount, preferably one that would draw attention to him.

He even had an appointment. The morning held considerable promise.

Harold left his unimpressive rig—another item that would have to be upgraded, now that he was marrying nobility—out of sight when he neared the stables.

He tugged down his straining waistcoat, then entered the posh facility. It smelled of leather and fresh hay—so unlike the manure and sweat of the farmers' stables where he'd grown up.

A young man sat in a small office to the left of the entrance. He stood as Harold entered.

Harold thrust out his chest. "Harold Wetherby," he announced. "Here to see about that stallion I've heard is for sale."

"Mr. Wetherby," the young man said. "Yes, I see your appointment in our book. Tim Kemble here, Mr. Derringworth's assistant manager. So, it's the stallion you're interested in?"

An assistant. His appointment hadn't merited the owner. Harold cleared his throat, irritated. "Yes, the stallion, of course."

"Of course. If you'll follow me, we'll have a look at him."

They passed an empty stall, then several that housed beautiful geldings and mares, before Kemble paused. "The stallion, he's quite a beast. Descended from Warrior Prince. Now, if it's a gentleman's horse you're after, you may wish to have a look at Marty here." He gestured inside a stall. "Fine gelding."

Harold flicked the animal an impatient glance. The horse *was* fine, but he suspected Kemble had mentally deemed him, Harold, unworthy of the finest animal the stables currently had to offer.

"Anyone there?" A deep male voice sounded toward the entrance.

"One moment, Mr. Wetherby." Kemble rushed off to greet the new visitor.

Harold ground his teeth.

"Your Grace! This is a surprise." Kemble's voice carried through the stable. "And an honor, may I add. If we'd known you were coming, I'm sure Mr. Derringworth would have arranged to greet you personally."

Harold peered toward the entrance as Kemble returned at the side of a man Harold immediately recognized. The Duke of Beaufort. Powerful and respected, the man could have anything in the world just for the asking. Harold hated him. Or would have, if he hadn't wanted so badly to *be* him.

"What can I do for you?" Kemble was asking.

"My brother-in-law tells me you may have a stallion worth looking at."

Harold felt his chest swell. The duke was interested in the very same horse as he was. Yes, he, Harold Wetherby, former nobody, was a man on the rise.

"Indeed. Fine creature." As they drew close to Harold, Kemble started, having seemingly forgotten his presence. "Right. In fact, Mr. Wellesley and I were just headed back that way. Mr. Wellesley, what did you think of Marty here?"

"Wetherby," Harold corrected stiffly. "And I'd prefer to see the stallion."

"Certainly. Only . . . Your Grace, do you mind?"

Harold bristled—*he'd* been here first, with an appointment. But the duke gave a nonchalant shrug.

"Then come with me, gentlemen."

At the end of the hall was a stall twice the size of the others. The stallion inside was massive, its coat a gleaming chestnut tone.

In truth, Harold had never been comfortable

around large animals, but when he saw the duke glance at the horse and give the manager an approving nod, he quelled the urge to cringe.

He nodded at the stallion as well, then stoutly declared, "Now that's more like it. I want something that'll impress my fiancée."

"You're to be married?" the assistant asked, finally looking away from the duke long enough to spare Harold a glance. "Congratulations."

The stallion tossed his head and snorted. Harold took a nervous step backward before catching himself—he did *not* wish to lose face in front of Beaufort.

"Storm Runner, he's called," Kemble told them. "He needs a firm hand."

The duke nodded. "A firm hand, perhaps, but the animal has clearly been kept in beautiful condition."

Harold forced a loud laugh. "Needs a firm hand, eh? So will my fiancée. A beauty, but headstrong. I'll train them both together."

The assistant manager opened his mouth as though to say something, but promptly closed it.

"Yes, indeed." Harold cracked his knuckles, already anticipating the moment he could relay this afternoon's events to his friend Cutter at their club. Here he was, sharing horse talk and manly jokes with the Duke of Beaufort.

On a roll, Harold continued, "An animal just has to be shown who its master is before he—or she—will mind him. Then it's a smooth ride. Heh. I do enjoy a good ride." He winked and reached over the door of the stable to stroke the stallion, but the animal tossed its head and backed away.

He waived a hand toward the horse. "'Course, I'd be

willing to bet Storm Runner here will come around before Elizabeth does."

"Elizabeth?" the duke asked quickly.

"Oh, yes," Wetherby went on, his chest swelling further, "Elizabeth Medford. Perhaps you've heard of her? A baron's daughter. Fine old family. Pretty chit, too, though, as I said, a bit headstrong. Nothing, of course, a man like myself can't handle."

The duke's expression was unreadable. Could he possibly be jealous? Unreasonable though she could be, there was no denying Elizabeth was attractive. In their recent argument, Elizabeth had all but admitted an interest in Beaufort. But no bloody way Harold would let her out of his clutches now. He resolved to press her uncle to make the announcement soon.

There was just one thing left to seal this as the perfect afternoon. Harold bobbed his head toward the stallion. "What do you want for him?"

The assistant manager fidgeted. "Mr. Wetherby, if it's a good, er, ride, you're looking for, perhaps a racehorse isn't your ideal fit."

The duke glanced between them, expression still blank. Harold recalled Beaufort had a reputation for ruthlessness, and complete lack of emotion, at the card table.

Harold folded his arms. "What do you want for the horse?"

Kemble squared his shoulders and gestured toward the stallion. "Well, Mr. Wetherby, a horse with a breeding record like Storm Runner . . ." his voice trailed off meaningfully.

Harold's neck heated. Damn it, this *assistant* was not going to make him look bad in front of the duke. "What do you *want* for him?"

The young man glanced anxiously at the duke, then back to Harold. "Perhaps, if you are interested, you could make an appointment—"

"I'm prepared to talk now," Harold said with clenched fists.

"The asking price," Kemble told them, "is twelve hundred pounds."

The duke, a man known for extravagance in all facets of life, didn't flinch. Harold, on the other hand, had to swallow, hard. The nincompoop of an assistant was trying to *rob* him.

"That is a handsome amount. I say"—Harold forced himself to breathe normally—"perhaps if you were to put the animal through its paces, show me what it's capable of . . ." He needed to buy some time.

Perhaps he could spot some flaw, force the assistant to lower the price. Because if a stallion from the Derringworth stables truly went for twelve hundred pounds, Harold was way out of his league.

"Of course, I am happy to take Storm Runner out," Kemble replied. "I assure you, when you see him in action, you'll see his price is fully justified. I'll just get him ready."

Before he could do so, the duke held up a hand.

"Sold."

"Pardon?" Kemble asked.

"What?" The question exploded from Harold before he could consider the wisdom of asking it.

The duke spoke to the assistant, ignoring Harold completely now. "I've done business with Derringworth's long enough to know you stand behind your animals. Storm Runner's worth at least that much. I'll send my solicitor with a bank draft for the full amount first thing tomorrow. Is that sufficient?"

"Now wait a minute—" Wetherby sputtered.

But neither man paid him any attention.

"Of course, Your Grace," Kemble said. "Absolutely."

Anger bloomed in Harold as he realized that all along, his presence at the stable, and in front of the duke, had been merely tolerated. Come to think of it, the duke hadn't actually laughed at his jokes. And when it came time to transact business, apparently he was invisible—at best.

"Unbelievable," Harold muttered, and stormed out.

The two remaining men watched him go.

"Your Grace," the assistant manager said, "I can't begin to tell you how sorry I am . . ."

"Not to worry," Alex told him. "He was no one of significance."

Kemble nodded. "Exactly. Please, let me assure you that Derringworth's does *not* cater to such clientele. I only pity the woman to whom he's betrothed."

"Indeed." Impossible to believe that *boob* was marrying the fiery redhead. The arrogant ass couldn't even handle purchasing a horse. There was no way he'd get his hands on Elizabeth Medford.

Chapter Three

"I'm in the most awful fix, Bea."

"Whatever has happened?"

"I've run out of time," Elizabeth answered. "You know the circumstances in which my father left us. It seems the rest of the ton knows as well. My prospects are . . ." she swallowed, "diminished."

"I am sorry, E.," Bea said, squeezing Elizabeth's hand.

Elizabeth could tell she actually was sorry, unlike so many others that mouthed the words while secretly relishing the downfall of a peer. It was one more reason she counted Beatrice Pullington a true friend.

When Elizabeth had arrived on Bea's doorstep the night before, fully packed valise in hand, she'd been welcomed without question. Bea had installed her in a comfortable guestroom and seen to her every need, and Elizabeth had succumbed to exhaustion after her turmoil-filled day.

Now it was midmorning, and the two women relaxed in the small salon of Bea's town house while they batted about ideas for Elizabeth's future.

"It isn't just that. My mother's brother, Uncle George, is head of the family now. He's insisting he can't support all of us, and he's going to marry me off to my single remaining prospect—Harold Wetherby."

"Wetherby." Bea wrinkled her nose, cocked her head in thought. "I don't know him."

"Not personally. He's some sort of remote cousin of my mother's. He doesn't move in the higher circles. But I've told you about him, Bea."

Slowly, Bea's eyes widened with understanding. "*That* Wetherby? The one from that picnic, the one who—"

"The same."

"No," Bea said weakly, reaching for her tea and taking a fortifying sip.

"I'm not going back. I'd sooner work for a living."

"Doing what?"

"That's the problem. I thought maybe I could be a seamstress."

"A seamstress?" Bea looked doubtful.

"I'm good with a needle," Elizabeth said.

"Yes, but E., the best modistes will want references, and you'll have none. You wouldn't want to work for the sort that would hire you without a reference." Bea poured a fresh cup of tea for each of them and offered Elizabeth a plate of biscuits.

The lack of references was a dilemma Elizabeth hadn't anticipated. "What do you suggest? There are few ways a woman can earn a living and remain anonymous."

"Sadly true. I know a woman who earns her living writing books . . ."

"I've no head for that, Bea. And, besides, it would take too long. I need something soon."

"Well, you're welcome to stay here as long as you like. It's no hardship."

"I know, and I do thank you for it. I don't know where I'd have gone if not here. But I can't stay in hiding forever, and I'd just as soon move on. Whatever work I find, it must be somewhere my uncle won't think to look for me."

Leaving the safe haven of Bea's house would be difficult, especially knowing that whatever life held for her next, it was unlikely to even remotely resemble the life she'd known before her father died. What line of work was appropriate for the runaway daughter of a disgraced, deceased baron?

"I could be a governess," Elizabeth suggested.

"Truly? A governess?" Bea made a face. Her own marriage had not been fruitful. "Caring for someone else's children? What if they're spoiled or unruly?"

"Oh, Bea. I love children."

"But E., do you think you've the disposition for being a governess? It's just, you're a bit headstrong—though I love you for it—and I think that sort of thing is frowned upon in governesses."

"I'm sure I can overcome that. I haven't the luxury of getting into scrapes anymore," Elizabeth replied. "But I would probably have the same problem in getting references."

"Very likely. If a seamstress must have references, imagine what—wait! I know just the person who might take you on. She may recognize you, but she's a kind soul, and I overheard someone at a tea the other day saying she was looking to hire a governess. She lives in the country, so you're less likely to be seen."

"Who?"

"The Viscountess Grumsby."

"Grumsby, Grumsby . . ." Elizabeth thought aloud, trying to place the name. "The Duke of Beaufort's sister. *Alex Bainbridge's sister.* I couldn't possibly!"

"E., I know you had a tendre for him, but now that nothing's come of that, I fail to see the problem."

"It isn't just that." Miserably, Elizabeth relayed the details of her most recent encounter with the duke.

"My." Bea took another fortifying sip of tea, then grinned. "That was daring. Did I say before that you were a bit headstrong? I believe I misspoke. You're not a bit headstrong, you are *entirely* so!"

Elizabeth's cheeks heated, but she smiled back.

"Though, really, you're in the same place now as you would have been if he'd agreed," Bea continued. "A bit uncomfortable if he happens to visit, of course, but no reason you can't stay mostly out of sight."

True. Only, if he *had* agreed, Elizabeth thought, she'd have been able to live out her dreams before descending to the lower rungs of Society's ladder.

"At any rate," Bea said, "it's worth a try. As I said, Lady Grumsby lives in the country most of the time, which will protect you from most prying eyes."

"But what if Alex has told her about me?"

"Unlikely. If he wasn't willing to have his name bandied about with yours in scandal, why would he say anything?" Bea airily waved a hand. "He's probably forgotten it entirely."

Elizabeth wasn't so sure about that, but as she could think of no better option, and the thought of leaving town for a while held a certain appeal, she agreed to the plan.

Within hours, Beatrice sent a message to Lady Grumsby. In the letter Bea gave Elizabeth her full endorsement for the position, though, as she confided,

"I may not be the best of references, having never hired a governess myself."

Since it was possible Lady Grumsby would recognize her anyway, Elizabeth agreed with Bea's recommendation that she *not* use a false name. She just prayed her mother wouldn't find out. Lady Medford took her noble status quite seriously.

The next few days were spent anxiously awaiting a response. As she could hardly stroll about the streets of London without being seen, Elizabeth kept to the house. Bea had more freedom, and, with Charity's help, managed to retrieve two of Elizabeth's plainest frocks from the Medford home. They'd already been dyed gray for the half-mourning period following her father's death.

"If you're to work as a governess, you must look the part," Bea said as she helped remove the white lace that gave the gowns their only fashionable touch. "Word of your disappearance hasn't yet leaked to the ton. Your sister tells me the family's keeping it a secret, hoping to find you first and make the whole matter go away. The scandal would be huge. I, of course, swore I knew nothing. But, E., are you sure you're doing the right thing?"

Elizabeth's most recent encounter with Harold leapt to mind. Unconsciously she touched the now-fading bruises below her collarbone. "Definitely."

Bea patted her arm. "As long as you're sure."

Finally the good news came that Lady Grumsby was indeed interested in interviewing Miss Medford. Bea helped her friend pack, and Elizabeth purchased a seat on a traveling coach departing the following morning. No more private carriages in her future.

The coach was slow and bumpy, and at one particularly steep hill, the driver asked the passengers to walk alongside the vehicle, easing the burden on the team of horses. Never before had Elizabeth traveled like this—no companion, no chaperone, and no conveyance of her own.

She was dusty and exhausted by late afternoon, when they stopped at a coaching inn. Thankfully, the Grumsbys had sent one of their servants with a wagon to convey her the remaining distance, for spending the night alone at the inn—even if she'd acquired a private room—was too daunting a prospect.

In spite of the early start, it was nearing dark by the time they drew near Garden Home, the estate belonging to the Duke of Beaufort's sister and her husband. Given the innocuous name, Elizabeth had been expecting a pleasant but modest estate. Instead, the wagon rolled past vast manicured lawns, and finally drew near a sprawling mansion that seemed a conglomeration of every architectural style England had known in the past four hundred years. Oddly, the effect was intriguing, softened by the profusion of spring blooms that sprouted from numerous welltended flowerbeds.

The servant Elizabeth rode with had a delivery of milk and butter for the kitchens, and he drew the cart around back. She thanked him for his trouble, then climbed down slowly.

If this didn't work, she had no alternate plan.

The matter of the viscountess's relationship to Alex Bainbridge was still discomforting, but Elizabeth had resolved—assuming she was offered the position—

to simply stay away from any gatherings he was likely to attend.

With trepidation, Elizabeth knocked at the rear entrance to Viscount Grumsby's manor.

A maid came to the door and looked Elizabeth up and down. "Yes?"

"I'm here to interview for the position of governess."

The maid modified her facial expression to one of greater respect. "Yes, mum. Lady Grumsby expects you'll be tired from the travel. I'm to show you to a room, and you'll interview first thing in the morn. Just this way."

Elizabeth bit her lip but followed the maid down a corridor, unused to being treated so casually by the help. She'd best get used to it, though, for a governess's station, while above that of a maid's, was far lower than that to which she was accustomed.

The maid directed Elizabeth to a small but comfortable room, and after leaving briefly, returned with warm water for washing, followed by a dinner tray. Elizabeth ate, grateful her hosts seemed to have thought of everything. Still, she spent a restless night, wondering what she would do if this latest plan failed.

Elizabeth woke early and was fully dressed—not to mention anxious—by the time the maid reappeared at her door. After a quick breakfast, she was led back to the main hall.

The maid indicated a small, padded bench against one of the walls near a door that led, presumably, to a salon. "Wait just here."

Elizabeth sat, imagining how best to present her limited qualifications when she was called in.

The maid disappeared through the doorway and reappeared moments later. "Lady Grumsby will see you now."

Elizabeth slowly let out the breath she hadn't realized she was holding and entered the salon, a pleasant room decorated in shades of ivory and pale blue. A lovely brunette, a few years her senior, sat on the edge of a delicate chair near a writing desk. Her physical appearance made her relationship to her ducal brother immediately clear.

Mindful of her new social status, Elizabeth sank into a curtsy. "My lady. I had not realized I would be interviewing with the lady of the house."

"My children are important to me. Finding a governess for them is not a task I deem appropriate to entrust to just anyone."

Elizabeth smiled, approving of the woman's sentiment.

"And you are Miss Medford?"

Elizabeth hesitated. She prayed the name Medford was common enough that the viscountess would not think to associate her, a girl applying for the position of governess, with the baron's daughter of the same name. "Yes, my lady."

"Right. Well, Miss Medford, I would not normally interview someone without references, but Lady Pullington did suggest I speak with you, so I suppose that's a reference of sorts. And it is the Season, when most governesses have already hired on to other families, so I am considering all applicants. My last governess left rather suddenly, to care for an ailing relative. You may sit." She gestured to a small chair, cushioned in pale yellow. "Please tell me of your qualifications."

Elizabeth opened her mouth to speak, determined

to bluff her way through this, when a sudden frown creased the viscountess's forehead.

"Wait a moment. You said your name was Medford? You're no relation to—no, you couldn't be. My neighbor was filling me in on all that's happened so far in the Season and the name Medford came up, and I just thought . . . and your red hair . . ."

Elizabeth was caught. She shifted uncomfortably on the small chair. However daring she'd learned to be, she wasn't an outright liar. "Yes, my lady. I am Lord Medford's daughter."

"No! But what are you doing applying as a governess?" Lady Grumsby's eyes reflected embarrassment for them both.

"It's rather a long story. Please, my lady, I assure you I am sincere in this application. My circumstances are no longer what they were. I need this position, and I love children. I am willing to work hard, to care for them and teach them as much as I know." Passion filled her voice as she pled with the woman not to turn her out. This was her last, best hope.

Viscountess Grumsby folded her hands and gave Elizabeth a long look. "Have you been compromised?"

"No, my lady. But my family can no longer support two unwed daughters, and I've no wish to be a burden, nor do I have any suitable opportunity to wed." Elizabeth hoped the viscountess would not pry further, for to explain that she'd refused her family's choice of suitor and left home would not reflect well on her character, no matter how abusive that suitor might be. Better to let Lady Grumsby think she'd been an utter failure in the marriage mart.

"I see. I am sorry to hear of your family's misfortune." Lady Grumsby's expression gentled, and Elizabeth breathed a sigh of relief. "You understand the responsibilities of a governess? 'Tis hardly the life you are used to."

"Yes, my lady. I understand."

"Well, if you were raised in Society, then I cannot fault your education. My children are young yet, but I do wish them exposed to good morals and learning."

"Mine was most adequate, my lady."

"I will grant you the position on a trial basis. If, after a period of three months, I, and the children, find you suitable, you may stay on."

Elizabeth smiled genuinely. "Thank you, my lady. This means a lot to me. I shall not disappoint you."

"Lovely. I shall be most glad of your assistance with the children, for I am expecting guests in a fortnight. A small house party during my brother's visit."

Elizabeth's stomach flipped, but she maintained a pleasant smile. Alex Bainbridge was coming. The man before whom she'd utterly humiliated herself.

The man who could have her fired with the merest word.

So much for a peaceful existence in the country. It appeared she would be put to the test immediately.

Alex spurred his mount across the final stretch of open field. The stallion tossed its head, then flexed its muscles beneath him as it responded to the command. Alex reveled in the crisp air rushing through his hair. His eyes teared at the corners as the horse gained speed, flying over the acres of the Grumsby estate.

He could think of nothing he'd rather be doing on this perfect May morning. He'd purchased that stallion at the Derringworth stables on behalf of his brother-in-law, Brian Grumsby. Normally, he'd have examined the animal thoroughly before making an offer, but he'd been too irritated by that sorry lout Wetherby to bother negotiating.

Brian hadn't balked at the price, but knowing Alex was the better horseman, had merely asked him to put the animal through its paces, once it had been delivered, to evaluate whether the amount had been fair. Alex welcomed the task, and the excuse to spend some time in the country.

The physical exertion of this morning's ride helped wrench his mind from the dissolution of his past, and the clean, open air and fields eased the feelings of suffocation that had lately plagued him in London.

His brother-in-law had acquired a fine, strong horse. It was young, and a bit lacking in polish and endurance, but that would come with time and maturity.

Alex let his mind wander as the ground disappeared beneath the flash of hooves. In London he was constantly hounded by businessmen, fawning nobles, and aspiring women. The business he enjoyed, and he'd long since grown used to the others, but sometimes a man just wanted to be left to himself. He'd been feeling that way more and more often of late.

The fact was—and he was man enough to admit it—he'd come to a point in his life where he wasn't quite sure of his direction. His estates and investments were operating smoothly. After fifteen years of watching his ventures pay off, he was confident in all his business decisions. But he was no longer inspired, no longer driven to prove himself. Nor was he interested in living the life of leisure and dissipation so many of his fellow noblemen embraced. He'd certainly tried it. But the cards grew old, the women tiresome. And the one time he'd made a mistake, it had been disastrous.

No, he needed something different, something new. He just didn't know what.

The country house with its manicured grounds came into view. After he cooled off the horse, he would have a nice visit with his sister and say hello to her children, who adored their only uncle. The other guests would arrive soon. He hadn't been thrilled to hear of the party, but Marian rarely entertained and was counting on his presence. He wouldn't let her down by returning to London.

As he approached the gardens, Alex reined in the horse. The children were out enjoying the morning with their governess, each tugging on one of her hands as they excitedly pointed out flowers, bugs, and other delights. Young Henry struggled to hold the leash of an exuberant black Labrador puppy, a recent gift for his sixth birthday.

Their governess was a plain woman, in gray cap and gown, but her attentiveness to the children was admirable. Alex saw her nod and laugh as his niece, Clara, held up a tiny bird's nest for examination. So absorbed was she in her young charge's treasure that she failed to hear Alex's approach. The puppy, on the other hand, went wild with excitement, broke free of Henry's grip, and ran pell-mell through the garden before rushing back to the trio.

Poor Henry grabbed for the trailing leash as the puppy dashed between Clara and the governess, toppling them both as he was brought up short. Masses of red hair tumbled out of the governess's cap, which now sat severely askew.

Alex caught his breath. Only one woman he knew

had hair like that. But what in blazes would *she* be doing here? He dismounted quickly.

Plain, indeed. The children's governess, he saw as he strode toward the garden, was none other than Elizabeth Medford. She dusted herself off gingerly and checked Clara for bruises while Henry admonished his puppy.

"Don't scold him too hard, Master Henry," she said. "He's just a pup, after all, and what is a pup to do when a great, scary horse rides up?"

Elizabeth looked up, and Alex saw her eyes widen as she recognized him. Her cheeks filled with color and she shook her head slightly.

Alex nodded, acknowledging her silent plea. He had plenty of questions for the brash Society miss-turned-governess, but he would not embarrass her by raising them in front of the children.

"Uncle Alex!" Blissfully unaware of the tension between the two adults, Henry jumped up and down in an effort to get his uncle's attention.

"Your governess is right, Henry," Alex said smoothly, bending for the little boy's hug. "Here, let me show you a better way to hold that leash."

Elizabeth's eyes were boring holes in the back of his neck, but he absorbed himself in puppy care. From the corner of his eye, he saw her straighten her cap and withdraw to a small garden bench as he played with the children. Her meek attitude completely belied the brazen chit he remembered from that morning in Hyde Park. The serviceable gray serge gown also made clear that she was not merely a guest of his sister who'd taken the children for a stroll.

What on earth had happened in the last two weeks

to change her so completely? And how had she landed in his sister's employ?

Whether Miss Medford wished it or not, he was going to find out more.

With a promise to return soon, he sent the children running back to Elizabeth.

He quickly found a lad to care for the stallion—thankfully the beast hadn't wandered far—and strode into the house, ignoring the servants' subtle glances at his dusty boots and jacket. He needed to find Marian.

His sister sat in her favorite salon, the blue-and-white room, working peacefully at her embroidery.

"What is *she* doing here?" Alex boomed.

Marian jumped, dropping her needlework. "Who?"

"*Her*. Miss Medford."

"I took her on as governess to the children."

"Clearly. But—" Alex searched his mind for how to say what needed to be said. He strode toward his sister. "Do you even know who she is?"

"Of course I do," Marian said calmly. "Sit down, Alex. There's no need for dramatics. I fail to see why you're upset. It isn't the poor woman's fault her circumstances are so reduced. Would you rather I'd turned her away?"

"No." Alex raked a hand through his hair, ignoring the invitation to sit. "Yes."

Marian narrowed her eyes at him, no stranger to the rumors about her brother's many romantic liaisons. "Is there anything *else* I should know about her?"

Alex's shoulders slumped. "No." In spite of Elizabeth's outrageous proposal—a proposal he could *not* stop thinking about—nothing had actually happened.

And he'd agreed not to mention their conversation, so there was really nothing more to say.

Marian's gaze softened. "She's good with the children, Alex. She just wants to live quietly, forget the past, and do her job. That's all I ask as well. I imagine it's difficult for her. Just let her be."

Slowly, Alex took a seat. Elizabeth was a schemer. He was sure of it. A beautiful one, to be sure, but no young lady of the ton would willingly trade her privileged life for the work of a governess. Had her only marital option been that boor he'd met at the stables? He'd not heard Elizabeth described as one of the ton's Incomparables, but surely she'd had suitors besides the one she'd been so desperate to avoid. And if she was absolutely determined *not* to marry, any number of men would happily support her in a comfortable style for the favors she'd rashly—and freely—offered *him*. Of course, her reputation would be shredded. She was too intelligent not to realize that.

Nor did he believe it pure coincidence that she had hired on with the sister of the man to whom she'd made that insane proposal.

No, Elizabeth Medford was definitely up to something. He just didn't know what. And, clearly, Marian had been just as taken in by Elizabeth as Alex had been by her father.

"So, who have you invited to this party of yours?" he asked to change the subject. "It's a small affair, right? After all, the Season is still on."

"A smallish affair," Marian confirmed. "About twenty guests." A matchmaking look Alex knew too well lit his sister's eyes. "Miss Landow and Miss Symington will be in attendance, along with a cousin of theirs just returned from France. I can't recall her name just now. Unmarried," she added helpfully.

"I see. Please, do not tell me this party has been concocted for the purpose of finding me a lifelong companion."

"A fiancée." Marian's features took on the fierceness of one going into battle. "No, that's not why I'm having the party, strictly speaking. But it wouldn't hurt you to look. When are you going to settle down, Alex? Your youthful follies were fine for, well, a youth, but it's been some time since you've seriously courted anyone."

"I'm not interested."

"You need an heir," Marian pressed.

"You speak as though I've one foot in the grave already."

Marian's expression softened. "No, of course not. I just want to see you happy. And no matter what you claim, I don't believe all your little *affaires* are actually making you that way."

She had a point. But admitting it would only add fuel to her fire. "We'll see," he said instead.

Alex's plan to uncover Elizabeth's true motives was not progressing well. He'd learned disappointingly little from his sister. Confronting Elizabeth in person proved difficult, for the tempting governess had made herself quite scarce. As soon as the guests for the house party had arrived, Elizabeth and the children had retreated to the nursery, or wherever it was children went with their governesses these days.

When she did appear in the open, she had the children in tow, and they were usually off to the gardens or the pond—somewhere, Alex realized, she was unlikely to be recognized by the other guests.

On Saturday afternoon, Alex watched as Elizabeth walked with the little ones in the garden, pointing out the various plants and shrubs. A nature lesson, he guessed.

The other houseguests were on an outing in the nearby town, but Alex had begged off, citing estate matters and correspondence. He'd dispatched those matters with ease, leaving the remainder of the day to his leisure.

Elizabeth laughed, presumably at something one of the children had said. She'd allowed her bonnet to fall back, and the rays of the sun kissed her cheeks and gleamed on her hair.

She was an enigma. Three weeks ago, he'd thought her no more than a spoiled, defiant daughter who didn't know what was best for her—and who came from a family of schemers. Most of London knew by now that the Medford coffers were empty, the family teetering on the brink of ruin. He was well aware of his own role in bringing them to that state, but what had Miss Medford actually hoped to accomplish when she'd approached him in the park? And why *him?*

True, she wanted to avoid marrying the arrogant pig he'd encountered at the Derringworth stables, but Elizabeth could have gone to any other nobleman— any other *man,* for that matter —and made him the same proposal she'd made to him. He couldn't imagine many, besides himself, would turn her down.

But, apparently, she hadn't sought out another man, a fact he found oddly satisfying.

She had, however, been serious enough about avoiding

the unwanted marriage to accept work as a governess and risk being ostracized from her family.

Judging from the genuine smile she gave the little girl holding her hand now, she didn't appear to be sulking over that decision. He had to give her credit for that.

Was her behavior with the children the true Elizabeth, and that morning in the park with him only a fluke? Alex considered himself an excellent judge of character, but he'd made a grave mistake with her father, and Elizabeth confused him even more. Even so, he wanted her.

Alex resolved once more to speak with the unusual Miss Medford. If only he could get her alone.

Chapter Four

Though the Grumsbys' house was spacious and well constructed, the walls could not completely mute the sounds of the ongoing party. Elizabeth willed herself to ignore them, but the occasional clink of a glass and low rumbles of laughter were excruciating reminders of how much she had lost.

She'd thought she'd reconciled herself to her new station. But knowing *he* was downstairs, likely surrounded by fluttering women vying for his attention . . . remembering how desperately she'd wanted his attention for herse . . . well, she simply could not concentrate on responding to Bea's most recent letter.

At least the duke had left her alone since that first morning, reducing her opportunities to further embarrass herself. Not to mention reducing her own opportunities to gaze longingly at the man who obviously found her charms lacking.

Did he think her a charlatan in her new role as governess? Thank the heavens he hadn't said anything to Lady Grumsby about their last encounter, or she'd have been fired and back in Harold's clutches for certain.

Perhaps it was like Bea had said, and he'd dismissed her from his mind entirely. If only she could do the same about him.

Instead, Elizabeth wished that for one day, she could have the luxury Alex Bainbridge did—not the material items, but the luxury to behave however recklessly he desired, and emerge unscathed.

Another rumble of laughter sounded, and she imagined him at the center of an admiring group.

Finally she gave up all pretense of writing. If Bea didn't receive a response immediately, she was unlikely to worry.

Elizabeth couldn't sit still any longer. She pulled a light shawl around her shoulders and quietly left her room. A walk in the gardens was in order. To be so near the duke, and yet so far, made her heart ache. But she'd stay well away from the party. She'd no desire to see the other guests—it was only too likely she'd be recognized and pitied.

The faint scent of earth and new growth lingered in the air as she stepped away from the house. She breathed it in, relaxing slightly. The moon hung low and bright in the sky. She and the solitary orb had something in common: they were alone. She forced her mind to focus on it, letting the tinkling sounds of the house party wash over her like harmless waves.

She was away from Harold, and she had employment. She'd just never realized how lonely her new life would be.

Inside, Alex smiled obligingly at the comely miss—what was her name?—with whom Marian had set him up. He stifled a yawn.

Alex loved his sister dearly, but this party was beyond mundane.

"I think I need a bit of fresh air," he lied.

The young lady brightened, no doubt imagining a romantic interlude. "Shall I accompany you, Your Grace?"

"No."

Her face fell. She gathered her skirts and, with a hasty curtsy, rushed off to join the gaggle of women surrounding his sister. Perfect. Marian would undoubtedly hear firsthand about his beastly behavior. Alex tossed back his wine, wishing it was brandy. Marian could scold him if she wanted, but he wasn't about to start encouraging every vapid miss that came his way. His heart wasn't in it.

Before another of Marian's guests could attach herself to him, Alex made a hasty exit, heading outdoors to back up the claim he needed air. He could always come back in through another entrance and seek the solace of his rooms.

Perhaps he'd become too accustomed to more wicked pursuits, because tonight, when the "entertainment" consisted of sipping wine and politely listening to pianoforte performances, he felt as though he were dying a slow death.

As he rounded a path outdoors and spied the silhouette of a young woman standing alone in the garden, the evening became infinitely more interesting—particularly because the gleam of moonlight on auburn hair immediately gave her identity away.

Unconsciously, he softened his step. This time, she'd not be able to avoid him.

He waited until he stood just behind her before asking

the question he'd been pondering since discovering her in his sister's employ. "Why are you here?"

She whipped around, eyes large. "Your Grace."

He inclined his head.

"I was just, that is"—she gestured toward the sky— "the moon is lovely tonight."

"So it is. But that only answers part of my question."

"I beg your pardon?"

"What brings you here, Miss Medford? To Garden Home?"

"You know the answer to that, Your Grace. I am governess to your nephew and niece."

"Of course."

"What do you mean, 'of course'?" Her chin went up. "Your sister was kind to hire me, and I am thankful for the position."

He admired her unique combination of spirit and humility. She wasn't too proud to admit she was grateful to have work, but she was strong enough to defend her choice. And now that he'd met Harold Wetherby, Alex had an inkling of why she'd made that decision. But he wanted to hear it from her. Why *had* she run away, when so many other women in her plight would have submissively married the prig?

"I had the pleasure of meeting your fiancé," he announced, keeping his tone jovial.

She frowned. "My fiancé?"

"Wetherby informs me you two are to marry."

Even the moonlight couldn't hide her deep flush. Embarrassment, or something else? Anger, perhaps?

"Oh, yes. We're very much in love," she choked out.

"So Wetherby says," Alex lied. "He is . . . really something. However did you manage to catch him?"

A strangled laugh escaped her throat. "Sheer luck, I suppose."

"Oh, come now," he teased. "A beauty like yourself? Wetherby must have done away with all your other suitors to even have a chance."

"Something like that," she said faintly, and pulled her shawl closer around her shoulders.

Ah. So she *hadn't* had other offers. At least none her father had accepted prior to his death. Elizabeth was attractive, but her lack of dowry was public knowledge. Guilt pricked him, and he resisted the urge to draw her close and protect her.

Instead, Alex decided to raise the stakes of their verbal game. "So, tell me. How does Wetherby feel about his fiancée working as a governess?"

Some unidentifiable emotion flickered in her eyes, but she kept her stance proud. "I was quite grief-stricken when my father died, and not at all ready to wed. Harold understands that. And he understands the necessity of working to support oneself, having done so himself."

Alex was willing to bet Wetherby would happily live off another's largess, given the opportunity. But that was not his main concern.

"Ah. So he does know you're here."

She hesitated.

The game was up.

"Elizabeth? The truth, if you please."

She looked away, her posture so rigid that, especially in the moonlight, she could have been made of marble.

"All right. If you must know, Harold does not know my new location," she murmured.

"And you wish to keep it that way," he surmised.

She'd rather toil in obscurity than marry that cretin. It was a decision few of her sex would make, but one he could respect.

"You won't say anything to him, will you?" she pled, stepping closer and placing one hand on his jacket. There was real fear in her voice.

He placed his hand over hers. Wetherby was more of a bastard than he'd thought, if he frightened her so. Alex gentled his tone. "No. I will say nothing."

She breathed a sigh of relief. She made a tiny motion to withdraw her hand, but he held it firm.

"But you must make me a promise in return."

"My lord?"

"I've yet to have a dull encounter with you, Miss Medford. Which sets you apart from most of your female counterparts."

"Thank you, I suppose," she answered. Her tongue darted out nervously to wet her lips.

A flash of heat, of pure sensual awareness, passed through him. He released her hand in surprise. "It was indeed intended as a compliment," he told her.

"But what must I promise you?"

Never taking his gaze from hers, he gave her his most wicked grin. "Stop avoiding me."

Her features registered surprise. Alex was tempted to kiss away the expression, but settled instead for a light brush of his fingers against her cheek before he strode back to the house. He'd learned what he needed to know—there was no point in scaring her off.

His sojourn in the country had suddenly become far more entertaining. *If* Elizabeth had the guts to keep that promise.

* * *

The Viscountess Grumsby didn't know it, but she was torturing Elizabeth. The small house party was supposed to last a week. It was the morning of day three, and Elizabeth felt trapped.

She'd been on edge ever since Alex Bainbridge had galloped, literally, back into her life. Blast her awful red hair. But for it, he might not have recognized her so quickly. The moment she'd looked up into those mocking dark eyes, she'd been struck by both embarrassment and longing. This was the man privy to, and in some way responsible for, the most excruciatingly humiliating moment of her life.

And yet one look into that sinfully handsome face, one moment spent observing his obvious caring for his niece and nephew, and Elizabeth was once more lost. Only this time she couldn't afford to humiliate herself. Her position depended on model behavior.

Decorum. Responsibility and decorum. She'd breached them once in her proposal to Alex, and once more in leaving home. A third indiscretion would surely mean her destruction.

And after their conversation in the garden last night, Elizabeth worried that indiscretion was *exactly* what the duke had in mind. If only the idea wasn't so tempting.

If Viscountess Grumsby had any notion of the thoughts Elizabeth harbored toward her brother, she'd be cast out without reference. And while being a governess was not a life of luxury, Elizabeth was content, at least for now. The Grumsby children were sweet-natured and eager to learn and explore. The lord and lady of the house treated her kindly. Her own family had, thus far, left her alone. Eventually, Elizabeth figured, she would come up with a more permanent solution for her future.

In the meantime, her governess's work provided just the haven she needed.

Elizabeth sighed and closed the door to the nursery. She'd just turned the children over to their nurse for a midday meal and rest. The Grumsbys' guests were gone on an afternoon outing. She could relax.

"I thought I'd never find you alone."

Elizabeth gasped and turned. Her heart gave a little *thud*. There, on the stair landing, stood the man she'd just been trying to forget.

"Your Grace."

"You can be quite evasive, Miss Medford."

He sounded amused.

Elizabeth kept her gaze about six inches below his chin, unwilling to see the mocking expression she knew he wore. "I don't know what you mean, Your Grace. My position here keeps me quite busy."

"You haven't been avoiding me?"

To answer she'd have to lie or reveal too much, so Elizabeth kept silent. She dared a quick glance upward. The look in his eyes told her he knew.

"Whatever happened to your promise?"

She lifted her chin. "I don't believe I actually made that promise."

"You disappoint me, Elizabeth."

She disappointed herself as well, for the secret joy she took in his presence. *Decorum,* she thought once more, but the mental reminder was drowned out by the pounding of her heart, which had doubled in pace when he stepped near.

"Well," he said with a slow smile, "it appears you have a temporary reprieve from your many duties. Perhaps you will humor me with a stroll in the garden?"

"I've just recently come in from the garden," she replied, trying to keep from sounding peevish.

"I see. Well, perhaps you'd allow me to show you the library?"

"What are you doing here?" she asked instead.

"I might ask the same of you."

The deep timbre of his voice sent a shiver down her spine. "You haven't—" She swallowed and tried again. "You haven't told anyone what I did?"

"No. Though I do believe I am owed some answers. I am—how shall I say?—concerned, with what I learned last night. To the library, then?"

She was caught. After all, she'd promised, sort of, not to avoid him. He knew her secrets. She needed to keep his good favor. In all the years she'd hoped Alex Bainbridge would seek her out, she'd never imagined it quite this way. The bright side, she told herself, was that she *had* been meaning to look at the library.

"I would be most pleased," she acquiesced, trying not to think about what exact answers the lofty duke thought himself entitled to.

He gave her a satisfied grin and offered his arm, as though she were still Miss Medford, the baron's daughter, and not Miss Medford, governess to the nobility.

Feeling it would be churlish not to accept the gesture, Elizabeth placed her hand in the crook of his arm and allowed him to escort her downstairs and to the library. She already knew its location, of course, and was quite capable of conveying herself there, but for just a moment she chose to forget the past several months, to forget the vaguely threatening note in the duke's voice or the fact that he'd once rejected her utterly, and allow this fantasy to play itself out.

It was the middle of the day and there were servants about. Surely no harm could come of this.

"Ah, here we are," Alex said as he led her into a large, well-appointed library. Bookshelves, each filled to capacity, lined three walls. On the fourth, large mullioned windows overlooked the lawns of the estate. The chairs and chaises scattered about the room were designed for comfort. It was the perfect place to lose oneself in a book, or even just in thought.

"'Tis a lovely room, Your Grace," Elizabeth said. "Thank you for showing it to me."

He shot her a knowing look. "You wouldn't be anxious to be rid of me, would you, Miss Medford?"

"Of course not." It was a lie, and he knew it as well as she. She pressed her lips together and took a deep breath. "You said you wanted answers. Well, here is your answer, Your Grace. That moment in the park was folly. A rash and unwise move on my part. I have never done anything else like it, nor do I intend to.

"As for the man who fancies himself my fiancé, I have never agreed to marry him—or anyone else, for that matter. I need this position, and I will work hard to keep it. Again, I thank you for showing me the library."

He threw her a grin and swept a gallant arm toward the many shelves. "You're welcome. But I've hardly begun. Here, now, what shall we examine first?"

She sighed. There would be no getting rid of him. Worse, there was a wicked part of her soul that rejoiced with each moment he stayed.

He bypassed a wall full of scientific texts, then stopped suddenly before a shelf of Byron. "Ah! I know. You have a fondness for poetry, if I recall."

Elizabeth was no budding poet, but she *had* attended a poetry recital held by the duke's spinster cousin a couple months ago. The whole event had been awful, from the lackluster refreshments to the crowlike voice in which the duke's cousin delivered what, presumably, were poems.

No doubt Alex remembered because, in Elizabeth's haste to leave when the wretched event was over, she had tripped over a sagging flounce at the hem of her gown and stumbled into him. And while she'd seen any number of ladies swoon gracefully into the duke's arms, *she* had landed there out of pure clumsiness.

She gazed up at him now and caught the telltale twinkle in the duke's eyes. She grinned helplessly. "I do love a good poem."

"Well, I cannot claim to share my cousin's . . . *ahem,* . . . *skill* in recitation, but I can show you my sister's fine collection of poets."

"No performance?" Elizabeth feigned disappointment as Alex directed her to the shelf packed with leather-bound volumes. "Likely it's for the best. If I recall, I was so carried away by the last one I attended, I lost my bearings and nearly ran you over." She kept her tone light as she turned to look at the poetry books.

"Of course, I quite forgot. Perhaps I should steady you, then, as you peruse these tomes, in order to prevent a reoccurrence."

Elizabeth sucked in her breath as his hands settled gently on either side of her waist. The temptation to lean back into him, absorb his scent and strength, was nearly overwhelming. She bit her lip, hard, in hopes the pain would distract her.

"I shouldn't allow this," she whispered.

"If I recall," he countered, "you were willing to offer much more."

"That was before." But she closed her eyes as his thumbs gently stroked her sides. "I just told you—"

"Shh. You are an unusual woman, Elizabeth," he murmured, his head bent so she could feel the warmth of his breath behind her ear. "I confess you have quite captured my interest."

They were slipping into dangerous territory. Elizabeth knew it and tried to change course. She reached out to finger a volume of poetry, though by which poet, she had no idea. "You toy with me, Your Grace."

"Nay, never that."

"I know well you find me less than tempting." Elizabeth spoke with more conviction than she felt.

"You're wrong. I think you a temptress of the most dangerous sort."

His breath tickled her ear, awakening a longing for him to touch that same spot with his lips. She tried to focus instead on how crushed she'd felt when he'd rejected her that morning in the park.

She turned to face him. "Forgive my skepticism, Your Grace. It's only that I find it hard to believe that when I was a respectable member of the ton, when I *offered* myself to you with no strings attached, you found me lacking. And now here I stand, a mere governess, and your interest is piqued?"

He shrugged. "I don't like Society women."

The blunt tone made Elizabeth study him closely. "You toy with me, Your Grace," she repeated.

"I assure you, I do not. Society women are cold and calculating. They measure and analyze everything, down to the slightest comment or the color of a person's gloves, in their quest to rise to the top."

Elizabeth tilted her head sideways. He had a point. Her own mother was one such woman.

"You, on the other hand, fascinate me, for you were willing to give all that up. And then, I've seen you with the children. You are so much more natural with them, and I've seen you show them real affection, even though they are not yours. Which Elizabeth is real? The brazen miss that concocted that outrageous, though sorely tempting, idea for her own ruination? Or"—he lightly touched her cheek—"the one who stands before me, a caregiver who puts others' needs before her own?"

He drew her inexorably toward a nearby settee, until Elizabeth had no choice but to sit. He sat beside her and laid his hand lightly over hers.

Any reply Elizabeth had been forming fled her mind.

"See? You know I am right. Look, here we are, away from Society, having an actual conversation. How many conversations have you had at a ball that didn't revolve around what someone was wearing, who danced with whom, and how to interpret that as currency in the marriage mart?"

Elizabeth laughed. That was *exactly* what most conversations at a ball were like.

"You have a lovely smile. Although," he mused, fingering the plain gray fabric of her gown, then lightly touching the hair she'd scraped into a tight bun, "I did prefer your appearance as a young lady of the ton."

Elizabeth did not have time to be offended at the implied insult, for he continued in that thoughtful tone. "Odd, isn't it, how in Society women strive to appear soft and inviting, when underneath they are hard and brittle?

Yet you, as a warm-hearted governess, are expected to appear utterly proper, even drab."

"I'm sure that is appropriate for a governess," she replied primly, though his lingering touch on her hair sent little flutters throughout her body.

This was wrong. But she was powerless to stop him.

"Perhaps." His hand covered hers again. "But it makes me wonder . . . what would happen if I pulled those pins from your hair? Would I have a woman before me who was soft and warm both inside and out?"

"I'm sure I don't know," she whispered, as his hand came up to test his theory.

Common sense dictated she retreat, quickly, to the safety of her quarters. But the future spanned endlessly before her, devoid of passion. Was it so wrong to claim just one moment's pleasure for herself?

She made no move to stop him as he slowly pulled one pin, then another and another from her hair. Piece by piece it fell, until the whole mass of it lay tumbled about her shoulders.

"Yes, here is the beauty I recall. Like a waterfall, set magically aflame."

His tone turned husky and sent a shiver of anticipation up Elizabeth's spine.

"Cold?"

He stroked her arm gently, and the heat of his hand warmed her to the very blood.

She gave him a sideways smile. "I believe you may have a bit of poet's blood in you after all, Your Grace, for that was surely the most fanciful compliment I've ever been paid."

Her smile vanished, all teasing forgotten, as he bent his head to hers. His lips met hers briefly before he pulled back. The dark, smoldering gaze she met when she raised her eyes took her breath away, just before he hauled her against him and crushed his lips to hers.

His mouth moved against hers with barely restrained passion, molding, tasting, testing. Elizabeth was drowning in sensation. He held her fast, one hand buried in the hair at the nape of her neck as he tipped her back to deepen the kiss.

His tongue gently parted her lips, then probed, dipping in to taste, to stroke, until a sharp need began to pulse low in her belly. She reached out, her hands gripping his firm shoulders, seeking an anchor in the storm of sensation. Somehow she was no longer sitting, but lying against the settee, with the delicious thrill of Alex's weight above her. She returned his kiss as best she knew how.

When his hand moved to stroke her, moving up her bodice until it cupped her breast, she moaned low in her throat. Alex continued the pleasurable torment, teasing her through the fabric until her nipple hardened into a tight bud.

Only when he dipped into her bodice, and she felt the shock of his caress on her bare flesh, did Elizabeth remember any sense of propriety.

She jerked back, twisting from him until she landed in an unceremonious heap on the floor beside the settee. She stared at him, trying to catch her breath. The awkwardness of her position hastened the return of her senses. Luckily she was too mortified by her lack of propriety to be embarrassed by her lack of grace.

What had she just done?

Alex stared back, his eyes full of dark heat. Slowly he straightened and stood, formally offering a hand to assist her.

Mechanically, she took it and allowed him to haul

her to her feet. She straightened her clothing, then began searching for her hairpins, all the while not saying a word to the man she'd just passionately kissed.

Even as she berated herself for her behavior, she already missed his touch on her skin. What must he think of her? Oh, Lord, she was a fool. Much as she might wish for the freedom the duke enjoyed, she did not have it. Dallying with the Duke of Beaufort would surely get her fired from her governess's position. She snatched up her scattered pins and hastily jammed them into her hair.

Alex, who'd remained silent until now, gently stilled her hands. "Here, now. There's no need to stab yourself. It can't have been that bad a kiss."

Alex may have been used to such casual dalliance, but Elizabeth was not, and she did not know how to respond to the light teasing in his tone. How could he be so nonchalant? Had the kiss not affected him as it did her? Perhaps not. After all, he was far more experienced. To her horror, tears welled in her eyes.

She turned away to hide them, but not before the duke noticed. He cupped her chin to turn her head back, then stroked her cheekbone with his thumb. Elizabeth closed her eyes and held very still, wanting more than anything to go to him, to let him fold her in his strong arms and comfort her. It made no sense, for he was the cause of her discomfort, but her emotions were too jumbled to care.

Finally she managed to whisper, "I should go."

To her combined relief and disappointment, he stepped back. "As you wish. There's more to you than I would have guessed. I find you very intriguing, Miss Medford."

Elizabeth, desperate to recover some normalcy, reverted to their formal roles and dropped him a curtsy.

He regarded her with amusement, evident in the slight quirk of his full lips and the crinkles at the corner of his eyes. He bowed.

"You may leave now, Elizabeth. But do not think for a moment I will not seek you out again."

Chapter Five

Harold Wetherby stared at the letter on his desk and seethed.

"Bloody Medford," he growled.

"Bad news?" Jim Cutter sprawled in a chair across the room, idly examining a newspaper.

It was rude to examine one's correspondence with a guest present, but he and Cutter shared the same opinion of societal manners. Besides, Cutter was a friend—or at least the closest thing he had, which was to say they shared similar ambitions and tolerated one another's presence. Both rented town houses in the not-quite-fashionable district, and both wanted—felt they *deserved*—better.

"I loaned Lord Medford a goodly sum, a few years back," Harold answered. "Could scarcely afford it at the time, but I needed the man's support, his connections." He shrugged.

"Never paid you back?" Cutter guessed.

"No. Died last fall, suddenlike. Carriage accident in a storm."

Cutter nodded sympathetically.

Harold glared at the letter again—a polite note from the solicitor handling the Medford estate. The money was gone. And, apparently, he had no chance of recovering his losses.

He slammed his fist on the desk.

"Damn it." It didn't matter that he could afford the loss now. The baron had *used* him. And while Harold himself wasn't above using people, he didn't like having the tables turned.

Cutter wisely absorbed himself in the newspaper.

Harold ground his teeth. He had ambitions. As a child he'd hated being the "poor relation," hated the way people dismissed him, or thought to invite him and his mother to an event only when someone "extra" was needed to even the numbers. As a youth he'd used his girth, and his fists, to gain respect, or at least fear, from the other boys. But he'd soon figured out he wanted more.

"What galls me," he finally said, "is how someone like *him* is considered polite Society, while no matter how *I* study, how well I invest, how I *advance* myself, I'm still an outsider to the ton."

Cutter raised his newspaper in a mock toast. "To the English aristocratic system." He pitched the paper into the fireplace.

"Bet that daughter of Medford's isn't smirking now," Harold said, finally latching onto a thought that cheered him. "She's taunted me for years, with her careless acceptance of her place in Society. Thinks herself too good for me."

Anger flooded him as he remembered their last encounter. Elizabeth had been flirting in Society, barely out of full mourning, and she'd done it to avoid *him*. Because to her, he was nothing.

Harold ground his teeth again. He had Cutter's attention now.

"Threw my suit back in my face," Harold confided. "As though she could afford it. She had the nerve to slap me. As though she had a better offer." He snorted.

Cutter shrugged. "Haven't seen any engagement announcements for her in *The Times*. Everyone in town knows she's practically penniless."

Elizabeth had failed.

She'd soon learn what it felt like to have to scrape and bow for every ounce of approval. She'd soon understand how it felt to have doors closed in your face simply because you weren't wealthy enough—or, in his own case, because he hadn't been born in line for a title.

Harold smiled—the thought of Elizabeth's discomfort gave him pleasure.

Cutter stood. "I'd best be off," he said. "I've an appointment with my tailor. I can see my way out. Sorry about your funds, Wetherby."

Harold nodded, waving off his friend and choosing to ignore the faint distaste he thought he detected in the man's tone.

He was far more interested in the new idea taking hold of his mind. Elizabeth Medford could still be of use to him.

Her father could no longer pay his debt. But *she* could. Maybe not in pounds . . . but how much better would it be to have her obeying him, serving him, as she'd been so loathe to do before? He'd touch that sweet body, *own* it, and in the meantime, he'd use whatever connections the Medfords had left to further his political purposes. Before, he'd courted her, minced about, hoping to curry favor.

But now, with *proof* the family owed him, he had leverage.

Harold smiled. He would call on them directly.

The duke was true to his word. Even after the Grumsbys' other guests returned to London, he remained. Everywhere Elizabeth went, it seemed he was there.

She wondered how long he could possibly prolong his visit. Could she outlast him in this game of cat and mouse before succumbing to those meaningful, desire-laden gazes he shot her when no one else was looking?

It was wrong. It was dangerous, to feel this way. But she'd wanted Alex Bainbridge to notice her from the moment she'd attended her first ball and seen him standing there, starkly predatory and surrounded by all-too-willing prey. He'd been everything she, as a female and the eldest Medford daughter, was not allowed to be.

She'd been standing at the edge of the Peasleys' ballroom, drinking lemonade after a disastrous waltz with an overenthusiastic partner, when her gaze had been inexorably drawn toward the duke.

She'd stayed back, content to observe, for Beaufort traveled with a faster, more daring set than she was comfortable with. Another man in his party told a joke, leaning into the admiring crowd to deliver the punch line. It was quite scandalous, judging from the duke's laugh and the shocked expressions of several of the young ladies—whom Elizabeth doubted were actually very shocked. One of the aspiring women used the opportunity to arrange a delicate swoon, aimed directly toward the duke's arms.

He'd caught her gracefully, of course, but he'd looked up as he'd done so and caught Elizabeth's eye. He'd winked.

Before the slightest notion of proper behavior had entered her mind, Elizabeth had rolled her eyes.

The duke had thrown his head back and laughed. Amazingly, Elizabeth had managed to maintain her composure, in spite of being shocked at her own audacity. She'd simply smiled and glided away.

He hadn't spoken to her that night.

But from that moment on she'd watched, and dreamed, always with the knowledge that Alex Bainbridge, Duke of Beaufort, Marquess of Worcester, and holder of who knew how many lesser titles, moved in circles far above her. Each year, every matchmaking mama in London prayed her daughter would finally be the one to snare him.

When he did decide to marry—and he would have to, to pass on his estates—it would certainly be to someone unforgettable, a diamond of the first water. Not to someone like Elizabeth Medford.

She glanced down at the stiff gray skirts that composed her governess's uniform. They were a clear reminder of her new station. She may have lost her heart to Alex Bainbridge years ago, but it was vital she didn't lose her head as well.

Careful, Elizabeth reminded herself. She had to be very, very careful.

This morning the children were out with their father, a man Elizabeth had come to respect. She'd taken advantage of her freedom by actually choosing one of the poetry volumes from the library—she'd been too distracted last time—and bringing it to her favorite bench in the garden. But her mind wouldn't focus on the words. Instead it drifted away from the flowery phrases and settled on Alex Bainbridge.

She'd stopped trying to avoid him—not only was it impossible, but after the intimacy of their kiss, she longed for his presence. So she wasn't surprised to see him strolling toward her.

She sat straighter, consciously gathering her defenses. She could ill afford another indiscretion.

The reminder did little, though, to squash the bubble of joy that rose inside her as he strode her way.

"A fine day for reading, Miss Medford. You make a lovely picture on that bench, surrounded by the roses."

"Your Grace." She stood and curtsied. The man was a master of flattery, but she knew better than to take it, or him, seriously. He'd charmed legions of women. She was only the latest in the long line of women who had, temporarily, captured his attention. But, oh, she wanted to believe she was different. That she meant more.

"Please, sit," he said.

She did, and he planted himself beside her. If anyone made a lovely picture that morning, it was he. More handsome than lovely, Elizabeth mentally amended. He was clad in a fine lawn shirt and breeches, his jacket a deep claret. The wind toyed with his dark hair, and she resisted the urge to smooth it back into place.

"Would you care to accompany me on a drive tomorrow afternoon? I believe our last conversation in the library was interrupted, and I'm anxious to continue it."

Interrupted, indeed.

"You're too kind, Your Grace, but I simply couldn't."

"Why not? Tomorrow is Sunday, and I know for a fact my sister makes a point of spending Sunday afternoons with her children. It would seem you are free." He frowned. "Unless, of course, you're trying to avoid me."

"No, Your Grace, of course not." The answer slipped out before she could think of a better one.

"Then you'll come?"

"Er . . ." She should tell him she'd already made plans. But for what? Silently Elizabeth cursed the mental lapse that robbed her of common sense whenever he was near.

His frown cleared, replaced by a satisfied, lazy smile, as if he'd already anticipated her capitulation. He placed his hand over hers, his thumb stroking small circles in her palm. "I know of a lovely route we could take. The flowers have all just begun to bloom. Rather like yourself—a beautiful bloom unfurling before my eyes." His eyes twinkled.

Elizabeth grew warm. "Your flattery is outrageous, Your Grace. Besides, it would hardly be proper."

"Is that your concern, then? Propriety?" He stroked the inside of her wrist.

Elizabeth melted. Desperately she tried to remember the many reasons why getting involved with Alex Bainbridge was a very, very bad idea.

Propriety. Yes, that was it.

"Of course," she managed, but her voice came out a whisper.

Alex grinned wider. Obviously, he knew exactly what he was doing to her.

She turned away, but he clasped both her hands in his.

"There's no need to play coy. I know you are not adverse to my attentions, else you would never have come up with that fascinating proposal. Let me see . . . how did you put it? Oh, yes. You asked me to ruin you."

She stood indignantly. "It is most ungallant of you, sir, to bring that up," she admonished, though from the amusement in his eyes, her scolding had little effect.

He gave her arm a tug that landed her back on the bench—this time much closer to him.

"Besides, that was when I thought your involvement would be beneficial," Elizabeth continued, trying to ignore the fact that their thighs were nearly brushing. Thank goodness for the layers of her skirts. "Now that I've managed to avoid my unwanted suitor and secure a position on my own, there's really no need for you to even think of me."

"I disagree." He slid even closer, and the heavy-lidded intent in his eyes told Elizabeth he meant to kiss her. "I'm quite certain there is, uh, *need*."

She scooted back, heat rising in her cheeks.

"There would be advantages for you, you know."

She cocked her head, uncertain how to respond.

"Let me be bold. I would have you as my mistress, Elizabeth."

The *cad!* Elizabeth grasped at the shreds of her dignity. "Hardly a position to ascribe to," she said haughtily. That wasn't true, though. Any number of women would gladly accept the position, even if, or *particularly* if, an offer of marriage was not forthcoming.

Alex knew it, too. "*Au contraire, cherie.* As my mistress, you would be supported in far more luxury than you can support yourself as a governess."

She looked away.

"Come, Elizabeth," he said, his tone gentling, "we

both know you are not suited to governess's work. You are a creature of passion."

With one strong finger he traced her ear, her jaw—a touch that, had he known it, confirmed his assessment of her.

"And yet," she replied, drawing her spine as stiff and straight as possible, "a governess holds a respectable position. My family may be upset with me, but at least I am not ruined in the eyes of all Society. And if I am to remain respectable, I must be a governess of unimpeachable reputation, sir."

"It was not so long ago you were more amenable to being ruined. May I point out that my offer is actually much better?"

She shrugged. "Obviously I was a bit desperate when I succumbed to such thoughts. Luckily I came to my senses and found something more stable. If I were your mistress, I would be in constant danger of losing my position, for your interest in me would soon wane." The string of mistresses he'd left behind was legendary. Elizabeth raised her eyebrows. "Then where would I be?"

He brushed aside that argument with a wave of his hand. "You underestimate yourself."

He was flattering her, but she steeled her will. "I cannot know that for sure, Your Grace. Better I look after my reputation."

"Still, you are attracted to me."

The confidence in his voice made her want to smack him. Of course, it was true, and he knew it. "That's hardly the point."

"Then why did you kiss me in the library?"

He had her there. She could point out that he'd initiated said kiss, but they both knew how she'd responded.

"You don't need to decide now." He stood. "I'll pick you up at two o'clock tomorrow. We'll go driving in the country." His features softened for a moment. "My carriage will be devoid of insignia—you needn't fear being seen."

"You'll be wasting your time, Your Grace," she told him, though her voice lacked conviction. "I won't come."

He gave her a tolerant smile. "Oh, I think you will."

She studied the ground. He knew her too well.

He pressed a kiss to her hand as he left. "I shall be counting the hours."

Elizabeth remained on the garden bench, desire warring with her trepidation. She stared blankly at the volume of poetry she'd brought outdoors. There was no way she could read it now.

Alex rubbed his temples and stared at the letter on the desk. Upon returning from the garden, he'd found a pile of correspondence waiting for him. His secretary had thoughtfully gathered it for delivery to the Grumsby estate, knowing his master was not one to let business linger.

Alex momentarily wished the secretary was slack in his duties, for he had no desire to see this particular letter.

Even after death, the Baron Medford continued to be a thorn in his side.

He was well aware the man had died still owing him a considerable debt. In fact, this letter didn't address the half of it—most "gentleman's debts" were never recorded. Alex was mildly surprised to learn the scoundrel had kept track at all. Now, Medford's solicitor had sent a letter explaining the status of the estate after his death. To put it succinctly, there was no estate.

Alex tore the letter in two. Disgusting. Men in Medford's situation had no business gambling. He'd frittered away a respectable, if not especially large, fortune on "investments" that amounted to little more than outright gambling, then worsened the matter with his actual gaming.

Trying to recover the funds would be futile. At this point, Alex would be content simply never to be reminded again of his connection to Lord Medford.

Medford's daughter, on the other hand, was another matter entirely.

Elizabeth baffled him. When he'd offered her the position of mistress, he'd done so, at least in part, just to see her reaction. And she'd surprised him. He'd had her pegged as a schemer, but what was she after? One minute she melted passionately in his arms, the next, primly informed him she preferred a respectable life of near-poverty to the pampering she would receive under his protection. Why?

That wild mane of red hair belonged spread across a pillow—preferably his—not tucked up under a governess's cap. He'd lost precious hours of sleep imagining where that kiss could have led.

But he'd made a promise to dissociate himself from any further involvement with anyone bearing the name of Medford. That promise had driven him to turn down Elizabeth's offer that morning in Hyde Park.

Now that he knew her better, it was a promise he was seriously coming to regret.

Alex poured himself a brandy. Hell, what was one more broken promise after a lifetime of sins?

If anything, he was beginning to think Lord Medford,

in a weird and twisted way, had been onto something when he'd tried to thrust Alex and Elizabeth together.

A gruff, cynical laugh escaped him. He *must* be losing it, if he was beginning to trust Lord Medford's judgment. He tossed the brandy back, savored the slow burn as he swallowed.

He'd once considered Medford a close acquaintance, perhaps even a friend. But that was before he'd learned the man's true nature.

They'd gambled together, with Alex assuming the baron could cover his mounting losses. Eventually, Alex had mentioned something about payment, not liking to leave things lingering too long. Medford had stalled, which had tipped off Alex that all was not as it seemed. Finally, the man had approached him, with an apology and a proposal so vile, Alex still had trouble believing it.

Lord Medford had met Alex at White's that evening, then waited until Alex's fellow card players had all abandoned the table and the servants were out of earshot.

"This is a hard thing for a man to say," Medford had muttered, not meeting Alex's eye, "but I simply can't cover those debts right now. It's a bad time." He laid down his cards.

Alex briefly felt sorry for the older man. Irritated, certainly, but also sympathetic, as he assumed the problem was temporary. "How long do you need?"

"Well, that's the problem. I simply can't say." He looked up. "But I thought perhaps there was another way we could even the score."

"I'm listening."

"You may have my eldest daughter in marriage."

"What!" Alex shook his head to clear his ears.

"I thought if we joined families, then the debt wouldn't matter. And Elizabeth is an attractive girl."

"See here, Medford, your thinking is awry." Alex forced the words through a clenched jaw. "For one, the days of the man paying a bride-price are over. They were over centuries ago. But that is what you're essentially asking me to do. Generally, it works the other way around. Women come with a dowry, which makes them more attractive to a man." Alex didn't need any woman's dowry, but that didn't change the principle of the matter.

"But Elizabeth is special," Medford said. And Alex hated the desperation in his voice.

"I don't even know the chit!" Not only did he not know her, he had no intention of marrying anyone in the near future.

"Does that matter for a ton marriage?"

"Medford, you disgust me. You're trying to turn your losses into profit. Just think—you'd be out of debt, you'd have an unwed daughter off your hands, and, to top it all off, you'd have an alliance with one of the premier families in England. Exactly how do you see this as a way to, as you put it, 'even the score'?"

Medford twisted a playing card in his hands and remained silent.

"Now, perhaps if she were willing to work off your debt in other ways . . ." He spoke with deliberate crudeness, wanting to see Medford, weasel that he was, squirm a bit. But though Alex was no stranger to debauchery, he had no intention of dragging an innocent girl into this matter.

"Now see here," Medford bleakly replied, his face pale, "Elizabeth is a respectable girl. She ought to marry. You, Your Grace, must be thinking of an heir."

Unbelievable what the man thought he could get away with. There was no way Alex was marrying a woman he'd never met. "That's not your concern."

"No." The baron swallowed. "I'm sorry." He began muttering to himself.

Alex picked out a few phrases, including "wouldn't be the end of the world," "figured it would come to this," and "after it was said and done, could still marry her off to an older man who didn't mind a chit with a bit of experience."

Alex turned away. He knew some families viewed their daughters as a liability, worth only the social advancement they might gain from marriage, but he certainly didn't want to hear this man say so aloud.

"I suppose we could consider that option," Medford said finally, "if Elizabeth were willing, and if we could somehow keep her mother from knowing—"

"No," Alex said shortly. "Forget I said anything. It's both preposterous and vile. Just pay me when you have the funds."

Alex had then left quickly, anxious to remove the baron from his sight. Many nobles ran short of funds occasionally, but there were far more genteel ways to handle it. Alex had wanted only to make the man squirm until he agreed to pay up—and with money, *not with his eldest child. This man was a gambler, a schemer, and, judging from what he'd been about to agree to, a panderer. Disgusting.*

What galled Alex the most was how he'd misjudged the man. Alex prided himself on his ability to tell a man's character, but here he'd been dead wrong. He'd never knowingly gambled with a man who could not afford to lose. It kept things civil. But the baron's easy demeanor, so unlike the hollow-eyed, drawn faces of others who were desperate, had fooled him enough that he'd not thought it necessary to look any deeper—at least until that last night. The man had possessed extraordinary skill at deception.

Alex moved to a more exclusive gaming club, and his contact with Medford had mercifully been cut off. A peaceful eight months had gone by, and though Alex had not been repaid, he'd believed he was rid of the scoundrel.

That is, until one wretched night in October . . .

Alex shook himself from his reverie. The circumstances surrounding the baron's death didn't bear thinking about.

Suffice it to say he'd made mistakes that could never be repaid, and certainly not by seducing the dead man's daughter.

Alex shoved the torn remnants of the solicitor's letter into his wastebasket and stood, noticing the sun sat somewhat lower in the sky than when he'd begun sorting his correspondence. He tiredly rubbed the back of his neck.

Why, of all the families in England, did the red-headed minx have to come from *that* one?

He could simply not show up tomorrow for the country drive he'd promised her. That would cut things off cleanly. But then he'd never know whether *she'd* had the guts to show up. And he wasn't sure he wanted to live with the wondering.

So if she did show up, he'd find a way to live with the guilt.

Chapter Six

By two o'clock the following afternoon, Elizabeth was a wreck. A million times she'd promised herself she would not, would *not* set foot in the duke's carriage. A million times she'd cursed herself for a fool. A million times she'd checked the clock in the hall, her heart beating faster the closer the designated hour drew.

Finally, her good sense admitted defeat. If she didn't meet the duke today, she would spend the rest of her life wondering what she'd given up.

At first she'd dressed in her usual governess's attire, thinking it might help quell the duke's ardor. Or her own. But then, Alex had to know she owned other gowns, and would think her ridiculous for wearing her uniform. And in front of Alex Bainbridge, she did *not* want to appear ridiculous.

To be completely honest, she also wasn't really sure she wanted her ardor quelled.

But what did one wear for such an assignation? Her nicest things had been left behind, either at home or at Beatrice's house, and there was no time to retrieve them.

Nor did she wish Alex to think she was pretending to a social rank she no longer possessed.

So she'd chosen a simple but flattering gown of muslin. It once had been pale yellow, but she'd had it dyed a muted gray as a compromise between her need to mourn her father and her need to be charming in Society. Of course, she'd since dispensed with both those needs, but the frock was still a favorite.

She'd scraped her hair into its usual bun, then, remembering what Alex had said in the library about leaving it loose—but not wanting him to think she'd paid too much heed—she softened the effect by loosening the knot and letting a few tendrils curl about her face.

As a result of all this double-guessing, Elizabeth was running late. It would never do for a governess to keep a duke waiting, no matter the nature of their relationship, so she thrust her feet into her shoes, glanced one last time in the looking glass, and flew down the stairs.

Alex was meeting her at the end of the drive, at the edge of the estate. She hoped that anyone seeing her leave the house would simply think she'd gone for a walk on her afternoon off.

The carriage waiting at the end of the drive was not Alex's usual phaeton, but a plain, discrete black conveyance. As he had promised, there was no ducal crest emblazoned on the side, and the driver wore no recognizable livery.

Elizabeth smiled as she approached. Even if anyone saw her enter, they would not know whose carriage it was. She appreciated his thoughtfulness. He might be used to tongues wagging at his every move, but her current position depended on those same tongues remaining still.

The driver helped her into the coach, then closed the door behind her, nodding politely.

Alex watched Elizabeth climb inside, feeling inordinately satisfied that she hadn't backed out of their meeting. That, in itself, told him all he needed to know.

He was well aware that this outing, in addition to keeping her out of the public eye, had the side benefit of allowing for considerable intimacy. As he watched her settle into the seat opposite him, he was grateful indeed for that side benefit.

Their kiss in the library had only whetted his appetite. He'd intended to kiss her, certainly, but he'd had no idea of the overpowering need her response would evoke in him. A need he'd barely even recognized until she'd pulled away and his head had cleared. A need that had had him on the verge of losing control.

A need that later had him breaking both his vow to avoid anyone bearing the Medford name and his vow to lead a less debauched life. If reforming meant he would never touch her again, never taste her, it simply wasn't worth it.

She sat primly across from him now, hands folded neatly. He intended to remedy that, he thought, envisioning her in his lap.

"Elizabeth, I am so pleased you could join me," he greeted her politely. She might be an outcast of the nobility, but she was still a gently bred young woman. That thought gave him pause, as he suddenly realized that if he truly cared about such things, he wouldn't have invited her on this outing at all.

Nor, if she were adamant about such rules, would she have accepted.

"It was kind of you to offer, Your Grace."

The carriage gave a small lurch as the driver pulled away. Alex had instructed him to tour the countryside randomly, with no particular destination. The driver, a well-trained servant who knew who lined his pockets, had asked no questions.

Alex took a moment to study his prey. In spite of her prim posture, Elizabeth looked flushed and alluring, her magnificent hair threatening to escape its confines. Before the drive was over, he would ensure it did. Her gown was a bit too plain for his taste, but he was far more interested in the soft skin beneath it anyway.

Elizabeth was becoming his obsession.

He tried to think of some sort of light conversation to put her at ease. The truth was, they had little in common, and he didn't think that whispered descriptions of the places he'd like to touch her could be considered light conversation. And he certainly hoped his attentions *wouldn't* put her at ease.

"How fare my niece and nephew?" he finally asked.

She gave him an odd look, but answered. "Quite well. They're charming children. Henry has begun his study of mathematics and is progressing splendidly."

"Good," Alex answered automatically.

He lapsed into silence. Elizabeth did the same, though tension seemed to hang in the space between them. She looked away, but a moment later, he caught her sneaking a glance at him. She flushed.

"It's, er, a lovely day to view the countryside," she offered, smoothing a nonexistent wrinkle in her skirt.

Alex leaned forward and drew the curtains. His knee brushed hers, eliciting from her a startled "Oh!"

"I find the view inside far more alluring," he murmured.

To his surprise, she met his eyes as she responded, "I confess I, too, am enamored of the view in here." Her voice was scarce more than a whisper, but she didn't look away.

He'd admired her daring, and her honesty, from the time they'd first danced at the Peasleys' ball. Now he admired her more. She was obviously nervous, but she was no shrinking maiden. She knew why she was here, and he respected her for that. Did he imagine it, or did her eyes actually rove his form?

His body responded as though her hands, and not her eyes, stroked him.

"It is dim in here. Perhaps if I sat closer, so as to ease the strain on your eyes," he teased as he smoothly shifted to the seat beside her.

He saw her swallow, hard, but he was not about to let her off so easily. Instead he bent his head to trace kisses along the line of her neck. She sat very still, as though uncertain how far she could carry her part in the intimate game they played.

Though he knew her to be bold, Alex realized she probably had little experience with intimate matters—after all, even when she'd asked him to ruin her, she'd seemed vague on exactly how one accomplished such things.

Well, he could teach her. If she was willing to learn. He retraced the line of her neck, noting with pleasure that she inclined her head ever so slightly to provide him greater access. He nibbled her earlobe, then dipped his tongue to explore its sensitive recesses.

Her hands fisted in her skirts and a tiny sound escaped the back of her throat. Yes, Alex thought hazily, she would be a willing student. His lips left her ear and began a path aimed at the lush curve of her mouth. She turned her head and met him halfway, and he gave a grunt of pure male satisfaction as he captured her lips in a hungry kiss.

He ceased planning, calculating, as her willing response drove such thoughts from his mind. Her hands clutched at his shoulders as she pressed toward him, and he fisted his hand in the hair at the nape of her neck to hold her there, stroking her lips with his, over and over, until they parted beneath the onslaught of his desire.

He tasted her, gently, and she moaned at the touch of his tongue to hers. He dipped in again, and again, exploring her fully now, telling her without words of the more intimate things he had in mind.

Suddenly she broke the heady kiss to trail smaller ones along his jaw, as he'd done earlier to her. Alex groaned at the loss but tilted his head, taking pleasure in the knowledge that she wished to touch him. His body was hammering in needy desire, unsatisfied by the chaste kisses to his jaw. Finally, when he could stand the pleasurable torture no more, he turned his head to claim her lips once more, hungry now. He delved her mouth fully, his tongue driving the kiss to new, more intimate heights as he tipped her back onto the cushioned squabs. His hands sought her bodice, molding and cupping her breasts.

Someone moaned in desire, he couldn't be sure whom. He abandoned her mouth in order to kiss the creamy swells above her bodice, his hands working to free her from what seemed an interminable amount of clothing. Her hands were in his hair, on his shoulders, encouraging him and begging him to hurry, to fill the need consuming them both.

Just as he'd nearly accomplished the task, the carriage gave a great lurch, breaking their embrace and tumbling the two of them to the floor.

The conveyance tipped precariously to one side, and Elizabeth's eyes widened in alarm. They both braced themselves, but with a final shudder, the carriage righted itself and stilled, coming to rest at an awkward angle.

Alex released his grip on the back of the bench and blew out a breath. He worked the latch and threw open the door, muttering, "What the hell?"

An even more colorful stream of invectives could be heard coming from the driver outside.

Alex stepped down just as the driver threw a stone at a quickly retreating dog. "Bloody mongrel!"

"Dog ran between the wheels?"

The man startled at his master's presence, then visibly tried to compose himself. "A thousand pardons, Your Grace. The team sidestepped to avoid the creature, and drove us into a rut. My fault. Afraid the afternoon sun, and the open road . . . I should've been more alert. Wheel's bent."

Alex examined the wheel, which was indeed bent. He raised his eyes to find Elizabeth standing next to him, still delightfully mussed from their kisses.

"How do you feel about a nice long walk?" he asked regretfully.

Marian Grumsby was pleased her brother had extended his visit. He'd claimed he enjoyed the open space, the peace of the country life. She'd happily welcomed him to stay as long as he liked. But she was not a fool.

Alex never stayed outside the city for long. There were too few entertainments—particularly those of the licentious variety.

Then again, her brother had not been himself for about eight months now. And the steady stream of gossip about his debauchery had nearly dried up. Marian didn't know if that was cause for concern or celebration.

Oh, the wit and urbane charm was still there, but he was moody and distracted. Restless. And she wanted to know why.

She knew better than to ask directly. Even as a child Alex had been a private person, more so as an adult. She'd seen him in deep conversation with her husband a few times during this visit, but if Brian had learned anything of interest, he was keeping mum— and that was driving her mad.

She'd replayed the last eight months in her mind, but she was too removed from her brother's life to guess what would have affected him so. A business venture gone bad? A woman? Something was bothering him, but what?

Unfortunately, her hopes for discovering his reasons were thwarted by his announcement at dinner Sunday night.

"I've decided to return to London tomorrow."

Marian set down her wineglass. "Have we finally bored you, then?"

"Of course not. But I've neglected matters of business and estate too long."

"It's barely been two weeks," she teased. "Surely your mansions are not tumbling to the ground already."

He smiled back, though the expression held a hard edge that made Marian wonder, not for the first time, if her brother had ever known true happiness.

"It's been a pleasure," Alex told her. "A welcome respite from the city."

She felt him withdrawing, slipping away again, and she mourned the loss of the easy friendship they'd had as children. Would she ever regain it? "At least promise me you won't go so long between visits next time."

"You have my word. Henry and Clara are delightful, and I've a mind to ride Brian's new stallion again, once it's better trained."

She accepted his answer gracefully, realizing her brother was unlikely to bare the contents of his soul over dinner.

When she'd finished eating, she excused herself to tell the children a story and tuck them into bed. The nurse would have seen to it they were fed and bathed, but Marian cherished those last few moments each night, when they snuggled sleepily under the covers and she smoothed their brows. Only when she and Brian were traveling or attending an engagement did she relinquish those coveted chores of motherhood.

Alex watched his sister go, wondering if he was even capable of the kind of love she obviously held for her family.

Brian signaled a servant for port and cigars.

When the two men were alone, Brian swirled his port, intently studying the dark liquid.

"I've seen the way you look at her," he said meaningfully.

"Marian?" Alex echoed. Revulsion flooded him. She was his *sister*.

Brian laughed. "Of course not—though you should have seen your face just now. I know your soul is black, Alex, but if I thought for one moment *that* were the case, you wouldn't be here." He selected a cigar. "Unless I invited you here to kill you with my bare hands. No, I was referring to our pretty young governess."

Alex, a longtime card player, knew when to keep his expression neutral. He didn't deny the accusation—Brian was no fool. Instead, mirroring his brother-in-law's sudden fascination with his glass, he traced the rim of his own, coolly meeting Brian's gaze as though waiting for him to finish.

The men passed a minute in silence. Brian lit his cigar, took a few experimental puffs.

"Marian told me she's Quality," Brian finally said. "I hardly ever go into London during the Season, so I'm not familiar with her family. I take it you are."

"We'd met."

"And?"

Alex shrugged. "I gambled with her father a few times before he passed."

"I see." But the assessing look in his brother-in-law's eyes said he knew Alex wasn't being entirely forthcoming. "I thought perhaps you'd been personally acquainted. You do, after all, have a reputation with the ladies."

Alex had a good idea where Brian was going with this conversation, but he wasn't going to make it easy on him. "Miss Medford was not among my closest acquaintances, though I'm sure we attended some of the same functions."

Brian shifted tack. "Marian tells me her qualifications are excellent."

"I'm sure they are."

"It's important to her—Marian—that the children are looked after well."

"Marian's a good mother."

Brian shifted in his seat, his discomfort apparent as he adjusted his jacket. "Must be tough on the girl if her family's fallen on hard times. Marian says she prefers to keep to herself. Attractive chit like that, having to work for a living."

"A shame," Alex allowed. "Though she seems to manage it all with grace."

Brian leaned back in his chair. "I'm a simple man, Alex—I just like to keep peace in my household. And it occurred to me that you probably unsettle her, remind her of how much she's lost." The merest hint of warning invaded his pleasant tone. "Better to let her be. She doesn't have much left to lose."

Alex narrowed his gaze. The rebel in him, the duke, bristled at having his behavior challenged. The *man* in him held a grudging respect for his brother-in-law's devotion to his family and staff.

Brian cleared his throat, sipped his port. "Well, no matter. You've already said you leave on the morrow."

Elizabeth was confused. She'd been certain, absolutely certain, after their aborted carriage ride, that Alex would redouble his efforts to seduce her.

Instead, he'd disappeared.

Telling herself it was for the best didn't help. She'd been on the verge of complete capitulation—and had been eagerly anticipating how he might contact her next—only to wake on Monday and discover he'd departed for London.

She'd stumbled through morning lessons with

Henry and Clara, gladly turning the children over to
the nurse at luncheon. Now she paced her little room,
wondering what had gone wrong.

She should be relieved Alex was gone. Every moment
spent alone with the duke was a threat to her reputation. But her heart refused to listen to her mind's logic.

After what had happened in the carriage, why had
he not stayed to complete the seduction?

She flushed guiltily. It was true she'd dreamed of the
duke for years, but recently her dreams had taken a
rather wicked turn. She wanted to know what it was
to lie with a man. Beatrice had described the act to
her, but Elizabeth could not imagine that the kisses
she and Alex had shared could lead to the painful, im-
personal process her friend had endured. Now, she
might never know.

But it was more than that. His touch, his kiss, made
her forget everything else. Made her forget how she'd
spent her life being a disappointment to her mother,
how her father had deceived her, how her whole life
had shattered after his death. How the men who'd
once courted her suddenly turned away when she
came near. With Alex, she felt desirable, worthy.

He'd left without so much as a farewell. Had she
meant so little to him? Was he truly as the rumors
painted—a shameless seducer of women? It pained
her to believe it.

Perhaps something had come up. A matter of business, or politics, that required his immediate presence
in London. And if that was true, she reasoned, it
would only arouse suspicions for him to linger, then
seek out the governess for a particular good-bye. Still,
with Alex gone, the days stretched emptily before her.

Luckily, Elizabeth received a letter in the post on

Tuesday that turned her mind from the sensuous but unpredictable duke.

The familiar loopy writing on the envelope brought a smile to her face, but it faded as she read the contents of Charity's missive.

Dearest E.,

It's simply not the same without you home. Mother isn't speaking to anyone, except perhaps Uncle, and only then when Uncle ceases his interminable lectures on "proper" behavior. They suspect I know where you are, but I haven't said a word, which only increases their wrath. Not that I blame you for leaving. Lady Pullington told me where to write, and I'm so happy you've found a position.

And in spite of it all, I'm doing well. Except for the most embarrassing thing. I was returning from the park with Mary Sutherby and her mother this morning, and we were coming up the steps just as a messenger stopped at our house. Well, I told him I'd take the message, saving him the trouble of delivering it formally. Of course, you know how curious I am. I couldn't just give it to Mother, though it was addressed to Lady Medford. So after Mary was gone, I used that trick you taught me—using steam to soften the seal. Anyhow, it was from another of father's debtors. They aren't very happy.

Elizabeth, do you remember the brooch father gave you the year you made your bow? I feel terrible telling you this, but the shop he purchased it from sold it to him on credit. He never paid. The letter said they'd respectfully waited until the family had time to settle the estate, but now they must request payment. What am I to do? Of course I know there isn't any money to cover it. I hate to tell Mother and Uncle, for it will only anger them further.

Do you still have the brooch? Do you think the store would accept its return? I'm so very sorry to ask it of you, E., but I haven't any jewelry of my own, or anything I can think to sell that would fetch a price. Please advise.

Oh, and do be well, Elizabeth. I'll conspire with Lady Pullington to visit if I can.

Your loving sister,
Charity

Elizabeth read the letter twice, folded it carefully, and tucked it into the small trunk in her room next to the nursery. She rummaged at the bottom of the trunk, finally extracting a small velvet pouch. She sat back and poured the contents into her hands.

The brooch winked up at her, a cluster of small, delicately set emeralds. *"To match your eyes,"* Papa had told her. She'd been so proud when he'd presented it to her. *"My little girl, all grown up,"* he'd said.

Elizabeth's throat grew tight. Whatever else he'd been, her papa *had* cared about her. She refused to believe otherwise. Of course, she now knew he shouldn't have been presenting her with such trinkets. The brooch resting in her hand had never even been paid for. Perhaps he'd intended to pay for it eventually. She wanted to believe that.

But more than a year had passed between its purchase and her father's death—meaning her father's funds had been low for far longer than anyone had known. She'd been raised to think that taking something you couldn't pay for was stealing. It hurt to think of Papa as a thief.

The brooch seemed to grow heavier, the twinkling stones mocking her. She slipped it back in its pouch, noticing the name of the shop, Gertman's, embroidered in gold thread on the velvet.

There was no way her governess's wages would cover fine jewelry. As much as it hurt, she would have to pray the shop would accept the item's return in place of payment. At least it was in her possession.

Elizabeth went to fetch writing paper. She composed a note to the jeweler, requesting a meeting, and another to Charity, telling her sister not to worry.

Chapter Seven

"Will ye be wantin' aught else, Yer Grace?"

Alex shook his head impatiently.

"We do 'ave a private dinin' room, if ye prefer."

The solicitous owner of the White Hart had already informed him of that fact, twice. "No, thanks."

Alex hadn't intended to stop at the inn at all. He'd been on his way to pay a surprise visit to his sister—knowing full well it was Sunday and that Elizabeth would have the afternoon free. He wasn't ignoring Brian Grumsby's subtle warning, exactly, but two weeks in London without Elizabeth had convinced him it was worth the risk.

Except that when he'd passed the White Hart, he'd seen none other than Miss Elizabeth Medford, pretty as you please, strolling up to the door.

Curious, he'd followed her inside, realizing she hadn't spotted him.

She'd scanned the room. An unfamiliar man with pale brown, thinning hair and spectacles stood upon seeing her. She hurried over and took a seat across from him.

Alex's gut clenched as he followed her.

Her eyes flared in surprise—or was that fear?—when she'd finally seen him. "What are you doing here?" she asked.

"I was about to ask the same of you."

She squared her shoulders. "It's none of your concern, Your Grace."

The mousy man across from her appeared horrified by her demeanor, but Alex grinned. "Everything about you concerns me."

"On that, we will have to disagree." There was an arch quality to her voice, but she bit her lip as she glanced back at her table partner. She was nervous. "Your Grace, I have business to conduct. May I respectfully ask you to take your presence elsewhere?"

"Certainly," Alex agreed. "As soon as I've had a meal. I'm famished."

With that, he'd taken a seat three tables over. Damned if he'd leave before he figured out what she was up to. He ordered a stew he had no interest in, then watched Elizabeth as the innkeeper hovered about, anxious to please.

At the moment, Alex would have *loved* to make use of the private dining room, if only to haul Elizabeth inside and shake some sense into her.

What did she think she was doing, meeting a man who, by all appearances, she didn't even *know*? Of course, as tempting as it was to scold her, he knew her reputation would be utterly destroyed if she was seen entering a private dining room occupied solely by the Duke of Beaufort.

The innkeeper finally wandered off to tend to his less illustrious customers, which at this hour consisted

of Elizabeth, the strange man, and a single other table
occupied by two men in traveling gear.

Alex stared down at his cup as he rethought the
wisdom of pursuing the delectable Miss Medford. In
truth, he admired her spirit, her risk-taking. He had
no doubt that that spirit would translate to passionate
lovemaking—if it didn't land her in serious danger
first. He eyed her table.

The traveling duo stood, patting their bellies in appreciation of the hearty food, and exited.

Alex shifted his chair slightly, trying to get a better
look at the man across from Elizabeth. He watched as
she pulled out a small pouch, showed the contents to
the man. Their voices were too low to hear—no doubt
because of his presence, but it was clear they were negotiating.

The man picked up a small magnifying glass and
held a brooch beneath it.

Ah. Elizabeth was selling her jewelry. Alex felt a
pang of sympathy that surprised him. Until he realized
she was choosing to sell her possessions rather than
become his mistress, and was even risking a clandes-
tine meeting with a strange man at a public house to
do it.

If only she wasn't so stubbornly independent, they
could dispense with such nonsense. He'd happily
cover her expenses, if only she'd give in to the pleasure they both desired. Alex shoved his hands in his
pockets. It was asking too much of an innocent. He
knew it, but every time he saw her, the need to possess
her, protect her, grew stronger. That need was winning
the war with good manners. Perhaps, once she fully
understood the pleasures of lovemaking and the ben-
efits such a position would afford her . . .

"It can't be!" Elizabeth exclaimed.

Alex narrowed his eyes.

The man across from her shrugged apologetically. "I assure you, Miss Medford, I tell the truth."

Her shoulders slumped.

Alex could hear the conversation now, and he listened intently.

"If you know the whereabouts of the true brooch, my shop will accept its return. But this is not it." He returned the piece. His neck flushed as though he were uncomfortable.

"My shop will accept its return." Alex watched Elizabeth's fist close slowly over the brooch. She wasn't here to *sell* jewelry, but to return it?

"Nooo," she moaned softly. She leaned forward, head in hand. "It must be real. It was a gift."

Realization struck him, along with a flash of pity.

Alex stood and crossed the distance to Elizabeth's table. "Can I be of assistance here?" he asked.

She shook her head without lifting her face from her hand. Then, suddenly seeming to remember her manners, she looked up and stood, curtsying hastily. "Forgive me, Your Grace. I was distraught."

"And the cause of your distress?"

She shook her head again. "A personal matter."

The shop's representative stood as well but wisely remained silent.

Alex remembered his reputation for extravagance with the fairer sex. In this case, it would serve him well.

"It pains me to see a lady in distress," he gallantly declared. "If the cause is the lovely brooch you were so recently examining, I am happy to see the matter settled."

"But—" Elizabeth began.

"If the merchant does not wish the return of the

piece you hold, perhaps I may be allowed to make it a gift to you?"

He shot a look at the jeweler's representative. Both men knew the bit of glass clutched in Elizabeth's fingers was worthless.

But the merchant once again showed good training by keeping his face expressionless as he informed the duke of the price.

Alex nodded. "Send the bill to my secretary. I'll see to it forthwith."

He handed the man a twenty-pound note. "For you. I want no mention of my involvement, nor of your meeting with this young lady, in your records."

"Of course not, Your Grace."

"Then I trust this matter is settled."

"Yes, Your Grace, thank you." The merchant bowed and left hastily, no doubt gleefully thinking of how he would spend the very generous sum the duke had bestowed upon him.

Alex turned to Elizabeth. Her cheeks bore bright patches of pink as she kept her gaze lowered.

"I'm so ashamed," she whispered.

"What cause have you for shame?"

"The brooch. It wasn't real. I never thought . . . my father gave it to me. It was special. Except—except I think he must have subsequently sold the real piece and substituted this one, for the merchant said this"—she unclosed her fist—"is naught but glass and paste."

He felt her embarrassment. "It isn't your fault."

Finally she met his eye. "Thank you for what you did. You are very chivalrous, Your Grace, and have saved me considerable discomfort. I can't repay you right now, as I'm sure you know. But I promise I'll save enough from my wages—" her words spilled out in a torrent.

"Shh." He put a finger to her lips. "You do not owe me."

"But—"

The innkeeper came out from the back and filled his arms with the other diners' used dishes, glancing between Elizabeth and the duke. "Back in a moment," he said, disappearing again with the dirty dishes.

Alex quickly closed the remaining distance between them, cupping her shoulders gently.

"Elizabeth, you torment me. These past two weeks I've thought of little else." He maintained his gallant tone, though his words held more truth than he cared to admit. He stroked down her arms and took her hands in his, hoping the innkeeper was wise enough to take his time in back.

He leaned in for a kiss—just a quick one, he promised himself, since the room had emptied of other patrons—but a movement near the door distracted him.

A man stood in the doorway, his head turned in profile as he spoke a last word with the stable boy before coming inside. A man Alex had hoped never to see again.

What the hell was *he* doing here? Alex's forehead broke out in a sweat and his stomach clenched.

The peasant garb the man wore was different from the livery he'd been in when Alex had seen him last, but the face was unmistakable.

Fuston. The Medfords' former coachman—the man who'd driven the baron on the night of his "accident."

It was imperative, Alex realized with a start, that Elizabeth *not* see him. If she did, she would most certainly recognize him. And she might ask questions. Questions about her father.

Questions Alex would prefer remained unraised.

Alex flew into action, clasping Elizabeth to him and seizing her lips in a searing kiss that sent her staggering backward. He clasped her tighter, moving backward himself and pulling her with him.

He could feel her confusion, her pent-up desire. Her lips matched his, even as she struggled to regain her footing, protesting the awkwardness of the embrace.

Alex ignored the protest and continued pulling her with him toward the back of the inn, never breaking the kiss. They passed a very surprised innkeeper, but a quick frown from the duke and the man pointed toward an open door.

Alex felt behind him for the handle, his tongue tangling wildly with Elizabeth's as he maneuvered them both into the room and shut the door behind them, closing them into the private dining room he'd insisted he didn't need.

"Hell."

Elizabeth's eyes widened at his language.

"My apologies," he muttered. He drew in a ragged breath, surprised by the intensity of his body's reaction to a kiss that couldn't have lasted more than thirty seconds.

She smiled up at him. "I'm flattered, my lord, to think you've missed me so terribly. But I'd have followed you willingly. Was your haste truly so great?"

"You've no idea, my sweet," he murmured, finally gentling their embrace. He wasn't about to let her go, though. Not only was his desire awakened, but he was still in control of his thoughts just enough to remember he didn't want her questioning their sudden rush into this room.

There was little chance Fuston had gotten a good enough look to identify them. There was even less chance he would follow them back here. Which meant Alex simply needed to find a way to pass enough time for the man to leave before he and Elizabeth exited.

She pressed little nipping kisses along his jaw, and her hands slid inside his coat to stroke his back.

Need consumed him. Hell. What good was a private room if one didn't put it to use?

He dipped his head and the kiss she'd aimed at his jaw landed square on his lips. Her eyes widened and she smiled. He couldn't remember ever kissing a smiling woman before. It was rather nice.

He hauled her against his length. She was all warm, soft woman. For two weeks—nay, longer—he'd thought of nothing but this. His own body hardened with the need to make her his. Elizabeth's smile evaporated and her eyes widened further at the evidence of his passion. This was better than nice.

He slid his hands down her back and she rocked against him, a seeking, uncertain movement. That uncertainty triggered a warning in the depths of his passion-drugged mind. In spite of his wicked intentions, a shred of honor remained in his soul, and it reminded him now that Elizabeth was an innocent.

"Ah, Elizabeth," he rasped. "You should tell me to stop." With regret, he shifted her away from him.

Elizabeth paused, her breath ragged, her body flooded with the need to touch and be touched. Most of her life had been dictated by what she "should" do, and it had never made her happy. Only these past months, when she'd flouted the dictates of Society and made her own life, had she any inkling of freedom or joy.

Or pleasure.

She stared at the duke, undecided. Tempted. His eyes promised endless heat. His hair was rumpled where her fingers had been moments ago. To continue down this path would mean her ruination. Then again, she was already an outcast. She couldn't bear the thought of turning away from the one man who made her feel beautiful, desirable. The kisses they'd shared before had only fueled her belief that without him, life was empty.

For the past two weeks, she'd lived with the ache of not knowing whether she would see him again. She'd been miserable. And then this afternoon, he'd arrived out of nowhere. He'd been her hero, her rescuer.

He could be gone again tomorrow. But today, he was hers. And she would claim him.

Slowly she shook her head. "I can't tell you to stop," she whispered. "I don't want you to."

He exhaled harshly. He'd been holding his breath, she realized with a rush of gladness. He wanted her as much as she did him.

She stepped close again, bereft without his touch. He chuckled. "Wanton."

She flushed but met his gaze, hungry for another kiss.

He gazed back, eyes dark with passion, and slowly traced one finger down her neck and collarbone. His touch was almost delicate, in stark contrast to the strength of his hands and the intensity of his expression. A series of shivers radiated down her spine.

This was a game of seduction. She didn't know the rules. But she wanted to play.

His lips met hers for another kiss, one leisurely and thorough, and she abandoned thought, content to focus on the exquisite pleasure of his taste, his tongue exploring and caressing the roof of her mouth.

His hand came up to cup her breast, and she gasped at the pleasure. His thumb brushed over the crest, and

Elizabeth wantonly bemoaned the layers of clothing separating her skin from his touch.

But he was a step ahead of her, for while his lips coaxed hers and one hand buried in the hair at her nape to hold her steady, the other sought out the hooks and ties of her bodice, undoing them with dexterity. She wrapped her arms around his back and pressed closer, hampering his work even as she urged him on.

"Hurry," she whispered. She stroked his back, the breadth of his strong shoulders, and reveled in the scandalous things he was doing to her. Her hips fit snugly against his thighs. She rubbed against them.

"Ah, God, Elizabeth," Alex groaned.

She stilled. "You don't like it."

"On the contrary, darling, I do. Far too much. And if you keep doing it, we'll end up doing something quite different from what I have in mind."

That gave her pause. She'd assumed . . . What *did* he have in mind?

She didn't have time to ponder it. As her bodice came loose, he tugged it down, his head dipping as he traced hot kisses down her neck, her décolletage, and finally her breast. His kissed her there gently, and when she didn't pull away, he increased his attentions, laving her with his tongue. Rough, warm, wet velvet. He closed in on her nipple.

Pleasure stabbed through her. She arched her head back as her knees threatened to buckle. He dragged her to one of the room's padded chairs and continued his attentions.

Desire coursed through her, pooling at her woman's center. Alex grabbed a fistful of her skirts, dragging them upward until his hands were on the bare skin beneath. He stroked higher.

"Trust me," he growled, as his fingers came in contact with the apex of her thighs.

She resisted the urge to clamp them shut and was rewarded as his touch there intensified her pleasure tenfold. She pressed her hips against his hand, seeking more. He laughed and dragged his head from her breasts to her sex.

Elizabeth gasped. "You can't—"

He raised his head to meet her gaze. "Trust me," he repeated.

"Yes," she whispered.

He bent again and his lips took over where his fingers had left off.

Elizabeth moaned and let her head fall back. She was going to die of pleasure, of need, if he kept this up. But should she expire, it wouldn't be a bad way to go.

His tongue stroked her intimately and she fisted her hands in his hair to hold him there, needing more. More. Just—

He plunged his fingers into her. He stroked, as his tongue closed around the tiny bud at the head of her sex.

Elizabeth shattered in an onslaught of sensation, her body racked with shudders of pleasure. Alex gathered her close as she went limp.

Slowly she returned to earth, and it dawned on her that Alex's attentions had all been for her. She wasn't naïve enough to think that what they'd just done would satisfy him.

In fact, it was anything *but* what she'd expected, given the whispered descriptions of marital relations she'd overheard. He hadn't experienced the same sensation, the same release, she had.

She wanted him to.

Elizabeth stood, unsteady, and reached out a shy hand to stroke his obvious erection through his trousers.

Alex sucked in a sharp breath as he watched the young temptress before him. She was beautiful in the aftermath of her pleasure. Her cheeks bloomed color, her bottom lip swollen from kisses. Her gown drooped at the bodice and her skirts were in disarray. She was perfect.

And then she touched him. Stroked him, as he had her. She fumbled with the opening at his waist.

He hadn't planned to . . . but dear God, if she didn't stop . . .

Need took over. The hell with his plans. Desire, lust, hammered at him with insistent rhythm.

Her fist closed around his swollen member. He groaned.

He needed to be inside her. Now.

He already knew how wet she was, how ready for him. He lifted her to the edge of the table, hooked her leg around his hip after quickly shedding his trousers. "Please," she whispered.

Sweet Jesus. Blood pounded in his ears, drowning out the rest of her plea. It didn't matter. He knew what she wanted—what they both wanted.

He kissed her full on the lips, positioning himself at her entrance.

Slowly. He needed to go slowly. But then she rocked her hips toward him.

He could wait no longer.

Wrenching up her skirts, he pressed forward, entering inch by tortured inch. She was so tight. His body shook with the desire to simply thrust into her, burying himself deep, over and over until he was spent. But he didn't want to hurt her more than necessary. Gently, he lowered her to the ground, bracing himself above her.

"I'm sorry," he whispered, and pushed forward, entering her fully.

She sucked in her breath at the pain, then stilled. He forced himself to do the same.

"It's always this way the first time, my sweet."

She took another deep breath, smiled bravely, then wiggled beneath him, making small, uncertain, seeking movements.

He followed her cue and slid deeper.

"Oh," she breathed.

He withdrew slightly, then moved in again, then again, increasing the pace, noting with pleasure when she matched her movements to his. He clasped her hips tighter as his body clamored for release. Her back arched.

"Alex." She tossed her head fretfully. "I need—"

He knew. He needed the same thing. They were close, so close . . . He increased the pace and placed one thumb on the swollen nub at the entrance to her sex.

She came in a shower of tremors surrounding him, just as he plunged once more and found his own release, one so powerful it robbed him of breath and shook the very foundations of his beliefs about the sexual act.

Long moments later, Alex once more grew conscious of his surroundings. He and Elizabeth lay in a tumbled heap on the floor. Hardly a dignified position for a duke and a gently bred young woman—or for anyone, for that matter. Though he felt no remorse for what they'd done, he did suffer a pang for how they'd gone about it. Damned awkward business. Elizabeth deserved better.

He slowly disentangled himself and stood, helping her up as well. Her lips were still swollen from his kisses, her eyes filled with sated desire and newfound knowledge.

What had he done? Even a courtesan would expect better treatment. And Elizabeth was certainly no common tavern wench, accustomed to a quick tumble in a stolen corner. She'd been an innocent.

He cupped her face. "Elizabeth, I'm sorry. I don't know what came over me," he told her ruefully.

Elizabeth stared back, uncertain of his meaning.

Did he regret what they'd just done? She couldn't bear the thought. Perhaps she'd disappointed him. He had years of experience dallying with the fairer sex, whereas she'd been hopelessly naïve. But she'd so wanted to please him.

"Please, please don't apologize," she begged, laying her own hand along his jaw. "I can learn. I'll do better."

He frowned. "It wasn't that."

"Then what? Tell me, so I can please you."

"Oh, Elizabeth." A laugh rumbled from his chest. "You do please me. More than you should. I meant I was sorry for my loss of control, for acting the common clod. Nothing else."

Pleasure flooded her at the idea she'd affected him so strongly. "You, my lord, lost control?"

He noted her teasing tone and tweaked her nose. "Don't push a man further than you must, once he's admitted a fault. In fact, I shall be happy to demonstrate to you the full extent of my, er, control, in a more appropriate location."

Her eyes widened. She was fairly certain she knew

what he meant, and she could feel the liquid heat pooling at her woman's core at his suggestion.

Alex gave her a wolfish grin. "You may wish to refasten your hair before we exit, my sweet." He held out a pin.

Her cheeks grew warm as she tried, without a looking glass, to force her hair back into some semblance of order. Alex was of little help—though he did manage to refasten all the hooks of her bodice.

Finally, when she'd managed as best she could, he opened the door, peeked out, then took her arm and whispered, "Casual, my dear, as though nothing has happened," before swinging the door wide open.

Following his own advice, he strolled out beside her, while she struggled not to wonder if their liaison would be apparent to all.

It probably would.

Oh, Lord, what if they were seen? The full ramifications of their act hit her with the force of a steam engine. Her heart thudded as though trying to escape her chest.

They came upon the innkeeper at the edge of the public room. Thankfully, he was the only person there.

Alex grabbed him by the wrist and growled, "If you value your establishment, you will forget immediately that either of us was ever here. Is my meaning clear?"

The man nodded quickly, rubbing the finger-shaped marks on his arm when Alex released it. "Of course, Your Grace."

Alex went out ahead of her and called for his horse to be readied. "I'd be happy to escort you back to my sister's. I was on my way there when I passed by the inn and saw you entering."

"But you have only the horse?"

"He'll carry two."

"We'd be seen leaving together."

He shook his head. "No one but the staff is here, and the old man values his business too much to go telling tales. Around back there's a trail leading into the woods. It comes out on my sister's estate."

Elizabeth nodded. "I suppose . . . but there would still be servants about when we reach your sister's. No, Your Grace, I think it better if I walk. It is not far."

"In that case, I shall accompany you. A woman traveling alone is at risk."

She had a feeling she knew the reason for his gallantry—and it wasn't the risk to her on the mile-long walk.

The inn boy signaled that the duke's horse was ready. Alex glanced at the great beast. "He could easily carry us both," he offered once more.

She quickly shook her head. Riding atop a horse, pressed intimately against the duke, his arms holding her steady . . . Elizabeth swallowed. That was the last place she needed to be. Instead, she took off walking while Alex claimed his mount.

She wasn't ready to discuss what had just happened, or what it meant for her future as a governess.

Why did she have no willpower when it came to Alex Bainbridge? She'd *known* what he was about. He'd been clear about his intentions when he'd touched her at the Grumsby estate. His reputation was known to every woman in England. When he'd disappeared for two weeks, she should have come to her senses, guarded her heart.

But one gallant act, and one fiery kiss, and she'd given in to every wanton desire she'd ever had. She'd *asked* him to make love to her. Worse, she knew she'd do it again, given the chance.

She heard the soft clop of hooves on the dirt road behind her, but she kept walking.

"I thought you might want this."

Alex loomed above her, leaning down from his horse to hand her a small velvet pouch. Her father's brooch.

"You left it in the room we . . ." He cleared his throat. "Well. I realize it's not what you thought when you came here today, but perhaps it still holds some value for you."

She accepted the pouch, cupping it in her hand and examining it as she walked. It was easier than looking up at the duke. Walking alongside his great horse made her feel smaller than ever.

"Elizabeth."

She shook her head, not trusting herself to speak. These feelings were too new, too raw. She needed to think—about what she'd done, and what she'd do next.

"All right. We don't have to discuss this now. But soon, Elizabeth, we will need to talk."

She nodded, grateful for the reprieve.

Finally she tucked the velvet pouch into her reticule. The brooch wasn't even real, she thought again, embarrassed. Her father had lied to her about so many things.

She glanced up at the duke, who had accepted her request for silence and now rode companionably beside her. Dear God, he was handsome. The late-afternoon sun struck his profile, burnishing his inky hair and highlighting his sharp features.

She couldn't be angry with him. She knew how willing a participant she'd been in her own seduction. And whatever faults he might have, at least Alex Bainbridge— unlike her own family—had not lied to her.

* * *

Back at the inn, Jim Cutter sat down and ordered ale. It reminded him of his humble roots. He indulged only at times like this—when he was certain none of his London acquaintances would observe him.

The White Hart was just far enough from the city to be safe. And apparently he wasn't the only one who thought so.

The Duke of Beaufort wouldn't recognize lowly Jim Cutter, but Cutter had definitely recognized the duke. He'd barely arrived when he'd seen the duke and his woman emerge. Wisely, he'd stepped out of sight, then waited until they were gone before entering.

Interesting, that.

There would be little use pumping the innkeeper for details—any man of business worth his salt knew how to keep secrets. But Cutter didn't need much explanation.

Unless he was mistaken, that was the selfsame chit Wetherby had declared missing. "Gone to visit a sick friend," he'd grumbled. "Bah. Avoiding me, more like."

Cutter snorted. The duke appeared in robust health. Not that he'd blame any woman for avoiding Wetherby. The man was a prig at best, though one of ambition—a motive Cutter understood and shared.

He prided himself on being observant. More than once, an interesting little tidbit like the one he'd just observed had come in handy in his never-ending scramble to social prominence.

Based on what he'd learned of the Medfords from Harold, added to the conversation he'd overheard between the duke and his card-playing friends at

White's some weeks ago, he didn't believe the lovely miss was merely avoiding Wetherby.

No, Jim Cutter got a very different picture of just why he'd seen Elizabeth Medford leaving a public house with the Duke of Beaufort.

A very different picture, indeed.

Chapter Eight

Alex bid Elizabeth farewell at the rear entrance to his sister's rambling home. He wanted to touch her, hold her close, taste her once more before letting her go. Instead, he slid down from his horse and gave her a formal, but distant, bow.

She curtsied in return. "Thank you for seeing me safely back."

"An honor, Miss Medford." *Elizabeth.* He wanted to use her Christian name. He certainly knew her well enough. But they stood in plain sight, where any number of servants might overhear them. What a ridiculous charade.

"Well . . ." she said softly. "I suppose I'd best go."

She flicked an uncertain gaze toward him, and the confusion in those green depths tugged at his cold, blackened heart.

"I'll see you again soon," he told her, his voice low. "I've no desire to wait another two weeks. I confess you're something of an obsession with me."

Her cheeks flushed beautifully and she hurried inside. He smiled.

Alex sighed. If his sister discovered he'd been here without visiting her, he was in for a lecture. He'd have to at least stay for dinner. Not that he minded, under normal circumstances. But knowing Elizabeth was so close, and his brother-in-law's eye so watchful, was going to be torture.

The honorable thing would be to offer for her. But there was far too much history between their families for that—even *if* he was a man of honor. If the full truth was ever known, the scandal would ruin them both, and everyone related to them. Better to keep it in the past.

She had every reason to hate him.

If she had any sense at all, she would. He'd taken her virginity at an inn, as though she were common, cheap. Then he'd disappeared again—when she'd awoken Monday morning, he'd already left for London.

She *should* hate him. She just couldn't.

Elizabeth kept remembering the gallant way Alex had paid for her father's brooch, and the way he'd insisted on escorting her home. And none of that even began to describe what she felt when she thought of his intimate caresses. Her schoolgirl fantasies paled in comparison, while her newfound knowledge had been keeping her awake at night, heat pooling in places she didn't dare touch herself, wondering when she'd see him again.

It might not be the life she'd once envisioned for herself, but Elizabeth was happy. Or at least that's what she told herself.

After all, she hadn't *expected* him to stay around, raising the suspicions of everyone in the house—they all knew the duke was an infrequent visitor at best. Still, it would have been nice if he'd left a note.

On Thursday morning, he did.

The letter arrived in the regular post. Once she turned Henry and Clara over to their nurse for lunch, she hurried to her own quarters. The suite next to the nursery wasn't lavish, but the room was cheerful enough, and paid for by her own work. Light filtered in from the small window, making the dust motes sparkle in the air. Tucked beneath her pillow, the letter waited.

She opened it with trembling fingers. The stationery was unmarked, but inside, the duke's bold scrawl covered the page.

Elizabeth,

I trust this letter finds you well. You fill my thoughts. I am anxious to see you again. Know that I would send you flowers and jewels—only a small measure of my affection—but I am afraid they would not escape the notice of my sister's worthy staff.

Your position there is troublesome, for I find myself wanting more of you than what my sister can, unknowingly, of course, spare. But I will not press you on that matter, for now. I hope you've no plans for your next afternoon off, for I am sending a carriage to deliver you to me. Please forgive the presumption. I'm most anxious to see you.

Alex

No polite closing. Just his signature. How like him.

Elizabeth squeezed the letter against her bosom, giddy with anticipation. He *did* want to see her again! She took a quick spin around her room.

She opened the letter to stare at it again. *"Forgive the*

presumption." *Hah!* she snorted. The man was a duke, one of the most sought-after in England. Presumption, and the expectation of forgiveness, were second nature to him. He knew perfectly well she'd climb into any carriage he sent.

She would. Elizabeth wouldn't bother fooling herself about that again. She couldn't resist the temptation of another afternoon in the duke's arms—especially not now, when she knew what to expect.

But she did have a few things to consider first. Slowly she folded the letter and tucked it at the bottom of the valise she'd brought when she'd first come here.

The Grumsby children were lovely. But was this— caring for other people's children, with only a few stolen moments for herself—all her future held?

She lay down on the narrow bed and rolled her shoulders a few times to ease out the kinks. Chasing Henry and Clara about the grounds tired her. Nature lessons were a favorite of both children, especially since, once they'd covered the planned material, she usually gave into their pleas for a game of chase or blindman's bluff. She shouldn't complain, though— they were sweet children, if active.

Rather how she'd once imagined her own children. Loneliness pricked her and she shut her eyes. She'd always wanted a family and children of her own. That wasn't likely to happen now, but she had the joy of Henry and Clara Grumsby—both surprisingly affectionate youngsters—in her life. She spent more time with them as their governess than most women of the ton did with their own children. It wasn't the same, of course, and would never totally erase the ache for a child of her own, but it was something, and it was good.

And as far as the men in her life—well, things in that area had improved vastly. She was not married to Harold. Thank God. And as a governess, she was finally out from under the thumb of her uncle George.

So far, her decision to run away hadn't brought dire consequences down upon her family. Elizabeth's friend Beatrice had sent word that the Medfords were simply saying that Elizabeth had gone away to the country to visit a sick relative. They were angry with her, according to a separate note from Charity, but apparently not so much they'd air their dirty laundry before the rest of the ton. Good. Elizabeth didn't want people to shun her sister because of *her*.

Best of all, she had the one man she'd dreamed about for years. Alex Bainbridge. And the real thing was far better than those naïve fantasies of old.

True, he wasn't hers in the most legitimate way. She could never marry him. But he did care for her—she could sense it. It was more than she'd ever really expected.

No. Elizabeth opened her eyes to stare at the ceiling. Try as she might, she couldn't convince herself that last was true.

This *wasn't* more than she'd ever expected. She'd been raised as a privileged daughter of the *ton,* a daughter for whom a good marriage—or at least an advantageous one—and children were *not* too much to expect.

She almost wished she hadn't had that childhood. She wished she'd known about her father's foibles all along, so the disappointment at giving all that up would taste a little less bitter now.

She had Alex's attentions for now, but for how long? And what would she do when he moved on?

Elizabeth punched her pillow, unwilling to think about that eventuality.

It could be worse. Much, much worse. She could be married to Harold.

She would just have to keep reminding herself of that and learn to be content with her lot in life.

In three days she would see her duke again. A moment spent in Alex's arms would erase the cares of her daily life.

Yes, Elizabeth told herself again, life was good.

Three Sundays passed, and with each one, Elizabeth met Alex for a few brief hours. She grew to understand that in between spurts of rakish charm, Alex was brooding, distant. She wanted nothing more than to reach him at those times, ease the pain of whatever had hurt him. He cared for her—that much she was sure of. But there was more to Alex than she'd ever guessed, and each moment spent together made her yearn to know more. And, Lord, how she missed his touch.

He'd told her he found her spirit and laughter refreshing, so when Sunday next arrived, Elizabeth didn't hesitate before donning the most frivolous frock she'd brought with her: a green muslin costume her friend Bea said brought out the color of her eyes. It wasn't fancy by the ton's standards, but when she fastened her hair in curls at her crown and wound a matching ribbon through them, she thought the effect quite nice.

Alex's unmarked carriage waited at the edge of the Grumsby grounds. She appreciated the precaution, though she still worried that eventually, someone would notice a pattern to her outings and start asking questions.

Today, the coach took her directly to Alex's cousin's nearby hunting lodge. The building was kept comfortable at all times, but neither the cousin nor staff was in residence. A perfect place for a tryst.

And tryst they did. For the moment the carriage pulled away, Alex's lips were on hers, his hands searching for the hooks and ties to her garments as he shut the door behind them. Her carefully styled hair came tumbling down in seconds, the festive ribbon lost, a victim to their passion.

She pressed closer, seeking his touch, the feel of his skin on hers. Was this desire for him insatiable? It felt as though they'd been apart for ages, not a mere week.

They made it up the stairs, stumbling, laughing, kissing, and shedding clothing as they went.

There was urgency in Alex's lovemaking today. An intensity she didn't understand. But when he finally slipped inside her she ceased questioning. God, yes. This—he—was what she'd been missing.

Yes, this was worth all the risk.

But afterward, when they'd spent themselves not once, but twice, and lay sated in each other's arms, the odd feeling returned.

Alex held her, but his gaze was on the ceiling. Elizabeth reached out to run her fingers through his thick dark hair.

"My lord?" she asked tentatively. "Have I done something wrong?"

"Of course not, darling," he murmured, capturing her hand and pulling it from his hair to his lips to take little nibbles of her fingers.

Elizabeth smiled but continued to watch him. Even

though *she* felt bonelessly, deliciously exhausted, there was still a tension in her lover's body. He was restless, distracted. She knew it in spite of his reassurances.

She lay silent for a while, stroking her fingers up and down the wide expanse of his chest, the firmness of his arms, and mentally urged him to relax, or share with her his concerns.

When he finally spoke, it wasn't to whisper foolish endearments in her ear.

"Elizabeth, my sweet, there's something I must tell you."

"You've arranged with your sister for an extended visit?" she asked hopefully, trying to tease away the uneasiness she'd sensed. Their afternoon was drawing to a close, and the upcoming week, a week spent away from him, loomed endlessly before her.

"Unfortunately, no."

A weight fell in her stomach, pulling her down. "What is it?"

"I must travel on a matter of business."

"You're going away?" On business? That didn't make sense. Noblemen weren't businessmen—though she knew Alex did invest, quite successfully, in a number of ventures. Rumors of just how successful he'd been often flitted about the ton.

"A shipping venture I've invested in requires my oversight," he confirmed. "Our vessel recently returned from India, damaged by a storm. The repairs aren't going well, the crew is restless, and my partner is trying to arrange replacement of some of the exotic goods that were lost. On top of that, there is some question as to the captain's integrity. I'd thought to let my man on the coast handle it, but the matter is more complicated than I'd anticipated, and there are considerable funds at stake."

She appreciated the insight into his business—she had a feeling it wasn't something he shared with most women. But it didn't answer her most pressing question. "How long will you be gone?"

"Three weeks. No more."

She nodded dumbly, the weight she felt in her stomach growing heavier. She understood, but this pending absence made the week she'd thought they'd spend apart pale in comparison. They'd only just become lovers. She ached for more of him, not less.

Alex took both her hands in his. "Elizabeth, if you would drop this charade of being a governess and become my mistress in earnest, I could bring you with me. 'Twould make for a far more pleasant trip."

"It's not a charade." But more and more it was. Much as she loved the Grumsby children, she *lived* for the moments spent with Alex.

She looked away. Swallowed.

"I know, Elizabeth. You truly care for my sister's children. I would not have you change that—in fact, it's one of the things I like best about you. But it's bloody awkward for a man of my position to play second fiddle to two small children."

At that she gave him a small smile, unable to imagine her powerful duke playing "second fiddle" to anyone. "We agreed this would be on my terms," she reminded him.

He expelled a forceful breath, his frustration evident. "Elizabeth, your terms make no sense. I can keep you in far more luxury than what you have now."

"But you cannot offer me respectability."

"This, what we're doing now, sneaking around

behind everyone's backs, is more respectable?" he asked incredulously.

She looked away again. He had a point. "Still, I cannot."

If their relationship remained a secret, the shame remained hers alone. If she was kept as a mistress, word would spread, and her family would lose the last shreds of respectability to which they still clung.

She couldn't do that to Charity. There was still hope for her sister's future.

She'd wanted Alex from the moment she'd met him. Maybe she hadn't known what *wanting* meant, back then, but she did now. And she wasn't willing to let him go.

But the choice he was asking her to make—she just couldn't do it. Between her father's actions and her own, her family had borne enough shame.

"If that is your decision, Elizabeth, I will accept it. And I will see you when I return."

Elizabeth nodded, and did the only thing she could think to do: kissed him with enough passion to last the next three weeks, and possibly to make him hurry his business matters along.

Marian Grumsby loved country life—most of the time. Her husband and children filled her world with love and joy, and they were happiest away from London. And, truth be told, she didn't want to do what so many other mothers did during the Season: simply leave the children for weeks on end. But occasionally, she missed the soirees and teas enjoyed by the other ladies of her acquaintance.

So when Lady Alicia Wilbourne, a girlhood friend, invited her to come to London for a holiday, she eagerly accepted. It was a blessing, Marian thought, to know she could have a few days' fun while the children were well cared for at home.

Hiring Elizabeth had been unconventional, but so far it was proving a perfect solution. The girl was good with the children, and her upbringing unquestionable. Which meant Marian could attend a few parties and catch up on all the latest gossip with her friends without worry.

She'd opted to stay at her mother's town house, as she usually did when visiting London—preferable, in her opinion, to imposing on friends she rarely saw. The dowager duchess was infrequently there, as she spent the vast majority of her days taking the waters at Bath. But the house had a small staff, who was always pleased to see Marian, and she had peace and quiet in between social events.

This afternoon's schedule held a garden party at Alicia's home. The weather had, remarkably, cooperated, and when Marian arrived, the Wilbournes' yard was decorated with white tents and flowers.

Lord Wilbourne, a middle-aged man with a quickly receding hairline, strolled the grounds, a plate of hors d'oeuvres in hand. He gazed fondly at his younger wife as they greeted their guests.

Upon seeing Marian arrive, they immediately headed her way.

"Lady Grumsby! Back from rusticating at last," Lady Alicia Wilbourne greeted her.

They'd come out during the same Season, and while Marian had initially pitied her friend for her parents' decision to marry her to Robert Wilbourne, Alicia didn't look unhappy in the least.

"Yes, for a short while," Marian said.

"Then you must be simply dying for conversation. I can't imagine how you spend all your time in the country. Come." Alicia gestured to a group of prettily attired women. "I've other guests to greet, but you remember Lady Tweedley, and Lady Robesford, and Miss Josephine Baxter." She led Marian to the group of women and, after a moment, returned to her hostessing duties.

The other women obligingly made room for Marian without a pause in the conversation.

". . . sent her packing," Lady Tweedley finished. "She was his mistress for, what, two years? Gone. He hasn't been seen with her in weeks."

"Oh, Harriet, however do you hear such things?" Lady Robesford asked, though her facial expression and the expressions on the other women's faces suggested they were far more fascinated than shocked to be discussing a member of the demimondaine.

"Perhaps he's finally looking to marry. If only it were five years ago."

Five years ago was when Lady Tweedley had married.

Marian wasn't entirely certain who they were discussing, but she had a good guess. It was a known fact that Harriet Tweedley had—prior to marriage, anyhow—always fawned after Alex Bainbridge.

Marian sighed. Had she really come all the way to London just to hear the usual gossip about her own brother? She almost wished he'd marry simply so the ton would find something else to talk about.

"Actually, I've an idea *why* he sent her packing, and it wasn't to marry," Miss Baxter, an incurable gossip well on the way to old-maidhood, put in.

"Oh, do tell," Lady Robesford breathed.

Miss Baxter glanced around as if confiding a great secret. "I heard," she said, pausing for effect, "he's been seen with Miss Medford. And the young lady's chaperone—if she had one—was nowhere in sight. Miss Medford was also seen entering a carriage driven by a man my source recognized as one of the duke's servants. One can only imagine why he would send a carriage for her."

"Elizabeth Medford?" Lady Tweedley asked.

"The same."

"It couldn't be. She's off to the country to visit some sick relative," Lady Robesford said.

Marian was finding it hard to breathe—and it wasn't just because her maid had the strength of an Amazon when it came to tightening stays. No, she had a very bad feeling about this conversation. But her feet were planted to the spot. She couldn't move.

Miss Baxter shrugged, smiling the smile of a gossip who relishes each shred of news she reports. "So I, too, have heard. But what relative? I heard there was a falling out when Elizabeth refused her last suitor, and she ran off."

"Impossible! The family would be ruined," Lady Robesford declared.

"The family is already ruined. Have you not heard? The baron died without a penny or an heir. Anyhow, I saw the suitor leave with my own two eyes, and he didn't look pleased. And Elizabeth hasn't been seen since. *Except*, of course, with Beaufort."

Beaufort. Marian blinked. Yes, they were talking about her brother. And, apparently, her governess.

"Oh, dear!" Miss Baxter exclaimed. "I only just realized you were standing here, Lady Grumsby." Bright splotches of color appeared on her cheeks.

Marian kept her face carefully neutral, her spine rigidly erect. So. The gossip in the ton revolved around Alex. That in itself wasn't so unusual. But this time it involved *her* as well, for her children were being looked after by the very woman rumored to be gallivanting with her hell-bent sibling. Her body hummed with tension, the desire to escape, but she refused to give in. None of the other women knew Elizabeth was in her employ.

She gave them an acknowledging smile. "Understandable. My brother can be quite an absorbing topic."

The other women looked uncertain as to whether to be relieved or not.

Marian took pity on them. After all, she was certainly used to hearing gossip about Alex. These friends of hers just didn't know why this particular gossip was unwelcome. "Do you know what *I* heard?" she asked.

They looked at her expectantly.

"I heard he's booked passage to India and is promised to marry a princess there, the daughter of a man with whom he's engaged in trade."

Miss Baxter's mouth dropped open.

"Of course, I know that not to be true, for Alex told me just the other day he wished to escape from London and spend some time at my estate. And not yesterday our mother was despairing over his lack of interest in marriageable ladies. And my home, while lovely, is hardly an Indian palace. But it did make for an entertaining rumor." With that, Marian excused herself from the gossipy trio.

She approached Lady Wilbourne. "Alicia. It is a lovely party. Though I hadn't thought to come so far from home only to hear news of my own family."

"It is a remarkably fine day," Alicia said, looking at the sky. "As to the duke, well, he does seem to be the topic *du jour*. Not that that's unusual. My husband plays cards with him, you know, and Robert told me the duke mentioned something that made him think these latest rumors might not be unfounded.

"Still, I suppose you tire of hearing of your brother's escapades. Shall we talk about the theater? There's a marvelous new play showing."

Marian shook her head. "I'm afraid I've the headache and must make my excuses. I do thank you for hosting this fine gathering."

Alicia looked sympathetic, and soon Marian was in the coach on the way back to her mother's town house.

She'd *so* been looking forward to her sojourn in the city, but she knew she'd not be able to enjoy it now. Even though she'd given the women good reason to question any gossip they heard, she knew that if *they* were talking about it, then most of London was as well.

As much as she'd like to believe the rumors were unfounded, she'd seen the way her brother occasionally gazed over at Elizabeth when he thought her unaware. And though Marian had gently ribbed Alex for leaving only a few days after the party ended, she'd actually been surprised at how long he *did* stay. Perhaps her governess had been the reason. She'd convinced herself they must have met when Elizabeth was still active in Society, that it was nothing more than old friendship. Except her brother wasn't known for *friendships* with women. And the gazes Marian had intercepted had been filled with heat. She just hadn't thought her older brother would be so foolish as to act on that heat.

In spite of the wild rumors that always circulated, Marian knew he usually limited his affairs to widows or members of the demimondaine. Perhaps he'd tired of such limitations.

Marian sighed as she repacked the things she'd brought to London.

Elizabeth was a good governess. But Marian put her children first in everything. And there was no way she could allow her children to be chaperoned by a woman of questionable reputation, deserved or not.

Chapter Nine

"What a disaster."

"You haven't seen the worst of it," Alex's partner said, as the two men stood on deck surveying the on-going repairs to the storm-damaged ship. After bidding Elizabeth farewell, Alex had stopped briefly in London before continuing to the port at Ramsgate, where his on-site partner, Tom Golden, had already begun setting things in order.

"No?" Alex had a feeling he wasn't going to like whatever came next. Of course, he hadn't expected this trip to be pleasant. "All right. Enlighten me."

"Come on."

Alex followed him below deck to the hold. As expected, many of the crates bearing fine Indian silks and curiosities from the Far East were ruined.

"I already knew the cargo was worthless." He shrugged. "No man can beat Mother Nature in a fury."

"It's not just that. Look." Tom pulled a length of fabric from one of the few undamaged crates. "Feel this."

Alex ran his hand over the fabric, then frowned.

"What is this? It's substandard. George knows better than this."

George Marks had worked as his foreign buyer for years. The man was extensively traveled and knew how to distinguish top-quality silks from their average counterparts the way most men knew a hammer from a shovel.

Tom took back the silk and tossed it into the crate. "George resigned, the day after the ship made port."

"Blast. Why?"

"Said he'd decided it was time to become a family man, but I don't buy it. The captain was there when we spoke, and Marks didn't make eye contact with him the entire time."

"Blast," Alex repeated. "Where's the captain?" That's why he'd come originally. Tom's letter stating the ship was damaged had been worrisome, but the fact the captain apparently didn't care to oversee the repairs was doubly concerning.

"Dorset."

"What?" He could feel the vein at his temple pulse as his frustration multiplied.

"His home, it seems. Beaufort, there's a problem here, and I fear it's far more complicated than a storm-damaged vessel. I know how you are about your investments, and I thought you needed to see for yourself."

"Indeed." He nodded. "You did the right thing, Tom. It's not you I'm angry with." He paused for a moment, forced himself to think. Dorset was several days' travel from the ship's current port, but sending a messenger would only prolong this process. And there were some messages the duke preferred to deliver in person. "You see to the repairs. I'll see to the captain."

Alex shook his head in frustration as he strode off the dock. He'd hoped to surprise Elizabeth by returning early. God, he missed her. Instead, it appeared he'd be surprising the captain of his ship. And then looking for his replacement.

"Miss Medford, you are released from my service."

Dismissed. The words reverberated in Elizabeth's mind like the tolling of a bell.

"I am sorry," the Viscountess Grumsby continued, her tone kind but firm. "You are a good governess, and the children love you. But your relationship with my brother has become public knowledge, and all the ton is gossiping about it. I was willing to risk hiring you in spite of your background as long as you worked quietly, but now I cannot risk my family's reputation by keeping you in my employ. I'm sure you understand."

Elizabeth's insides squirmed in misery and embarrassment. She opened her mouth to speak, but the other woman put up a hand to stop her. "It doesn't matter if it's true or not, Elizabeth, only that Society thinks it so." She gave Elizabeth an appraising look. "Though I've seen the way my brother looks at you, and I daresay the gossip is not without merit."

Elizabeth lowered her eyes. She had no defense. "I am sorry to have caused such trouble, my lady. I'll pack my things and be on my way at once." She dropped a dutiful curtsy and left the room.

A hollow buzzing filled her ears as she numbly packed her few belongings. Elizabeth could hardly blame her—if she was in the viscountess's position, she'd have done the same thing.

She was a fool. She'd ruined the only opportunity for

respectable employment she was likely to receive. And all for a man she could not marry. A few moments of stolen pleasure, and she'd wrecked her life utterly.

How had the gossip leaked? The innkeeper? Elizabeth doubted it. Alex's threat had made the man visibly tremble. Some other servant?

It didn't matter. The only thing that mattered was that somehow, their relationship was known. If Lady Grumsby had heard of it in London, the talk must be everywhere.

There were precious few things to pack. Elizabeth had left most of her old life behind when she'd assumed this position. She took her valise downstairs to the back entrance of the manor. The local butcher was just climbing into his cart, having completed a delivery to the Grumsby estate. She quickly arranged to ride with him as far as the White Hart Inn. What she would do when she got there, she'd yet to determine.

The cart smelled strongly of blood, but the ride was free and the butcher not given to conversation, so Elizabeth was thankful.

At the White Hart, she could hardly look inside without thinking of all she and Alex had done in the private dining room. Her breath quickened in shame and desire. Those moments had cost her everything, but, oh, what she wouldn't give to relive them.

She quickly purchased a seat on the mail coach to London and waited outside. Perhaps Bea would take her in, hide her while she gathered her wits and found new employment. Though now the matter of references would be more difficult than ever.

Oh, why had this happened while Alex was away? He'd not given her any way to reach him. Not that he owed her such considerations. After all, she was not his wife, and she'd even refused to let him keep her as his only mistress. But now she longed for his presence. He was always so confident, so decisive. He would know what to do.

Then again, Elizabeth reflected, the duke's answer would likely be to renew his argument to let him keep her. As much as she cared for him, it was an arrangement she did not cherish. Taking him as a lover had been risky, certainly, but it had been her choice. It was not the same as allowing him to pay for what they did together.

Elizabeth missed her sister, too. But to go home would be to admit defeat. And her uncle was as likely to shut the door in her face as to let her in.

The coach arrived, and Elizabeth wearily climbed inside, barely noticing as she bumped knees with other passengers in the crowded interior.

All her life she'd been pressured to act responsibly. Much as she hated to admit it, her mother had a point. Just look at the mess she'd made of her life the first and only time she'd strayed from that advice.

The mail coach stop in London was several blocks from Elizabeth's destination. When they finally arrived, she climbed down, then stood a moment, uncertain. Never had she walked through the streets of London without even a maid to accompany her. Would anyone recognize her? What would they think? She didn't dare risk sending for someone to fetch her. She was counting on pleading her case in person, begging Beatrice Pullington's forgiveness and mercy. Bea had already helped her once, and Elizabeth had ruined that opportunity by her indiscretion. Was it too much to count on her friendship a second time?

Elizabeth glanced once more at the bustling street. She still wore her governess's uniform. Perhaps if she kept her head down and hurried, no one would be the wiser.

· Her bag seemed heavier now that she had to carry it through the streets, but she didn't dare slow her pace. So far, her plan seemed to be working. Even when she did look up to keep her bearings, no one gave her a second glance.

She neared the park. If she cut through, she could reach her friend's residence more quickly. Even better, she was less likely to be seen, for she was on the side of the park that, though it contained paths, was not man-icured and was therefore less frequented by the fash-ionable set.

The street cleared and she hurried across, intent on her goal.

But as she stepped onto the park path, the toe of her slipper caught on a stone. Momentum, and the weight of her valise, conspired against her. She went down hard.

Worse, as Elizabeth picked herself up from the ground, she discovered she'd fallen directly at the feet of a man who'd just been leaving the path.

He reached down a hand to assist her. She took it, cursing herself for being so clumsy.

The man who'd helped her looked no better than she. Haggard lines furrowed his face, and she smelled alcohol on his breath. It was only mid-afternoon. She muttered a hasty thanks and turned back to the path.

"Miss Medford?"

Curses. She stopped and looked at him once more.

He was dressed as a gentleman, but not one of her acquaintance. "I'm sorry, have we met?"

"Perhaps not. You *are* Miss Medford, are you not?"

Was there any point in denying it? "Yes."

The man's eye took on a gleam. He glanced at the valise she carried. Elizabeth knew that he registered her lack of chaperone from the way his brows lifted as he looked around them. "You are unescorted?"

She sighed.

"Perhaps I can be of assistance."

She didn't trust the way he looked at her, the way his gaze lingered in places it shouldn't. "It seems we are headed in opposite directions . . . Mister?"

"Cutter. My apologies. Name's Cutter."

In spite of Elizabeth's observations about his intended direction prior to their collision, Mr. Cutter followed her as she continued toward the Pullington home.

Her stomach tightened in unease. She hadn't wanted to cause a scene on the street, but now that they'd moved farther into the park, there was no one else around should she need help. She hefted her bag and quickened her pace.

"Why such a hurry?" Cutter asked. "Keeping the duke waiting?"

"I don't know what you're talking about."

She would have problems enough when she reached Bea's and began trying to piece her life back together, Elizabeth thought darkly. Couldn't she at least get that far without incident?

"There's no need to deny it. Your relationship with the duke is the talk of the ton." His words were slightly slurred.

How, on God's green earth, had she had the misfortune to run into this man?

"Mr. Cutter," she said impatiently, "you are mistaken.

There is no relationship. Furthermore, I am not in need of your assistance."

"I see. The duke lost interest already? Well, now that you've worked off your father's debt, you're free to choose a man more to your liking." He put a hand on her arm.

Elizabeth stopped. The man was clearly foxed. Why else would he ramble such nonsense? "I haven't the faintest notion what you mean. Kindly unhand me."

"Don't play innocent with me," he sneered. "I'm not interested in a virtuous woman. The duke himself told me."

"Told you *what?*" she asked, even as she thought how ridiculous it was to question a man so obviously inebriated.

But Cutter spoke with conviction, as though, beneath the alcohol-sodden layers, there was a kernel of truth. "How your dear father offered *you* as payment for the gaming debt he owed Beaufort. Can't say I approve, but now that the deed is done . . ."

"No. He wouldn't have," she said faintly, her stomach clenching. But how could she be sure? So much about her father was not as she'd thought. But there was one thing she did know. "And if he had, His Grace would never have stooped to accept such a bargain."

"Oh-ho. Defending Beaufort over Daddy? You think he'd ignore such an offer, laid in his lap? Why? He's a man, after all. And surely you must know he has a reputation."

Eyeing her bosom, Cutter continued his verbal assault. "You are not without certain charms. Though I must say, when you become my mistress, I will have you do more to display them."

Elizabeth said a mental prayer of thanks for her modest governess's gown. "I'm sorry, Mr. Cutter, but your interest in me is misplaced. I have no intention of becoming your mistress."

"Too good for a mere mister, eh? I'll have you know I can pay handsomely."

"Don't be crude. My favors are not for sale," she replied coldly, doing her best to edge away. Why, oh *why*, had she thought to cut through the park?

"Look," he said, his tone turning nasty, "now that you've done it to help dear old Daddy, there's no going back. His Grace grows quickly tired of his mistresses. I'm sure you know that. He's probably already moved on. Why else would you be alone on the street, valise in hand?

"Consider the debt paid. Since His Grace was not supporting you for those favors you hold so dear, you've no reason to be so loyal. Surely you're not such a fool as to believe he'd grown to care for you."

Her nails dug into her palms as she resisted dignifying his attack with a response. This man could never understand what she and the duke had shared.

Cutter snickered. "I assure you, Beaufort doesn't develop lasting affections. *I*, however, might. We could have a pleasant arrangement, you and I." He ran his hand up her arm.

Elizabeth pulled away, hard.

"Listen to me," she hissed. "I am not interested. If you speak another word, I shall be ill. Here, on your shoes. I'm going to leave now, and I suggest you do not hinder me. If I scream, we are not so far from the street I cannot be heard. And if you speak one more word of such filth to me, I shall not hesitate to give your name to my uncle upon returning home. He is not a forgiving man. Understood?"

She stalked off before the gaping man could reply.

Angry. He was just angry that she hadn't jumped at his improper offer. He was foxed, obviously, and angry. That's all there was to it, Elizabeth told herself, over and over. The threat of her uncle's retaliation was an empty one, she knew. He'd just as likely hand her over to Cutter and wash his hands of her.

Exiting the park, Elizabeth prayed she'd never have cause to find out.

Only a few more blocks. Her heart slowed its reckless pace.

But even though she held her head high, her chin firm, an awful feeling crept through her.

She knew *she* hadn't been involved in any agreement, but what about her father? Could he really have offered her to Alex? Had he even owed the duke a gaming debt?

She squeezed her eyes closed, faltering in her brisk pace.

Yes, likely he had. She'd learned enough about her father to know his problems ran deep. But selling his own daughter . . . no father could be so cruel. Could he?

And the thing with the duke . . . that simply didn't make sense. If there'd been a bargain, she'd have been informed. She'd have been told she had no choice. Instead, she thought, she'd practically thrown herself at Alex, *asked* him to ruin her, and he'd refused. Only when she'd become a governess, months after her father's death, had he pursued her.

A new, ugly thought occurred to her. It often took months to settle a nobleman's estate and accounts after his death, particularly when there was no heir. What if Alex had turned down the offer while her father was alive because he planned to hold out for monetary payment of the debt? At some point after the baron's death, the duke would have been notified that there was no money to pay. Would he then have reconsidered using Elizabeth, using *her*, as payment?

She didn't want to believe it. But so many of her illusions had been shattered in the past few months, it was impossible not to wonder. If only she knew the date that Alex had found out her father's payment would not be forthcoming. Then she could compare it to the date he'd begun pursuing her and see if there was any relationship.

Unfortunately, there was no way she could come out and ask him without accusing her father of having made the offer, and accusing Alex of being a man who would consider it.

The whole thing was just too awful to contemplate, really.

Chapter Ten

"Miss Medford? Please wait here while I announce your arrival to Lady Pullington." The butler deposited her just inside the entrance to the formal salon, then swept away.

Elizabeth fidgeted. Bea's staff had known her for years. On previous visits she'd been shown immediately to the small "family" salon. This reserved welcome made it clear the rumors had reached the ears of the Pullington servants.

Had she been wrong to come here?

Seconds ticked by interminably. Finally Elizabeth heard the rush of Bea's footsteps on the stairs. The door was flung open, and before Elizabeth could say a word, Bea clapped her in a sisters' embrace.

After a long moment, her friend stepped back. Bea was, as usual, the picture of fashion in a cherry-colored day gown and matching slippers. Her expression, however, was that of someone rather put out.

"Bea, whatever's wrong?" Perhaps she had problems of her own. Elizabeth's palms dampened as fresh doubt surged through her. If her best friend turned her away, she'd nowhere left to go but home.

Bea pouted. "It seems you've had a grand adventure, and didn't share even the tiniest morsel of detail with me, your poor, dull, widowed friend." She grinned.

Elizabeth tried to smile, but to her horror, felt her eyes well instead. "Some adventure. Oh, Bea, I'm in the most awful fix. I probably shouldn't even be here—associating with the likes of me will tarnish your reputation irreparably. Though," she added, "I am infinitely, if selfishly, grateful to see you anyway."

"An awful fix? It seems I've heard those same words from you not long ago."

"This is ever so much worse."

Her friend nodded slowly. "I imagine. Come," she said, pulling Elizabeth out the door and across the hall to the family salon. "Tell me all about it."

The recounting was quick. Under other circumstances, Elizabeth would have been tempted to divulge details, but at the moment, she was too worried about her future to revel in sharing the delicious thrill of the duke's embrace—especially when it was unlikely she'd ever again experience it.

When she neared the end of the story and told Bea of the disgrace in which she'd left the Grumsby home, Bea scooted closer on the settee and hugged her gently. Elizabeth leaned her head on her friend's shoulder, relieved to know the whole world had not turned against her.

"E., you're my dearest friend and I love you no matter what scandal surrounds you, but I admit I'm not certain how to help you out of this one."

"I fear my uncle's wrath, should I return home," Elizabeth admitted.

"Then you shan't go there. You'll stay here, of course."

Elizabeth lifted her head. "I'd be ever so grateful. It's only until I come up with a new plan. I shall be entirely discreet, too—no one will ever know you've taken in a ruined woman."

Bea squeezed her hand. "Poor dear. The rumors are quite nasty, as rumors tend to be. Hiding away will only strengthen wagging tongues, you know. But don't worry about me." She grinned. "My own life has been exceedingly dull of late, and a brush with scandal may be just the thing to liven it up."

Elizabeth knew her friend well enough to discern the worry behind her smile. "You are a true friend, Bea."

"Well," Bea said carefully, "thus far, none of the rumors I have heard have come from anyone who actually saw you with Beaufort . . . only servants' gossip and the like. Perhaps we could persuade the rest of the ton the rumors are untrue?" She sat forward, and Elizabeth could tell her friend was warming to the idea.

"Bea, it would never—"

"I suspect I'm the only person, other than Charity, privy to the exchange you and the duke held in the park—the one where his interest in you was, em, well . . . lacking?"

Elizabeth's cheeks heated. "I have no reason to believe anyone else knows of it."

"We could re-tell that episode, then. Leave out the part about what you were actually proposing, of course, and simply focus on the duke's disinterest. No offense to you, dear, but surely the ton will find it easier to believe the duke was out of your reach than that this whole affair could be true."

"Lady Grumsby fired me," Elizabeth pointed out.

Bea deflated. "Yes, there is that." She sat back again.

The two young women sat in silence for a moment.

"So . . . the duke's interest in you was not so lacking as it first appeared." Bea's lips quirked, and the light in her eyes revealed only curiosity, not malicious intent.

Elizabeth felt another surge of gratitude to her friend.

"Alex's interests were . . ." Her flush deepened and she pressed her hands to her heated cheeks, as thoughts of the duke flooded her with desire and longing. And frustration. How could he have left her to face all this alone? Her spirits sank once more.

"I see," Bea said softly, sparing her further explanation. She stood, pulling Elizabeth to her feet as well. "You shall have your old room here for as long as you wish. I imagine you're exhausted, so why don't you have a rest before we decide anything else."

Alone in her room, Elizabeth sank onto the bed and gratefully closed her eyes. But when she awoke, her problems still loomed large. Bea's hospitality was a godsend, but she refused to endanger her friend's reputation by advertising her presence at the Pullington house.

The result was Elizabeth spent most of her time indoors, whiling away the hours at embroidery or other pointless tasks, away from the beady eyes and wagging tongues of Society.

On her second day at Bea's, Elizabeth wrote to Alex. After several drafts in which she poured out her love, her sorrow, how much she missed him, and how horribly unfair it was that this happened while he was gone, she decided on a different course.

The final letter was short.

Your Grace,
Everyone knows. I've lost my position with your sister.
                                          Elizabeth

She made no mention of what she'd been told by Mr. Cutter in the park. Who knew if it was even true? The fact that she was now shunned by all of Society was plenty.

She had no idea how Alex would react. She didn't even know where to reach him, so she hired a hack and took it to Alex's London address.

"Please," she told the butler, trying not to wonder what the man was thinking behind his impassive expression, "I need to get this letter to the duke. I understand he's not here, but can you see that it gets to him, soon?"

"Of course," the man said.

Elizabeth felt marginally better on the way home. Her situation was grim, but surely Alex would know what to do.

But as days went by, she heard nothing from him. She knew he was somewhere on the coast. Anxiously she tried to calculate how long the letter would take to reach him, and how long before she could expect a response. She even built in an extra couple days, just in case the butler hadn't been prompt in passing on the letter.

Still, nothing. Either the letter hadn't reached him, or he'd not deigned to respond. She doubted his servants would be so slack as to ignore a letter from a woman they must know was involved with their master. Which left the possibility that Alex was too busy, or too uninterested, to respond. Either way, it hurt.

After two weeks, she forced herself to stop checking the post the moment it arrived. She tried instead to resign herself to hermitage, for that was essentially what her life had become.

She knew—oh, she knew—how willingly she'd given herself to the duke. And for that one moment in the sun, she would pay the price of a lifetime. Loneliness.

Now that finding a respectable governess's position was out of the question, Elizabeth sent inquiries to several modistes, asking whether they had need of assistance. Plying needle and thread seemed her best hope of supporting herself.

"Any responses?" she asked Bea, who was sorting through the correspondence on her small writing desk.

"No, nothing yet." Bea picked up another envelope. "Oh. Lady Mettlethorne is hosting a card party. I should like to attend, but . . ." She trailed off with a furtive glance in Elizabeth's direction.

A pang of—what? Regret? Jealousy?—shot through her. "Please, don't feel you need to stay in on account of me. I'll be fine."

"Well, all right, then." Bea flushed, sparking Elizabeth's curiosity.

"What is it about this party? Who did you say? Lady Mettlethorne?"

"She's a friend of my mother's."

"Oh. But what . . . *oh!* Is there any possibility a certain son of hers will be in attendance?" Mr. Colin Mettlethorne was attractive, not much older than Bea, and, if Elizabeth remembered correctly, eligible.

Bea flushed deeper.

"By all means, go! And I shall expect to hear every detail when you return."

* * *

Elizabeth briefly considered waiting up for Bea the night of the card party, then dismissed the notion as foolish. She was well aware that such events often lasted through the night—both her parents had attended them regularly. Her mother had been at one the night her father died.

Elizabeth shuddered, unwilling to relive the events of those midnight hours, and forced the melancholy thought away.

Bea had done an excellent job in supplying her with novels and stitching materials to help pass the time. Her eyes grew tired long before her body, though. With no company to liven her lonely existence, she ended up pacing restlessly about the house before finally sinking into the oblivion of sleep, her dreams tortured by the strong arms of a dark but elusive lover.

The following morning, Elizabeth awoke more determined than ever to end this purgatory. Alex was gone, she told herself, but all hope was not lost. She would become a seamstress, earn her living, and, perhaps, in time, meet a respectable merchant and marry. Not for love—no one could ever make her feel the way her duke did—but with the hope of family, and children, at least. A simple life, well outside the elite circle in which she'd been raised, but one still open to her.

Her determination was redoubled when Bea finally drifted down for breakfast, a dreamy look on her face.

Elizabeth's lips quirked. "I take it the events of last night were enjoyable?"

"Quite." Bea's cheeks pinkened prettily.

"Mr. Mettlethorne was in attendance, then?"

"He was." Bea sat down at the small table with Elizabeth and poured a cup of tea.

"You are being maddeningly short of words."

Bea smiled. "I am sorry. It's only . . . I don't know what to say."

"Is he courting you?"

"Not yet."

"Do you wish him to?"

Bea studied her cuticles. "I don't know what I wish. When I first made my bow, my parents were already in discussions with Lord Pullington. I never had time for more than the briefest flirtations before I married." She sipped her tea. "I've no wish to repeat the experience of my marriage, but perhaps . . ."

Elizabeth sipped at her own tea, weighing her response. She had no words to describe the exquisite pleasure of taking a lover one truly desired—nor could she imagine what Bea must have felt on her wedding night. "Yes, perhaps," she echoed inadequately.

But when the first calling card to arrive that morning belonged to one Mr. C. P. Mettlethorne, the pleasure that lit Bea's eyes was unmistakable.

Elizabeth was grateful the gentleman had sent his card rather than calling in person. She'd have been mortified to put Bea in the awkward position of either turning him down or asking her to hide in her room. And what if something more developed between them? Bea, more than anyone, deserved a chance at romance. What sort of liaisons could she have while harboring a fugitive from polite Society?

She looked out the window, pretending not to notice the careful, almost loving way her friend set

Mettlethorne's card on her writing desk. Today, Elizabeth determined, she would call personally on the dressmaking establishments she thought most likely to hire her.

Outside, an unadorned coach rolled to a stop in front of the Pullington home. Though the vehicle was plain, it was also familiar.

Sure enough, her uncle George's form appeared in the door, followed by that of her mother.

Elizabeth tapped Bea on the shoulder, pointed, then slipped quietly into the servants' hall, preferring to avoid confrontation until she knew their purpose. Her position in the hall kept her out of sight but within earshot.

A moment later, she heard her uncle loudly announce, "Lady Medford and Mr. George Gorsham. We seek audience with Lady Pullington."

"Very good, Mr. Gorsham," the butler replied. "Let me show you to the salon while I see if my lady is available."

"Tell her the matter is urgent."

"Certainly." The butler moved off, but not in a hurry.

Bea took her time entering the salon, and the moment she did, Elizabeth's uncle descended.

"Lady Pullington. I understand you are a close friend of my niece."

"I am."

"Right. Well. To come to the point, I wonder if you have any idea as to her whereabouts?"

"Her whereabouts?"

Elizabeth smiled in her hiding spot. Trust her friend not to give her away.

"Yes." Uncle George cleared his throat. "We've said

for some time Elizabeth was visiting sick relatives. In truth, she left on her own. And—there is no delicate way to put this, my lady—with the rumors surrounding her, it's become imperative that I find her."

"We're concerned for her," Elizabeth's mother put in.

Elizabeth softened a fraction, but then her uncle continued.

"Yes. Time to put an end to this nonsense. Get her under control before she shames the family further."

Anger flooded Elizabeth to hear her uncle disparage her so in front of her friend.

"The London gossips can be vicious, it's true," Bea replied noncommittally. "But what makes you think Elizabeth wishes to return home?"

Elizabeth could imagine her uncle's face redden as he sputtered, "By God, the place of an unwed female is with her family."

There was an awkward pause.

"Perhaps she is uncertain of her welcome," Bea said softly.

"Do you know where she is, or do you not?"

Suddenly, shame filled Elizabeth. She was no coward. Bea shouldn't have to be the one to answer for her, nor to pay for her mistakes. But that's what she was allowing to happen, the longer she hid in her friend's home.

Elizabeth straightened her skirts, less because they needed it than to give her nervous hands something to do.

She was tired of living in hiding. There'd been no word from Harold Wetherby in the months she'd been gone, or Charity would have found a way to tell her. Likely he wanted nothing to do with her anymore. Thank heaven for small things.

Going home would not be pleasant, but at least it wouldn't be dangerous.

Nor did it have to be permanent, Elizabeth told herself as she stepped from her hiding place. As soon as she found respectable employment, she could be on her own again.

She walked slowly into the salon, interrupting the tense conversation. "It's all right, Bea. You needn't make excuses for me any longer. I'll go home."

It was strange. Before "the scandal," Elizabeth was always on the receiving end of endless lectures about her responsibilities and her mother's expectations for her. Now, though she'd moved back into her old room, no one seemed to know what to do with her. Clearly, she was doomed to spinsterhood, but no one spoke about it. Uncle George hadn't offered to support her—not that she wanted him to. Nor had anyone suggested she seek employment. With Bea's assistance, she'd arranged to interview for a seamstress's position next week, but she'd no intention of telling her family before she knew the outcome.

Besides Charity, there was hardly anyone to talk to. Many of the servants, aware of the Medford family's impending financial doom, had left to seek employment elsewhere. Emma, once as much friend as servant, was among those who'd left. So was the butler, who'd been replaced by a surly man who acted far loftier than merited, for a man willing to settle for the limited wages the family could pay.

All in all, it was a quiet, strained household.

On Tuesday morning after her return home, she sat in the salon, pretending to work at her needlecraft, while the rest of the household pretended she wasn't there.

Elizabeth sighed and stared out the window, embroidery forgotten. She *had* to think of something. She was willing to admit she'd acted foolishly in falling for Alex, but if she didn't cobble her life back together soon, she'd spend the rest of it under her uncle's thumb.

The door opened and Charity clomped in, then flung herself dramatically on the settee. "Ugh. Mother's got to stop. I can't blame you for leaving, E. I might do the same."

"No! Charity, what are you talking about?" Her lovely sister really did appear disgruntled.

"She's trying to make me a match. I haven't even had a Season, but she says that won't matter to certain gentlemen. Her only qualification seems to be that the gentleman is wealthy enough not to care whether I have a dowry."

"Yes," Elizabeth said dryly. "I'm aware of that qualification. Though I was unaware she'd set her new hopes on you."

"I don't see why we can't all just retire to the country. Uncle George's home is not so very small, nor do I require as much upkeep as he seems to believe."

"Don't you want to marry eventually?"

Charity sat up. "Perhaps. But not like this. Do you know what she told me today? Lord Hetterton expressed possible interest. Whatever 'possible' means, she did not say, but do you know how old that man is?"

Elizabeth tried to dredge a face from her memory. "Hetterton? Oh! Yes. Why, he must be approaching fifty. Where did you encounter him?"

"A tea I attended with Mother. He spent nearly an hour telling me of his spinster sister's fondness for small dogs."

"Ugh. How dismal."

"Well, thankfully he's not knocking at the door yet. Though, honestly, I don't think Mother or Uncle are in the mood to listen to my preferences in finding a suitor."

Guilt gnawed Elizabeth. "This whole debacle is my fault. You shouldn't be in this situation." All her life Elizabeth had been the responsible one—at least until the past few months. And while she didn't mind her own reputation being smeared, it bothered her that, ultimately, her sister would be the one to pay the price.

Charity shrugged. "As I said, I don't blame you for running. I encouraged it, right? Wetherby was vile. You just *couldn't* marry him." She wrinkled her nose. "Hetterton isn't vile, or even a complete toad. Dull, but not unkind. I just never imagined marrying so soon, or someone so old."

Her sister's plight stayed with Elizabeth the remainder of the afternoon, and she was still dwelling on it when her uncle summoned her shortly before dinner.

"Elizabeth, I have excellent news."

She eyed her uncle. Their definitions of excellent were considerably different.

"Harold Wetherby will be joining us for dinner. He's been traveling, and, with luck, may not have heard of all your escapades. I urge you to behave well toward him. He may consider renewing his suit."

"He's hardly likely to forget I disappeared just before our engagement was announced."

Uncle George folded his arms across his sizeable middle. "You were distraught. You were very close to your father, and his death had an impact on your already delicate sensibilities." His lips twisted nastily around the words, making it clear he didn't buy a word of what he was saying.

Elizabeth raised her eyebrows. Too bad her uncle hadn't considered her "delicate sensibilities" when he'd castigated her and threatened to beat some sense into her upon her return.

"Uncle—" she began.

"Young lady, do not argue with me. Harold doesn't move in the higher circles of the ton, so he may not be privy to the gossip concerning yourself and Beaufort. You do not deserve another chance, but you may get one. It would ease the family circumstances if you did not waste it."

Ah, guilt. He was trying to shame her into being nice to Harold. Well, it might ease *her uncle's* circumstances if she married Harold, but Elizabeth failed to see how it would ease her own. Although, there was Charity to consider. A renewal of Harold's suit would take the pressure off her sister. If Elizabeth could stomach it.

"Comb your hair and put on a fresh gown. You must do your absolute best to appeal to the man. And do not think you can fool me with anything less. You're attractive enough. Make him notice your charms."

Harold was the last person she wanted noticing any charms she might possess. And what was wrong with the gown she was wearing?

She sighed inwardly. As the "ruined" ward of the family, she'd no position from which to argue. All the more reason to find a way to support herself—and soon. She gave a thin smile. "I'll see what I can do, Uncle."

He narrowed his eyes. "See that you do. And be prompt about it. I want you ready the moment he arrives. He mustn't think you one of those vain, tardy women who deem it acceptable to keep a man waiting."

Elizabeth grumbled but went to make herself presentable. She didn't put any particular effort into it, but her uncle would find no fault with her pale gray silk gown, or the matching ribbon wound through the nest of hair gathered at her nape.

She drifted listlessly back down to the salon. The hour was yet early; it was unlikely Harold would arrive for some time. Her embroidery sat abandoned near the chaise. She eyed it distastefully. Who cared if there were rosebuds at the hem of her sleeves? Still, she picked it up, if for no other reason than to avoid an "idle hands" comment should her mother walk by.

She gazed vacantly at the fireplace, vaguely registering that the Limoges vase that used to sit on the mantle was gone. And the roses of the wallpaper were less faded in one square area where a painting had been removed.

Sold. A last, desperate attempt to slow the family's descent into genteel poverty.

She swallowed. The lack of pretty things didn't bother her nearly as much as the feeling she was trapped.

"There you are!" Charity entered, carrying a plateful of scones, which she thrust in Elizabeth's direction. "I thought you might like some of these."

The fact that her sister carried the tray—there were too few servants left—was another reminder of the changes.

"Thank you. Has Harold arrived yet?" Elizabeth asked.

"No. I just heard from Uncle that he was coming."

The two young women stared at each other, each one's misery mirrored on the other's face. It pained Elizabeth to see her normally irrepressible sister so dispirited.

"I hate Father," Elizabeth declared.

"Elizabeth!" Charity glanced around as if expecting a lightning strike or vengeful ghost. "You do not. 'Tis ill to speak so of the deceased." She set down the tray and handed her sister a buttered scone.

Elizabeth sighed. "I'm sorry. I did love him. He laughed with me, took me on outings, and never scolded my lack of grace the way Mother always did at my lessons. But I hate that he put us, me, in this position."

"I know."

"He acted as though everything was perfect, and I could marry whomever I pleased, whenever I pleased. I would have much preferred he be honest about our circumstances."

"Perhaps he truly thought his misfortune temporary, and that he'd recover without anyone knowing. After all, it would be a hard thing for a man to come to his family and tell them he's let them down."

"He wouldn't be the first," Elizabeth pointed out.

"True, but that doesn't necessarily make it easier."

"I know." Elizabeth sighed and bit into her scone. "These are very good. I'm certain I won't be able to touch my dinner. Not sitting across the table from Harold."

"Let's not speak of that yet."

"You're right. It'll come soon enough." She polished off the scone, then stood and paced. "I'm just so angry, Charity! At Father, Uncle, Harold, everyone. Even Mother. Couldn't she at least have given Father a proper funeral? Surely that was more important than this charade she insists on, staying in town with her head high when we can barely afford to get by."

Charity tugged at her hair, an old, familiar habit that signaled her own distress. Elizabeth sat again.

"I don't understand it either." Charity bowed her head. "I never got to tell him good-bye. I asked if she'd open the casket, but she'd had it sealed and locked."

Elizabeth frowned. It had bothered her, too, not to see her father's body as she made her final farewells. They said he'd been thrown from the carriage in the accident, but surely they could have cleaned him up enough for a proper funeral. Was her mother truly as cheap and uncaring as that?

Not wanting to upset Charity further with her misgivings, Elizabeth put an arm around her sister. "Oh, honey. I'm sure he knows we wanted to say good-bye. And I'm sorry I said I hated him. I'm just upset right now."

"It's understandable." Charity nodded. "I'd be angry, too, in your place."

"Ugh. Why *does* Uncle George hate me so much?"

Charity's eyes softened. "It isn't just you. He was beastly to Mother while you were gone. Berated her constantly—said she thought herself better than the rest of the family, marrying into nobility, as she did, and look where it had gotten her."

"Oh, dear." Elizabeth wasn't on the best of terms with her mother, but she disliked her uncle more.

"He sees us as a problem to be taken care of, preferably with as little of his own money as possible. That's why he's so unkind to you. Marrying you off to Harold would rid him of one of us, at least, but you won't do it."

"Not willingly." Elizabeth gave her sister a quick squeeze, then pinned on a smile. "First things first. Help me think of a way to get through tonight."

A spark of Charity's usual spirit gleamed in her eyes as she quipped, "Lots and lots of wine?"

Charity may have been joking, but when at last Elizabeth was seated at the dinner table that evening, she clutched her wineglass as if it were the only lifeline between her and purgatory. The temptation to run again, to escape to anywhere but here, had nearly gotten the best of her.

Harold dominated the dinner conversation, relating the details of his recent travels to the Continent at length. It sounded to have been a rather dull trip, Elizabeth thought, but her uncle George kept plying him with questions about who he'd met and what promising connections he'd made.

Elizabeth hoped fervently one of those connections might be a fiancée, relieving her of any future obligations, but Harold mentioned nothing of the sort. Occasionally he paused in the monologue, shoveling food into his mouth and leering at her while he chewed.

Elizabeth quickly decided it was better to keep her gaze lowered to her plate. When one of the men addressed her, she answered succinctly, using as few words as possible.

Her mother and Charity remained mostly silent, though occasionally Elizabeth looked up to catch a sympathetic glance from her little sister.

Once, she saw Uncle George nod approvingly toward her. Apparently he was under the impression her behavior constituted an attempt to be demure.

Well, no need to relieve him of that impression, Elizabeth thought, taking another long sip of wine. For now, all she had to do was get through this dinner. After that, she'd rather sew a thousand gowns for the women who used to be her friends than marry the swine sitting across from her.

Midway through the meal, Elizabeth was feeling pleasantly lightheaded.

Toward the end of the meal, however, she thought perhaps she'd been a bit too liberal with the wine . . . How many glasses *had* she drunk?

It hadn't seemed like that many, but she dreaded having to stand when it was time for the ladies to retire. Her balance, never a strong point anyway, was certain to be off. Already her chair seemed to be floating in a bumpy sea.

"Elizabeth, why don't you and Mr. Wetherby remain here while the rest of us retire?" Uncle George suggested. "He told me before dinner that he wished to speak privately with you, and I must say I approve."

At the moment, Elizabeth thought drowsily, that didn't seem such a bad idea, for it would save her the indignity of having to rise and reveal her tipsiness. Then again, she'd be alone with Harold. "I'm certain he won't mind if you stay," she asserted, though the words came slower than normal.

"No, no," her uncle replied. He nodded at the other two women. "Come, ladies."

Elizabeth watched as the hazy figures of her uncle, mother, and sister drifted from the room, until she and Harold were the only ones remaining.

Her toady suitor moved closer, taking the seat next to her. "Finish your wine, Elizabeth." He held out the glass.

She shook her head, and the room spun. Bad idea.

"No, Harold. I believe I've had enough. Why did you wish to speak with me?"

Funny. Her words were slurred, and the room seemed to waver in her vision. She blinked to clear it, then blinked again.

"We'll talk," Harold said. "But first I propose a toast. To us?"

Warning bells warred with her already pounding head. "There is no 'us,' Harold," she informed him. Or thought she did. She couldn't be sure, for the room gave a great lurch, and the table rose up to meet her.

Chapter Eleven

She was dreaming again. She knew it, but couldn't seem to lift the thick sea of fog that held her down.

They were traveling. Occasionally a rough bump jostled her into consciousness, enough to recognize she lay on the floor of a moving vehicle, probably a carriage, her arms positioned awkwardly behind her. *Tied.* Her tongue felt thick, her throat dry. Once, maybe twice, someone held a flask to her lips, and she drank thirstily.

Inevitably, the fog would descend again, and carry her back to unsettling dreams.

This time, it carried her back to the night of her father's death. She whimpered, knowing the events that were about to unfold, but unable to stop them.

She watched herself—another, more innocent self—descend the stairs, glance outside at the night storm, and move into the kitchen for a late snack.

And then she *was* the other self, and it ceased to be a dream.

* * *

"*Bloody hell, Fuston, what's happened?*"

Never in her life had Elizabeth Medford heard the relentlessly formal butler use such language. Silently, she crept into a shadowed corner of the back hallway.

A shaft of moonlight from a small window fell on Fuston, the coachman, who trembled in his torn and stained livery. "Accident. Was naught I could do. The horses—they took a fright—" he stammered, eyes darting everywhere. "A creature, wolf, mebbe, ran out on the road . . . but the horses . . . out of control . . . went off in the ravine. I only just jumped clear before the carriage overturned. The master was—was—" Fuston swallowed audibly, unable to continue.

Icy dread flooded Elizabeth, but she dared not reveal herself before knowing what had happened to her father.

"How bad?" Even in his just-awakened state, the butler sounded imposing.

Fuston shook his head and wrung his hands, looking terrified.

Elizabeth's breath left her and she sank to her knees, imagining the worst. The biscuit she'd nabbed for a midnight repast fell unheeded from her fingers, landing with a tiny thump on the floorboards.

Both men stopped and looked around at the noise, but the shadows kept Elizabeth hidden. Blood pounded in her ears as she strained to hear more.

"Did you fetch a physician?"

"There was no need," the coachman whispered.

Growing dizzy, Elizabeth pressed her knuckles to her lips, muffling the tiny moan that escaped at the coachman's words.

The butler sucked in his breath. "We'll need to inform the baroness at once. She departed in Lady Jameson's coach this evening, without leaving word of her actual destination. We can start at the Jameson residence."

Elizabeth doubted they would find her mother there . . .

Lady Jameson played whist with her mother often enough, but Lord Jameson did not approve, so the all-night games were hosted by others. She was on the verge of interrupting when the butler spoke again.

"There will need to be arrangements made. Where is the master's body?"

Elizabeth's insides seemed to hollow out at the blunt mention of her father's mortal remains.

Fuston, however, looked truly panicked. Beads of perspiration pearled and ran down his face. "Here. But there's a bit of a problem . . ."

He looked around, and Elizabeth pressed herself farther into the shadows. Finally he pulled the butler in close and whispered something she could not hear. The shaft of moonlight fell on both men now, and she saw astonishment on the older man's usually masklike features before he turned and rushed out the door, dragging poor Fuston behind him.

Elizabeth remained in place, limbs numb, unable to absorb the conversation she'd just heard. Her father . . . He couldn't be . . . She could not fathom a world without his reassuring presence. Her mind screamed for her to run after the two servants, beg them to tell her it wasn't true. But they'd mentioned a body. Her heart and mind refused to reconcile this news with the only reality she'd ever known.

It could be hours yet before her mother returned, but Elizabeth had little interest in finding and offering solace to the cold baroness. Nor could she remain crouched in the hallway forever.

The fabric of her dressing gown whooshed *softly in the now-empty hall as she stood, trembling, and went to wake her sister.*

Where was Charity?

* * *

Elizabeth shifted restlessly. A sudden lurch shook her from the terrifying memory.

The carriage had stopped.

Feebly, she tried to push herself up. But her arms, tied behind her for so long, were too numb. She forced her eyes open.

The fleshy form of Harold Wetherby wavered before her eyes as he lifted her from the vehicle. A wave of nausea rolled over her as he tossed her over his shoulder and strode toward an unfamiliar house. She shut her eyes again.

Elizabeth sat bolt upright. She'd been dreaming. This time, she'd been back at one of last Season's balls.

Her mother, admonishing her that a lady must always be polite to a gentleman, had nearly shoved her toward her pudgy, self-indulgent cousin. He'd led her onto the balcony, ostensibly for a breath of air . . . She could feel his fleshy fingers pressing into her rib cage . . .

No.

Better not to remember.

But as she blinked and looked about the unfamiliar bedroom, an awful feeling of unease settled in her gut. Her mind was groggy. Why couldn't she remember where she was? Or anything of how she got here?

Last she could remember, she'd been at home, sitting through an unpleasant dinner with her mother, Uncle George, and Harold. She'd drunk more wine than usual but surely not enough to muddle her head this much.

No. That wasn't right. She had vague memories of traveling, of being horribly uncomfortable, but unable to move. Where *was* she?

The room she was in was small, the window shuttered. It was daytime, for cracks of light filtered in.

Elizabeth eased herself from the bed, using a small table to steady herself as an onslaught of dizziness struck her. She opened the shutter and breathed in damp country air. Frowning, she turned again to the room. It was decorated in pale blue, the bed and furniture adequate but not lavish.

She was certain she'd never seen any of it before.

Footsteps pounded outside the door. Someone was climbing a set of stairs. The door opened to reveal her cousin, a tea tray in one hand, his heavy face flushed with the effort of the climb. He'd changed clothing, she noted, though the absurdly embroidered waistcoat did nothing to improve his features. But the change of clothing proved one thing. He'd *planned* this.

He gave her an arrogant grin. She didn't return it. "Harold."

"Miss Medford." His tone dripped with sarcasm at the formality. "I see you've survived the night."

"Where am I? What have you done?" She hated the fear in her voice.

"Relax, Elizabeth. I thought it best if I took my fiancée somewhere quiet where we might renew our acquaintance."

"I've no wish to renew your acquaintance. And I'm not your fiancée." Anger, indignation, filtered through her fear.

"My, my." He set the tray down on a side table, then leaned indolently against the door frame. "I see I was correct when I told your uncle you might need some time to adjust to the idea. But you are, indeed, my fiancée. We signed the betrothal two nights ago."

"And where was I? Am I to have no say in the matter?"

"You were . . . resting." He did not meet her eyes.

"Drugged, you mean. You *drugged* me." Blood began to pulse at her temples as she realized what he'd done.

"It was for your own good. What with your abominable behavior these last months, we could hardly expect you to see reason."

"Reason?" she screeched. "You think this passes for reason? Drugging a woman you intend to marry and hauling her off to . . . where am I, anyway? And what day is it?"

"Today is Thursday. Your location is . . . somewhere private."

"Somewhere I can't escape, you mean." She shook with anger, with humiliation.

"It's only until you adjust."

"Adjust? To what?"

He pushed off the door frame and walked toward her. His large hand cupped her chin, forced her gaze to his. "To marrying me. To being obedient. To placing my pleasure, *my* will, above your own. As a woman should."

She yanked her chin away. "You're mad."

He stepped closer, his features twisted in a sneer. "I assure you I am not. You *will* learn obedience, if I must beat it into you. It would be better for you to accept that."

The wall behind her cut off her retreat. Elizabeth turned her head rather than face him.

Her mind was still muddled from the aftereffects of whatever potion he'd used on her, but she struggled to think her way out of this.

"An obedient and proper woman would not countenance staying alone with a man she thought to marry," she declared, shoulders squared.

"Proper?" He gave an ugly laugh. "Do not toss that term at me, for all of Society is gossiping over your behavior. Your uncle thinks I don't know, but I am not a fool, Elizabeth."

Elizabeth wasn't about to give in, even if it meant acceding, at least on the surface, to his statements about her character. "Is it not my behavior you wish to change? Perhaps it would be best to start by setting a proper model."

"Regrettably, we must forgo that aspect of propriety." He gave her a leer that suggested he didn't find the situation regrettable at all. "You've proven yourself untrustworthy and unpredictable, and I believe matters between us are best settled apart from others.

"Besides, a stay alone with me will, in the eyes of the church, only hasten the need for marriage." His hands encircled her waist, then snaked up to her rib cage, his thumbs pressing at the underside of her breasts.

"Stop it." She jerked back, but the wall stood firm behind her.

He squeezed lightly, panting.

"Your touch makes me ill. If you do not release me, I shall cast up my accounts upon your shoes."

Harold stepped back quickly with a glance at his overpolished shoes, the leer of moments before replaced by the flush of anger. "Don't think this is over, Elizabeth. The world already knows you're a slut, so you can't put me off with talk of propriety. I intend to have that delectable little body of yours. Maybe not now, but soon enough. I'm in charge here. If you wish to have your freedom again, or a visit with your sister, perhaps, you'll learn to please and obey me."

"I'd sooner perish," she spat.

He gave her a pitying smile. "I'm sure you'll come to

rethink that position." He turned and left the room, picking up the tray of tea and bread and taking it with him. Only when she heard him fumble with the latch did Elizabeth realize he'd locked her in.

Bastard. Harold's actions, though despicable, did not surprise her. They were right in line with his character. But the fact that her uncle, at least, must have agreed to the plan . . . Elizabeth hated them both so much her hands shook.

Well, she would not be subdued that easily.

She went again to the window. Outside she saw a small yard, then rolling green fields, then forest. The morning mist still lay in the hollows between hills. No road, no village. But perhaps her window simply faced the wrong direction to see them.

Or else Harold had taken her some place very remote indeed.

Between the house and the forest, there was no place to hide. She would have to be quick. The room that imprisoned her was on the second story. A thick hedge grew beneath. She bit her lip, considering. If she hung from the ledge, the hedge would break her fall—though the landing would likely be unpleasant. But not so unpleasant as waiting helplessly in the room for a rescue that might never come.

She could do this. Elizabeth looked again, but there was no sign of Harold. She slowly eased out of the window and lowered herself until she hung by her fingertips. Holding her breath, she let go.

Fabric tore as her skirt caught on a peg, but other than that, she landed unharmed.

As soon as her legs were under her, she ran for the forest.

It was farther than it had looked from the window.

Her lungs burned. She dared not slow until she'd reached the cover of the forest.

Finally, the open field was behind her. Slipping around the trunk of a tall tree, she leaned against the rough bark to catch her breath. The dew had soaked her slippers and the hem of her skirts. She was still wearing the clothes she'd had on for dinner back in London. They were hardly made for rough travel.

Slowly the sound of her heart pounding receded, and all she heard were water droplets dripping from the leaves. Everything seemed unnaturally still.

From the slight chill in the air, and the surrounding trees, she guessed Harold had taken her north. Though where, exactly, she had no idea.

She peeked from behind the tree trunk. No one in sight. Without a particular destination in mind, she slipped from the tree that hid her to the next, and the next, keeping the fields in sight so she wouldn't lose her way. If only she could find a road, or a cottage— anywhere she might ask for help.

Hooves thundered toward the edge of the forest.

Elizabeth ran for deeper cover, but it was too late.

Harold's gloved hand swooped down and struck her to the ground as he pulled his horse to a sudden halt.

She landed hard, the wind knocked from her lungs. Desperately she scrambled backward, gaping like a fish as she struggled for breath.

Harold's face was purple with fury.

"Foolish slut! Did you honestly think I wouldn't guess you'd try the window?" He leapt from his horse with surprising agility, considering his heft. He grabbed her arm and hauled her toward him, bending her over his knee like a misbehaved child.

His hand came down hard on her backside. Suddenly she could breathe again. The blow hurt, but Elizabeth bit her lip to keep from whimpering.

"You will," he grunted with exertion as he smacked her again, "learn obedience. I will not have a disrespectful wife."

"Why did you leave the window unlocked if you knew I'd escape?" She tried twisting away, but his meaty forearm held her pinned.

"It was a test. To see if you could behave reasonably. But I see I was correct when I told your uncle you would require training."

"Beast." She spat the word.

He ignored the insult, instead hauling her to her feet as he grabbed a length of twine from his saddle and lashed her wrists together.

She yanked her arms away before he could secure them.

"If I must render you unconscious, I will not hesitate."

Elizabeth stilled, but her mind continued working furiously to find a way out of this situation. Unfortunately, nothing immediately came to mind. He could physically overpower her, and with him on horseback it was impossible for her to escape on foot.

Harold lifted her onto the horse, grunting with the effort, then mounted behind her. She cringed at the close contact with his sweaty mass but remained silent. Angering him further now would only make things worse.

Harold turned the horse back toward the house. He allowed the animal to amble along slowly, using the time to run his hands along Elizabeth's sides. Bile rose in her throat as she felt his growing erection press into her backside.

The twine cut into her wrists, but no matter which way she twisted them, she could not loosen the binding.

Only when she was certain she couldn't stand another minute of his filthy groping, they reached the house.

It was an unassuming, two-story structure painted in pale blue. Large enough to house a family, perhaps a servant or two. It certainly didn't *look* like a prison.

The front door opened and an unfamiliar man stepped out. He had a greasy look about him, groomed but not clean. After searching her memory, Elizabeth placed him as the coach driver who'd aided Harold in abducting her. Another enemy.

Harold dismounted in the yard. Elizabeth resented mightily that she had to wait for him to lift her from the horse.

The servant came over and took the reins from Harold. "Right quick you were in recovering her, sir."

Harold's chest puffed and he put an arm about Elizabeth's waist. "She's willful, but no match for me."

She jerked away. The servant gave a nasty chuckle and led the horse toward the barn.

Her whole body felt abused—a feeling that did not lessen as Harold dragged her back into the house and up to the room she'd so recently escaped.

"Now, Elizabeth, I suggest you rethink your ways," he told her when they stood once more in the hated room. "Though chasing you down is exhilarating, I prefer a more submissive female for a wife. I'll untie you now, but I hope you've learned a lesson from this." He began working at the knot, but not before giving her backside a solid pinch.

Elizabeth kicked at his shins, but her dainty footwear was no match for his riding boots. "Not only am I not your wife, I've made it abundantly clear I will not marry you." The moment her wrists were free, she sent an elbow flying into his ribs.

"I am sorry to hear that," he grunted, not sounding sorry at all. He released her with a hard shove that sent her stumbling against a wall. "You've become an obsession with me, my dear."

"Clearly." She rubbed the circulation back into her wrists.

"All my life I've been told what things I couldn't have. Things I wasn't good enough, noble enough, for. And you, a baron's daughter, thought you were so far above me. Parading around in your finery, treating me like a poor relation when all along, your father was spending your fortune in the gaming hells. Well, look who's the poor relation now. Not so lofty now, eh?"

Elizabeth couldn't remember ever intentionally lording it over her poorer cousins, most of whom were decent people, but one thing Harold said was true.

She thrust out her chin. "Money or not, you'll never be good enough for me."

"Your hauteur is impressive, but we both know that's not true. If it weren't for me, you'd be out on the streets."

"I'd find that preferable to here. I'm perfectly capable of fending for myself."

"Oh? Then why did you come crawling home when your last little adventure turned sour?"

"I must not have been thinking," she muttered.

"On the contrary, that was perhaps the most rational decision you've ever made. If only you'd followed up by learning to be grateful and obedient. You may as well resign yourself, Elizabeth. No other man will have you now."

Elizabeth shrugged. Men, she'd learned, were vile creatures. Not a one could be trusted.

"Consider your next actions carefully, Elizabeth.

You'll have plenty of time." He stalked out, once more locking the door.

Her stomach grumbled, reminding her that the last time she'd eaten had been the fateful dinner before her abduction. Did Harold intend to starve her into submission?

She recalled the tea tray he'd kept from her earlier. Apparently, he did.

When Harold's clomping footsteps receded into silence, she allowed the tears of frustration that had been building all day to flow freely.

How had she reached this state? Ten months ago she'd been the carefree daughter of the Baron Medford, and even one month ago she'd been happy enough as a governess and a lover to one of the most powerful, coveted men in England.

But neither her father nor the duke had been the men they'd seemed, and now she was nothing more than the pawn of a man she thought less of than toad spawn.

Women were *supposed* to place themselves in the care of men. Well, look where that had gotten her.

She wasn't being fair, at least to Alex. He *had* offered her more protection than she'd been willing to accept.

She shook her head. What a fool she was for the duke, even now, looking for ways to exonerate him. She should know better. Even if Alex hadn't used her to pay her father's debts, the way that drunk, Cutter, in the park had suggested, he was still a man who routinely seduced and left women. He might have offered her money or jewels, but would he have guarded her heart, her person, with as much care? Clearly not—she hadn't had so much as a note from him since he'd left on business.

From now on, she would trust no one but herself.

Elizabeth was not given to long bouts of self-pity. When her tears were spent, anger grew in their place. Anger at herself.

Her fury with Harold had not abated, to be certain, but now she berated her own foolishness in attempting to escape without a plan. She'd panicked and fled, and, predictably, been caught.

Elizabeth gripped the windowsill of her prison bedroom and narrowed her eyes. Next time she would do much better.

Chapter Twelve

Alex grinned as Viscount Grumsby's country manor came into view. He'd been away on business for far longer than he'd anticipated. Finally he'd gotten the mess straightened out. The ship was nearly done with repairs, the captain replaced and his partner appeased. Profits were off, but they'd recover on the next expedition to India. Everything looked promising. Only one problem. He'd sorely missed Elizabeth. And not just physically, which surprised him.

No, he'd missed her spirit, her sense of adventure. He'd missed the way that, in spite of her family's downfall, she always looked forward, not back—something he'd struggled with lately.

Hence the visit to his sister and her husband before he returned to London.

The drive leading up to the house seemed longer than usual, and it was with relief that he finally pulled the phaeton alongside the house and tossed the reins to the groom who ran up to assist.

"Have the carriage put away, and see to the horses.

It's been a long road." He sprang down, suddenly full of energy, and strode toward the house.

Inside, the butler informed him that the lord and lady of the house were out for the day. No matter. It would save him the pretense of visiting with them before he could speak to Elizabeth.

"And the children?"

"Outdoors, my lord, with their governess."

"Perfect."

Alex retraced his steps, then headed back to the gardens, where Elizabeth most often played with his niece and nephew. Sure enough, he heard the laughter of children just before a small boy came hurtling toward him.

"Uncle Alex. Hurrah!" Henry cried.

He swept the boy up and tossed him into the air. Henry squealed in delight.

"Again!"

"In a minute," Alex told him, looking around for Elizabeth. But all he saw was Clara bending over a flowerbed next to an older gray-haired woman.

"Henry, where is your governess?"

"Just there, Uncle." Henry pointed to the older woman.

Alex frowned. "No, I mean, where is Miss Medford?"

"She's not here anymore."

"What do you mean, 'not here'?" Where the devil else would she be? His feeling of buoyant anticipation evaporated.

Henry shrugged. "She said she had to leave. I didn't want her to, but she did anyway. She was fun, Miss Medford was. But Mama says we're to obey Miss Grifford now."

Gone? What the devil had happened? Disappointment flooded him.

"Uncle Alex, will you toss me up again?"

"Not right now, Henry," he said absently. "Go and play with Clara."

"But, Uncle Alex—"

"Henry, I've matters to attend. Go play with your sister."

The boy's face fell as Alex turned and strode toward the house. He'd make it up to the lad another time. Right now he was sorely distracted by the disappearance of one Elizabeth Medford.

"To what good fortune do I owe this visit, Alex?"

Alex ignored his sister's trivial politeness. "Where is she?"

Marian quirked a brow. "She?"

Heaven help his sister if she meant to play games with him. "You know exactly whom I mean. Where is Elizabeth?"

He'd been unable to pry any useful information from the servants, so, pacing the rooms of the house incessantly, he'd waited for Marian's return. Had Elizabeth left to avoid him? Had she received some better offer of employment? Or—he swallowed hard—an offer of marriage?

Thankfully, his sister had cut short her outing and returned before he'd worn a path in the floorboards.

"Where is she?" he repeated, while Marian untied her bonnet with maddening slowness.

"I let her go. Alex, give me a moment. I've hardly walked in the door. If you'll follow me to the salon, we can discuss this over tea. I find traveling leaves me quite parched."

"What do you mean, 'let her go'?" Alex demanded of his sister, blocking her from proceeding to the salon. He'd be damned if he was going to wait while a servant brought tea. He needed to know what had happened to Elizabeth, *now*.

Marian pressed her lips together and squared her stance. "I had no choice. All of London was abuzz with gossip concerning her." She gave him a sharp look. "And, of course, you, Brother."

Alex looked away, unable to deny her unspoken accusation, but uncertain how knowledge of his affair with Elizabeth could have leaked.

"Your rash actions have cost me a good governess." Marian cast him an admonishing glance. "Let me speak frankly, Alex. I know you're used to having any woman you desire, but you usually take care she comes to no harm. Why Elizabeth? She was a nice girl, even if her family was unfortunate, and the children loved her."

"I'm sorry. I know the children liked her." Striding to the door, he asked, "Did she say where she could be located in the future?"

"Indeed." She folded her arms.

"And?" It took considerable willpower not to throttle his younger sister.

But Marian wasn't done with him. "After her father's death, everyone simply pitied Elizabeth for her new circumstances. When she left home to work as a governess, Society cut her off—or would have, had her whereabouts been known.

"But it wasn't until *you* seduced and then left her that respectable women began dragging their children to the other side of the street rather than be seen with her, Alex." His sister shot him a look of withering scorn. "Her reputation has been ruined beyond reproach. She has no future."

Marian could berate him later to her heart's content. Now, all he wanted was to find Elizabeth.

"Mar-i-an." He enunciated each syllable, his impatience barely contained. "Where did she go?"

"Home, I believe. That is . . . *if* they were willing to have her back."

"Right." He turned and exited through the door his sister had entered only moments ago, leaving her gaping at his unprecedented lack of manners.

"Groom!" he called as he made for the stables. The same lad he'd met earlier ran up. "Have the phaeton put to and the horses readied. I'm leaving for London immediately."

The boy's eyes widened. "Aye, my lord." He hurried off, though Alex thought he heard him mutter "only just put them out," as the groom went to do his bidding.

Alex impatiently ground the toe of his highly polished boot into the dirt while he waited. Damn. How had all this happened while he was away? And why hadn't someone thought to inform him of it?

His horses neighed in protest as Alex slapped the reins of the hastily readied vehicle. They were tired, but he drove them hard. He knew his young lover had been desperate when she'd left home. He could only imagine how desperate, and betrayed, she must feel to return. And it was his fault, damn it.

He had an apology to make. Likely one involving jewelry. But he was not willing to let Elizabeth go so easily.

Guilt pressed down on him as his sister's words registered. Elizabeth's reputation was in shreds. It wouldn't be the first time a female had fallen from Society's good graces, though he couldn't recall any who had done it with quite the dramatic flair of his Elizabeth. That thought almost brought a grin to his face, though he doubted she would share his humor.

In fact, she had every right to be angry with him. His unstable mood soured again as he realized his own role in the young lady's ruin. He was responsible for more than just seducing her, though she didn't know it. He'd tried to set things right, but when it came to Elizabeth Medford, he was always one beat out of sync. And since he couldn't seem to stay away from her, he'd just have to try again.

After several broken hairpins, Elizabeth decided lock-picking was far more difficult than the heroines of her favorite novels had led her to believe.

Which meant she'd have to be clever, perhaps trick Harold into believing she'd succumbed. If she could "earn" the freedom to wander the premises, she could plan an escape route, or even find a way to send for help. She had no money. Still, there had to be a way.

Plotting kept Elizabeth from paying attention to the gnawing hunger growing in her belly. But by the time the evening twilight cloaked the fields, and the luscious smell of roasting beef wafted up the stairs, nothing could turn her attention from her appetite.

She hadn't eaten since the night she'd been kidnapped. She wasn't quite sure how long they'd traveled before reaching their current location, but Harold had told her the betrothal had been signed two nights ago—meaning it had been quite some time since she'd had a real meal.

Because, during *that* cozy family dinner, she'd had little appetite, thinking Harold meant to press for an engagement. If only she'd known what was actually coming, she'd have paid more attention to her plate and less to her potion-laden wine.

When the light outside dimmed further, and still Harold had not revisited her, Elizabeth resorted to pounding on the door. She would need energy, a clear head, for what she'd planned for tomorrow. That meant a meal tonight, and right now her bloody captor was keeper of the kitchen.

She heard his footsteps with a mixture of relief, anger, and fear.

The door opened partially—enough for her to see him, and see that his girth blocked any chance of rushing past him. She was certain that was intentional.

"Yes?" he asked curiously, as though he'd no idea what she might want.

Bloody cur. She hated him for making her beg.

"I thought perhaps you meant to share your evening meal with your fiancée." She referred to their union with all the sincerity she could muster, though the thought of sharing anything with Harold nearly made her gag.

In truth, she didn't plan to be around long enough for the reference to matter.

"Dear me, I must have forgotten," Harold said. "Though your behavior this morning hardly led me to believe you would be amenable. Perhaps you'd care to apologize for that?"

She hated him even more. "I'm sorry for the inconvenience I caused."

He gave her a satisfied and knowing smile. "Still, I

think it's best if you stay up here a while longer. I'll bring up a tray."

Fine. She didn't care where she ate the meal, so long as it consisted of food. Of course, he was also denying her the opportunity to explore her prison.

He returned, bearing a small tray. "Since I have already eaten, I shall simply keep you company." He passed the tray to her, then seated himself in the room's most comfortable chair.

When Elizabeth saw how little food he'd allotted her, she wanted to cry. Only pride kept her tears at bay.

"I've heard it said you ladies have delicate appetites, so I hope this won't be too heavy for you, my dear."

The tiny amount of beef and bread wouldn't have been too heavy for a sparrow. It was enough to whet, not satisfy, an appetite.

Elizabeth gave him a smile as though everything was just perfect, and proceeded to eat as primly as possible, in spite of the desire to gulp it down and plead for more.

Harold watched through narrowed eyes. The moment she was done, he stood and retrieved the tray.

"I trust you'll have a good night's sleep, dear Elizabeth. Mayhap tomorrow we can continue this improvement in our acquaintance."

"Mayhap." She smiled through clenched teeth. When she escaped—and she *would* escape—she needed a place to go. The Duke of Beaufort was a rake who'd broken her heart, but she felt certain if he knew her dire straits, he'd not deny her his protection. Whatever it took, she had to get a message to Alex.

* * *

The duke's horses were lathered and dragging their hooves by the time he arrived at No. 9 Milton Road. Between the trip to his sister's, and then to London, not to mention Ramsgate and Dorset, Alex wasn't looking his best either as he launched himself from the phaeton and up the steps of the Medford residence.

A butler in faded livery showed him in, and Alex stalked impatiently as he waited for the sight of the woman he'd so missed. But the person who greeted him no more resembled Elizabeth than a street pebble resembled a ruby.

"Your Grace, an unexpected pleasure."

Alex was not in the mood. "Who are you?"

"George Gorsham, Lady Medford's brother, Your Grace."

Ah. The "Uncle George" Elizabeth had referred to so disdainfully.

"Where is Elizabeth?"

Elizabeth's uncle didn't quite meet his eye. "I'm afraid she's not here."

"What do you mean, 'not here'?" Alex felt like an echo. Where the bloody hell was she?

"My niece has retired to the country for the time being. I'm afraid she found city life a bit much."

God's teeth, the man was unhelpful. "Where in the country, exactly? I want an address."

George rubbed his palms on his pants, then clasped them nervously. "I cannot tell you, Your Grace."

"Can't—or won't?" Alex asked, his tone ominous.

"Can't. I am sorry. But perhaps, if you've business with Miss Medford, I might be able to get a message to her."

Alex took a step closer to give the other man the full effect of his height. "How, Mr. Gorsham, do you intend to get a message to Elizabeth if you do not know her address?"

"I—I don't know it, I swear," George said, now wringing his hands. "But I know someone who would, and if I hear from him, I could relay the message."

"There's no need of that. My business with her is my own. Who is this person who can tell me her whereabouts?"

"Harold Wetherby."

"Wetherby? You *must* be joking." Harold was the last person Elizabeth would confide in.

"No. She is with him."

"Alone?" His pulse quickened and a muscle in his clenched jaw began to twitch.

George didn't meet his eye. "Er, I couldn't say."

Alex grabbed the other man by his cravat. "Did she go willingly?"

George didn't answer, though the pressure Alex was exerting on his neck may have hindered any response. But Alex didn't need an answer. He knew how Elizabeth felt about her cousin. Finally, as George's eyes bulged, Alex released him. George slumped into a chair and fought to regain his breath.

"If Elizabeth comes to any harm at the hands of that black-hearted cur, I will hold you personally responsible." He left the man gasping as he stalked from the room.

Tracking down Elizabeth had just become imperative. If he had to hire every Runner in the city, he would find her.

To Elizabeth's dismay, it took three more days of mental games and constant hunger before she'd "earned" the freedom to wander the grounds. Even

then, Harold granted her barely enough food to sub-
sist, and that only when she was submissive. When she
did leave her room, her captor and his greasy servant,
Bormley, lurked near enough to prevent another
escape attempt. The latter was less attentive than
Harold, though, and under his "supervision" she'd
managed to sneak quill, ink, and paper beneath her
gown and then back to her room. Not all at the same
time—stealth required patience, and more days had
passed before Elizabeth had collected the materials
needed to compose a simple missive.

Lack of full meals left her energy flagging, but her
resolve hardened. Alone in her room after a week of
captivity in the remote country house, she pulled out
a sheet of writing paper.

Memories of Alex's deep voice, his eyes darkened
with passion when they touched, swamped her as she
wrote. Should she declare that he still held her heart?
No. Elizabeth pressed her lips together. Men expected
a combination of passion and practicality, not love,
from a mistress.

> *Your Grace,*
>   *At one time you offered me your protection, should I
> accept the position of your mistress. I foolishly turned you
> down. Yet I miss the passion we shared, and long to be
> near you again. My circumstances have changed, as you
> may know. I wish to accept the offer you once made, if the
> position is still available. I cannot say when. My cousin
> holds me, I know not where, against my will. I intend to
> escape, and pray that when I come to you, you will not
> turn me away.*
>
>   *Ever Yours,*
>   *Elizabeth*

She took a deep breath and folded the paper. A few drips from the candle sealed it.

And, oh, how far she'd fallen.

These last days had proven one thing: Harold would stop at nothing to make her his. With each day his vile hands grew bolder, as though he knew her strength, her ability to fight him off, was waning. She was running out of time. Sacrificing her pride, begging Alex Bainbridge for a position she'd once scorned, was infinitely preferable to this—if only she could get to her former lover.

There was hope. Last night she'd been awakened by an argument downstairs.

"You promised me double wages for helpin' you bring your woman out here," Bormley had griped. "I ain't even seen regular wages for two weeks. Not that I could spend 'em, out here. Feel like I'm the one bein' kep' prisoner."

Harold had answered in lower tones, but from what Elizabeth had gathered, he hadn't been able to appease his servant. Which meant opportunity was ripe—any man low enough to work for Harold in the first place was a man low enough to accept a bribe.

She tucked the letter into the bosom of her gown and left her room. By the time she reached the tiny parlor, her shadow had appeared. This time it was Bormley, looking disgruntled. Perfect.

She opened the door and stepped into the yard, knowing he'd follow.

The cottage Harold had chosen for this adventure was truly remote. It lay at the end of a narrow dirt lane, with no other homes in sight. The lane itself wound through the hills into the distance. She hoped it led to a village. Under other circumstances the house would have seemed pretty enough, with its shuttered windows and whitewashed fence, but she could look at it only with revulsion.

She continued across the yard and around the corner of the barn, out of sight of the house.

"Ye're wanderin' a bit far this mornin'," her shadow warned.

She slowed until he caught up. "I wished to speak with you."

A calculating gleam lit his normally flat eyes. He waited.

Elizabeth straightened her shoulders. Make this about him, not her. "Let me speak plainly. I heard your argument with Wetherby last night. He's using you. Double wages? Not likely. He's not a generous man. He's the sort to pay you off, then turn around and say you stole it."

Bormley folded his arms.

"We could help each other out," she pressed on quickly. "Help me escape, and I'll see you rewarded."

He curled his lip, eyeing her up and down. His gaze lingered at her bosom, but finally he said, "You've got nothing I want. Everyone knows you're penniless."

"That may be so, but I've friends who would pay dearly for my return."

He sneered. "What sort of . . . friends?"

How she hated catering to someone so low. "I can't imagine, Mr. Bormley, that working for Wetherby is ideal for a man of your skill. You are, perhaps, a man of ambition. Help me, and you'll never have to do his bidding again."

He cocked his head, clearly interested. "How do I know I'll get paid? An' what exactly do you want me to do? Wetherby's got a sharp eye."

It was true. Harold watched her constantly, expecting her to run again. She needed him off guard.

And then it hit her.

Was it asking too much? She had to try.

"When you and Wetherby brought me here, he gave me wine laced with something . . . a sleeping draught, perhaps. Is there any remaining, and if so do you know where it's kept?"

He eyed her steadily, unreadable. "There is, and I might."

"If Wetherby were . . . distracted, it would help greatly." She remembered the letter tucked in her dress. "Can you deliver a message?"

"Not likely. I'm near as much prisoner here as you, 'less the boss decides to send me on an errand."

"I see. Never mind." She'd have to manage that part herself. "When I'm ready, I shall give you a signal— I shall let my handkerchief fall."

She began walking again, not wishing to remain hidden behind the barn for too long. As Bormley had pointed out, Harold was already suspicious.

"An' the payment?"

"The Duke of Beaufort will see to it, I assure you." She prayed her faith in Alex was true—even if he didn't love her, he'd not stand to see her harmed.

Her coconspirator gave a slight nod. "I'll see what I can do."

It wasn't a promise, she noted. But it was something.

As they rounded the corner, coming back within sight of the house, the servant dropped back a few paces. If Harold observed them now, nothing would suggest they'd been plotting behind his back.

Could Bormley be trusted? She had no illusions that he would consider helping her out of Christian charity.

She only hoped greed, the lure of profits greater than those Harold could provide, would drive him to her aid. For once she was grateful the gossip about her scandal with the duke had spread so far. If Bormley had heard it, he'd be more likely to believe she had the connections to pay him off.

She hugged her arms protectively, only in part to ward off the cool morning mist. Though the sun was out, the chill in the air suggested an early fall.

"Cold?"

Her stomach clenched as Harold approached, but she kept her expression neutral. "A bit."

"Perhaps you should go in and warm yourself before we go."

"Go?" Her hopes soared dizzily. They were going somewhere? He hadn't mentioned this before, but she didn't care. She would be away from her prison. Maybe even have a real meal . . . for surely he'd not keep food from her in public?

"Yes, did I not say?" His sing-song tone made it evident he enjoyed tormenting her. "I have a surprise for you, Elizabeth."

What sort of surprise? More starvation? Another beating?

"I am most eager to learn what it is," she managed. She'd have to be on guard.

"No, no, my sweet," he laughed condescendingly. "You must wait. But I assure you, you will find it most, ah, engaging."

His play on words sent shivers up her spine. Elizabeth dug her nails into her palms. This wasn't part of her plan. She needed more time.

She moved toward the house, passing Bormley on his way to the stable. She met his eye, desperately trying to convey new urgency, yet unable to speak openly in front of her captor. She took out her handkerchief, held it briefly to her nose, then let it slip through her fingers and flutter to the ground. She bent to retrieve it, watching Bormley for any reaction.

The slippery servant returned her gaze with an inscrutable look. Panic welled in Elizabeth's chest.

She stepped inside and collected a warmer shawl, a handmade piece she'd found in a trunk in what she'd come to think of as "her" room. To whom it had previously belonged, she couldn't say, for Harold had told her nothing of the ownership or past occupants of the house.

She warmed herself by the drawing room fire while Bormley readied the landau and horses. Would he come through for her? Or was he even now revealing her plot to Harold?

"It's time, Elizabeth."

Stiffly, she went to the vehicle, still trying to determine whether this change in events signaled opportunity for escape or only more danger. Bormley helped her up, but his blank expression gave nothing away.

As Harold hefted his considerable girth onto the seat beside her, Elizabeth's hopes diminished.

The servant moved to take the driver's perch, then suddenly veered off course. "One moment, sir," he called, hurrying back into the house.

Her heart thundered in her chest and she sent up a quick prayer. Harold gave an impatient grunt.

Rushing from the house, Bormley handed up a flask and a small, cloth-covered basket. "For your journey, sir."

Hope flared and Elizabeth flashed him a look. Was it only her imagination, or did he nod this time? And what did it mean?

Harold took the offering, and his servant bowed and climbed onto the driver's perch. A slap of the reins, and they were off.

For the first part of the journey, she sat stiffly by her captor's side. He'd not told her anything more about their destination, nor had she asked, unwilling as she was to upset whatever good humor had prompted him to take her out in the first place. Curiosity ate at her, though, as she tried to fathom his intention.

"Drink?" Harold offered her the flask, his manner unusually companionable.

She shook her head, and watched as he took a swig, then rummaged in the bread basket.

The landau rolled past small farms, their fields nearly ready to harvest. Bormley had left the cover down, and Elizabeth was glad she'd brought the shawl. They passed a few other travelers on the road. Would they think her mad if she called to them for help? No, she had to wait. She couldn't afford another ill-fated escape.

Finally, she saw the steeple of a village church off in the distance.

A village, with real people, and a marketplace, and, and . . . tears rushed to her eyes at the longing for such normal, everyday life. She could stand Harold's silence no longer.

"Are we going to the village?" she asked, hating the pleading sound of her own voice. Between imprisonment by Harold and the isolation she'd endured in London, both at Bea's and at her family's house, she'd been too long starved—not just for food but for human contact.

"Yes, to the church."

"For service?" What day of the week was it? Sunday? She'd lost track.

"Of a sort."

Her hands twisted in her shawl as her unease grew.

"Consider your actions carefully, Elizabeth," Harold admonished her, "for it is not only your own fate that rests upon your decision."

Elizabeth frowned, questioning.

"Think of your sister."

"Charity?" Her surprise was real. "What has she to do with this?"

"The way things stand now, you've ruined her chances at a decent future."

Shame flooded her. It was true. Though Charity had told her she could take care of herself, Elizabeth knew her own actions had cost her sister dearly. The Medford family's reputation had been shaky after her father's death, but now it was in shreds. And none of it was Charity's fault.

"Of course, we may be able to fix that."

"I cannot see how."

"Society is unforgiving, but when they wish, they are quite capable of forgetting a person's foibles, especially if that person sees the errors of their ways and settles into a respectable, legitimate marriage." He took another swig from the flask.

Elizabeth yanked her gaze from his, staring instead at the road as the vehicle rolled slowly along the road. The golden-brown fields and farms swam in her blurred vision as tears welled in her eyes. He'd said they were going to church. Now she knew why.

Still, there was time. The banns had to be read on three Sundays before they could marry.

"Marry me, and when the gossip settles, I will sponsor Charity for a Season of her own."

She shook her head in protest, her throat too thick for words.

"Think carefully, Elizabeth, before you make a decision you will regret."

She would do anything for her sister. But Harold's offer was empty, for though he might be able to afford sponsoring Charity, he did not have the necessary political and social wherewithal to launch her successfully—especially given the gossip surrounding her family.

Harold was wrong. Gossip might die down, but people did not forget. Not unless they feared the social clout of the person asking them to forget.

When Elizabeth remained silent, Harold gripped her upper arm, hard. "If you are still unconvinced, we could return to your home, where I will inform your uncle that, in spite of our interlude in the country, I find you unsuitable. And that I prefer to marry Charity instead."

Something inside her snapped.

"Never!" She pummeled him with her fists. "You will not touch my sister."

He batted away her fists.

Furious, Elizabeth grappled with him, desperate to regain control over the madness that had become her life. "Bormley, stop this vehicle now!" she shouted, but the servant did not so much as acknowledge her.

Harold's face twisted in anger. He outweighed her by at least five stone, and in the weakened state brought on by near-starvation, she was unable to compete with his bulk.

Realizing her folly, Elizabeth retreated to the edge of the bench and prepared to leap from the carriage.

A stunning blow knocked her back against the seat, then onto the floorboard in front of Harold's knees. Her jaw hit the opposite seat with a *crack*, just before his meaty fist yanked the back of her hair, forcing her chin up to look at him. Her head rang with pain.

"If you jump, I *will* marry Charity. And I will touch her any way I bloody well please. She's pretty, and young. She will likely be far easier to train. How many missed meals, how many beatings will it take, do you think, before she welcomes me into her bed?"

This did what all his other threats, beatings, and even starvation had not accomplished.

She had no choice. Harold would *not* get his hands on her little sister. Elizabeth's own folly had landed her in this position. Even if it hadn't, she could never knowingly allow her sister to bear this fate.

Her head throbbed and her body ached from the blow, but she pressed her lips together to stifle the pain.

If only she could get to Alex, Charity, too, would be safe, provided for under the umbrella of his protection.

The tears spilled over and her throat felt tight, but she managed a slight nod. Let him think what he would.

"You're doing the right thing, Elizabeth," Harold told her, and she hated the smugness in his voice. "It took you a while, but I knew you'd see reason eventually. In fact, that's the reason for our outing this morning."

Guarded, Elizabeth turned to look at him.

"I've arranged a special license to be married." He sounded proud of the fact.

"Special license?" she croaked.

"Yes. The vicar will be waiting for us at the church."

She struggled to breathe. "You mean to do this

thing today?" A special license eliminated the requirement for banns.

"No time like the present. A bit more speed, I think," he called to the front, and the servant urged the horses into a trot. He gave her an arrogant grin. "You've given your assent."

Elizabeth flicked a glance at the flask. Was there any hope left? Harold showed no sign that the wine he'd consumed had any unusual effect.

A new idea occurred to her.

She couldn't count on Harold passing out from the potion. But *she* could. She was already lightheaded with hunger. Surely she could feign a passable fainting spell.

Bormley drew the vehicle into the little churchyard and stopped. Harold eased his frame from the carriage and . . . Elizabeth blinked. Had he swayed when his feet hit the ground?

It didn't matter. She had a plan—albeit a temporary one. She climbed down and followed him, in seeming obedience, into the dim church.

The vicar couldn't proceed with the wedding if the bride was unconscious, could he?

Chapter Thirteen

Investigating Elizabeth's disappearance took far longer than Alex had hoped. He resisted the urge—barely—to ride madly about the countryside searching for her. To search without a plan was a fool's errand. She could be hidden anywhere.

Instead he hired the best investigators, paid them extra for speed, then hounded them incessantly.

After two days of hearing nothing, Alex was desperate to tear his mind from worry and guilt. He met Lord Wilbourne at White's for a night of cards and drinking, with considerable emphasis on the drinking.

"You're playing abominably, Beaufort," Wilbourne told him, only an hour into the play.

Alex shrugged and tossed back another brandy. Where the *hell* had that bastard taken Elizabeth?

Wilbourne dealt them a new hand, which he quickly won. Alex continued drinking.

Three hands later, all won by Wilbourne, and Alex had finally reached a state where he couldn't focus enough to worry.

Wilbourne set down the cards. "It goes against my

conscience to bet against a man who is clearly more focused on killing himself with drink than on playing the game."

"Right," Alex managed.

"I believe the proprietor is wringing his hands even now, worried he may not have stocked enough of your favorite brandy. Something on your mind, Beaufort?"

Vaguely, Alex registered the note of concern in his friend's voice. "Can't find her," he muttered.

Robert Wilbourne studied his drunken friend. "Her?"

"Elizabeth."

Now, *that* was interesting. Robert had never seen the duke drink himself into a stupor before—let alone over a woman. And not just any woman. He'd heard the rumors.

Alex tiredly raked a hand through his hair, then let his head fall back against the chair.

Robert glanced around. They were in a relatively quiet corner of the gentlemen's club—a good thing, because whatever was bothering his friend, Alex wasn't in any state to be overheard.

"She's the one, isn't she? The one whose father sold her out?"

Alex stared at him for a moment, as though trying to remember. "Yes," he finally said. "But I didn't—"

"Of course not."

"But later . . ." Alex groaned and finished off another brandy.

With the slightest hand gesture, Robert signaled the waiter not to bring anymore. It was going to be hard enough getting his friend home in his current state.

"God, she's something. She's . . . different. I think I . . . I *need* her," Alex said, his words clear but slow in coming. His head dropped into his hands. "Christ. This is all my fault."

"How is it your fault?"

Slowly he shook his head, still in his hands, from side to side. "I did it. All of it. She doesn't know. I *ruined* her. And now she's gone."

The duke was rambling—Robert couldn't follow his alcohol-soaked confessions. What he did understand, though, was that Elizabeth Medford was more than just another of Alex's illicit, meaningless affairs. "Where'd she go?"

"Don't know." Alex rubbed his temples. "Can't think. Kidnapped."

"Kidnapped?" Robert echoed.

"Wetherby. Bastard." Alex looked up, eyes red-rimmed, but his voice gaining strength. "I've got . . . least a dozen . . . Runners looking for her now. I'm going after her." He put out an unsteady hand. "As soon as the bloody room stops spinning."

Unless Robert was much mistaken, Alex's ramblings meant one thing: the Duke of Beaufort, London's most dissolute rake, had fallen in love. Hard.

"Beaufort," Robert said gently, "I'm going to call your carriage. I'm going to help you into it. When you get home, sleep it off. Then go find your woman."

After nearly a week of empty reports from the men Alex had hired to look into Wetherby's affairs, one man at last returned with a report of a textiles factory and a small residential property to the north, owned by one Harold Wetherby.

Filled with renewed purpose, Alex secured specific directions and set off immediately. He could travel faster riding alone than in a carriage, so he did. It was a fair distance, but after riding through the afternoon and night, he was in the vicinity of the residence.

It wasn't much. A two-story home in rural England. He checked the investigator's description one last time, then approached cautiously. His heart pounded. He wanted nothing more than to rush up and see for himself that Elizabeth was all right, but common sense told him such an approach might actually provoke Harold further.

No one heralded his arrival in the small yard. There was a stable, but he heard no animal sounds, save for those coming from a few chickens pecking in the yard.

His feeling of anticipation gave way to one of uncertainty. Something was amiss here. Did he have the wrong place? He doubted it, having always been astute with directions. Besides, there was nothing else around.

The house was quiet. Too quiet. His knock went unanswered. No servants about.

A brief search of the house confirmed it empty, though its occupants had not been gone long. The remains of one person's breakfast still sat on a table, and the scent of a woman—Elizabeth, he was certain—lingered upstairs.

A sense of impending doom struck him as he went back outside and confirmed the stables were also empty.

Alex retraced his route. A little investigative work of his own revealed new tracks, a conveyance of some sort, leading down the road in the opposite direction from whence he'd come.

He nudged his mount back onto the road, kicking him into a gallop. The stallion tossed his head in protest. He nudged the animal again. "I know you're tired, but we've no time."

The horse gave one more flick of his head but picked up his pace. Alex patted him as a knot grew in his gut.

Had he taken too long to find her? Where was Elizabeth? God help Wetherby if she'd been harmed in any way.

It had been many moons since Alex Bainbridge, Duke of Beaufort, had darkened the doors of a church, but as he kept his eyes on the tracks he followed, his mind turned to prayer. More than anything, he prayed Elizabeth had not suffered for his foolishness. His conscience was already sorely tried by its burden of guilt. He could bear no more.

The tracks led him to a village, and then to a chapel.

His unease turned to near-panic as he saw where the tracks ended. He flung himself from his mount and ran to the chapel without even thinking to secure the weary beast.

His push sent the lightweight wooden door banging into the adjacent wall. As his eyes adjusted from the bright sun, Alex made out three figures standing near the altar. One wore black, and the other two stood before him in the time-honored formation of a wedding ceremony. The bride's blaze of auburn hair was unmistakable. Rage filled him.

"You cannot proceed!" His voice echoed, bouncing off the stone walls. He quickly closed the remaining distance between himself and the three at the altar.

Elizabeth, the vicar, and a portly man with receding brown hair turned to gape at him. Wetherby. Alex recognized him from their encounter at the Derringworth stables months ago.

"I believe this is my church, and I will proceed as I

see fit," the vicar replied. His furrowed brows belied his mild tone.

"If you value your position in the least, you will desist," Alex told him in the most authoritative tone he knew.

"I think," Wetherby slurred, "I need to sit down." As he spoke the words, his hand landed clumsily on the altar in an attempt to steady himself.

Alex turned to the woman he'd just rushed pell-mell across the countryside to find. "Elizabeth, what is going on here?"

But her attention was turned to Wetherby, whose face had gone slack. His hand slipped from the altar, and he crumpled heavily to the floor.

Something was odd here. Alex longed to simply gather her in his arms, but first he needed an answer.

"Elizabeth," he urged, "tell me you never meant to marry that cur."

For a moment her eyes stayed fixed on Wetherby's crumpled form.

Then, lifting her chin, she met his gaze with something of triumph in her own. "Never."

She was paler, thinner than he remembered, but his fiery temptress remained unbroken.

Alex smiled for the first time in days. "Let us go, then, before he recovers."

"Oh, I don't believe that will be for a while."

The vicar cleared his throat. "Excuse me, sir, but who are you? And what precisely is going on here?"

Elizabeth answered for him. "He's Alex Bainbridge, Duke of Beaufort. And as for Mr. Wetherby, I believe he's had a taste of his own medicine and found it . . . overwhelming."

"Duke?" the vicar squeaked. His glance darted between Elizabeth and her overweight, would-be husband. Her captor. Who showed no sign of awakening from his fainting spell.

The vicar's brows knit together as he nudged Harold with his toe. "Young lady, has this man been poisoned?"

Her cheeks pinkened. "Only a sleeping draught."

Alex felt his chest swell. He was so damn proud of that woman. Still. "You cut the timing a bit close, don't you think?" he whispered to her.

A shiver passed through her.

"This situation is highly unusual," the vicar declared as though taking an official position on the matter.

"Indeed," Alex said dryly.

Harold groaned, drawing the attention of the other three. He passed a hand over his forehead, then slowly pushed himself to his feet. His gaze landed on Elizabeth and he scowled. "The wine," he muttered. "You little bi—" he bit off the last part of the slur.

Elizabeth took a step back. Alex moved in front of her, his ire rising once more as he observed how nervous she became around a conscious Wetherby.

"You may proceed," Harold informed the vicar. "I want this thing done."

"Like hell," Alex said.

"Gentlemen—" the vicar began.

"We've matters to settle." Alex's words, and his raised hand, stopped the vicar midspeech.

Harold sidled over, still swaying. "Elizabeth's family appreciates me taking her off their hands."

Alex clenched his jaw, unable to believe the man's gall.

"You see," Harold said, "in marrying *me*, she'll regain some of the respectability she lost in consorting with *you*."

Alex's fist connected with the fleshy jowl of his

nemesis. Harold staggered—though from the blow or
the lingering effects of whatever potion Elizabeth had
slipped him, Alex couldn't tell.

"Now, now!" cried the vicar, though he backed several steps away from the angry men. "This is a house
of God."

Both men ignored him.

Alex watched as Harold struggled for balance and
clutched his jaw.

"Get out," Alex bit out, not trusting himself to further speech.

But the swine lumbered back and thrust out his
chest. He grabbed Elizabeth's arm. "She's mine now."

"As I told you, the lady does not wish to marry you."

"She's ruined. What other option does she have?"
he blustered.

"One far superior. She's marrying me."

Suddenly the small church went silent. Elizabeth,
Harold, and the vicar all stared at him, the latter two
with their mouths hanging open.

"Is this true?" the vicar finally asked Harold.

"I know nothing of it," he answered, but his normally ruddy face had lost most of its color.

"Young lady?"

It took all Alex's patience not to answer for her. *Yes.
Just say yes,* he silently begged her.

He'd not been planning a proposal when he entered
the church that morning. It had just slipped out. But
now that it had, he knew, deep in his core, it was meant
to be. If only Elizabeth would agree. They could work
out the details later.

Dust motes danced in the light that filtered through the
church's narrow windows, and still Elizabeth was silent.

The vicar turned back to Harold. "At any rate, I

can't perform the ceremony under such circumstances. I fear I must recuse myself."

"We had an agreement," Harold hissed.

"He's a peer of the realm," the vicar hissed back.

Alex ignored them. "Elizabeth?"

"My lord," she whispered. "I know you didn't mean it. It was a mistake. And you, being a gentleman . . . but you don't have to—"

"Yes, I do."

"But Society will—"

"Society be damned." He placed a finger over her lips to hush her. When she stilled, he grasped her hands and knelt.

He'd done more to hurt this woman than she even realized, but he loved her. And starting this moment, he intended to make it all up to her.

"Elizabeth, I meant it. Forget everything else. Will you marry me?"

She bit her bottom lip and looked at him hard, as though taking his measure. She cocked her head, and he could see the mistrust in her eyes give way to hope, and then the corners of her mouth turned up in the first true smile he'd seen from her that morning. She took a deep breath and gave him the answer he so longed to hear.

"Yes, I'll marry you."

Harold punched his fist into the altar, then recoiled as the marble proved too solid to shatter before his frustration. Rubbing his knuckles, he staggered from the church.

The vicar withdrew more quietly, leaving Elizabeth alone with Alex.

She sank slowly to the steps before the altar, reeling with emotion. The events of the morning would have had any lesser woman reaching for her smelling salts. In fact, she'd been only seconds away from pretending to faint, thereby stopping the sham of a wedding, when Harold had done so instead.

And of course there was Alex. He'd looked so magnificent, storming into the church. How had he known where to find her?

It didn't matter. He *had* found her. Her heart swelled. He cared.

His proposal had given her a moment of pause, though. After all, he was a cad. He'd seduced her, and the whole of London knew, or at least suspected, it. And there was that thing Cutter had said, about her being a part of some deal between Alex and her father.

But she loved him.

Cad or no, she would marry Alex Bainbridge. Besides, his proposal rendered most of those prior faults irrelevant.

She longed to trace the hard line of his jaw, to step into his arms and melt into the strength of his embrace.

But first, she owed him an explanation. "Your Grace—"

"I liked it better when you simply called me Alex."

"Alex," she began again, determined to tell him why he'd found her in a church, seemingly about to marry another man.

But how, exactly, did one explain such a thing?

"What happened this morning . . ." she tried again.

"We can discuss it later. Just tell me one thing." Alex reached out to touch her fading bruise. "Did he hurt you?"

Elizabeth looked down, unwilling to lie but ashamed of the truth. After a long moment she met Alex's gaze again.

His eyes were hard. "He will pay," he told her, his voice

clipped. With one hand he tipped her chin, then studied her neck, patted her arms. "Where else did he hurt you? *How* else did he hurt you? Shall I summon a physician?"

"Nay, I am already mending quite well."

"But perhaps, just in case . . ." His hands fretted over her body.

Seeing the duke brought low by worrying over *her* melted Elizabeth's reserve.

She stilled his hands with her own. "Oh, Alex, just hold me."

He did, snatching her into his arms with barely checked force. He stroked her hair, her back, over and over while he held her. "God, Elizabeth. You've no idea. When I returned to my sister's and found you gone—"

Whatever else he'd been going to say was lost, for his lips found her forehead, her brow, as he covered her with kisses.

Elizabeth inhaled his scent, absorbed his strength. There were a thousand questions to ask about the future, but they would wait for now.

"Tell me again," he murmured against her neck, nuzzling at her earlobe.

Elizabeth tipped her head to allow him greater access. "Tell you what?"

"That you'll marry me."

"I'll marry you," she breathed, unable to believe that Alex Bainbridge, Duke of Beaufort, had proposed to her. If this was a dream, she hoped it would never end.

The vicar stood in the shadows of a stairwell, watching the handsome couple at the altar.

He would lose the generous sum Wetherby had promised him for performing the marriage ceremony, but there was no doubt in his mind that the red-haired young lady had made the right choice.

Chapter Fourteen

What had he just done? How had this slip of a girl transformed him from London's worst libertine into a man who dashed across the countryside to propose marriage?

The funny thing was, it felt *right*. As though marrying her would make him whole.

Alex looked at Elizabeth, standing beside him. She appeared a bit dazed. Not that he could blame her.

"Let's go," he told her, taking her hand and leading her from the little country church. He squinted his eyes against the bright morning sunlight. There was no sign of Wetherby. Good.

Alex's horse stood near the gate to the church cemetery, looking disgruntled—no doubt he'd been expecting a rubdown and some oats after tearing across the countryside.

Alex walked over and picked up the reins, his eyes drifting over the tombstones as he did.

Lord Medford was probably rolling in his grave. When he'd offered Elizabeth up to the duke to settle his debts, could he have had any inkling of how well suited the two were?

Alex would have smiled, but the irony was too grim. If he *had* agreed to marry Elizabeth when her father first proposed it, the baron might still be alive. And Elizabeth certainly wouldn't have suffered the trials of these past months.

It was better she didn't know the extent of her father's betrayal. She'd suffered enough.

Alex's horse presented another problem.

"I was so intent on finding you, I didn't think how I'd get you back to town," he apologized. "My horse is good, but I doubt either you or he would be comfortable riding double all the way back to London."

He glanced around the village. Besides the church, it boasted a few shops and homes, and a small inn. "Stay here a moment—promise me you won't move an inch."

Elizabeth did exactly as he asked. After the tumult of the morning, she wasn't sure she could move an inch if she had to, other than, perhaps, to collapse in relief and wonder.

Alex was gone mere minutes before he came striding back, looking mildly put out.

"There are no carriages for hire until the next town over—perhaps two or three miles. You'll have to ride in front of me. My horse can carry us both that far," he told her.

She nodded. But she had a more pressing need than transportation. She stared at the ground, her neck and face heated, hating for Alex to know just how Harold had weakened her. "Alex, before we go, is there somewhere we can eat? I'm hungry."

"Hungry? The noon hour is still a way off."

"I know, but . . ."

She knew when he understood the truth of it by the way his eyes darkened. "That *bastard*," he bit out savagely. "If I *ever* get my hands on him—"

"Alex."

He stopped. "My apologies. Of course, dearest. We'll find something to eat."

Grateful tears pricked her eyes. She blinked them away, but when Alex returned ten minutes later with a thick ham sandwich and an apple, they flooded forth. She cried even as she ate, sitting on the ground in front of the little church.

To her surprise, her stomach filled long before she wanted to be done.

"It's all right," Alex said gently. "I guess you haven't had a good meal in some time. If you try to overdo it now, you'll just make yourself sick."

She nodded but clenched tight the remains of the sandwich.

Alex held her close. "God, Elizabeth, I'm so sorry. I should have been there for you all along. This should never have happened to you."

"You came for me. You're here now."

"And I'm not going anywhere." He carefully pried the food from her hands and wrapped it in a cloth napkin. "We'll bring this with us. When you're ready, you can have it. You don't ever need to worry about going hungry again." He kissed her temple, her lips. "Are you ready to go now?"

"Yes. Please." With that most basic need satiated, she wanted nothing more than to get as far from her memories of Harold's torment as possible. Except . . . "Wait. There is one more thing. Bormley—that's Harold's servant. He put the potion in Harold's wine this morning, at my request. I promised him payment for aiding my escape. Only," she studied the grass at her feet, "I haven't any way . . ." she trailed off, embarrassed at her request.

"Consider it done." Alex glanced around. "He's gone now. But I'll see to it—you need never think of the matter again."

Finally, Alex helped her mount the horse. Her senses jolted as he settled behind her and nudged the horse to a walk.

It was intimate, and improper, riding like this, with her bottom nestled against his hips, snug between his thighs.

But they *were* to be married—and there was really no other way. She tried to relax into the rhythmic gait.

After the intense scene in the church, Alex seemed hesitant to talk. Elizabeth didn't know what to say either. So much had happened in the past few weeks. She didn't want to relive it all right now.

She twisted around to look up at her new fiancé. His jaw was so strong, his eyes so intense. His unruly dark hair begged for a woman's touch. This man owned estates throughout England, invested in ventures at home and abroad, and wielded more power than anyone she'd ever known.

And he'd come to rescue *her*. He'd offered to marry *her*.

She should be deliriously happy. Except—except she just couldn't help but remember the incident with the man she'd encountered en route home after losing her governess's position. Mr. Cutter, drunkard though he may have been, had unsettled her, shaken her faith that Alex's intentions were sincere. Had Alex actually bargained with her father to accept *her* as payment for gambling debts the baron couldn't cover? The thought made her ill.

He'd only pursued her *after* her father's death, she reminded herself. But it was still possible he'd received notice from her father's estate, saying the debt could not be repaid, and only then decided to make good on her father's other "offer." But he'd never mentioned anything of the sort to her . . . because it was shameful, or because it wasn't true?

When he'd first pursued her, was it out of true interest or simply to "collect" on the agreement? And how had Cutter known of the situation? Had Alex actually discussed this with others? How many members of Society were secretly snickering—or, hopefully, appalled— that her very own father saw her as a fancy bargaining chip?

She was certain Alex cared for her now, but how much?

Was he marrying her out of love or guilt?

Dear God, what if his silence now was because he *regretted* his hasty proposal in the church?

Alex glanced down to see Elizabeth looking at him. The sun shone like flames on her hair where it escaped the confines of her cap, and he had a sudden urge to kiss the pert tip of her nose. But her eyes seemed shadowed.

"What is it?"

She shook her head and turned to face forward again.

"Elizabeth?"

She sighed. "What you did back there . . ."

"Was something I should have done long ago," he finished for her.

"Should have? Or wanted to?"

"What do you mean?" Something was obviously bothering her.

"What made you pursue me in the first place?" she asked suddenly.

That was easy. "When I returned to find you gone, and heard what had happened . . . that Wetherby had taken you . . . it was the only thing to do. I only wish I'd been able to come faster."

"No, no. I mean, why did you pursue me before all that? I mean, I nearly begged you to ruin me, and you refused. What made you change your mind?"

She was fiddling with her skirts. He could feel the tension in her body.

She did have a point.

"I can't explain it," he said slowly. "Your offer tempted me sorely, and later, when I discovered you under my sister's employ, away from the falsity of Society . . . I couldn't stop thinking of you. I know we did not begin on the most honorable of terms, and I apologize for that. My desire got the better of me."

She turned to him as fully as their position allowed, narrowing her eyes. "It wasn't because you were exacting payment from my father?"

Bloody hell. He swallowed, hard. How had she heard about that?

But no, he'd never *done* that. If anything, her father's offer had nearly kept him from pursuing her at all.

Alex saw in her eyes it would do no good to feign ignorance. "No," he told her, gently but firmly, "I was not trying to recoup your father's debt through you."

"But he did offer me." She said it flatly.

"Yes." Alex felt sick. But he wasn't going to lie.

How could it feel, to know your father would do such a thing?

"I refused, and avoided further contact with Medford after that," he told her. "I wasn't even certain who you were at the time. At the Peasleys' ball, I asked you to dance out of true interest. Imagine my surprise when you turned out to be his daughter."

"But he was dead by then. You knew he'd never be able to repay the debt honestly."

Alex frowned. "My sense of honor is not so entirely lacking as you suggest, my lady. The loss irritated me, but I would not expect a daughter to pay for her father's misdeeds. If anything, that is why I refused your unconventional offer at first."

"And later?" She seemed unconvinced. "If there was no agreement, then how did Cutter hear of it?"

"Cutter?"

She explained the incident in the park.

"Ah, Elizabeth." He pulled her tense body back against his. His body was reacting to their intimate position atop the horse, but for once he kept his mind focused on what was best for her.

Even if he hadn't accepted Medford's awful proposal, he *had* wronged Elizabeth. She needed words right now, not his lust.

"That *was* my fault. On a night when I'd drunk too much—in an effort to forget you, and your outrageous proposal I'd just turned down—I made a brief mention of your father's words. I was clear, even then, that I'd never agreed to it. I don't believe I even named you, or your father. But Cutter must have heard of our affair and come to his own conclusion. I should never have mentioned it, and for that I am truly sorry."

She nodded in seeming acceptance.

"Both of us have acted in ways that do little credit to our character," she said softly. "I ran from home, and shamed my family by engaging in a scandalous affair."

He leaned his head against hers. "I cannot fault you for running. I understand now, far more than before, why you were so desperate to avoid a fate tied to Wetherby."

He kissed the top of her head, stroked her hair. "Nor, Elizabeth, would I undo anything we've done together, regardless of how it came about."

"Nor would I," she whispered.

Alex began nibbling at her ear. "It was you I wanted, Elizabeth, not some strange form of revenge against your father. I'm sorry I didn't do the honorable thing and ask for your hand before claiming your body. You've no idea how I missed you while I was away. And then to return and find you gone . . ."

"I sent you a message," she told him. "Just after I lost my position."

He drew back slightly and shook his head. "I never received a letter. My business travels sent me in directions I hadn't anticipated. Most of my correspondence never caught up."

"Oh."

Her pulled her close again. "I would never have ignored your troubles, had I known of them. Please believe that."

"I do," she whispered.

"And believe also, that those weeks away made me realize that more than anything, I wanted you by my side. Not just for a stolen afternoon here and there, but always.

"Forget your father's bargain—it was the desperate

rambling of a man brought low by his own weaknesses. But it has nothing to do with what's between us.

"Let me make things right. Be my wife." He dipped his tongue in to trace the contours of her ear, then the delicate hollow behind it.

She shivered. "Yes."

"Elizabeth, we're nearly there."

She stretched sleepily and opened her eyes. It hadn't been a dream. Alex Bainbridge, her *fiancé*, occupied the bench across from her in the enclosed carriage. And in his hands he held a letter. One all too familiar.

With a start, she came fully awake. "Where did you get that?"

"This? It slipped from your gown as you slept." He turned it in his hands as though it were a foreign curiosity.

The seal was unbroken, she saw with relief. She held out a hand, palm up. "Please, may I have it back?"

"It's addressed to me."

He *couldn't* read it. Not now. Not when everything was finally perfect, and he'd asked her to marry him. If he found out she'd been willing to settle for so much less, would he still love her? She couldn't bear to have her heart broken a second time.

"Please, Alex." She stretched her fingertips toward the letter. "It's of no importance now—only a note I'd composed to you before you arrived at the church." Her voice shook.

"What does it say?"

"I . . . well . . . only that I hoped I might count on your aid, once I escaped. Please, may I have it back now?"

Reluctantly, he handed it over. "Of course I would come to your aid, in anything. Sweeting, your cheeks are quite red. What else does the letter say?"

She dropped her gaze.

"I saw how you were treated out there. I promise, nothing you could tell me would lower my opinion of you. You are the bravest, cleverest woman I know." He shifted seats to sit beside her, drawing her into his arms.

"I'm so ashamed," she whispered.

"Darling, as you've already said, it's of no consequence. You can tell me."

She took a quivery breath. "I was frightened, out there, for even though I planned to escape, I had nowhere to go once I managed it. Home was no longer safe, and I hadn't any letters of reference, so I—I wrote to you, and said that if the offer you once made me still stood, I would accept it now."

She raised her eyes to his, and found only understanding, and love. Not condemnation.

"I am honored that you thought to turn to me in your hour of need," he said, his voice choked. "But I stand by what I said earlier. You belong by my side as a cherished wife, and nothing less."

She gave him a tremulous smile. His gaze dropped to her lips and she leaned in, needing his touch, his love.

His mouth captured hers with tender hunger. Her arms slid around his neck as she arched closer, parting her lips to receive his kiss fully. How had she ever thought to live without this man?

The carriage stopped.

"Have we arrived already?" she asked with regret. Though they'd been travelling for two days, stopping only at the coaching inns for meals and fresh horses,

Elizabeth had welcomed the interlude as a temporary haven between her imprisonment and the scrutiny she would face by returning to London—with the Duke of Beaufort, no less.

"Not quite. I asked the driver to stop at my London house, but only for a moment. I wish to change carriages."

It was true the rented carriage was not as luxurious as the duke's own, but Elizabeth knew he had another reason.

Sure enough, within moments Alex's driver—this time his normal driver, in full livery—brought a luxurious carriage with the Beaufort crest conspicuously emblazoned on the side. Their next stop was the Medford home, where they intended to make their engagement both official and public knowledge.

Elizabeth made the change to the new vehicle, but as it drew closer to her childhood home, she had second thoughts.

"Must we do this?" she pled. "Couldn't you just haul me off to Gretna Green and be done with the matter?"

Alex smiled and leaned in for a kiss. A brief taste, and he pulled back. "A tempting notion indeed, but no. If we're to have any hope of showing our faces in London, it's best this be done properly." A shadow crossed his face, as though something more were troubling him.

He'd said "we," but she knew his concern was for *her*. The ton would forgive a duke anything, especially Alex Bainbridge. They would not be nearly so kind to her.

Their carriage turned onto the street her mother lived on.

"I don't want to go in there."

"I know," he said tenderly, cupping her cheek. "But I am going with you. And I promise I've no desire to linger." A shadow crossed his face, then just as quickly disappeared.

Elizabeth sighed. Though she'd already promised to marry Alex, he'd insisted on asking her mother and uncle formally for permission. Given how readily they'd betrayed her before, she didn't see the point.

Why did her duke have to choose *now* to become chivalrous?

But she owed him so much. She could at least do this for him. She allowed him to help her from the carriage, then steeled herself at the barrage of emotions that threatened to consume her when the butler opened the door and led them in.

They waited in the rose salon, not bothering to take seats. Only moments passed before her mother and her Uncle George hurried in, curtsying and bowing. Elizabeth almost smiled at their anxious expressions. It wasn't every day a duke came to call—especially not hand-in-hand with the daughter of the house—the daughter who was *supposed* to be imprisoned in the country with an altogether different man.

"What an honor, Your Grace," Lady Medford said, only a hint of strain in her voice. "And Elizabeth, welcome home."

Elizabeth tried not to be hurt that her mother had acknowledged Alex first.

"An honor, indeed," Uncle George murmured.

Alex gave them each a lordly nod, reminding Elizabeth that though he might tease and play with her, he was every inch a duke. As long as he remained standing, her relatives did, too, looking uncertain. She smiled and kept her hand in his.

"Of course, you are welcome here, Your Grace. But my niece . . . I'm afraid I don't understand. Where is Wetherby?" Uncle George asked.

She felt Alex stiffen in anger. For her, everything that had happened back at that house seemed strangely distant, as though it had happened to another woman rather than to herself.

"Don't ever speak that man's name in my presence again," Alex ordered.

She suppressed the urge to shiver at his tone. Instead, she drew herself tall and spoke. "Whatever your intentions were in forcing me to spend time with that man, I must inform you that he and I most definitely did *not* suit."

Alex was not nearly as restrained. "That blackguard belongs in jail. I can think of nothing, save one thing, I'd enjoy more than seeing him—and anyone who conspired with him—behind bars. Or dead," he declared.

Uncle George managed to keep his expression neutral, though, Elizabeth noticed, his knuckles, gripping the back of a chair, had turned white. Her mother looked apologetic. Perhaps the plot had been contained to the two men.

"What one thing would you enjoy more, Your Grace?" Lady Medford asked uneasily.

He softened his tone. "Marrying your daughter."

A swift look passed between the duke and Lady Medford, then Alex gave an almost imperceptible bow.

Though Elizabeth sensed something important had just happened, she didn't understand the exchange. Her uncle appeared to have missed it entirely.

"This is the purpose of my call," Alex told them calmly. "I'd like to request Elizabeth's hand in marriage."

Some of the tension seemed to leave Lady Medford's

body as she smiled. It wasn't the giddy excitement one would expect for the mother of the girl who'd just landed the most coveted marriage proposal in England, Elizabeth noted dryly, but her mother *did* smile.

"Elizabeth, are you amenable to his request?" her mother asked.

She looked up at Alex, hoping he could see in her eyes how much she loved him. "I am."

"But Ha—" Uncle George remembered himself just in time, though the near-slip earned him a dark look from the duke. "I mean, certainly, I can think of no greater honor for Elizabeth. Of course, you have my permission."

Elizabeth sincerely doubted her uncle thought she *deserved* that honor, but she determined not to worry about that.

"You have my blessing as well," her mother added.

Alex bowed. "I thank you, both."

"You'll stay here, of course, until the wedding, Elizabeth," her mother said.

"No."

Lady Medford's shocked gaze flew to the duke.

"No, mother," she explained. "I'm staying with Beatrice Pullington. I'm sorry, but after what happened the last time I returned home, I've no desire to do so again."

Her mother had the grace to look guilty.

"And when will this wedding take place?" Uncle George asked.

"Three weeks," Alex declared.

Uncle George narrowed his gaze. "Is there a *reason* for such haste? Must the ceremony take place sooner, rather than later?" His tone made it clear that he, at least, had not forgotten the scandal surrounding the young couple.

"No!" she hastily asserted—just as her fiancé said, "Yes."

Elizabeth's jaw dropped and she yanked her hand from Alex's. "But—"

Lady Medford sat down, heavily, on the beige settee.

"I see." Uncle George's voice dripped with scorn.

"I don't think you do. Though your lack of faith in your niece comes as no surprise." Alex drew himself to his full height. "The matter is simple. I care deeply for Elizabeth, and she's been through a great ordeal. I want her under my roof, under my protection, as soon as possible."

Elizabeth relaxed and slipped her hand back into his.

"Then you're not . . . ?" her mother asked weakly.

"No," she confirmed.

Lady Medford nodded and breathed a sigh of relief. "Three weeks is hardly any time at all, but if His Grace wishes it, we will abide."

"Certainly," Uncle George confirmed, though his disgruntled expression belied his words.

"Elizabeth will have my full staff at her disposal. They can assist in any aspect of planning she wishes. I'm certain they are up to the task."

"Of course," Lady Medford said. "But a gown . . ."

"I'm sure that can be accomplished, too," Elizabeth told her. She didn't say it, but if her mother had any notion of helping her prepare for the wedding, she was going to be in for a disappointment. Bea and Charity, loyal friend and sister, were all the help she desired.

Alex seemed to sense her discomfort in discussing

details, now that the biggest hurdle was out of the way. "Lady Medford, and sir, I thank you again for Elizabeth's hand. We've had a long journey and are quite exhausted. I'm sure you understand. I'll instruct my secretary to have any correspondence from you delivered to me personally, with haste, as I'm sure we'll be in contact as the wedding draws near."

Another round of bowing and curtsying, and they were back outside. Elizabeth took a deep breath, a weight lifted from her chest.

Suddenly she grinned, tempted to throw her arms around Alex and kiss him right then and there. For the first time in nearly a year, her future looked bright.

Chapter Fifteen

Working things out between Alex and her family was only the beginning of Elizabeth's challenges. There was still the matter of working things—specifically her besmirched reputation—out with the ton.

First, she had to make sure Beatrice Pullington hadn't succumbed to the lurid tales and turned against her. When she'd told her mother she'd stay with Bea, she'd not yet actually spoken with her friend.

Alex's carriage took her to Bea's home, dropping him off at his town house first.

"Elizabeth, if there's any trouble—any at all—with your friend, please come straight back to me," he'd implored her. "I want to know you're safe and cared for, and I won't rest easy until I've got you under my roof for keeps."

She'd placed one small hand on his jaw. "Thank you, Alex. Of course," she'd teased, "I imagine that's not your *only* reason for wanting me under your roof."

"Go on, you minx," he'd growled as he climbed out of the carriage. "Tempt me not!"

The carriage had whisked her away, with daydreams

of the many ways she hoped to soon tempt Alex Bainbridge filling her mind for the short trip to Lady Pullington's home.

Bea's house looked the same as ever, but Elizabeth felt like a different woman as she pulled the bell.

The butler answered, and Beatrice appeared moments later, looking slightly apprehensive. "Elizabeth. You're back! I was so worried. Come in, come in. Are you all right, then?"

Elizabeth held out both hands to greet her longtime friend. "Perfectly all right. Better, perhaps, than you may even know." She grinned mischievously.

Bea's eyes widened. "What happened? There have been rumors, but you know how that is. And was that the *Duke of Beaufort's* carriage I saw pulling away? Oh, Elizabeth, do tell."

Elizabeth quickly filled her in, ending with her as-yet-unannounced engagement to the Duke of Beaufort.

"Oh, Elizabeth!" Bea repeated, her face filled with joy for her friend. "How amazing. And after all you've been through, you absolutely, absolutely, deserve this."

Elizabeth grinned, relieved to confirm Bea was, as she'd known in her heart, a loyal friend.

"When is the wedding?"

It gave her the opening she needed. "Three weeks. But, Bea, I need a place to stay until then. I despise myself for imposing on our friendship again, but—"

"Say no more. You're not imposing. Of course you can stay here."

"I don't know what I'd do without you, Bea."

Bea hugged her. "I don't know what I'd do without *you* to liven up my life. I'd probably be a dreadfully dull old widow!"

"Never!" Elizabeth exclaimed in mock horror, and both women giggled.

"Is your family not amenable to the marriage, then? I can't fathom why not."

Elizabeth sobered, then explained her imprisonment in Harold's country house.

"No! How beastly! Your mother knew? Your uncle?"

"My uncle, certainly. Mother, well, I'm not sure. But I can't go back home, Bea. Not after that."

"No, I suppose not," Bea agreed. "Are you really all right, then?"

Elizabeth thought of the wonderful man waiting to marry her. "I am now."

Bea ushered Elizabeth straight to the room she'd stayed in before, and Elizabeth settled in happily.

Although she was deliriously happy to be marrying the man of her dreams, Elizabeth feared her reputation was beyond repair.

Lady Grumsby disagreed.

"You'll *have* to reenter Society. There is nothing else for it." Marian Grumsby spoke with certainty. She was one of Elizabeth's first callers—after Charity, who'd arrived barely an hour after Elizabeth had settled in at Bea's.

They sat in the small salon. Bea was out for the afternoon but didn't mind at all if Elizabeth received callers. "This is your home, as long as you're here," she'd said.

Lady Grumsby, to Elizabeth's relief, had been very enthusiastic about the engagement.

"I knew there was something different about the way he looked at you," she'd crowed. "And of course I'm not angry with you. How could I be, when you and Alex are so obviously right for one another? I can—and did—find another governess. I could never find a better fiancée for Alex." Her gaze became gentle. "Or a better sister for me or aunt for my children. Do you know how many women have been thrust in front of my brother since he was old enough to notice the fairer sex? And never once did he show any desire to form a lasting attachment with any of them—save you."

Marian's words were comforting, but as for her insistence that Elizabeth attend balls and teas as though nothing had happened . . .

"I couldn't." Elizabeth shook her head. "Alex and I will simply live quietly in the country. I mean, look around you. I've so estranged myself from my own family that I'm not even living in their home."

Marian shook her head, her pretty brunette curls bouncing. "Elizabeth, there is no way to say this politely, but I wouldn't want to live with your family either. Except perhaps your sister. I understand she's lovely. But, honestly, the matter of where you live the last few weeks before your wedding is not nearly as important as whether or not you appear to be in hiding.

"The Duke of Beaufort is an important man, and you'll be expected to entertain as befits that station. You cannot simply retire to the country. My dear brother may have agreed to that because he's so besotted with you, but in the long run it would do him harm. You don't want that."

"No." Elizabeth stared at her tea. She didn't. She wanted happiness for Alex, wanted him to have a wife he could be proud of.

"There's another reason," Marian cajoled. "Think of

your sister. As long as you are ruined, so is she. But if the ton can be persuaded it was all a big mistake, she may safely make her come-out and likely have a number of fine suitors to choose from."

Elizabeth gave a hollow laugh. "Lately, it seems as though whenever someone wishes to coerce me, my sister is used as bait." She briefly told Lady Grumsby of Harold Wetherby's threat after she had again refused to marry him.

"How awful! Elizabeth, I never meant—"

"No, no." Elizabeth waved her hand, smiling in earnest now. "I know you didn't. I *do* care for my sister, very much." Of her relations, Charity alone was a loyal friend. She deserved the best, and Elizabeth *had* endangered her future terribly. If there was some way to make that up, she would do it. Even if it meant facing the cold stares and wagging tongues she was sure to encounter from the rest of the ton.

After all Elizabeth had done—flouted nearly every one of Society's strictures—it would be attempting the impossible.

"My lady," Elizabeth said, "I fear my mistakes are so grave, they cannot be overcome in the eyes of Society."

"You must call me Marian, now that we're to be sisters." The lovely brunette's smile was genuine.

"Marian?"

She shrugged. "My mother was a bit fanciful. Named me after Robin Hood's ladylove."

"I like that very much."

"Anyhow," Marian continued, "the eyes of Society are not so discerning as all that. People would rather believe they made a mistake in judging you than risk falling out of favor with my brother. Being the Duke of Beaufort does have some advantages."

"It will take more than that."

"Which is why I am here. You'll have me, my husband, and Lady Pullington to champion you, at the very least. And all of our reputations are beyond reproach."

Elizabeth stared at the floor, not missing the implication that her own reputation did not share such favored status.

Marian laid a hand on her shoulder. "I didn't say that last to shame you. I think you're a brave and fine woman. You must be, for Alex to care so deeply for you."

"Marian, I am most grateful for your assistance, though I admit I am still uneasy."

"Undoubtedly. But you mustn't let anyone else know that. You must, *must,* hold your head high. They will pounce on your fear like starved cats on a mouse if they sense it.

"It would be nice if your mother were also to support you, though, of course, her word carries less weight both as your mother and due to your father's circumstances."

Elizabeth nodded. "I believe she could, at least, be prevailed upon to stand by my side at a ball. She will not wish to offend the duke." She and her mother had spoken little since her return to London, save for the visit with Alex. Their relationship was still strained, though Elizabeth did at least harbor hope that her mother had not been involved in the plot with Harold.

"Then that settles it." Marian smiled. "We shall make your reentry three weeks hence, at the Holbrooks' ball."

"But Alex wishes to be married in three weeks," Elizabeth protested.

"What? Impossible!" Marian exclaimed. "Unless, of

course, it is . . . well, necessary?" Her face flushed at the indelicate question.

"No, not in that way."

"Then you must convince him to wait."

"Convince the Duke of Beaufort he must wait?"

Marian laughed. "Good point. Even a few extra weeks would buy the time you need. Though, the longer the engagement, the better—at least from the ton's perspective."

Elizabeth sighed. As usual, the ton's perspective was not one she shared. But she *did* want to be a wife Alex could be proud of. "I can try."

"My brother will grant you anything you ask," she predicted. "It's settled, then. At the Holbrooks' ball, you will reenter the ton with your head as high as though you had never left.

"My husband can serve as your escort—I'm sure I can convince him—and we'll fashion a way to explain the whole scandal away. It will help that it's only the Little Season, for the crowd will be lighter."

"But what will we *tell* them?"

"About what?" Marian airily waved a hand, as though the gossip Elizabeth needed to face down were trivial.

"Oh, I don't know," Elizabeth said on a choked laugh. "About my relationship with your brother? About my sudden disappearance in the midst of last Season, and now my return? No matter how high I hold my head, people are bound to ask questions."

A discreet knock at the door interrupted them, and Bea poked her head in. "I'm back—mind if I join you?"

Marian bounced up. "Perfect! Please do. You can help us plan."

Bea scooted in and took a seat. "Plan what? I love schemes!"

"Elizabeth and I have just been discussing that she may not have such an easy time upon reentering Society. There has, as you may know, been considerable gossip. We were hoping you could help us form a plan of attack, of sorts."

Beatrice beamed. "There's nothing I'd like better."

Though Elizabeth had dropped the matter of her father's betrayal, it still bothered Alex. Of course, he knew far more about it than she did.

Never in a million years would he have envisioned himself engaged to the scoundrel's daughter, but in truth, his engagement to Elizabeth made him feel as though he'd long been traveling a path off track and had suddenly been set on course. He was happy.

For the first time in months, he had a sense of peace and interest in his own future. He could imagine a son with Elizabeth's vibrant red hair, or a daughter with her dreamy green eyes. He looked forward to escorting Elizabeth publicly, instead of sneaking around. She embraced life fully and wasn't afraid of risks. She made him see things afresh.

Yes, the future was looking up. He just hoped the past could be forgotten.

But before he could forget, he needed to be certain he'd left no loose ends.

A quick private audience with Lady Medford confirmed that lady's desire to avoid further scandal over the deceptive man she'd married.

"Elizabeth still harbors fond memories of her father,

in spite of what she knows," Lady Medford reminded him. "Why rob her of that peace?"

Alex agreed. His second errand was much simpler. An anonymous bank draft of a generous amount, sent to one former coachman, sealed the matter. Fuston was wise enough to know where the money came from, and that it purchased his silence. They'd discussed it before. This was simply a reminder.

With the past put safely behind him, Alex felt lighter as he stopped next at Lady Pullington's house. Inside, he knocked softly on the half-open door to the salon where his fiancée sat talking with his sister and her friend. The butler had offered to announce him, but Alex had waived him off.

One glance at Elizabeth and he wanted her with an intensity that unnerved him.

While on the way back to London, once they'd finally secured a carriage, she'd been too exhausted from her ordeal to engage in any real intimacy.

He'd done little more than hold her while she slept, her peaceful body in stark contrast to his, rigid with unfulfilled desire.

And since their return, she'd been staying at Lady Pullington's town house, where she seemed always to be surrounded by female friends, twittering excitedly about wedding plans.

It was almost enough to make a man run for the hills.

Instead, Alex pushed the salon door wider and entered. All three women stood, interrupting the charming scene.

"Alex," Marian beamed. "We were just discussing how your lovely fiancée ought to reenter Society."

Alex glanced at Elizabeth. She looked doubtful.

Guilt twinged him—this was one more discomfort of
Elizabeth's that could be traced to him. Thank God
that, unlike his other mistakes, the effects of this one
could be undone.

"Perhaps I'd best leave you to plot. You're the
expert on societal strictures," he said to Marian. Alex
had absolute faith his sister would soon have his
fiancée back in the graces of every clucking matron in
the ton—as long as Elizabeth could withstand the excruciating scrutiny she was about to be placed under.

"No, really, we've nearly finished," Lady Pullington
told him. "Lady Grumsby and I were just about to visit
the stationer. Right?"

"Please, call me Marian. And, yes, I believe we've
made our decision—the Holbrooks' ball it shall be.
Chin up, dear Elizabeth."

Marian and Bea exchanged looks, then hastily
exited the room.

"I believe they mean to give us some privacy," Elizabeth observed, a twinkle in her eye.

He crossed the room to her, took both her hands in
his. "Elizabeth, you don't have to do this. Society can
be cruel, and you've been through enough."

The bruise on her jaw was gone now, but the
memory of it—and what she'd told him she'd lived
through these past weeks—was more than enough to
make him want to spare her further pain. "I've plenty
of estates in the country where we can live."

She stepped closer, until she had to tip her head
up to make eye contact. "I want to do this, Alex. You
deserve better than a wife you have to hide in the
country."

He waggled a brow at her. "The better to keep the
other gentlemen away."

She grinned at his teasing tone, then sobered. "I love that you believe in me. But I have to do this for myself, and my sister. To restore my family's reputation—if it can be done."

He knew she was right. And he knew it would be hard. "I'll stand by you no matter what."

"You are an honorable man, my lord," she told him softly.

Alex stared at her for a moment. "No, I'm not."

He'd taken her virginity at a public inn as though she were a common tavern maid, then failed to keep their affair utterly secret. Failed to protect her.

And even if their recent engagement meant those indiscretions could be forgiven, there were other things that could not.

He looked into her luminous green eyes once more, and saw that she didn't believe his response. Her faith in him shook him to the core, warmed the deepest reaches of his blackened soul.

Her lips parted. Alex's body quickened in immediate response.

"Perhaps," she said a little breathlessly, "you could take advantage of this moment as Marian and Bea intended, and make me forget I've got to show my face before dozens of self-righteous Society members who will vie to be the first to give me the cut direct."

"They wouldn't dare."

She arched a brow. "Apparently you do not know women as well as you think, my lord."

He moved closer, folded her into his arms. "I beg you, give me the chance to prove otherwise."

She melted into his embrace. "That's more like it."

God help him, he was going to spend the rest of his life trying to be the man she thought he was—and hoping she never found out otherwise. He crushed his lips to hers.

Alex and Elizabeth decided, upon the recommendations of Beatrice and Marian, to wait until after Elizabeth was back in the good graces of the ton to announce their engagement publicly. This meant Alex's original proclamation—that the wedding would take place in three weeks—had been modified. He'd generously doubled the allowance to six. He couldn't understand why the women had pushed for even longer—but he did understand that it was important to his fiancée.

"Surely," he'd argued, in between highly distracting kisses that sent Elizabeth's head spinning, "your magnificent team of coconspirators will have launched you to the very pinnacle of Society by then."

Elizabeth wasn't so sure. But she, too, was anxious to make her marriage a reality.

According to Marian and Bea, the Holbrooks' upcoming ball was the hurdle Elizabeth must leap if she wanted her reputation back. The annual affair was small, as it was only the Little Season, but influential members of the ton usually attended. If Elizabeth could gain their approval, she would have smooth sailing afterward.

Lady Medford agreed to attend at her daughter's side, in order to show family solidarity and to further dispel rumors. Elizabeth's mother was showing considerably more goodwill now that her daughter was to marry beyond her expectations, though she seemed uncomfortable whenever the duke was actually present. More than once Elizabeth had seen her mother's gaze turn pensive, almost wary, when Alex entered the room. But perhaps it was only a lingering worry the duke would hold Elizabeth's kidnapping against her. The current truce between Elizabeth and her mother had been formed only with the understanding that neither of them would speak the names of any of their male relatives, close or distant.

Preparing for the ball kept Elizabeth's mind from lingering long on such topics, thankfully. Bea and Marian would attend the event as well, and, of course, Alex, though they'd agreed he should not serve as Elizabeth's escort. That duty fell to Brian Grumsby instead, as Marian had offered.

Charity alone was left out. She'd indignantly pointed out she *was* eighteen now. It took a great deal to convince her she'd have an easier time at her first ball if her sister was a duchess and *not* the biggest source of gossip at the affair. She'd reluctantly settled for the role of wedding assistant, which Elizabeth happily bestowed on her.

The short timeframe—the ball, to be followed barely three weeks later by a wedding—sent all the women into a flurry of preparation.

Over the past year, Elizabeth's wardrobe had suffered considerably, first by being modified into mourning clothes, then into governess's attire.

But with a sizeable transfer of funds from Alex and a lot of cajoling, she'd been able to talk a modiste into preparing a ball gown, for a considerable price, at such short notice.

When the night of the ball finally arrived, Elizabeth's nerves intensified. Her stomach writhed like she'd swallowed a snake, and her hands shook at the thought of facing everyone.

She'd committed unforgivable breaches of propriety. No matter what she said, she feared anyone who looked into her eyes would see the truth: she *had* done everything they'd accused her of, including sleeping with the notorious Duke of Beaufort.

Even with the Grumsbys, her mother, and Bea at her side, she stood as good a chance of receiving the cut direct as she did of being welcomed back into Society.

Oh, how she wanted to flee again.

Bea's ladies' maid was in her element, helping both women perfect their look for the ball.

"Oh, stop fussing over me," Bea finally told her, once her hair was finished. "I can do the rest myself. It's Elizabeth who's got to stun everyone tonight."

"An' of course she will, my lady," the maid said, turning her attentions to Elizabeth.

Based on the advice of Marian and Bea, Elizabeth wore a gown of pale, creamy gold silk. It flattered her coloring, but held none of the bold overtones of the sapphire and emerald shades she normally chose.

"You want to appear lovely, but innocent," Marian had said. "No white, for it's not your color, and will only set minds to wondering if you are as virginal as your gown."

"And no crimson, nor anything dark," Bea had chimed, "for though they suit you, such colors would only remind everyone of your supposed passions."

"Perhaps I should select my gown to match the color of the Holbrooks' walls, so that I may blend in?" Elizabeth had quipped, certain she would spend most of the ball wishing she could do exactly that.

But now, as Bea and her maid helped with the

finishing touches, Elizabeth had to admit they'd chosen well.

The pale gold silk was cut in the Grecian style, a long column draping and covering her curves while still clinging to them. The gown fell in folds from one shoulder, leaving the other artfully bare.

"It's enticing because it's unexpected," Bea told her as she adjusted the shoulder to sit just so. "You don't want to show too much décolletage, but to cover up completely would make people think you had something to hide. This will keep them guessing."

"I don't know when I've ever put so much thought into a gown before," Elizabeth told her friend honestly.

"Well, the effect is lovely. And if you will just stop wringing your hands, no one will ever doubt that you belong at the pinnacle of Society."

But Bea looked nearly as worried as Elizabeth felt.

The pinnacle of Society. Elizabeth swallowed. As the duke's fiancée, that's exactly where she would be, ready or not.

She straightened her shoulders and forced her shaking hands to her sides. "Well, then, we'd best be on our way."

They collected Elizabeth's mother, who waited downstairs, then climbed into the readied carriage.

Usually the streets of London were crowded, but tonight, to Elizabeth's dismay, the coach made record time to the ball.

Elizabeth noticed with relief that the Grumsbys' carriage had arrived just in front of theirs. All too soon, their whole group handed their cloaks to the footmen and stood waiting for the butler to announce them.

The butler's voice seemed even louder than normal.

When he reached the end of their party and called out, "Miss Elizabeth Medford," a hush fell over the ballroom.

A scant moment later, the volume escalated as every man and woman present turned to the person next to them and began murmuring in low voices.

Elizabeth's heart sank. But before she could even worry about facing the crowd, she had to pass muster with their hosts. Who, unfortunately, were approaching fast.

Lady Holbrook was a solidly built woman with striking white hair and a no-nonsense expression.

"Grumsby, how pleasant to see you. And Lady Medford, Lady Pullington." She greeted them efficiently before turning to Elizabeth. Her eyes narrowed almost imperceptibly. "Miss Medford. I did not expect to see you."

"'Tis true I am only just returned from the country, my lady," Elizabeth replied softly, just as she'd practiced.

"Whereabouts in the country?" Lord Holbrook boomed, seemingly oblivious to his wife's reasons for prying.

"My cousin has a small property to the north." That much was true. "His wife was lonely and much desired company. And I admit that the flurry of last Season turned out to be a bit much for me, especially after the loss of my father. So I seized the opportunity to remove to the country and visit them for a spell."

"I see." Lady Holbrook's face softened marginally. But she wasn't done. "You know there were rumors after your disappearance."

Elizabeth glanced at the Grumsbys and dipped her head. "So I have learned. Though I believe, as is often the case, the rumors were more interesting than the truth behind my absence." She prayed her hosts couldn't hear the pounding of her heart. Lying always made her uncomfortable.

"I see," Lady Holbrook repeated. "Then you are not involved with Beaufort?"

"Lydia!" Her husband's eyes bulged at the brutally direct question, but she waived him off.

"Involved?" Elizabeth echoed, trying to summon a blush. Not a difficult task when she considered the true extent of their "involvement."

"I did meet him at Lady Grumsby's estate, where I visited after leaving my cousins. The duke was there helping his nephew train a new pup. He's quite an amiable man." She prattled lightly, like a schoolgirl who'd developed a naïve but unrequited crush on the imposing duke. Again, not a difficult act, given that that's exactly what she'd been a couple years ago.

"Amiable?" It was Lady Holbrook's turn to sound the echo.

Marian and her husband stood nearby, smiling benign smiles, as though every word Elizabeth spoke was the full truth.

"Yes, I've always found my brother-in-law personable," Lord Grumsby averred.

Elizabeth's mother and Bea smiled and nodded as well, though the story she'd told did not implicate them in any way.

Behind their little group, additional guests had entered and were waiting to greet their hosts for the evening.

Lord Holbrook stepped forward. "Well, Miss Medford, welcome back to London. I hope your health will be sufficient to see you through the Little Season," he said, taking his wife by the elbow and turning her to their newest guests.

Lady Holbrook looked as though she had more to say, but she dutifully went with her husband.

Elizabeth breathed a sigh of relief.

Slowly, the pounding of her heart subsided. She still had to get through the rest of the ball, but she'd passed the first test.

She scanned the ballroom as her party proceeded into it, but Alex had not yet arrived. She sighed and prepared herself to spend the next several hours either propping up the wall or taking refuge in the retiring room.

As it turned out, things were not quite so bad. The elderly Lady Tanner came over to join their party, followed by some of her friends.

"Young lady," Lady Tanner addressed her gruffly, "I hear you've given your family some trouble over the summer."

Elizabeth flicked a glance at her mother. "I believe we've settled our differences," she said softly.

"Oh?" the older woman said, looking to Lady Medford for confirmation.

For once, Elizabeth's mother did not let her down. "Elizabeth's always been a headstrong girl," she said. "But in the end, she's done well for herself."

Lady Tanner's eyebrows raised. "Shall I take that to mean there is an engagement forthcoming?"

"I'm not at liberty to say," Lady Medford replied with a mysterious smile that clearly implied she was withholding a juicy morsel of information.

"Well, then," older woman said, and gave Elizabeth a gruff nod of approval.

Lady Tanner and her cronies soon fell to gossiping

with Elizabeth's mother. The presence of so many of
Society's matrons near Elizabeth seemed to quell
some of the rumors about her reputation. She was by
no means the most popular female on the dance floor,
but she did not have to sit out every number.

Finally she heard the butler announce Alex's name.
Her heart caught in her throat as she watched her
handsome duke enter the room. His evening wear was
black, almost stark, but for a snowy-white cravat and
shirt. He looked dangerous. Dangerously appealing.

Elizabeth swallowed. Why had she agreed to wait an
extra week for their wedding?

"Are you certain two dances would be too many?"
she asked Bea.

Marian and Bea, her mentors in this wild attempt to
salvage her reputation, had allowed her to reserve
only one dance with Alex.

Bea smiled knowingly. "Two dances would be showing him particular favor."

"But we'll be announcing our engagement soon.
Oughtn't he favor me?"

"Better not fuel the rumors more than necessary,"
Marian advised. "If we're to stick to our story that he
became enamored of you while rusticating in the
country, and that you've been chaperoned at my estate
this whole while, we can't have people asking too
many questions."

Elizabeth nodded, disappointed.

The story they'd concocted was full of holes. Techni-
cally she *had* been with a cousin—Harold—in the country, though she preferred not to remember that. And as
far as having been in residence at the Grumsbys, well,
that had happened, too, though not in the order her
fabricated story alleged.

She hadn't been a *friend* of the Grumsbys until recently. She'd been their *governess*.

She just hoped she'd managed to stay out of sight on the few occasions her employers had had guests, and that no one had recognized her there.

Yes, the story was shaky, but there was simply nothing better they could think of.

When Alex came to claim his one dance, he kept his demeanor businesslike, as though she were merely a friendly acquaintance. Only the intimate gleam in his eyes when he took her hand told her otherwise.

She wanted nothing more than to slide her hands beneath his jacket, beneath the crisp white of his shirt, to hold him close and touch him fully. She'd never been graceful on her feet, and now, merely breathing in his clean masculine scent made her head spin. How on earth was she going to concentrate on *dancing*?

The first strains of music sounded and Alex grimaced. "A reel? You've got to be joking. Couldn't you have at least reserved me a waltz?"

She gave him a helpless smile. "Marian's orders. A waltz is too intimate. She intends to present me as the soul of respectability."

Alex took his position, several feet away. When they next came close, he gave her a wolfish grin. "I hadn't intended on marrying 'the soul of respectability.'"

Elizabeth missed a step. Alex's grin widened.

"Right," she finally managed, several beats later. "Well, had you been privy to our earlier conversation with our hosts, you'd have learned that you, Your Grace, are now the soul of amiability."

His brows lifted. "I've never been described as amiable in my life."

The nature of the reel allowed little further conversation, but as her fiancé returned Elizabeth to her mother, she whispered to him, "I find you quite amiable. At least as amiable as I am respectable."

He laughed, then gave her a sober smile. "I do have the utmost respect for you, Elizabeth. 'Tis only the thought of marrying someone nicknamed 'the soul of respectability' that makes me shudder."

"I shall endeavor not to live up to it."

"And I shall hold you to that promise." He handed her off to her mother. "Soon."

Elizabeth was too warm and tingly to care that the moment he left her, as usual, a throng of admirers surrounded him. It was something she'd have to accept, at least until their engagement was publicly announced.

Marian and Bea gave her matching triumphant smiles.

"I think," said Marian, "you have managed it."

Bea nodded. "I've been eavesdropping," she confided. "There are some who still wonder, but most figure you'd never have dared show your face tonight if half the things that have been said about you were true."

Elizabeth smiled back. If only they all knew.

Chapter Sixteen

Preparing for the Holbrooks' ball was nothing compared to preparing for her wedding.

Elizabeth and Alex announced their engagement a mere week after the ball. Though a few nasty rumors resurfaced, they were mostly bandied about by envious young women, each of whom had hoped to see her own name associated in the papers with that of the Duke of Beaufort.

The young men of Society favored the marriage, for it gave them a better chance at the unmarried females who no longer could hold out hopes of a proposal from Beaufort.

The rest of the ton seemed to accept it as well. People who had shunned Elizabeth weeks before now came to call, offering congratulations and, Elizabeth assumed, hoping to curry enough favor for an invitation to the event.

Bea's house had turned into a veritable blizzard of wedding-related paraphernalia, and Charity was present so often Bea had offered her one of the other guestrooms.

Fortunately, in Elizabeth's new role as fiancée to the Duke of Beaufort, every modiste in town was praying for her patronage. Never mind that the wedding was scheduled for two weeks hence, and most of them would have to delay other clients' requests in order to satisfy hers—they each wanted to be able to claim the distinction of having designed the Duchess of Beaufort's wedding gown.

But a wedding dress was only the beginning. There were any number of garments a duchess would need, she discovered. Walking dresses, riding habits, capes, ball gowns, and theater gowns were the bare essentials . . . not to mention the bonnets, capotes, gloves, and other accoutrements she must have to complete each ensemble.

And *nothing* she already owned would suffice, as Marian, Bea, and Charity unanimously informed her.

They'd packed her governess's gray serge and black mourning gowns and sent them to a mission for the poor. Her chemises, stockings, and undergarments went right with them.

When Elizabeth protested, arguing that her underthings were perfectly serviceable, the two ladies who'd been married laughed aloud.

"I can't claim to have had a passionate marriage, E.," Bea had told her, gaining a curious glance from Marian, "but even I know your duke won't wish to see you in old, plain cotton."

Elizabeth was no innocent, but she'd still been shocked when they'd whisked her to a French modiste and she'd seen what that lady deemed "necessary" to her wardrobe.

Filmy confections of fabric designed to reveal, to entice, more than to cover. Elizabeth had colored until her ears matched her hair, but the proprietress of the shop assured her that her new husband would be pleased.

After spending a truly obscene amount of Alex's money—though Marian promised her there was nothing her brother would rather spend it on—they left the shop.

Marian strode like a woman on a mission toward the nearby hatmaker's, but Beatrice quickly pulled Elizabeth aside. "E., are you absolutely sure this is what you want? I mean, I know how you've always felt about the duke, but marriage, well, it's different."

"Different how?"

"You'll have to answer to him, for one. And," her face grew red, "there's more to the marriage bed than kissing."

Elizabeth smiled, though her heart swelled with pity for Bea and the type of marriage she must have had. "I know, Bea. But"—she lowered her voice further—"I must confess marital relations with Alex don't hold any distaste for me. In fact, they're a reason favoring marriage."

Beatrice's eyes grew round at her friend's tacit admission that the rumors about the affair with the duke were true. "I see," she murmured. "Yes, I suppose with a man like the duke it would be different. I just want to know you're happy, E."

"Very," Elizabeth confirmed. "Now, let's catch up with Marian."

After the hatmaker, it was the glove maker, and then the perfumery, before Elizabeth finally pled exhaustion. Since her friends were drooping as well, they all agreed to rest and regather at Bea's the following day, when Elizabeth was due for a fitting for her wedding gown.

On the way home, Elizabeth's eye kept straying toward the packages containing her new undergarments. What would Alex think? Their intimate encounters before had been rushed, secretive. She'd never deliberately dressed to seduce him.

But across from her, an innocent-looking white box held a gown made entirely of sheer lace, with slits up to her thighs and nothing but a flimsy tie to hold the bodice together.

Yes, he would like that. She remembered the way his eyes darkened before he kissed her, imagined his touch with nothing but the lace separating them . . . for however long the gown stayed on. Elizabeth's fantasies made her shift uncomfortably in her seat, longing for the day when she and Alex would be married and could once again share a bed.

It wasn't a bed—or even an enclosed carriage, which might afford them some privacy—but when Alex offered to take her for a ride in his new curricle the following Tuesday, Elizabeth eagerly accepted. Since returning to London she'd had precious few moments with the man she loved, and most of those few had occurred in settings that hardly even allowed for conversation.

No sooner had they entered the park than a young man in a cheaply made suit ran up.

"I beg your pardon, Your Grace." He doffed his hat and gave an awkward sort of bow. "Miss Medford. I wonder if I might speak with you a moment."

"Who are you?" Alex asked.

The man looked embarrassed. "Tippen's the name, Your Grace. I work for Harrow and Morton, Solicitors."

Elizabeth pitied the man his obvious unease, though at the mention of his occupation, she felt a twinge of unease herself. "And why, Mr. Tippen, would you wish to speak with me?"

"Well, it's only that, er, our firm has business with your late father's estate—sorry for your loss, miss—and, er, we've been having quite a time of it trying to get a firm answer from his solicitors . . ." Tippen trailed off, his face red.

"I'm sorry to hear that," Elizabeth said politely.

Beside her, Alex fingered the reins in obvious impatience.

"Right, well. Miss Medford, I can't quite think of a delicate way to put it, but there's a rather large sum of money involved. And, er, my firm is quite anxious to recover it."

"I'm sure they are." Elizabeth was aware there were probably solicitors, tradesman, and merchants all over town wringing their hands over her father's unpaid debts. But this was the first time one had been bold enough to approach *her*—with the exception of the jeweler who'd made her father's brooch. And in that instance, Elizabeth had gotten involved only after Charity had intercepted the firm's letter. At any rate, she had no intention of getting involved again.

"I fail to see how I can help you," she told the man firmly. "Your inquiries are best directed toward the solicitors of my father's estate. If you are having difficulty gaining a response, perhaps a personal visit would be in order."

"I just thought—" Tippen stammered, face redder than ever.

"I'm sorry, I must be going," she said firmly.

At her words, Alex gave the reins a little slap and the curricle moved off, leaving Tippen standing at the park entrance, hat still in hand.

"I cannot fathom what made him approach you like that."

Elizabeth shrugged. "I'm sure he's only trying to do his job. No doubt he must answer to someone, and I imagine he's not anxious to explain the lack of progress on the Medford account." Her lips twisted in an ironic smile.

"Still. In a public park, when it's obvious to anyone you're on an outing. And in front of your fiancé, no less. A terrible breach of manners. What did he think to gain?"

She glanced away, uncomfortable. So much for the romantic outing she'd hoped for. "I imagine he thought to make you aware—in case you were not already—of my father's problems, perhaps in the hope you would cover his debts."

Alex's face darkened. "Surely you jest. I've already forgiven a lordly sum owed me by the baron. I've no intention, nor any responsibility, to cover his others."

Anxious, Elizabeth placed her hand on his arm. "No, I never meant you *should*. Only that perhaps it is what that man was after."

Alex's features relaxed, slightly. "Truly, Elizabeth. The position your father left you in is untenable. I cannot imagine how such an irresponsible, overreaching man—let alone the rest of your family—raised a daughter like you."

"He wasn't so bad as that."

Alex's look was disbelieving. "How can you defend him?"

Elizabeth sighed. Alex was a wonderful fiancé, but

he clearly did not care for her family. In fact, he had an odd habit of changing the subject whenever she mentioned one of them. *Especially* when she mentioned her father. Whenever he was brought up, Alex's expression immediately became shuttered.

She knew the reason, at least partly. It still hurt to know her father had offered *her* as payment to Alex. But she had other, better, memories as well.

She tipped her head to one side as she attempted to explain. "I know he spent too much on gaming. And I know he and my mother were not always happy with one another. But there was another side to him, as well. A kind, laughing side. And that I cannot forget."

"But if it weren't for his actions, you never would have been placed in the situations you've faced since his death," Alex argued. "Elizabeth, he tried to *sell* you to me."

She nodded. "I know. And I can only hope that, somewhere beneath the depths of his desperation, he did so out of some intuition for how well we'd suit.

"Alex, it may be hard for anyone else to see, but I remember my father as a good man, at least when I was young. When I was twelve, for instance, my mother enrolled me in dancing lessons. She was disappointed in not having a son, and determined her daughter would make an amazing match to compensate for not providing her husband with an heir. I'm afraid I disappointed her further, however. As you may have noticed, I am not particularly graceful."

"I never noticed."

But she could see the twinkle in his eyes.

She swatted him playfully. "Anyhow, the dance lessons were miserable. The instructor berated me, yelling the beats and the steps loudly, as though I were hard of hearing and if he simply raised his voice, I might be able to follow. After each lesson, my mother would chastise me for my lack of improvement.

"But one day, it was my father waiting at the end of the lesson. I was nearly in tears, as we'd been learning the quadrille, and I'd never managed to be in the right place at the right time. Father never said a word about my clumsiness. He only smiled and held my hand, and asked me if I'd like an outing to Vauxhall Gardens. Of course I said yes, and we had the loveliest time. He made me forget all about the horrible dance instructor.

"We listened to the strolling musicians, and he told me he thought it was foolish to dance to music when one might be making it. He knew how I loved to play the violin—even though that, too, was considered ungraceful. I could hear the beats just fine when I played, I just couldn't move my body to them.

"He bought me sweets from the vendors, even though Mother was strict that we not have them. By the end of the day my spirits were restored. Best of all, when we returned home and Mother questioned me about the lesson, Father stepped in and told her I'd done very well. He lied for me."

Elizabeth smiled. "I knew lying was wrong, of course, but for that one day I didn't have to face up to my failures. *That's* the father I wish to remember."

Alex sobered. "I am sorry, Elizabeth. I did not know him that way. I do understand, now, why you defend him. It must have been hard on you to lose him so suddenly. I'm sorry."

She gave him a small smile. "It's not your fault."

He said nothing.

"Besides," she continued brightly, "if he hadn't been

the man he was, faults included, then none of the things that have happened to me would have turned out this way. And, after all, that sequence of events did lead me to you."

"Yes, there is that." But his voice was oddly choked.

Elizabeth frowned. She'd done her best, but despite Alex's acknowledgment that he understood, his mood was still dark. Perhaps in the future, she should simply avoid the topic of the men in her family—provided they had no further encounters with overeager solicitors.

Before she could think of a way to cheer her duke, Elizabeth was distracted by a landau full of brightly attired young ladies, all of whom were waving at her.

Or, rather, she mentally amended as she registered their longing gazes, they were waving at her fiancé.

The vehicle carrying the young women slowed as it drew even with their own. Elizabeth sighed as Alex drew in the reins to their own vehicle. It would have been rude to do anything else, though for a moment she was tempted to reach over and give the reins a brisk slap.

Instead, she resigned herself to postponing her probing of the reasons for Alex's moodiness, then pasted a bright smile on her face for the inevitable round of congratulations—though she suspected these would be grudgingly given—and gossip to follow.

If the number of gifts arriving at the town house was any indication, Elizabeth's reentry into Society had been a success. Day after day, parcels arrived in a steady stream. Some gifts came directly to Bea's house—these were mostly from closer friends. Charity brought others in a daily delivery from the Medford home. Still others, she knew, would go to the home she and Alex would share after they were married.

What had been intended as a small wedding was turning into quite an affair, but Elizabeth had no cause for complaint. She was marrying the man she loved. A man who'd forgiven her lack of dowry and the unattractive traits of her family members, and had even rescued her at her worst moment.

To the rest of Society he might be a ruthless, if wealthy, rake, but to Elizabeth, he was a knight in shining armor.

But even a happy bride can be a nervous one. By the time the wedding date arrived, Elizabeth's nerves had resurfaced in full force.

The church was full to bursting. Carriages clogged the streets outside and last-minute arrivals looked for any vacant inch of pew on which to sit. Elizabeth, Charity, and their uncle stood in a small room near the front of the church, hidden from sight, as they waited for the ceremony to begin.

Anxious, Elizabeth peeked out. There was something unreal about all of this. She watched an usher discreetly escort a turbaned woman to one of the back pews, where she would not block the view of the other guests.

She, Elizabeth Medford, was marrying the Duke of Beaufort. Her family's reputation was ruined. Her personal reputation was ruined. She was penniless. She had red hair.

Somehow, Alex loved her enough to marry her anyway.

Suddenly Elizabeth imagined she heard the voice of Miss Prissom, her childhood governess and a woman fond of pithy sayings, whispering in her ear, "If something seems too good to be true, it usually is."

She shrank back into the waiting room and moved to an alcove near the window. She shook her head to clear it, and blew on her suddenly cold hands to warm them. How many of the hundreds of guests in the pews were whispering to the person next to them, wondering if, after all, there *had* been merit to the scandalous rumors about her and the duke?

She may have been accepted back into Society's good graces, but would they actually accept her as a duchess? What if someone discovered that mere months ago, she'd been employed as a governess? They would laugh at her, or behind her back.

Worse, they would laugh at Alex.

He deserved someone so much better than she. How could she ever be the model of grace and decorum a duchess was supposed to be? Dear Lord, what if she was an embarrassment to her husband?

Her duties began tonight, at the reception following the wedding. Thank goodness the Grumsbys were the official hosts—she'd never been a hostess, or a guest of honor, for that matter, in her life.

Elizabeth took a deep breath and forced her knees to stop quivering. First she had to marry the man. Everything else came after.

From her position near the alcove's window, she saw a carriage arrive bearing the Beaufort crest of arms and felt a momentary rush of relief. Alex was here. He was not going to strand her at the altar. After the constant wedding-related henpecking of her mother, Marian, Beatrice, Charity, and Alex's estimable valet, she'd been half-afraid he might. Instead, he leapt from the carriage and hurried into the church, leaving the driver to maneuver through the hopelessly clogged streets. She peeked out of the room again.

In the pews nearest the altar she could see Marian and Brian Grumsby smiling. Alongside them was an elderly woman who shared Alex's firm jawline. His mother, Elizabeth realized, come away from her sanctuary in Bath for their wedding. And across from the dowager duchess sat Elizabeth's own mother, looking nervous and proud at the same time.

Now, if she could only make it down the aisle without tripping, she'd count the day a success—though the yards of pearl-encrusted silk trailing behind her wouldn't make that easy.

Why, oh, why, hadn't she mentioned to Madame Benoit that she was hopelessly clumsy, and had that lady design a more appropriate gown? Never in her life had she so wished she'd been born with at least a modicum of grace. And, drat it all, her knees had begun quivering again.

Her uncle George stood stiffly at her side. Elizabeth was hardly on speaking terms with him after what had happened with Harold, but she'd had no one else to escort her, and no desire to set tongues wagging yet again by insisting upon walking down the aisle alone.

Charity stood at her other side, looking stunning in an aqua silk gown, her golden tresses piled atop her head. She gave Elizabeth a smile full of hope and excitement, and Elizabeth felt some of her sister's good cheer seep through her own nerves.

The last of the guests were seated. From what seemed like an interminable distance, she saw the vicar nod.

Charity glided forward, a picture of grace and youthful beauty, and took her place near the altar, where she would stand during the ceremony to assist Elizabeth with her gown's long train.

The music changed, signaling her entrance. Last chance.

Elizabeth placed her gloved hand lightly in the crook of her uncle's arm, and moved forward.

Alex stood at the end of the aisle, his expression admiring and approving.

Dear Lord, her soon-to-be-husband was so *handsome*. His smoky dark-velvet jacket was cut to perfection, his formal breeches likewise.

Elizabeth focused on him, willing away the faces of the crowd, each etched with avid curiosity. She lifted her chin. Let them think what they would.

Amazingly, she didn't trip, or faint, and she watched with unreal detachment as her uncle and Alex grimly clasped hands. Her uncle stepped away, and the ceremony began.

Alex took her hand in his. His grasp was warm and strong and oddly comforting as they stood before God and all of Society to take this irrevocable step.

Elizabeth repeated her vows, prayed she'd never have cause to break them. Alex repeated his, his voice low and confident, and again, oddly reassuring.

Together, they turned to face the vicar.

A shiver of excitement slid down Elizabeth's spine. Alex Bainbridge was her husband. Never in a million years had she dared to believe this would happen.

At the vicar's nod, Alex encircled her waist, his strong hands drawing her in for a warm kiss. Elizabeth closed her eyes, breathed in his scent, and kissed him back.

* * *

If the reception didn't end soon, Alex was going to be driven certifiably mad.

He forced a grin as yet another well-wisher clapped him on the shoulder, all the while wondering what the hell had happened to his wife.

His mother had already departed the celebration, but not before making it known—thank God only to him—that she firmly expected him to get to work, immediately, on producing an heir. "It's high time, Alex. Thank heaven you've finally chosen someone."

Alex had merely ground his teeth. He *would* be working on an heir, if his wife didn't keep getting whisked away from him before he could inform her of his desire to leave.

"I intend to make you proud of me," she'd told him earnestly when the reception began.

"You already do," he'd replied automatically, his mind on other, more intimate, matters.

The wedding, in his mind, served one particular purpose: no one could criticize him any longer for sleeping with Elizabeth. And, damn it, that was exactly what he wanted to do.

But it appeared his wife was bound and determined to fulfill the social role of a duchess. It dawned on him that this was important to her—it was what she'd meant about making him proud. He shook his head in disbelief. She was incredibly sweet, but, by God, didn't she realize such trivialities could come later?

He'd spent the past month in a near-constant state of desire, yet had managed only an occasional stolen kiss. Even as a schoolboy he'd never been so smitten, and for so long, with one woman. Yet, for someone whose reputation had been ruined, Elizabeth's family and friends had guarded her like hawks.

Alex tossed back the rest of his champagne, holding his frustration in check. Those same women had managed to resurrect Elizabeth into Society's good graces, a fact for which he was thankful.

Or, rather, he *would* be thankful, after more important matters were addressed.

Finally he spotted Elizabeth surrounded by another throng of guests, many of whom were heavily bejeweled females of advanced years. He wisely decided to wait just a bit longer—there would be no extracting her from *that* group.

"Growing weary of the celebration yet?"

Alex glanced over to find Brian Grumsby giving him a sympathetic grin. "Bloody hell."

Grumsby laughed. "No one would think twice if you and Elizabeth were to leave. In fact, I daresay most everyone's wondering when you will."

"We would," Alex growled, "if my lovely wife would so much as glance my way."

"Ah. Perhaps she's nervous. It's not at all uncommon, man, for a woman to be a bit jittery on her wedding night."

"I'll keep that in mind," Alex said dryly. What had this night come to, that *Grumsby* was offering him advice on the opposite gender?

Elizabeth was a passionate woman. Even if her new role as duchess unnerved her a bit, he knew *that* aspect of it didn't trouble her. Was it possible she was simply not as anxious as he? Or that she was truly so caught up in the gaiety she hadn't realized the time had long passed for them to leave?

Grumsby looked as if he had more to say, but just then Elizabeth finally did look up and meet Alex's eye, then nodded slightly and gazed toward the exit. Relief flooded him, and Alex left his brother-in-law in mid-sentence.

He strode quickly to her, clasped her hand in his, and without further ado, escorted her from the party amidst loud cheers from the many guests.

Ignoring them, Alex hurried her along the hall that led to the private family rooms.

"You are a vision," he told her, meaning every word. Her gown was a work of art, her hair dressed exquisitely. "Have I told you that tonight?"

Of course, in about ten minutes, perhaps five, he intended to see that gown in a heap on the floor and her hairpins strewn next to it.

"Perhaps once, my lord," she teased breathlessly, half-running to keep up with him.

He slowed his pace. Barely.

"It was a lovely party," she told him.

"Yes. Lovely."

"You seem in an awful hurry to leave it."

He stopped, faced her. "God's teeth, Elizabeth, can you not discern why?" He snatched her into his arms, kissing her in a manner designed to erase any possible doubt. Her hair and skin smelled of roses, and she tasted of fine champagne.

He was drowning. He'd never needed anyone like this before.

When he finally released her, her face was flushed, her eyes wide.

Grumsby's words came back to him. "You're not nervous, are you?" Alex asked curiously.

"Of course not." But she hesitated. No more than a fraction of a second, but it was there.

"Dearest, there's nothing to be nervous about. We—" He stopped just short of saying *we've done this before.*

Somehow it didn't seem right to remind her that their wedding night had been precipitated—though that didn't bother him in the least. He'd assumed that would actually make their lovemaking easier to enjoy.

Elizabeth *was* nervous. Oh, she wanted Alex to make love to her. For weeks her body had craved his touch. But mixed with her desire was the fear she would never measure up as wife to the Duke of Beaufort. At the reception, she'd been shocked by the sudden and complete transformation in how Society treated her.

She'd known she was marrying a duke. She'd just never managed to see herself as a duchess.

But now, people who'd never before spoken to her bowed and scraped and begged her opinion on even the slightest of matters. She was starting to understand what Alex had experienced his entire life. Not having been born to it, she was unnerved.

This was not the time to think about her new position, however, since Alex was tugging her along the hall again, and she was quite certain he had no intention of calmly discussing their roles in Society. Perhaps if he kissed her again, she, too, would forget such matters. Her heart lighter with the anticipation of that kiss, she smiled.

Finally they reached the wide double doors that led to the master chamber.

Emma, her longtime maid, had happily agreed to serve in the Duke of Beaufort's household, once she'd learned of Elizabeth's engagement. Now she and Hanson, Alex's valet, stood like sentinels waiting for them.

"Here, Your Grace." The moment they passed through the doors, Hanson made a move to help Alex with his formal coat.

Elizabeth almost giggled as her husband let out an audible growl. Hanson took a nervous step backward.

"I believe we'll be able to manage without assistance this evening," Elizabeth said softly.

"All those hooks," Emma murmured, eyeing her wedding dress.

Alex growled again, though this time Elizabeth was able to distinguish the words "leave us" at the end.

Taking the cue, Hanson and Emma disappeared, bowing and curtsying as they beat a hasty retreat, though Elizabeth saw Hanson cast one mournful glance back at his master's finery. No doubt he didn't trust Alex to care for it properly.

Probably for good reason.

Her lips quirked and she found herself, for the first time in this stressful day, grinning.

"What's so funny?" Alex asked.

She shook her head. "Poor Hanson. He won't be able to sleep tonight for worrying over your clothing."

Alex grinned, too. "Come here, wife."

"Are you sure you don't want me to change? Madame Benoit designed a nightrail especially for—" She bit her lip. "I mean, shouldn't a duchess be more . . ."

Alex stared at his babbling wife. She was still nervous. He closed the distance between them and placed his lips on hers, cutting off further clothing-related protests.

He kissed her softly, brushing his lips back and forth, and felt the rigidity leave her body as she melted, leaned in for more.

God, it was going to kill him to take this slowly. But she deserved to be savored.

He continued kissing her, working at the many hooks on her gown. His fingers fumbled.

"There are a great many of them," she apologized. "Should I—"

"Hush. The gown is perfect. *You* are perfect."

"Oh, Alex." She sighed. "I'm so very far from perfect. I don't know if I can ever be a proper duchess."

"I don't want a proper duchess," he told her, fighting the urge to smile now that he understood what troubled her. He cupped her chin, held her gaze. "I never have. And you, Elizabeth, are indeed perfect—for me."

"In that case," she managed, and he caught the glint of tears in her eyes as she dipped her head to kiss his palm.

His own throat felt oddly tight, choked with emotion. Alex returned his attention to the many hooks of her gown, moving around back of her where he could concentrate on the task.

One by one he undid the hooks, kissing each new place he uncovered. He kissed her neck, her shoulder blades. She arched her neck, leaned toward his touch. Inch by inch, the bodice loosened, until it came free entirely. The many layers of skirts were a much easier matter—a few ties to undo and they softly slid to the floor, leaving Elizabeth clad only in a thin silk chemise.

"Perfect," Alex repeated. He slid his hands up her sides, over her breasts, and clasped her to him, his growing erection pressing into her backside.

She gave a little moan at the erotic contact.

God, he ached to be inside her.

Instead, he forced himself to concentrate next on the pins securing her hair. One by one they followed her garments to the ground, until her hair tumbled en masse to her shoulders and down her back.

He picked up one wavy lock and kissed it, drawing a giggle from her.

"It's red," she informed him.

"It's *perfect*," he repeated. Finally he moved back in front of her, pulling her in for a kiss. Her tongue found his, and this time he was the one who groaned. Her breasts, her hips, pressed against him as she instinctively sought more.

He tore his mouth away and shucked his own garments, removing them with considerably less finesse than he'd spent on hers.

He heard her quick intake of breath as his breeches hit the floor. He hardened further. A flick at the straps on her shoulders and she, too, stood nude.

He scooped her up and carried her the few feet to the large bed, then laid her carefully down. "I want to feast on you."

"Mmmmm." Her eyes clouded with passion.

He kissed her jaw, her neck, then ducked lower, drawing one dusky nipple into his mouth. He tugged gently and felt her fingers dig into his back in an unspoken plea for more.

He'd give it to her. He'd give her everything she wanted and more.

But maybe not just this minute. Because she was making little wiggling, seeking motions with her hips, and his body was screaming with the need to take her. He'd waited more than a month. He couldn't wait any longer.

He nudged her legs apart. Instinct took over. He probed her entrance, his swollen shaft throbbing when he found her slick and ready.

He drove in, one swift thrust that brought them together fully.

"Alex," she cried, arching her back.

He withdrew, then surged forward again, finding the rhythm they both sought.

"Open your eyes, Elizabeth," he whispered hoarsely.

She did, and the passion, the love he found there, nearly unmanned him. He pushed them both toward the brink, caressing her breasts, her hair, touching, touching everywhere.

She moved beneath him, matching her own movements to his. God, yes. How had he not known from the beginning that she was his match in every way?

He thrust again, the last vestiges of control slipping as she urged him on. He was going to come, any second, and he wanted her there with him. She was close, he could feel it. He pressed his thumb to the bead of her sex and felt her shatter around him. With his other hand he clasped hers, held her tight, as with one final thrust he roared and poured himself, everything, into her.

He collapsed and rolled to the side, pulling her with him, still intimately joined. Still holding her hand. He'd never before held the hand of a woman as he made love to her. He wasn't going to question the implications of that now. Instead he tucked her head under his chin, holding her, protecting her, until he caught his breath.

He felt her smile against his chest. "That was quite impressive, my husband."

Minx.

"Wife," he growled laughingly into her hair, "we've only just begun."

Chapter Seventeen

Married life was perfect. In Elizabeth, Alex had found a mate who loved him for more than his rank, and who matched his spirit and adventurousness in every way. If anything, she was *too* adventurous—but there was nothing he'd rather do than spend the rest of his life protecting her and their inevitably mischievous children.

There was just one thing he had to do first. A matter left from the last of her adventures, which had nearly shattered her.

"I want him destroyed," Alex commanded.

The solicitor looked up. "Your Grace?"

"By the time you're finished, Wetherby won't have a shilling to his name," Alex instructed.

No man got away with the abuse Harold Wetherby had inflicted on Elizabeth. He'd told her he was meeting an investing partner today, but the truth was, he'd come to ensure Wetherby would never bother her—or anyone else—again.

The temptation to do the man physical harm gnawed at him, but he'd settled for a gentleman's revenge, one he knew would hurt Wetherby's obnoxious pride far more than would a physical beating.

"I see, sir," the solicitor said.

"I knew you would, Browne." It was one of the reasons he kept the solicitor on retainer—Browne had the ability to ferret out financial details on almost any situation about which the duke inquired.

"So far, I've determined he holds shares in several mines to the north, as well as some sort of textiles factory—men's garments, I believe—near Yorkshire. The working conditions at each are abominable."

"Undoubtedly." Alex wondered how many orphans, widows, and poor slaved daily to earn Harold's living. It was something he'd never have considered before, but seeing Elizabeth as a governess had given him new understanding of the precariousness of being an unwed, moneyless female. "Can you destroy Wetherby without putting his workers out on the streets?"

Browne appeared dumbfounded. "Your Grace?"

Alex waved a hand. "I know, I know, I've gone soft. But Wetherby is the one I want to suffer, not those who are already his victims."

Browne nodded. "It can be done, Your Grace, with a bit more finesse. Perhaps if you were involved, indirectly of course, in some rival ventures . . ."

"You take care of the details. I don't care how," Alex said. "But Browne? Work quickly."

Two weeks after her wedding, Elizabeth sat in Alex's study. He'd gone to meet one of his investing partners, promising to return soon. She hummed happily as she wrote out thank-you notes for a lovely silver tea service, a handsome wooden trunk, and a set of rather ugly candlesticks. Tomorrow, she and Alex would journey to Montgrave, Alex's country seat, where they would winter. She gave an impatient sigh. London was fine, but she eagerly anticipated spending the cold months snug at her husband's side, without the distractions of city life.

Hearing a scratching noise behind her, she turned to find the butler.

"Your Grace, there is a gentleman at the door to see you." His lips pursed at the word "gentleman." The servant cleared his throat. "I told him to go around back, as that appeared to be his proper place, but he insisted it was imperative he speak with you. He claims he used to work for your father."

Elizabeth stood, flexing her hands to ease the cramps in her fingers. "It's all right. I'll come see."

The butler looked slightly mollified that at least he wasn't being asked to show the unexpected visitor into the study. Elizabeth followed him into the hall.

The man hovering near the door wore simple, gray country clothes—no longer the livery of a noble house—but Elizabeth recognized her former coachman immediately.

"Fuston! Where have you been these many months?"

He shook his head. He looked ten years older.

"Whatever is the matter?"

"Miss Medford—that is, Your Grace, I had to come tell you someth—" Fuston stopped, twisting his hat in his hands. "But no, I shouldn't be here." Beads of sweat appeared on the man's forehead. "I'm not allowed . . ."

Elizabeth frowned. Something was very wrong here.

"What do you mean, you're 'not allowed'?" As far as

she knew, English citizens were still free to roam the country at will, including visits to former employers and their families or friends. It might not be common, but it was *allowed*.

"His Grace . . ." the beleaguered man whispered.

Worry set in, though she attempted to mentally thrust it aside. She and Alex had had their share of estrangements, certainly, but now they had finally worked everything out. She was a blissfully married woman.

But the fact that Fuston was here, now, after having gone missing for months . . . and he was obviously upset. She smoothed her skirts and glanced around, but the other servants had disappeared. They were alone.

"Your Grace, he's not . . . you shouldn't . . ." Fuston glanced at the door as though second-guessing his decision to visit her.

"Fuston, relax. Tell me what you came to say. It will ease your conscience, and then you can go back to wherever you've been staying." Surely, whatever the matter was, it couldn't be *that* bad. She hoped.

He nodded shakily, then beckoned her closer. Elizabeth obligingly leaned in.

"Your father, miss. His death was . . . 'tweren't an accident."

Elizabeth stepped back, unable to comprehend. Pressure built inside her temples and the bodice of her gown suddenly felt too tight, constricting her breath.

She shook her head. "No, it was a carriage accident. You said so yourself. And we saw the carriage. 'Twas utterly wrecked."

Fuston gulped and nodded. "Aye. I overturned that

carriage on purpose—at the Duke of Beaufort's direction. But your father was dead before the carriage ever left the road."

Elizabeth felt for the wall behind her, seeking balance in a world that suddenly seemed unsteady.

"I don't understand. You must be mistaken." Perhaps the poor man had gone mad. Or had forgotten himself with drink.

But he did not smell of alcohol, and, though he was obviously nervous, there were no telltale signs to prove he'd lost his sanity.

"Nay, miss. No mistake. Your father was shot."

"Shot?"

"Aye. I was sworn to secrecy. Paid to disappear from London. But when news of your wedding reached the country . . . Beaufort . . ."

"What has my husband to do with this?"

"'Twas him that done it."

Elizabeth finally found the wall behind her and pressed her palms against it. "You must be mistaken," she repeated.

Fuston shook his head, beads of nervous perspiration forming above his brow. "I'm truly sorry, Your Grace. But you see, now, why I had to tell you. Only I wasn't in time. We don't get the papers, or any news, in a timely fashion . . ."

She waived that aside. "What happened . . . to my father?" she breathed, unable to find her normal voice.

"I don't know the whole of it. Had me drive him to Beaufort's that night, did the baron, but what went on inside I can't say. 'Cept that, there was some loud voices, like they was arguin', and then a door slammed. Then more voices. They were outside, on the other side of the estate. I stayed by the carriage, an' I couldn't hear all of what they were sayin', but I knew the voices.

"Then a shot. A man, one of Beaufort's, I b'lieve, came up to the carriage jus' as I was gettin' down. Said the baron was dead, and the duke would pay me handsome if'n I could make it look as though 'twere a carriage accident what killed him."

"The body . . ." Elizabeth whispered.

Fuston bobbed his head earnestly. "The casket was closed for the funeral, nay?"

"I thought that was because he'd been mangled in the accident." It felt odd to be discussing her father's remains in this way. "Does my mother know?"

"I couldn't say. Lowdry, the old butler for yer family, he was the one what talked to her. But I doubt he told her. After all, we was supposed to cover it up for Beaufort, and yer poor mother might rest easier simply thinkin' it was an accident."

The coachman's story was too awful, too absurd, to be believed. "Did anyone actually see Alex—I mean, His Grace—that evening?" she asked, seeking to exonerate the man she loved.

"Not me. But his voice was one o' the ones arguin', an' 'twas him what paid me to leave after the matter was settled."

Fuston held up pleading hands. "Miss Medford, don't you see? You've married the man what murdered your father."

Somehow, Elizabeth had seen Fuston to the door. He'd been only too anxious to leave. Now she sat at the small writing desk, elbows propped on its surface, her head in her hands, as she stared at the letter she couldn't write. Unfinished thank-you notes for wedding gifts surrounded her. How strange they suddenly seemed.

Her first instinct had been to run. But she'd already done that too many times. For the past few months, she'd been running from her past. She was tired.

Besides, there was nowhere left to go.

She wished devoutly she could dismiss Fuston's tale as the ravings of a lunatic. Except the placid coachman had never shown signs of madness in all the years she'd known him. Whatever had happened the night her father died, Fuston's fear had been real. And there was no reason for Alex to pay off the coachman if he had nothing to hide.

None of this made sense. She *loved* Alex. He was her husband. She could even be carrying his child.

But how could the man she loved, the man she'd dreamed of for so long, be the one who deprived her of the only other man she'd ever loved?

Her father had been no saint, as she now knew, but he'd still been her father. Had Alex killed him?

She recalled their recent wedding, how he'd proudly taken her hand, repeated his vows. Surely a man with a murderous deed to his name could not stand in church with such confidence, such ease. Not unless his soul was blackened beyond caring.

She needed advice. But there was no one to ask. What was the responsible thing to do? Confront her husband?

Dear God. She wasn't afraid of him, exactly—he had no reason to harm her. But if Fuston's tale wasn't true, she would wound her husband's honor, his character, by even asking. He didn't deserve that. Unless, of course, it *was* true.

She laid her pounding head on the desk.

If she confronted Alex, she'd reveal Fuston's involvement, and perhaps put the coachman in danger. She couldn't do that.

Nor could she simply dismiss the incident as though it had never happened.

Hence the letter. Though what it would say, she had no idea. Raising her head, she twirled the quill absentmindedly between her fingers, then crumpled another sheet of paper.

They were supposed to attend a poetry reading tonight—another performance by the estimable Miss Lambert, Alex's crow-voiced cousin. She and Alex had jokingly agreed they could bear it together. Now she couldn't fathom making it through the evening.

Hastily Elizabeth scrawled a note claiming she suffered from a headache and pleading to be excused from the evening's entertainment, then found a footman to deliver it to the duke.

The note didn't address her most pressing problem, but it would buy her some time.

The claim of a headache was no lie. Her temples throbbed and the pressure on her skull was as if someone held her head in a vise. Wearily, she climbed the stairs and sought her bed. *Their* bed. She stared at the handsomely carved posts, the fine linens covering the mattress. He'd touched her here, caressed her with infinite tenderness. The image of his body rising over hers, his eyes full of heat and love, flashed through her mind as her heart protested her disloyal doubts.

Wearily, she climbed in and pulled the covers over her head, seeking oblivion.

She hadn't expected to actually sleep, but when Elizabeth opened her eyes again, dusk had fallen over

London. The throbbing of her head had receded some-what. She stood and went to the window. Outside, a car-riage rolled slowly by, and windows of other houses glowed softly where lamps were lit. Everything was normal.

Except for her.

She couldn't hide in her room forever.

Elizabeth forced herself to recall the night of her father's death, the scene she'd observed between Fuston and the butler while she'd hid in a dark corner of the hall. For months the scene had replayed itself in her dreams, but every time she awoke, she'd tried to put it behind her.

The things Fuston had said then—things she'd ig-nored in the shock of losing her father—came back to her now. The coachman had been terrified. She'd always thought it was because he felt responsible for the accident.

But if there'd been no accident, perhaps his true terror had been at being an unwilling accessory to murder. It made a certain, sick sense.

Except that it went against the one thing she *knew*.

Alex was a good man. An honorable man.

Her father, on the other hand, was a scoundrel who'd gambled beyond his means and then offered up his oldest daughter as payment for debts he couldn't cover. In truth, it was only because of her hus-band's honor that she hadn't been sold into that un-savory deal.

Elizabeth slowly drew the curtains, reminding herself of the many reasons she believed in Alex Bainbridge. She was not blind to his faults—at least not anymore. His rep-utation among the ton pegged him as a ruthless man—

in business, gaming, and nearly every other pursuit including women. It was a reputation not undeserved.

But in spite of that, Elizabeth *couldn't* believe him capable of cold-hearted murder. She knew Alex better than did anyone in the ton. As much as he presented that ruthless, cynical image to the rest of the world, she'd seen beneath it. She'd seen the way his niece and nephew lit up at the sight of him, and the way he responded to them with ease. Children were more astute judges of character, in Elizabeth's opinion, than many adults.

More importantly, she knew how he'd treated *her*. When her own family had failed her, he'd searched the countryside and rescued her from Harold. He'd offered her his name, his love, his body. Perhaps not in that order, but she'd been willing enough in their earlier indiscretions.

The point was, Alex was a good man.

She owed it to him not to destroy their trust, their relationship, based solely on the words of a former coachman who'd even admitted he hadn't *seen* exactly what happened the night of her father's death.

But she owed it to her father as well not to let his death go unexamined, if in fact he did not die in a carriage accident as she'd originally been told.

And so she came to a decision that did not make her proud, or even entirely comfortable.

She would not doubt or dishonor her husband with an open confrontation. No. She would prove Fuston wrong. And in order to do it, she would investigate on her own.

As planned, Alex and Elizabeth removed to the country at the end of October, having attended as many social events as they both could stand before seeking time for themselves. The whirlwind of activities had prevented Elizabeth from lingering on the terrible accusation Fuston had made against her new husband. But now, with the quieter months looming ahead, her mind turned increasingly toward her worries.

Montgrave, the seat of Alex's dukedom, was a vast, sprawling estate. The main house had been built in the 1600s, then updated by each duke in the line of succession, resulting in a stately mix of history and modern convenience.

Elizabeth loved it at first sight. At the same time, it overwhelmed her, adding to the maelstrom of doubts and insecurity that already plagued her. Was she an adequate duchess? Did her husband hold terrible secrets? And where did she begin, if she truly wanted an answer to that last question?

On the third day after they arrived, she'd sent a note inviting her sister to visit. She and Alex were supposed to be honeymooning, but the huge country house felt intimidating and empty at times—especially whenever her husband was engaged in the many matters of business that so absorbed him. She didn't think he'd begrudge her a family visit. Of course, she hadn't expected Charity to arrive quite so soon.

But Charity, anxious to be away from their mother and Uncle George, had readily accepted the invitation and arrived four days later—before Elizabeth had had time to investigate their father's death and put those doubts to rest. With her sister present, Elizabeth forced herself to put the Fuston matter out of her mind—for now.

"It is lovely to finally be away from town," Elizabeth confided to Charity on the seventh day of her sister's visit.

They were comfortably ensconced in the music room. Outside, a cool fall rain fell, making their tray of hot cider and scones especially appealing.

"I vow," Elizabeth continued, "if I'd attended one more function and seen one more matron of Society eyeing my middle, trying to determine if Alex had been forced into marrying me, well, I believe I'd have been provoked to violence."

Charity's eyes widened at Elizabeth's mention of such an indelicate topic. "Thank you for going to so many functions at all, E.," she replied. "I know it was, at least partly, for me that you bothered."

It was true. Charity could finally make her bow next spring, and Elizabeth wanted her to have every opportunity. And that meant making sure Alex retained his position at the pinnacle of Society—and joining him there, keeping her head high and outlasting the rumors that kept popping up.

Her own actions had sparked those rumors, Elizabeth had often reminded herself as she sat through yet another tea, and it would have to be her actions to repair the damage.

Elizabeth smiled warmly at Charity. "You deserve it, since I very nearly ruined your chances for any Season at all."

"No, father nearly ruined my chances for that, not you." Charity tugged at a lock of hair. Elizabeth knew it still made her sister uncomfortable to speak ill of their father.

"Well, you're the only loyal family member I've got, and I'm not about to forget it," Elizabeth declared. "I'm so pleased you've decided to stay with us for a while."

She helped herself to another scone from the tray they were sharing and gazed out the wide expanse of mullioned windows. The rolling grounds of the estate, though exquisitely tended, were turning brown with the onset of winter.

"It's lovely here," Charity said, dragging Elizabeth from her reverie. "But I've been corresponding with Mother and your friend Lady Pullington, and they tell me if I'm to order a full wardrobe to be ready in time for next Season, I'd best start planning soon. So I think I shall return to London soon."

"Truly? Must you?"

If Charity left, so did her excuse for not pursuing the investigation of their father's death. At the heart of the matter was the fact that Elizabeth was loathe to cast shadows of doubt across her new marriage. She was determined to prove Fuston wrong. But didn't the fact that she felt the need to do so prove she thought there *was* a possibility of truth to the tale?

But her father was, well, her *father*. And Elizabeth was running out of excuses.

Charity gave her a sheepish grin. "E., you and the duke are newlyweds, after all. Surely you don't want your little sister underfoot all the time."

"I never think of you as underfoot," Elizabeth replied loyally.

"Nonetheless, I believe Lady Pullington and Mother have the right of it, in this case. And I do look forward to selecting gowns, and ribbons, and such. It's been so long since we could do such things without worry over the cost, and truthfully I was too young to care a great deal back when we could before. Your duke has been more than generous to us, E."

"I know," Elizabeth said softly. "Alex is a good man."
Which made what she had to do that much harder.

A Bow Street Runner she was not. In fact, Elizabeth
reflected glumly, her skills as an investigator were proving woefully inadequate.

True to her word, and to the disappointment of her
sister, Charity had packed up and returned to London
two weeks ago. And so Elizabeth ground her teeth and
started asking questions . . . phrased as delicately as
possible, so as not to start the staff talking.

She had to proceed slowly. If she ran about asking
questions of all the servants at once, they'd surely
think her daft, and likely report her behavior back to
Alex. So she'd contrived any number of excuses to
seek out the various members of the staff, one by one,
and pose casual questions.

But she'd underestimated the enormity of her task.

Her father's death had occurred in late October, a
year past. Fuston had said he'd taken the Baron Medford to the Beaufort estate, not to Alex's London
house.

Though the Medfords had wintered in London that
year—her mother loathe to leave the entertainments
the city offered—Montgrave was not all that far away.
And extended house parties were often held at the
country home of the host. It stood to reason her father
had indeed come *here*.

But finding anyone who recalled that fated evening
proved nearly impossible.

The butler, when asked if Alex entertained often at
Montgrave in the winter, had stiffly informed her that,
as he'd only come into the duke's employ last May, he

could not speak with authority on the duke's habit, or any lack thereof, of entertaining during the winter months.

The housekeeper, when asked when the guest wing had last been used, said she didn't know, though she hastily assured Elizabeth the furniture and linens were carefully stored, and the rooms could be readied if the duchess wished them so.

The gardener, when asked Alex's favorite places to play outdoors as a child, had informed her he'd not known the duke as a child.

The only staff member she hadn't yet managed to question was Alex's personal valet, Hanson. The man kept to himself and was as tight-lipped as a nun in a room full of prostitutes. She suspected he'd been in Alex's service for years, and held more insight than did any of the other servants, but she never saw him outside her husband's presence.

Finally, Betsy, one of the lower kitchen maids, provided some insight as to why no one seemed to know a thing about their master.

"I'm sorry, Your Grace," Betsy said when Elizabeth asked if she recalled a friendship between the duke and the Baron Medford. "I 'uz on'y just hired on here in August." She loaded several loaves of bread into a large basket and folded a cloth around them, then shifted the basket onto her hip.

"Are many on the staff new, then?" Elizabeth asked.

"Indeed, my lady. Most of us just come on in these last few months."

"Have you any idea why? Was there a problem with the old staff?"

Betsy shrugged. "Couldn't say. His Grace didn't mention none, but per'aps he were cleanin' house,

as it was. Sometimes the nobility'll do that. Start fresh
so there's no lingerin' 'urt feelins' or anything."

"I see." But she didn't. "Thank you, Betsy."

Apparently, Alex had replaced the majority of his
servants since the previous fall. But *why?* Had her
father's death aught to do with his decision? Or had
he merely been dissatisfied with the performance of
the old group of servants and decided to replace them
all at once?

It seemed an odd decision, despite Betsy's reassur-
ance that sometimes the nobility "cleaned house"
that way.

Betsy shifted awkwardly, then nodded at her basket.
"I've got to carry this bread into town for Mrs. Culpepper. 'Er husband's been laid up with an injured foot,
and with 'im out of work, they could use a little extra.
The housekeeper says we've plenty."

"That's very kind of you. Please convey to Mrs.
Culpepper and her husband my hope that he soon
recovers."

Betsy curtsied awkwardly and went about her
errand, leaving Elizabeth to wonder what had caused
the duke to suddenly replace all his staff only months
after the death of her father.

She sighed. Alex was an attentive and loving husband. It was so tempting to simply forget this whole
matter.

But she'd *loved* her father. He'd always accepted her
the way she was—clumsiness, strong-willed nature, red
hair, and all. He'd held a lot of secrets, some dishonor-
able, behind his laughing, easygoing nature. Elizabeth
could accept that she hadn't known him fully, and that
his obsession with gaming had cost her family dearly.
She also knew that in spite of all he'd done wrong,

there was a part of her that would always care for him, and that part had a need to lay him to rest fully.

She had to try harder. If no one knew anything about her husband, then perhaps it was time she learned more about her father.

Chapter Eighteen

Alex glanced at Elizabeth out of the corner of his eye. She was perched on the corner of his desk, seemingly lost in a daydream. He was reviewing the financial sheets of his latest investment, an Indian factory that produced finely embroidered silks. Owning the factory would cut out the need for a foreign buyer, ensuring he was never again the recipient of a substandard shipment such as the corrupted Marks had tried to pass off on him earlier that year.

Having dallied with the fairer sex for years, Alex was well aware of their passion for finery, particularly finery not readily available to their female competition. He had every belief this factory's fabrics would fit the bill and turn a nice profit for him when sold through select milliners and modistes. As soon as the first shipment arrived, he planned to present Elizabeth with scarves and a gown to complement her vivid coloring. When London's ladies saw his lovely duchess, the race to copy the new trend would be on.

He jotted a figure, raw material costs, in his ledger.

Elizabeth shifted slightly. A light waft of lavender reached him.

He shook his head. Was that number correct? With his tempting young wife hovering beside him—fresh from a lavender-scented bath, no less—it was difficult to concentrate. Not that he was complaining. Finally he pushed aside the papers.

"The morning grows late. Would you care to luncheon with me, today, my lady?"

Alex flashed Elizabeth his most wicked grin. "Although it's too cold for a picnic, I've asked the staff to prepare one anyway. I thought we might enjoy it by the fire." He nodded meaningfully at the large hearth and the luxuriously thick rug laid before it.

He saw her eyes widen as she took his meaning. Her lips parted and her tongue flicked out to touch her bottom lip ever so briefly. Alex's blood heated.

But to his surprise, Elizabeth didn't return his grin. Instead she seemed to shake herself. "I, er, can't," she said, looking away. She ducked her head. "I've promised Mrs. Culpepper a visit."

"Surely you could be late." He traced a finger down the line of her throat, her bodice, and saw her shiver.

"Um. Well." She leaned into his touch, then suddenly straightened. "It's just, I did . . . rather . . . promise."

"Who is this Mrs. Culpepper? I don't think I like her."

She batted him playfully. "You oughtn't say such uncharitable things. She's one of the villagers. Her husband's been laid up, injured, for weeks, and they've a brood of five, and I thought the poor woman could use a bit of respite and some cheering up."

Alex's heart softened fractionally. He couldn't fault Elizabeth her kindness or charity, but damned if he wasn't getting tired of things getting in the way of the seductions he'd imagined would fill his newlywed hours.

Having Charity around had been trial enough. Cheerful though she was, the presence of a sister-in-law tended to stifle a man's plans for impromptu liaisons. Of course, knowing what life had been like for Elizabeth with her mother and her uncle George, he could hardly fault her for offering her sister the chance to escape the same.

Now that Charity was gone, though, he'd looked forward to having Elizabeth to himself. Wasn't that what the honeymoon period was for?

Certainly not for traipsing about to every function put on by the ton, though they'd done that, too.

And aiding the villagers was all well and good, but there would be plenty of time for that later.

Apparently his wife thought otherwise.

Elizabeth ducked her head again. "I shall return as quickly as possible. Perhaps we might have tea?"

He sighed dramatically, hoping to tease her out of her do-gooder ways. "I suppose we might. It doesn't have quite the appeal of a fireside picnic, but if that is all the time you can spare . . ."

"Oh, hush," she said and leaned forward to kiss him full on the lips.

He kissed her hungrily, felt her lips give beneath his, and dipped his tongue in to taste her, stroke her. Selfish though it was, he hoped every minute she spent at the Culpeppers' was filled with regret for what she *could* be doing here with him.

Finally Elizabeth pulled back. "I'm sorry, Alex. I shall make it up to you."

"I fully intend to hold you to that promise," he told

her as she gathered her skirts, scooted off his desk, and retreated from the room.

Damn. He leaned his head against the back of his chair. Was it possible Elizabeth didn't know why newly married couples kept to themselves?

He supposed not all of them did. Plenty of ton marriages were made without any strong feelings on the part of the participants. He'd avoided such a union for years. But he'd thought what he and Elizabeth shared was different.

Was it possible she didn't share his near-constant state of desire? No, it was there in her eyes when he touched her. He *knew* she did. So, why was she so difficult to pin down lately?

Elizabeth did visit the Culpeppers. She just didn't stay long. Since her husband's past remained a troubling mystery, she'd decided to approach her investigation by examining the last months of her father's life. To that end, she left the Culpepper home within minutes of delivering a small parcel of preserves and cheese.

She went next to the public room at the village inn, where she'd arranged to meet with the solicitor who'd handled her father's estate. Rather than draw attention by using a Beaufort carriage and driver, she'd chosen to ride the gentle mount Alex had purchased for her. Buttercup was a placid creature, but Elizabeth had never been an accomplished rider, and the ride was not a comfortable one.

Prying information from a man she'd never met before was equally uncomfortable.

Per her request, the solicitor, Mr. Pearce, arrived with a sheaf of papers detailing the baron's various accounts at the time of his death. The amounts, nearly all of them negative, were staggering.

Even more interesting were the names. One in particular, one she recognized, appeared repeatedly.

"Garrett."

Mr. Pearce shifted, seeming to rouse himself to sit straighter. "Yes, Your Grace?"

"Lord Garrett's name appears here," she said, pointing, "and again here. What do you know of him?"

"Little, I'm afraid. A third partner in a few of your father's failed ventures. I do know, and pardon my saying it, that Lord Garrett's estate was better able to absorb the losses."

"But did they actually know one another?"

She knew Garrett was a frequent card partner to Alex. If she could prove a link between him and her father as well, she might be onto something.

But the solicitor lifted one shoulder in a shrug. "I imagine they did, but cannot speak with authority on their personal relationship."

She turned back to the papers. "And my husband? I see only one mention of him."

"Yes, Your Grace."

"Was that debt ever paid?"

Mr. Pearce cleared his throat uncomfortably. "No."

"I thought I might find more mention of him here . . . I was led to understand they were gaming partners for some time, along with Lord Garrett." She was pushing, she knew, but desperation drove her.

The solicitor wearily rubbed a hand across his forehead. "May I speak openly?"

"Of course, please."

"I don't know what information you sought this

afternoon. But my advice would be to stop asking questions."

Her heart thudded. "Why?"

"You seem to seek a link between your father and your husband. I can tell you this: all noblemen have agreements, and disagreements, they choose not to record. Some more than others. If you go searching for answers, you may not like what you find—nor do I believe the duke, to whom you owe allegiance, would approve. Most men prefer their private matters left private. Leave the past in the past." He stood, straightened his coat. "I hope our meeting has been of some value to you, Your Grace, but I think it best if I leave now."

"But my father—"

"Your father was an unhappy man." He leaned close, his voice low. "But the man you have married? He is a ruthless man."

Elizabeth stood numbly as Mr. Pearce departed without further explanation. Her mind whirred with questions, but her body felt mired in sand. "Ruthless," he'd said. Well, she'd known that all along. It wasn't proof of anything.

She shivered as she stepped out of the inn and called for her mount.

The ride home was as uncomfortable as the ride there. Her worries remained unabated, and her rump would be sore on the morrow.

She was keenly aware that, if she'd been a better wife and had absolute faith in Alex, she could have spent the afternoon enjoying an intimate fireside picnic rather than traipsing about the cold gray countryside.

* * *

"Where in heaven's name have you been?" Alex stopped pacing his study and turned to stare at his wife, who'd just blown into the room like a gust of cold air. Where had she been *this* time? It was clear she'd been outdoors, for her cheeks were still pinkened and her hair mussed. She looked beautiful.

Or would have, if he hadn't just spent the last six hours wondering frantically where she'd disappeared to, or whether she'd met some untimely end. Even now, members of his staff were searching the grounds.

Elizabeth stopped short. He watched as she smoothed her skirts. Was it his imagination, or did her fingers tremble?

"I've only just returned from the village, my lord."

"The village? What foolish notion prompted you to go to the village with snow clouds looming just above our heads?" He knew his frustration showed, but she had no idea how worried he'd been.

He busied his hands pouring a large brandy, then forced himself into a relaxed stance, leaning against the wall next to the fireplace.

"I didn't realize those were snow clouds. There are clouds nearly every day in the winter, so I didn't pay them much attention."

A servant appeared quietly with tea and Elizabeth paused, then moved to the tray and focused on pouring herself a cup as she finished answering him. Her movements were stiff, her hands red and chapped from the cold. Alex would have been tempted to offer to pour it for her . . . if he hadn't been so irritated.

"I visited the Culpeppers again. And—and—I brought a basket of jams to the orphanage. Cook assured me we'd more than plenty, and I thought those children might like a treat—" She broke off, studiously stirring a lump of sugar into her tea.

"I see. Another of your noble journeys." A muscle ticked in his jaw. "Elizabeth, you may give away every last jar of jam in this house if you like, but not in the middle of December, with snow on the way, and without informing anyone of your whereabouts—let alone going without an escort."

Really, all this disappearing had to stop. His wife of barely two months was as elusive as a wood sprite. Which, in a way, she resembled at the moment—looking so delightfully windblown, her red hair reflecting the firelight. He should hire someone to do her portrait that way.

Alex rolled his eyes. When had he become such a pansy? He couldn't even get a straight answer from his wife, and yet he dreamt of fanciful paintings of her. Damn it, how did she do this to him?

Elizabeth sniffed. "You don't have to treat me like a child. I've seen to myself well enough until now."

"Oh, yes," he said, warming to his anger again. "A fine job you did of that. Let me see. You ran away from home to work for my sister, then ran *back* home, only to be abducted by your cousin . . . Yes, I think the evidence stands for itself.

"I'm tempted to lock you up for your own good. I suppose I should have realized, before we married, that you have a habit of disappearing. But, Elizabeth, you'll be the death of me—if not yourself—if you do not desist."

She sniffed again. "All right." She looked miserable.

Alex heaved a sigh, his anger abating. "Likely you've caught a head cold out there in this frightful weather. Come here." He offered her a handkerchief, then drew her into his arms and stood in front of the fire.

He rested his chin on her head, finally relaxing for real. She was back. For now.

He didn't understand her. When she wasn't eluding him, she was playful and passionate. And every time she did disappear, she seemed contrite afterward. He could never predict what each new day would bring. Was it too much to ask that she'd give a little thought to her own safety? Or at least confide in him, her own husband, so he could protect her? Bloody independent woman.

When had Elizabeth come to mean so much to him? So much that he'd been nearly paralyzed with terror at the thought of losing her?

In spite of Elizabeth's reassurances that she would stop disappearing for hours on end, Alex's gut was uneasy. Instinct told him his wife was slipping away. If not physically, then mentally, spiritually. But he had no idea what he'd done to prompt it. Or how to stop it.

His instincts were confirmed when, two days later, at dinner, she informed him she wanted to travel to London for a spell.

"Why?" he asked, flabbergasted. Who went to London in the winter, unless upon matters of business? Elizabeth was a duchess. *His* duchess. She didn't need to work for a living.

Elizabeth sat across the table from him. She poked at the edge of her fork until it was perfectly in line with the other silver. "Well, I, er, thought to visit my family."

"Charity was here just last month." And though he didn't say it aloud, she was the only member of Elizabeth's family he deemed worth visiting.

"Yes, well . . ." She fidgeted some more. "There is also the matter of gowns for next spring's Season."

"I can arrange for the modiste of your choice to come here."

That didn't make her happy either.

"That's very kind of you, my lord, but then there is the matter of accessories, such as hats, gloves, parasols . . ." She waved a hand. "And of course London has more in the way of diversion than the country. I can't say why, it's just, I've been feeling at odds lately. It is terribly quiet out here."

He gaped at her. Mere months ago, *he'd* been the diversion she longed for. *He'd* been the one to brighten her day. They'd had to snatch stolen moments together, and the "terrible quiet" she now described had sounded like a lovers' paradise. He'd looked *forward* to time alone in the country with her.

Was his wife truly so fickle? Already, she'd lost interest in him and needed "diversion"?

She'd sworn she loved him. Had it been a lie?

He pushed away his plate, no longer hungry. Too bad, for the cook's roast quail was exquisitely prepared and one of his favorite dishes.

Elizabeth's face drooped at his extended silence.

God, she was beautiful, even with the corners of her lips quirked downward. He hated to see her disappointed. Maybe if he gave in, maybe if she had the diversion she sought, she'd come back to him.

"All right," he agreed hollowly. "We'll go to London next week. I suppose we can do your shopping, and see your family for the holidays." It sounded like torture.

But finally she smiled. "Thank you, husband. I do believe our trip will be just the thing to, er, set me to rights."

He hoped so.

Chapter Nineteen

"What are we shopping for again?" Bea asked. "And why couldn't it wait? It's freezing out here."

"A new riding habit," Elizabeth answered. "And Alex promised me a fur-trimmed cloak."

Charity rolled her eyes. "You don't even enjoy riding. Though I suppose the cloak makes sense." She'd accompanied the other women happily enough, but when the carriage deposited them on Bond Street, she'd been the first to point out Elizabeth had timed her shopping for the coldest day of the year.

Elizabeth had hoped a day of shopping would take her mind off her problems, and possibly even allow her to discover Lord Garrett's whereabouts. She suspected that Garrett, being a bachelor, wintered in town. In fact, she was banking on it, for he was her last hope in her thus far ill-fated investigation. She needed to be certain he was here before putting the rest of her plan, flimsy though it was, into action.

Elizabeth ushered her companions into the mantua-maker's, where the proprietress clucked over them and the shopgirl brought steaming cups of tea. The hot beverage seemed to soothe Bea's and Charity's ruffled feathers.

Elizabeth absentmindedly selected fabrics, linings, and trim from the patterns and samples the proprietress eagerly showed her. "I'll not lie," the merchant said. "Business has been slow, with the cold, but it will surely pick up if others learn of your patronage, Your Grace."

Elizabeth smiled uncomfortably. She had no idea what she'd just selected, so it would be something indeed if other women rushed out to copy it.

None of the women was anxious to venture out again, but Elizabeth promised they would stop only for hot chocolate and sweets, then return to Bea's. She'd wasted enough time. With the streets so empty, she was unlikely to "run into" anyone who might be of use to her secret purpose. No, she'd decided on another way to corner Lord Garrett, as long as Bea agreed to help.

In the sweet shop, they were again the only customers.

"Elizabeth, is something wrong?" Bea asked, picking at an éclair.

"Why?"

"Well, I thought newlyweds kept to themselves. I can't speak from experience, of course, since my marriage was hardly a love match, but I thought you and Beaufort were . . . different."

Charity seemed suddenly absorbed in her hot chocolate, but Elizabeth knew her sister hung on every word.

"Of course," she forced herself to say lightly. "Alex is wonderful. It's just, Montgrave is so vast . . . sometimes I feel lost. I miss female companionship—my sister and my best friend."

Bea looked mollified.

"Bea," Elizabeth asked quickly, anxious to change the subject, "may I ask a favor?"

"Certainly."

"I want to surprise Alex with something he'd enjoy. Would you host a card party while we are in town?"

"A card party?" Charity piped up. "E., never tell me you've taken to gaming."

"No, not like that, not like father. I just thought, Alex does enjoy playing, and it might be fun to see people before we return to Montgrave." She lowered her eyes, her heart hammering in her chest. "I know the names of his regular partners. I'm just not entirely comfortable yet in the role of hostess." God, she was such a liar.

"I'd be happy to," Bea said. "Heaven knows, I've nothing else to plan. Who did you wish to invite?"

"Lord Wilbourne and his wife, Lord Stockton, and Lord Garrett," she said, ticking off the names. "Do you know if they are in town?"

Bea nodded. "The Wilbournes are in the country for the cold season, but I believe the other two are here. Anyone else?"

Lord Garrett *was* here. Surely he'd not turn down an invitation once he knew Alex would attend. As for others, Elizabeth replied, "Oh, anyone you wish—so long as they aren't novices. My husband does take his card-playing seriously."

"I have a couple female friends who enjoy whist— they would help even out the numbers."

"I suppose I'm to be left out again," Charity grumbled.

Elizabeth gave her a plucky smile. "As soon as you've successfully appeared in Society, I promise to introduce you to all sorts of scandalous behavior."

"Is that a real promise?" Charity looked hopeful. "Your affairs have been wonderfully interesting over the past months, E., if a bit scary, but I miss getting into scrapes together."

Elizabeth smiled, internally praying that she'd have nothing more scandalous to involve her sister in than a few card games. "I promise."

She'd happily get into scrapes with her sister—once she got out of the one she was already in.

Two days before the card party, London's cold spell finally snapped. Everyone spilled out of doors, grateful for the reprieve. The air was still brisk, but the sun shone brightly.

Elizabeth called on Charity, and the two went for a quick stroll through Hyde Park.

They were just returning to the Medford town house when Charity groaned. "Oh, bother. Uncle George is headed our way."

Sure enough, Elizabeth spotted his portly frame on the path ahead. For someone who'd made it clear what a burden it was to care for the three Medford women, her uncle certainly hadn't hurried back to the country now that his duties were over. If anything, Elizabeth thought, he seemed perfectly content to remain living in the London home her husband now paid for. It was the primary reason she'd avoided visiting her mother since the wedding. Even during Christmas dinner, which she and Alex had hosted and her uncle had had the gall to attend, she'd managed not to speak directly to him.

It was too late to turn onto another path, for within moments, Uncle George huffed up to them.

"Elizabeth—I mean, Your Grace. And Charity. Ladies, I've just received distressing news."

"Whatever is the matter, Uncle?" Charity asked.

"Perhaps you ladies should accompany me home, and we may discuss the matter there."

Elizabeth wasn't accompanying him anywhere. "Whatever it is, you may tell me here."

"Harold Wetherby is dead."

Elizabeth flicked a glance at Charity. By her sister's expression, they seemed of the same opinion. This news was interesting but hardly distressing.

"What happened?" she asked.

"I'm afraid the poor man drowned."

"Drowned?" Charity asked. "How awful."

"Awful," Uncle George repeated. "There was a letter left on his desk. The night of his death, he'd just received word that his factory had gone bankrupt, and the laborers at his mines in the north had all given notice. They'd left to work for a competitor who was paying more than Wetherby could afford. He was on the brink of ruin."

A flash of clarity struck Elizabeth so suddenly she gasped. Alex was behind this. She *knew* it. He had done this for her, to ensure she was safe from Harold forever. Even better, Alex's choice to go after his enemy financially was a strong indicator he wasn't given to cold-blooded murder. Her heart warmed with love for the lordly man she'd married.

"But how did he come to drown?" Charity, ever curious, asked, and a hint of Elizabeth's worry returned.

Uncle George shook his head. "I'm afraid he wasn't in a clear frame of mind that night. A dock worker witnessed his fall, but by the time he secured a boat and rowed out under the bridge, Wetherby was gone."

Elizabeth took her uncle's explanation to mean that Harold had fallen because he'd been drunk—or that he'd jumped. Either way, he'd not been murdered. Relief flooded her.

Try as she might, Elizabeth felt no remorse for Harold's loss. "That must have been a shock to you, Uncle," was the best response she could manage.

"Indeed." Uncle George looked suitably distraught. "The funeral will be three days hence. Your mother and I will see to the arrangements, as he had no closer family. Can you extend your stay in town?"

Elizabeth briefly considered it. The habits of a dutiful daughter died hard. No. She owed her uncle nothing, and Harold even less. "You may make whatever arrangements you like. I've no intention of attending. Nor will Charity." Elizabeth started to turn, then thought better of it. "And, Uncle? When you've done what's necessary, I suggest you return home. Surely your estate suffers your neglect. You wouldn't want it to suffer the same fate as Wetherby's interests."

She had the satisfaction of seeing his face blanch before she took Charity's arm and walked away.

Alex had no idea why, after insisting upon visiting London to shop and see family, Elizabeth extended their stay for a card party.

"But you see, it's winter, so not everyone could attend, and Bea is counting on us to round out her tables," she'd begged prettily.

Once again, he'd given in. When she'd told him she'd invited Lords Stockton and Garrett, he actually looked forward to the affair. It pleased him that his wife had gone to the trouble to see that his friends were invited to Bea's party. Perhaps she'd not grown as distant as he'd thought, though her behavior was still worrisome, and their life together far from what he'd imagined being newly married would be like.

That evening, his valet, Hanson, finished knotting his cravat and then said, "There you are, Your Grace. A fine job, if I say so myself. Will you be going out with your duchess this evening, then?"

Hanson rarely spoke, let alone asked questions. Alex was so surprised, he answered without thinking. "Yes, of course."

Hanson nodded. "Good, good. Look after your lady, my lord."

Alex frowned. Hanson wasn't verbose, but he'd been with Alex for years, and the duke knew him to be observant. "What's wrong with Elizabeth?"

Hanson shook his head. "I never said aught was wrong, Your Grace."

Alex waited.

The valet sighed. "I'm not a married man, and I don't profess to know women. But there's something queer of late, something in her eyes . . ." He ducked his head. "Your Grace, I apologize. I believe your duchess is perfectly fine after all. My eyes are getting old, playing tricks on me. I won't allow my thoughts to do the same."

Alex nodded brusquely and left, meeting Elizabeth at the door to her dressing room. His breath caught at the sight of her. She still did that to him.

She'd taken extra care with her appearance. Her hair was swept up on top of her head, a green ribbon twined through the mass of silken fire. He wondered what would happen if the ribbon was pulled, and was sorely tempted to try it. Her gown was a deep green, draping and clinging to her curves before falling in soft folds to the floor. He swallowed.

"You are beautiful, my sweet."

She looked up, a smile playing at her lips.

"But not quite perfect."

The smile disappeared.

"I believe this will help." He held out a small velvet box, opened to reveal an emerald pendant.

"Oh," she breathed. "How beautiful."

"Here." He fastened the clasp around her neck, breathing in the scent of lavender and woman. He stepped back before the urge to crush her to him got the better of him. "Perfect."

"It's lovely, thank you so much." She placed her arm in his. "Shall we go?"

"Indeed."

He'd hoped for at least a few moments of intimacy in the carriage to Lady Pullington's, but it was not to be. Elizabeth sat close to him, and told him several more times how she appreciated his gift, but she seemed distracted, fidgety. He tried to quell his growing impatience with her behavior, but with Hanson's odd warning lingering in his mind, he found it hard to do.

When they arrived for the party, Bea had tables set up in two salons and the library, though much of the large salon was dedicated to a long table laden with refreshments and an open area for guests to mingle.

Prior to his marriage, Alex would simply have settled in at a table and ignored the socializing in favor of serious card-playing.

But tonight, he was having trouble letting go of Elizabeth. He noticed, not for the first time, how her gown was cut low in the bodice. With his advantage in height, the hollow between her breasts was enticingly obvious, especially with the emerald pendant he'd given her nestled just so.

Alex plucked a glass of wine from a passing servant's tray. Damn it, *why* wasn't he at home, in bed, with his wife?

"Why don't you go ahead and play?" Elizabeth suggested sweetly.

Was she so anxious to be rid of him? He settled a possessive hand at the small of her back, in no hurry to leave her. Cards could wait. But just then, Lord Stockton clapped him on the shoulder.

"Beaufort. Good to see you. Heard a rumor you were in town—wouldn't have come here tonight otherwise."

Elizabeth gave Alex a pretty wave and slipped away from his grip. Before he knew it, he was seated at a table with three other men. He recognized them as veteran players. It wasn't the entertainment he would have preferred, but perhaps the night wouldn't be a complete waste.

"Surprised your young wife let you out tonight, Beaufort," one of the men remarked.

"Oh, come off it," another said. "Beaufort's a man can do as he pleases. Wouldn't let a little thing like marriage tie him down."

He would, Alex reflected, it was his *wife* who wouldn't. Had this trip lightened her spirits, as she'd claimed it would? It was hard to tell, he'd seen so little of her.

Lord Garrett arrived and took the last seat at the

table. "Excellent," he said as the men dealt him in. "Haven't found a game as good as this all winter. Beaufort, you've been missed. Glad to see your wife knows how to entertain herself."

"What's that supposed to mean?" Alex asked sharply. Damn it, why was everyone remarking on his marriage? He forced a deep breath. They were probably just ribbing him—they couldn't know Elizabeth's odd behavior had him worried.

Garrett gave him a blank look. "Meant nothing by it, Your Grace. I passed her out shopping the other day with some of her lady friends, and again in the park— don't know the gentleman she was speaking to. A bit older, he was. Anyway, nice of her not to keep you all to herself. White's has been terribly dull."

Alex gave a strained smile. Who the hell had his wife been meeting in the park? For that matter, who on earth went to the park in the middle of winter? Why hadn't she asked *him* to accompany her? A thought stopped him. Perhaps she didn't *want* him there.

She'd been so distant of late . . . all those disappearances, sometimes for hours. Where had she been? And with whom? Had he been only a means to an end for her? Was her true love elsewhere? His heart—an organ he'd only recently discovered he possessed—felt like lead. He picked up his cards, forcing himself to concentrate despite the anger and mistrust boiling up inside him.

Elizabeth watched anxiously as the party progressed. She'd promised herself that after tonight, especially if she learned nothing new, she would drop this crazy investigation. Her heart hurt over the growing distance between her and Alex, and over the knowledge it was her fault. Tonight, she would have a chance to speak with two men who knew Alex best, one of whom her father's solicitor had also mentioned. If they didn't know anything, there likely wasn't anything to be known—a gross misinterpretation on her old coachman's part, perhaps, but nothing more.

Finally, she saw the opportunity she'd sought. Lord Garrett, who'd played at Alex's table most of the evening, pushed away his cards and stood to stretch.

As he headed for the table bearing the punch bowl, Elizabeth followed.

She casually reached for a glass of fruity, alcohol-laden punch, just as Lord Garrett did the same.

"Oh, pardon me," he exclaimed.

"No, no. I'm sorry," she squeaked, her voice abnormally high. She was such a fraud. "Lord Garrett, yes?"

"At your service, Your Grace." He bowed gallantly, handed her the glass of punch she'd been reaching for.

"Why, thank you." She sipped, then swallowed with difficulty, too nervous to consider drinking any more. She gripped the glass tightly to conceal her shaking hands.

"I don't recall if I've had the opportunity to congratulate you personally on your recent marriage."

"Why, thank you, Lord Garrett."

"Never thought Beaufort would succumb to the lure of marital bliss," he joked. "Of course, he is a man of great wisdom, and great appreciation for beauty. Clearly he found something unique in you."

Elizabeth cast her eyes down, a smile at her lips. Lord Garrett, a few years younger than her husband, was clearly a charmer. But that was good. If he was friendly, this could be easier than she'd thought. If only she could lure him somewhere quiet, where they might talk at length.

Together they drifted toward the hall, where a few windows were cracked just enough to let in some air without letting in the winter chill.

"I must say, though," he continued, "it is a surprise to see you both back in London so soon."

"Only for a short visit. My husband and I had a few matters to attend to in town, and when my good friend Lady Pullington invited us tonight, it seemed like a nice change from the monotony of country life. We'll be returning to Montgrave soon. I confess, the past year has been rather tumultuous for me." She paused to catch her breath.

"Yes . . . your father," Lord Garrett murmured. "I'm sorry for your loss."

Hope flared in her chest. He'd brought up the subject of her father with only the smallest opening from her. Perhaps she could finally learn something.

"Did you know him?" Elizabeth asked. "I believe he used to play cards on occasion with my husband, as you do. Did he ever join your group?" she prompted.

Was she being too obvious? Her palms felt moist, her tongue dry.

Lord Garrett looked discomfited. "No, I'm afraid not. I don't believe the baron and your husband were playing together by the time I joined the group."

"Oh," she said, disappointed. "I thought I remembered something, a business venture of some sort, where my father might have mentioned you." She gave him a silly smile. "I must be mistaken—I've no head for such matters."

He smiled back, falling easy prey to her foolish-female act. "No, you are quite bright. In fact, now that you mention it, I do believe the baron and I were involved in a shipping venture or two."

"And Alex as well?" she asked hopefully.

He gave a rueful laugh. "No, if I recall, those ventures did not turn out well. The duke is far too wise to have made such mistakes."

"I see." He'd confirmed for her, at least, that the gambling relationship between her father and Alex had once existed. "You seem to know my husband well. Why did my father and Alex stop playing cards together? Was there some sort of falling out between them?"

Lord Garrett cast a glance back toward the large salon where guests were mingling and laughingly placing predictions about who among them would have luck at the playing tables tonight.

"Perhaps it is best forgotten," he said gently.

But Elizabeth couldn't stop now. Not when she'd finally spoken to someone who'd known her father, apparently, toward the end of his life.

She pressed closer, gave him the most soulful, appealing look she knew. "It's only, I don't often get to speak with anyone who knew him. The rest of the ton, as you, seems anxious to forget."

"I didn't mean that," Lord Garrett said quietly. "But I'm afraid, by the time I knew Medford, he was not a happy man, and I should feel terrible if I dampened your spirits with such a topic."

"On the contrary, my lord, it is a relief to speak frankly. I know my father had a side to him he hid from his family. We learned that the hard way, from those to whom he was indebted. My husband doesn't like to speak of it. But I thought if I knew more, I might be able to finally *understand* my father for the man he was. It's important to me to do that."

"I see." Lord Garrett studied his punch. "I've no wish to come between you and your husband, but I can tell you they argued—Beaufort was one of the men your father owed and could not pay. I'm afraid the duke didn't think very highly of your father when Medford broke the news. Your husband gambles, but never with money he can't afford to lose. He has little respect for those who do not play similarly."

Lord Garrett lowered his voice further as he spoke, until they stood mere inches from one another, heads bent in deepest confidence.

"After the argument, the two men avoided one another," Garrett told her, his lips so near her ear they nearly brushed, and yet she still strained to hear him. "I don't believe they had any further contact until—"

"I'm sorry to interrupt this cozy little conversation," a deep voice growled, startling Elizabeth so that she sprang back.

"Alex!"

"Beaufort," Lord Garrett greeted him with a smile.

"Garrett." Alex did not return the smile. His face was a mask of ice. "My wife and I are leaving."

"But Alex—"

"Don't argue with me." His voice was low in her ear, but menacing. She shuddered.

Lord Garrett looked between them. "Is something amiss?"

"My wife has the headache."

"I don't—" The beginnings of a protest slipped out before she thought to bite them back.

"Fine. *I* have a headache. Come, fetch your things."

Elizabeth followed her husband, casting a glance of bewildered apology back at Lord Garrett, who shrugged and headed for the card room.

Elizabeth had to hurry to keep up with Alex's long, angry strides.

A footman brought their cloaks, and soon they were ensconced in the duke's carriage, en route to his London home.

Alex sat stonily on the seat across from her. Darkness sheltered her from his glowering expression, but she could feel the waves of anger radiating from him.

"Now will you tell me what's wrong?" she pled, her voice soft.

"No."

"Why? What can it be?"

"Elizabeth!" The word burst forth before he clamped his jaw shut and turned toward the window. "I don't trust myself to speak yet."

A shudder passed through her. He was angry at *her*. She knew it. But why? Could he have uncovered the real reason behind her desire to go to London? She'd certainly tried to be discreet—after all, her heart still protested the idea that her husband could have been responsible for her father's demise. Or was there something else?

Elizabeth risked another glance at her husband. Lights from the homes they passed dimly illuminated the interior of the carriage—enough for her to see Alex's expression had not changed.

She hugged herself close. Had she been wrong to come here? She knew their relationship hadn't been good of late. But she loved him. She just—well, she just had to *know*. If not for her father's sake, for her own. She'd spent the first twenty years of her life being deceived by a man she loved. She had no desire to spend the remainder of her life the same way.

Finally the coach slowed, then stopped in front of their home. Alex allowed her to precede him out.

She entered the house uncertainly, handed her cloak without thought to the butler, then stood in the chilly entryway.

Alex removed his cloak as well. Finally he spared her a glance. "Upstairs."

Fear slowed her steps as she obeyed the single-word command. She'd never seen him this angry. Or this controlled.

At least he wasn't going to argue in front of the servants.

He went up ahead of her, then stood at the top waiting, his expression ominous.

Then again, she thought wildly, if the servants *were* present, there would be someone to protect her.

She'd believed, all these months, that she would find the evidence that would exonerate her husband. But witnessing his anger now cast a dark shadow of doubt on that belief.

The moment they entered the master suite, he rounded on her.

"Is he the one?"

"What?" His question floored her. "Who?"

"Garrett," he spat.

"What about him?"

"Is he *the one?*" His eyes narrowed. "For God's sake, and your own, do not tell me there is more than one."

Her mouth fell open as understanding dawned. He thought her unfaithful? "No. No, I would never—"

He waved a hand to cut her off. "Don't bother. I should have known better. From the moment you proposed that I ruin you, I should have stayed away. I thought it was just your father who was mad, who'd driven you to such lengths, but I see I was wrong."

His lips twisted as though the words he spoke tasted bitter. "You may have been innocent back then, but it has not taken you long to learn to ply your wares."

Her mouth fell open. "What does my father have to do with this?"

"He offered you to me. Remember? As payment for his debts," Alex spat, his face dark with rage. "I couldn't believe a father would do such a thing. But apparently he knew his daughter better than I thought. Oh, I'm sure he's happy now. Probably laughing his head off from beyond the grave. I actually *married* you."

"No," Elizabeth whispered—though what she'd just denied, she couldn't have said.

"Perhaps I should have just taken what he offered, back then, for then I'd have enjoyed your delectable body without guilt, without obligation."

"Obligation?" she echoed, her own anger rising. "You married me out of *obligation*? I made it very clear from the beginning—"

"You made nothing clear. I actually believed you an innocent, a victim of circumstance. A gently bred girl forced into a governess's position, forced to hide away her beauty and passion in the country where nothing could come of it. Well, you do have beauty and passion, my sweet. Would that you'd used them to more noble purposes." He turned away.

"You're not making sense," Elizabeth said, as calmly as she could, though her whole body roiled against his accusations, against the vast gulf of misunderstanding that separated them. "What have I ever done— besides love you?"

"Love me. Oh, yes, I can see that you do," he bit out

sarcastically. "Perhaps that is why you, my wife, are gone so often from our home that I've begun to think you cannot stand the sight of me. Oh, you loved me well enough to get my ring on your finger, to get my name added to yours," he said icily, "but your love disappeared rather quickly after that. You're no better than all the other debutantes who flung themselves in my direction. No better than a common whore, who, once paid, withdraws her affections."

He stalked the room, flinging an angry arm toward the bed as he ranted at her.

"Well, the greater fool am I for believing in your love," he said, bitterness creeping into his tone. "I'm sorry to admit your little scheme worked. It was clever, I'll grant you that. No one else went so far as to ensconce themselves in both my bed and my *sister's* house in order to grab my attention. Most contented themselves with fawning over me at balls and the like. But you, I thought you were different. You had me fooled. I thought you were *real.* I ought to know better, after so many years in Society."

"There was no scheme," Elizabeth whispered. His words stung like cruel whips.

"No? Then where is this love you proclaim?"

"I do love you," she whispered, her heart aching with both love and betrayal. She loved him—she just didn't know if she trusted him.

He knew it, too.

"Liar," he spat. "Only today you were seen in the park consorting with another man, and then tonight I catch you in confidence with Lord Garrett. Elizabeth, I might have made a mistake in believing your love was true, but I will *not* stand for a wife who cuckolds me. Do you understand?"

"I never—"

"You lie." His voice was impenetrably cold and unemotional, his face a mask of rigid planes. "Your father's wretched offer didn't work. And when he left you nearly destitute, you and your horrible mother *still* thought you could attach yourselves to a dukedom, and you were willing to stop at nothing.

"Well, I don't like being used, and I don't like being lied to. I can't imagine what you could possibly still want that would lead you to another man, but I do not care to find out. You're nothing more than a talented liar and a slut. Get out of my sight."

Elizabeth had no idea how he'd convinced himself of what he said, but it was clear that any further argument of hers was worthless. Gathering what scraps of dignity she had left, she rose to leave.

"You are wrong, Your Grace. Perhaps someday you will know this. Perhaps not. But I am certain of what is in my heart and my conscience. Nothing I did, nothing *we* did, was less than honest."

Perhaps *his* actions, or her father's, had been false, but all *she'd* done was get caught in the struggle to remain true to the two men whom she'd loved.

There was so much more she wanted to say, to tell him, but the duke had already turned away.

For a moment, she simply stared at him. He stood in silhouette near the window, the dim light of a brace of candles deepening the shadows around him. His broad shoulders were as straight as ever, but his head slowly bowed. In defeat? Misery?

She ached to go to him, to cast herself at his feet and beg forgiveness for betrayals both real and imagined. But she knew that, in spite of what she said, she'd betrayed his trust far worse than he thought. She also knew the duke was not a man to whom forgiveness came easily.

She had, in all likelihood, ruined the best thing she'd ever had.

Finally, Elizabeth exited the room, then stood blindly at the top of the stairs as her vision blurred with tears.

Chapter Twenty

Elizabeth had failed.

She'd failed to discover the truth behind her father's death—if there was even any to find. More importantly, she had failed in her marriage.

"Don't take it to heart, Your Grace," Emma said reassuringly. She was combing and dressing Elizabeth's hair with even more care than usual—not that Elizabeth had anywhere important to go. Elizabeth suspected Emma knew she was hurting and was offering comfort in her own way.

"Your duke will come around."

Elizabeth's shoulders wilted. "I doubt that, Emma."

It had been two weeks since they'd fought, since Alex had told her to get out of his sight, and he'd shown no sign of relenting.

He'd shown no sign of anything, to be honest. His anger had subsided, but now he treated her as though she didn't exist.

The morning after their argument, he'd returned to Montgrave without her.

By the time she'd followed him and arrived at the

country estate herself, he'd had the servants move all her things into a suite of rooms in a separate wing of the vast home.

It was humiliating. The entire staff knew the duke and his lady were not in accord.

Divorce was out of the question. But they would certainly not be the first, or only, married couple among the nobility to have a marriage in name only. A marriage that was a sham.

Emma pinned another fiery curl into place. "He's a proud man, your duke, but a man only gets that angry at someone he loves. Which must mean he loves you."

"He used to," Elizabeth whispered. "I don't believe he does anymore." And why should he? She'd betrayed his trust. Not in the way he apparently believed, but betrayed nonetheless.

She'd thought she was doing the right thing. She'd tried to trust Alex and still do her duty to her father, rest his soul. But she'd failed.

In fact, in some ways her betrayal was even worse, for rather than giving her affections to another man, as he'd accused her of doing, she'd questioned her own husband's integrity.

Especially now, having seen him angry, she could not put aside her doubts. As coldly enraged as he'd been the other night, she could well believe him capable of murder.

"Well," Emma said around a hairpin wedged in the corner of her mouth, "he has an heir to think of. Surely he won't neglect his duties there . . . and, pardon my boldness, Your Grace, but that might be your chance to win him back." She stuck the pin in. "You look particularly lovely this evening. Perhaps if

you go to him, remind him—if you take my meaning—
of what you once shared . . ."

Elizabeth forced a smile, but it didn't reach her
heart. An heir. 'Twas one of the reasons dukes married
at all. And yet Alex appeared supremely unconcerned
at his current lack of heir.

Elizabeth had not conceived in their first few
months of marriage. She'd thought maybe . . . but
then her courses had arrived two mornings ago. Yet
another area in which she'd failed.

She'd dreamt of the children they might have—a little
boy, perhaps, with Alex's dark hair and intelligence, or a
little girl she could dress in ribbons and bows.

But despite Emma's reassurances, Elizabeth was convinced Alex would sooner let the dukedom pass to
someone else than approach her again in *that* way. As
far as he was concerned, she might as well not exist.

"There now." Emma gave her hair a final pat. "Perfect. Why don't you take a walk before dinner, mistress?
'Twould do you some good, and it's unseasonably warm
for winter. I heard the gardener's been growing roses in
the greenhouse. Perhaps you'd like to see them."

Elizabeth gave her loyal maid a wan smile. "Thank
you, Emma. Perhaps I will."

"Will you eat in the dining room tonight, or would
you like me to ask them to make you a tray?"

"A tray, please," she said softly. Not that it mattered.
Ever since *the* argument, as she was coming to think of
it, Alex had been conspicuously absent from their
evening meals.

Given his reputation prior to marriage, she didn't
like to think of where he might be.

After a few nights of dining alone, she'd taken to
requesting a tray for her room. Far better than the

cavernous silence of the formal dining room. No matter how unscrupulously polite the serving staff had been during those solitary meals, it could not erase the awareness she'd eaten alone.

Emma nodded sadly. "I'll see to it, Your Grace." She curtsied her way out of the room, leaving Elizabeth alone.

Not that that was unusual, these days.

She *deserved* this, Elizabeth reminded herself. But that didn't make it any easier to bear.

Following Emma's suggestion, she visited the greenhouse. The roses were indeed lovely, and the gardener unfailingly attentive and enthusiastic in showing them to her, but Elizabeth could not muster the spirit to share his enthusiasm.

She longed for companionship. Longed for the intimacy and ease she and Alex had shared. That feeling that the two of them had a secret, one that allowed them to laugh secretly at the foibles of the rest of the world while enjoying only each other.

She longed for the way he could kindle her desire with just one burning look, or the way he could draw out the pleasure of lovemaking into a leisurely bliss that left her feeling both exhausted and exhilarated.

There was just no one else like him.

And finally it hit her. She was still running. Every time she was faced with a crisis, her instinct had been to run, to hide herself. This time, she hadn't done it physically, but choosing not to confide in Alex had accomplished the same thing. It had torn them apart.

She needed to apologize.

And she needed to tell him the truth.

Would he believe her? He thought her an adulteress. In truth he was the only man she'd ever known. But if she wanted him to believe that, she would have to tell him everything else—everything she'd kept bottled inside since that horrible afternoon Fuston had visited.

A shiver of fear passed through her.

Perhaps he had a simple explanation for what had happened that night of her father's death. Perhaps he'd laugh and think her foolish for listening to Fuston's story.

Or perhaps he'd feel even more betrayed that she'd been hiding such doubts from him the entire time they'd been married.

Or, worse, he'd tell her it was true.

It didn't matter.

She *had* to talk to him, to come clean. She would apologize for her doubts, her flighty behavior, and ask his forgiveness. There was nothing else left.

But she had to do it right. How best to approach him? She didn't want him angry. Nor could she bear his cold indifference.

If she came to him at night, in bed, offered herself to him physically first, would he listen to her? There had always been passion between them. She knew he'd not be able to turn her away. But he hated being used—and wouldn't she be doing exactly that?

Perhaps morning was best, in the clear light of day? But when? Breakfast? He rarely showed. Interrupt his work? She didn't want him irritated from the start.

Ugh. How had this distance between them grown so vast?

This was all her fault. It was up to her to make it right—if that was still possible.

When Emma brought her tray of supper, Elizabeth ate absentmindedly, pondering her dilemma. Finally she pushed away the tray, much of the food still untouched.

She still felt lonely. Maybe a visit to Buttercup would cheer her up. Though she'd never been much of a rider, she'd always enjoyed patting and talking to horses. And right now, she needed to be near another living being, human or not.

Head down, deep in thought, Elizabeth wandered across the shadowed lawns and toward the stables.

It had been sunny earlier, a nice respite from gloomy winter, but now that the sun had gone down, it was quite cold again.

Elizabeth shivered and wished she'd brought a heavier cloak. The sky had turned that shade of darkest blue it docs just before going black. She tipped her head up to search out the stars while her boots crunched through the dried grass.

She reached the stables. The door stood cracked open and a warm, beckoning beam of light shone out of the entryway.

She lifted her hand to swing the door wider so she could enter.

"Don't move."

Elizabeth stopped dead, her breath caught in her throat.

Then she realized the voice was not directed at her. It was her husband's voice, but he was talking to someone else. She peered through the opening.

A man stood frozen at the other end of the stable.

A man her husband was holding at gunpoint.

"On three, I'm going to shoot." The duke's voice was low, taut.

Why would he give the intruder warning?

"One."

Elizabeth inched forward and recognized the

terrified features of Old Tom, her favorite groom. He was no intruder.

With that realization came another, more startling.

Her husband *was* a murderer. And unless she acted fast, another innocent man would die.

"Two."

Elizabeth rushed forward.

"No, stop!" she cried. "Don't shoot! You heartless bastard, Old Tom's done nothing. I won't let you kill him. You've already murdered my father. Isn't that enough?"

Two shocked male faces turned to stare at her as she grabbed Alex's arm, wrenching with all her might to turn his aim away from Old Tom.

The gun went off, but the aim was wild. The bullet thudded into the stable wall. One of the animals panicked, streaking past her and knocking her aside as it rushed out into the night.

Elizabeth, intent on preventing another murder, hardly noticed the creature. She tightened her grip on Alex's arm. Her husband's first shot had missed because of her hold on him, but he was far stronger than she, and she knew him for a crack shot.

If he wanted to kill, he could.

"Don't kill Old Tom," she begged. "What has he ever done?"

To her surprise, Alex dropped the gun. "He's gone. It's no use now."

Elizabeth stared in confusion. The groom was right there, wiping the sweat from his brow.

There was something going on here she didn't understand.

She backed away, slowly. Her husband's behavior was unpredictable, but now that she knew him for a killer, she was terrified his anger would turn on her for interrupting the scene of moments before.

"Elizabeth, don't go out there." His command was stern, his frown fierce.

She shook her head and continued moving toward the door. "You're a madman," she whispered. "It was true all along. What Fuston said. I didn't want to believe him, but it's true. You murdered my father."

Old Tom's mouth fell open, but Alex's brows lifted to reveal his dawning understanding.

"Nay, mistress," Tom finally spluttered. "You got it all wrong. His Grace was aimin' for the dog, not for me."

Elizabeth stopped. "Dog?"

Vaguely she recalled the flash of fur.

"The great hairy beast what ran out the door when you shouted," Tom said. "He's been roaming these parts the last month or so, killin' chickens an' such. We weren't too worried, until we heard he'd bit a man over in the village, an' that man's gone raving mad an' is like to die. Couldna have such a dangerous beast roaming wild, an' when we saw him sneakin' into the stables tonight, yer husband thought to rid us of him. Only problem was, I had the misfortune to be standing between him an' the creature."

Elizabeth turned to her husband.

"I was aiming for the dog," he confirmed. "Tom, it looks like we've lost him for tonight. But I believe my wife and I have some things to discuss, if you'd be so kind as to leave us." He spoke to the groom, but his eyes remained on Elizabeth.

"O' course, Your Grace." Tom glanced between the pair, obviously curious, but, aware of his place, he made a hasty exit.

Alex let out a long breath and bowed his head, seemingly aging before her eyes. "Elizabeth."

"Your Grace." Dizziness washed over her. She believed Tom's explanation for the events she'd interrupted, but that didn't provide any answers to her greater question—and now that her husband was aware of her suspicions, she couldn't be sure how he'd react.

He shook his head as if in defeat, then spread his hands wide in appeal . . . or maybe just to indicate he meant her no physical harm.

"I am not a murderer. But I do not deny my role in the death of your father. Will you allow me to explain?"

Her heart sank at his words, and her knees felt unsteady, but she nodded.

He gestured toward a low bench. "Please, sit."

She obeyed as though in a trance. A tiny part of her brain argued for her to run, to escape the presence of this dangerous man, but her heart hurt too badly to care what could possibly happen to her next. She would not run again.

The duke settled beside her, lowering himself slowly, as though he were a man of great age and weariness.

"I was not aware you suspected, or knew, what happened with your father. How long have you known?"

"Since just after our wedding," she whispered.

"All this time?" he asked wonderingly.

She looked at him, searching for a sign of the man she'd so loved.

"I was unwilling to jump to conclusions, my lord, based on the words of one man alone. I prayed he was mistaken. You were the man who held my heart."

"Were?" he asked, then shook his head. "No, don't

say anything. I do wish you'd come to me with your fears, your suspicions. You are an amazing woman. Brave."

"I am a fool," she countered. "For I determined to find the truth on my own. I dared not ask the question of you, lest it be true. Yet in all my questioning, I've found nothing to contradict Fuston's words. And tonight, just now, you confirmed them yourself."

"Nay," he contradicted. "Not entirely. Although I do not deny the deed, I never had any intention of killing your father. I am responsible, but I am not a murderer."

She wanted to believe him, she did, but his words confused her more. "I don't understand."

"How much *do* you know?"

She studied her hands. "Only what Fuston told me. That you shot my father, and then made his death appear an accident."

"True enough, in its way, and yet not a full picture of the events that transpired."

Elizabeth waited, trying to quell the hope filling her heart, lest it grew strong only to be quashed again.

"On the night your father died, Elizabeth, I was hosting a party. A gaming party. Not an unusual event for me, though I'd not expected your father in attendance.

"The guest list was exclusive, and as your father's debts to me were already considerable, I'd discontinued our interaction some months before. But he arrived that evening as the companion of a guest I did invite, and I saw no need to create trouble. Perhaps he would win that night, and if not, what was one more member of the nobility with an unwise penchant for gaming? I simply decided *I* would not play against him that night."

"Yes, I know of my father's habit," Elizabeth confirmed quietly. Thus far, her husband's account made sense.

"Your father did not win that night, but he did consume great quantities of spirits. I fear they clouded his judgment in more ways than one."

"Your Grace?"

"Your father lingered until most of the guests had gone home. I'd managed to avoid him during the gaming, but at this point he decided to confront me. I'd finished seeing a good friend to his carriage and was headed back indoors when he called across the lawn." Alex frowned. "Elizabeth, I'm not sure how much of this you should hear."

Elizabeth met his eye. "I think it best you explain fully."

"'Tis said unwise to speak ill of the dead," he countered.

Elizabeth sighed. "I've come to understand my father was no saint. And these secrets have been kept long enough, done damage enough. Tell me what happened and they will hold no further power."

He raked a hand through his hair and nodded. "I am afraid your father, spurred on by the amount he'd drunk and his own knowledge of just how deep his debts ran, had reached a point of desperation. He attempted to recoup his losses at gunpoint."

"At gunpoint?" she echoed. "He threatened you? But why . . . ?"

"Because of you, Elizabeth."

She shook her head. "I don't understand."

"Actually, you know this part already. When he'd come to me before, several months prior, the proposal he'd made to settle his debts involved you. That was why we'd fought." Alex looked away, weariness etched in his features.

Elizabeth swallowed, then suddenly stood as a flash of realization struck her. "When you made me your mistress . . . you were . . . you were fulfilling those terms? You were recouping what you were owed? But that was after my father's death. No! You told me, when you rescued me from Harold, that you'd never—" Her voice broke and tears filled her eyes. She stepped back. "You cared for me, I know you did. Maybe not at first, but . . ."

"Hush, darling." Alex stood, too, and put tentative arms around her.

Elizabeth stood stock-still, the feel of his embrace foreign and yet so achingly familiar. Tears raced down her cheeks. How much of their relationship had been a lie? Had she ever known this man? Oh, but she had, her heart argued.

"I never agreed to your father's proposal. Never." His thumb slowly stroked, back and forth, along her jaw, and it was all Elizabeth could do to listen to his words. So many nights she'd longed for his touch, wondering—even as she'd reminded herself why she ought to despise him—if she would ever feel it again.

"I'm sorry to even bring it up—I only did so to explain exactly how things came about, the night of his death," he continued. "As I said, I'd cut off contact with him after it became clear he could not pay his debt in pounds. Never once, after I actually knew you, did I consider using you on such terms."

He cupped her chin and tilted her head toward his. "Not once," he repeated, his gaze fierce. "What we had— what we have—is entirely between us."

She believed him. Lord help her and all the other

fools, but she did. She took a deep breath and relaxed, slightly, in his arms.

"Wait a minute." This time, Alex was the one who stepped back.

He frowned thoughtfully. "You said a moment ago you'd been trying to uncover the truth about that night . . . Is *that* what you were doing those many times you refused to explain your whereabouts or what you'd been doing on your outings?"

"It is."

His face cleared but only for a moment before he dropped his forehead into his hands with a groan. "And for that I accused you of adultery," he mumbled from between his fingers. "Elizabeth, it is I that am the fool. A fool, a cad, and a man unworthy of your trust. When I thought you . . . It killed me, to think the one woman I'd dared love, I'd dared let myself believe in, would give herself to another. I apologize. I should have known you would not betray me so."

"Yes, you should have," she said softly. A piece of the great weight bearing down on her broke off and crumbled. "But I forgive you."

He looked up. "You do?"

"Yes. I can see how my behavior would have seemed odd. And both of us were keeping secrets . . . How were we each to know what those secrets were, or trust the other? I did betray your trust. Just not in the way you thought. And I, too, am sorry."

He appeared to consider that.

All her life, she'd thought she needed someone to believe in her, to love her. That was true. But she needed someone to believe in her *fully*. To believe in her enough to share the truth with her, not simply try to protect her from it.

"Alex, I need to hear the rest."

"All right," he said heavily. He led her back to the bench and they sat.

Alex tipped his head back and pinched the bridge of his nose, then released it and met her eye. "It was not one of your father's more admirable moments, but he seized on the details of that proposal and twisted them until he'd convinced himself that I was responsible for ruining you as revenge for those unpaid debts."

"How could you have ruined me? We'd hardly ever met."

"I know. But as I said, his mind was heavily fogged that night. I tried to reason with him, but his capacity for reason was limited. It became clear he'd no intention of relinquishing his weapon, and considerable intention of using it. He tossed me a second weapon, and demanded I give him satisfaction."

"A duel?"

"Well, it was nearing dawn, but we had no seconds, and he followed through on his demand before any such arrangements could be made."

"He shot at you?"

Alex nodded. "I am sorry to tell you this."

"You could have been killed!"

"Given his state, he'd have had a better chance of accomplishing that if he'd been aiming elsewhere. Though I'm not sure what he hoped to gain through my death, except, perhaps, that I'd no longer be anxious to collect on my debts.

"After his shot missed, he began reloading as he walked closer. It became clear—if there'd been any doubt before—this was no gentlemen's duel." He gave her a searching look. "Elizabeth, a man at close range, even a foxed man, can be quite dangerous. When he raised his weapon again, I gave him no chance. I fired first."

Her throat tightened and she couldn't breathe, let alone speak, as she envisioned the events the duke described.

"I'd aimed for his knee, but two things sent my shot awry. For one, it was a weapon unfamiliar to me, and every pistol is slightly different. Second, and most unfortunate, was that the moment I fired my shot was the very same moment the drink finally got the better of your father. He stumbled just as I fired, and his chest took the shot meant for his knee. I'm sorry, Elizabeth."

Her mind reeled. If what he said was true, then her father's death *had* been an accident—just not a *carriage* accident. A man threatened on his own property, a man who defended himself from that threat, was not a murderer.

But could her father truly have been so recklessly foolish as to have issued the challenge Alex described? And had he used *her*, his own daughter, as an excuse? She'd thought she'd come to terms with her father's errors, but this new revelation stung.

"Did he—did he die immediately?"

"Yes. By the time I reached him on the lawn, he was gone."

"You didn't mean to kill him."

He shook his head slowly. "No. I confess I held no love for your father—a man who gambled beyond his means, who would use his own daughter—but I did not wish his death. And yet I did cause it."

"If what you say is true, though, you cannot hold yourself responsible."

"Have you ever killed a man, Elizabeth? Intentional

or no, it is impossible not to feel the weight of responsibility. Still, I would not have you think me a murderer."

She saw the regret etched in his features, the weight of the guilt he'd been carrying reflected in his eyes.

"Do you believe me, Elizabeth?"

The story made sense, and yet, the whole scenario was so macabre, she was left unsettled.

So she opted for telling him the truth. "I want to believe. I do. Yet it is difficult to accept such things of one's father, in spite of all I know about him now."

"I wish you would believe based on my word alone, but I know that is difficult, especially as my behavior these last months has given you little reason for such trust." He covered one of her hands in his.

She didn't move, didn't withdraw it, but also gave him no positive response.

He nodded in acceptance, then sighed heavily.

"There is someone who can verify what I've told you," he said.

"There is?" That was a surprise. In all her weeks of discreet questioning, she'd hadn't turned up a soul who claimed to know a thing. "Who?"

"Your mother."

Chapter Twenty-One

"My mother?" Elizabeth echoed in blank shock.

"She was in attendance that night as well."

"But—"

"She came with Lady Jameson but intended to leave with your father," Alex confirmed. He smiled grimly. "I would never have invited her either—please don't take offense, my dear—but both your parents came as guests of those I *had* invited. The gaming community among the nobility is small, even more so during the winter, when many are away."

"But—"

"Perhaps she can better explain than I."

And so Alex led Elizabeth from the stables and called for his coach to be put to immediately.

The night was yet young by ton standards, but Elizabeth felt as though a hundred years had passed since she'd gone down to the stables that evening.

She climbed into the coach obediently, without thinking to pack a valise or bring even so much as her reticule, her mind focused only on what her mother could possibly say to explain the bizarre accounting she'd heard from her husband.

Alex sat next to her in the coach, their knees lightly touching, though he made no move to hold her again.

She wanted him to, though. The heat of him, his scent, his nearness made her throat ache with unshed tears. She'd missed him these past weeks. And her gut told her that tonight, he'd spoken true.

It was important to her to hear what her mother said before she did anything else, though. Elizabeth had the feeling she'd spent most of her life being kept in the dark—first by her father and her mother, and then by her husband. It was time that ended.

There was little surprise on the baroness's face when she greeted them. In fact, she looked like a person who'd resigned herself to a meeting both long-anticipated and long-avoided.

"Mother."

"Elizabeth. Your Grace." Lady Medford looked more exhausted than Elizabeth could ever remember. Of course, it was the gray hour before dawn by the time they arrived, but Elizabeth's mother displayed the exhaustion of ages, not merely a few missed hours of sleep.

Elizabeth decided there was no point in exchanging further pleasantries.

"Mother, tonight I have heard a tale my mind has difficulty grasping."

Her mother nodded. "I imagine you have. It was bound to come out eventually, once you married the duke."

"It's true then? About father?"

Lady Medford kept her eyes on Alex. At his slight

nod, she told her daughter, "It's true your father's death was caused by no carriage accident. It is also true he was killed by your husband. But the duke is not to blame."

"Father threatened him?"

Lady Medford's shoulders sagged, her voice lost strength. "He should never have gone to the party that night. And *I* should never have let him stay, once I saw him there. At the very least I should have stayed by his side, not let him imbibe so much. But that was not the nature of our relationship. We each went our own way, as we usually did, though we'd agreed to return home together later."

"And father . . ."

"Yes, he threatened His Grace. I'm sure if James hadn't been foxed, he'd have thought better of his actions. I did not know how desperate his—our—circumstances were until that moment."

"How is that possible?" Elizabeth was aware of Alex standing solidly by her side. For some reason she had the impression he was there to support her, rather than to draw satisfaction as her mother confirmed his story.

Lady Medford wrung her hands. "I knew he enjoyed gaming—sometimes too much. I never wanted to know more than that. Your uncle George is not a kind man, but he got one thing right. I thought I'd married up when I married James. Well, I had, of course, for James was titled. And in the beginning, we were well off. I just kept living that way—I never thought to suspect him, to question his habits. I never knew until too late."

Acceptance seeped through Elizabeth. And forgiveness. "I understand, Mother. I do. He was so easygoing, so carefree."

Alex finally spoke. "He fooled me as well. I would never have bet with him otherwise."

Elizabeth looked between them and saw resignation, acceptance.

"I was searching for James, to tell him I wanted to leave, when I heard his voice outdoors. I came to the door and saw—" Lady Medford wrung her hands. "I was terrified. I called to him, begged him to stop . . . He gave no indication he heard me. Maybe he didn't. I should have done more . . . I should have done *some-thing* . . . I was scared . . ."

"And you had no weapon," Alex reminded her gently.

"No."

"So you saw what happened—all of it?" Elizabeth asked.

"Yes."

"And you agreed to cover everything up. To make it look as though father died in a carriage accident."

"Yes," her mother answered. "It's never a pretty thing when one of the nobility dies under shameful circumstances. Especially when the cause of death is a gunshot. I could have pressed charges, and your duke could have done likewise. I didn't know the full extent of our family's problems until later, but I did know that an investigation into James's death was likely to create an even greater scandal.

"Alex was quick-thinking to devise the plan he did. It helped us avoid considerable shame, and I could hardly begrudge the duke the fact that it saved him from charges as well—I'd seen how James threatened him. All I asked was that Alex make me a promise: that after that night, after everything was covered up, he would never contact our family again. I wanted to forget."

Elizabeth pressed her lips together, taking in this information. Then another thought occurred to her. "Afterward, when I was looking for suitors, and you told me you prefer I stay away from Alex . . . this was why, wasn't it?"

Lady Medford nodded. "I hope you'll forgive me, Your Grace. But at the time your interest in Elizabeth did not seem serious, and we were rather desperately hoping to find her a solid match. And, I thought that the less she was involved with you, the less likely the past would come unburied."

"I see," Alex said. He took Elizabeth's hand.

"Of course, months later, when you arrived to ask for Elizabeth's hand, I considered that promise void. You two were clearly suited for one another."

Elizabeth recalled the unspoken exchange she'd seen between Alex and her mother on that occasion. It made sense now.

The older woman lifted both hands in appeal and spoke to the duke. "I can understand why it was necessary Elizabeth know the truth now, for deception strains a marriage. But it would comfort me somewhat if I knew the story would spread no further. If not for my own reputation, then for that of my other daughter."

"Yes, of course," Elizabeth said softly, feeling some sympathy for her mother for the first time in many months. "I'd not have father's name smeared further by the gossips, so long as my husband's reputation also remains clear. I can find Fuston and explain to him that he misunderstood. I don't believe he has any desire to gossip—he only feared for my well-being."

"In fact, he's been well paid *not* to gossip," her husband dryly put in. "Though I can forgive him his attempt to warn my wife." He moved his hand, letting it rest protectively on Elizabeth's shoulder.

Warmth seeped through her at his touch. It was all she could do not to turn to him and bask in his affection. Yes, this man had fired the shot that ended her father's life. But she understood now that he'd had no choice. She also understood that, long before that evening, her father had lost control, lost himself, in desperation and misery over a habit that had gotten the better of him.

"Still, you should have told me," she said to both her husband and her mother. "Perhaps not right away, but long before now. Before Alex and I were married. I'm not a child. I deserved to know. Especially as my life was to be so affected. These past weeks . . ." her voice broke as she thought of how strained their relationship had been of late.

"I know. And I am sorry," Alex told her once again. "If I'd had the faintest inkling what had you so upset, I would have—even if it meant driving you away for good. I wanted to protect you, and, I admit, I feared that, accident or not, mine was too great an offense to be forgiven."

"Can you forgive me?" the baroness asked.

Elizabeth faced her mother. Her husband she was prepared to forgive, but not her mother. She voiced her remaining objection with one word.

"Harold."

The baroness looked away. "I didn't realize how he treated you," she said quietly. "I thought you were simply being willful. You were, after all, always a willful child. We did need to find you a husband, and as you'd never shown great proclivity for wringing marriage offers before . . ." she trailed off.

"I'd never had urgent need before," Elizabeth reminded her. It was foolish to still feel hurt that her mother hadn't believed her capable of success on the marriage mart. After all, she'd had offers early on, before her father's death, and the man standing beside her as husband was proof she had what it took to capture the attention of the ton's most desirable catch.

Lady Medford sighed. "From where I stood it looked like you wanted to give up a solid offer from Wetherby in order to gamble on another that might or might not appear," she said. "And by then I'd had enough of gambling."

Elizabeth nodded, conceding that point.

"Still, no mother wishes to see her daughter beaten. Harold and your uncle concocted the plan to remove you to the country without my knowledge. Once George told me, I should have done something. But I convinced myself that if you two were left without interference, you might come to terms. It was a last hope, for by that time you'd destroyed your other chances through your own reckless behavior."

Elizabeth said nothing.

Her mother sighed again, and as the air left her body she seemed to shrink. Elizabeth realized for the first time how small a woman she was.

Had she ever really wielded the tyrannical might Elizabeth remembered, or had that been merely a figment of her own youth and imagination? Of her own guilt over not living up to expectations?

"I wasn't without my reasons, but I can see now I should have watched more closely," her mother finally said. "I could have listened when you told me of your dislike of Wetherby. I could have asked more questions.

If I'd known what was actually happening, Eliza-beth, I would have called a stop to it."

Elizabeth closed her eyes. This was the best she was likely to get from her mother. They might never see eye to eye, but neither did she want to live with permanent resentment. She opened her eyes again.

"I do forgive you," she slowly said.

Some of the worn expression seemed to lift from the baroness's features. And then, miraculously, she did for once exactly as Elizabeth hoped she would.

She curtsied and retreated quietly, leaving the married couple alone.

"But can you forgive me?" Alex asked, turning her to face him fully. "I know it is still a lot to ask."

The dimly lit room cast shadows over his face, intensifying his expression. Elizabeth reached up to trace the outline of his jaw.

God, how she loved this man.

"I can't undo the past, but I do want to share the future with you. No more secrets," Alex continued.

Elizabeth cut him off by pressing a finger against his lips. "Just hold me."

She took a deep breath as his arms came around her, enfolding her, protecting her. His chin came to rest atop her head. She inhaled his scent like a drowning man starved for oxygen. It had been so long.

They stood that way until Elizabeth's legs felt numb, but still she didn't want to move. Finally she shifted slightly, just enough to encourage blood flow to her limbs.

"Elizabeth?"

"Mmm?" She lifted her head slightly, unwilling to let him go.

"I want to take you home."

"Mmm." She held him closer, in complete agreement.

"But I want to make love to you first."

She grinned happily. "I believe I still have a room here."

"Excellent."

When Charity awoke, rays of sun peeked through the curtains. As was her habit, she sprang from bed, went to the window, and flung them open to greet the day.

This morning she had to shield her eyes, as sunlight bounced brilliantly off an emblazoned, black-lacquered carriage standing in the drive. She looked again, and saw it bore the Beaufort crest.

Elizabeth! When had she arrived? Charity had missed her sister terribly—especially since, at their last visit, she'd sensed Elizabeth wasn't entirely happy in her new marriage.

Oh, dear. Could that be why she'd arrived unannounced, in the middle of the night?

Charity flew down the hall to her sister's room, ready to share comfort and confidences as only sisters can do.

She raised her hand to knock. A muffled giggle made her pause. It was followed by a low growl. Another giggle and then what sounded like—Charity's cheeks heated—a moan of pleasure.

Charity slowly backed away, a smile spreading across her face.

Unless she was very much mistaken, her sister and the handsome duke were perfectly in accord now, and quite possibly in the process of creating the duke's heir.

Charity grinned and skipped back to her own room. She would enjoy being an aunt.